MW00761282

HELL IN A
BRIEFCASE

HELL IN A
BRIEFCASE
A MATT COOPER NOVEL

**PHIL
LITTLE**
WITH
**BRAD
WHITTINGTON**

BROADMAN
& HOLMAN
PUBLISHERS

NASHVILLE, TENNESSEE

© 2006 by Phil Little
All rights reserved
Printed in the United States of America

13-digit ISBN: 978-0-8054-4080-5
10-digit ISBN: 0-8054-4080-1

Published by Broadman & Holman Publishers,
Nashville, Tennessee

Dewey Decimal Classification: F
Subject Headings: ADVENTURE FICTION
                  FAITH–FICTION

06 07 08 09 10   10 9 8 7 6 5 4 3 2 1

Chapter 1

Marjeyoun, Lebanon.
Thursday, 21 November 2002. 01:30.

A full moon. A glow seemed to rise from the sand, allowing them to drive with their headlights off. The five Jeeps kept to 40 kph on the dark road that wound southward between hills and wadis. In the third Jeep, Major Skaff allowed himself the brief luxury of picking out Pegasus in the sharp winter sky before he compulsively scanned the rocky terrain for signs of Hezbollah fedayeen. He was leading this patrol to check out rumors of increased activity near Shaaba Farms, the disputed area where three Israeli solders had been kidnapped two years before.

The ridge road ran from the town of Marjeyoun down to Qlaia'a under the ominous gaze of Shqif Arnoun–the castle called "Beaufort" by the Crusaders–to the west. Christians and Muslims had fought for this ground for centuries, trading possession of the castle as their fortunes rose and fell. In the 1970s the Palestinian Liberation Organization had used the strategic placement of the castle to shell civilian settlements in northern Israel.

That was when Skaff, then a young recruit of the Southern Lebanese Army, had been a driver in a similar convoy, shortly before the civil war broke out between Christians and Muslims in 1975. Traversing this very ridge on a mission, he had come under fire from the castle. His evasive driving had saved the convoy and drawn the attention of General Lahd.

The intervening thirty years had been a generation of unremitting war. Israel, tiring of mounting civilian casualties and the Lebanese government's refusal to expel the terrorists, invaded southern Lebanon in 1982 and captured the castle. Eighteen years of occupation followed, during which Skaff had risen through the SLA ranks while working openly with the Israelis to keep the various Muslim factions at bay. When he had started, Hezbollah did not exist. Now the radical Muslim army controlled the south and dealt severely with the Christian resistance.

As the occupation had grown increasingly costly and casualties mounted, the pressure increased for Israel to withdraw. When the SLA collapsed in 2000, Israel destroyed what was left of the castle walls and pulled back behind the Blue Line specified by the UN. The SLA scattered. Thousands fled to Israel or went into hiding. Those who didn't were imprisoned and tried as enemy collaborators. As Hezbollah gained control of the area, the anticipated slaughter of Christians didn't materialize. But any SLA militiamen emboldened to return were also imprisoned.

As he scanned the distant ruins of the castle in the moonlight, Major Skaff reflected on change and constancy. Where PLO guns had once rained death on Israel and Lebanese Christians, now tourists snapped pictures and rushed home to post them on the Internet. And the same General Antoine Lahd who had brought him up in the ranks and fought beside him for decades had fled to Paris. Only a week ago he had opened a fancy restaurant in Tel Aviv called Byblos. It had a nice ocean view.

True, Lahd had a death sentence hanging over him for treason and war crimes, but so did Skaff. And so did many of the two thousand SLA in Lebanese prisons.

But some things had not changed. Southern Lebanon was just as dangerous for the men in these Jeeps as it had been when Skaff was driving instead of commanding.

Skaff was drawn from his reflections by a dark shape ahead. At the end of the ridge the road snaked through an outcropping of rock. He had passed through it many times, always with reluctance. This night he felt a peculiar sense of revulsion as he squinted at the misshapen lump of stone looming before him.

He nudged his driver and nodded toward the rocks. Hassan nodded back. He could feel it too. Skaff reached for the radio to signal the lead Jeep. A lifetime of guerrilla fighting had convinced him that such premonitions were not without merit. His transmission was brief, but they were already entering the outcropping when he put the radio down.

Five seconds later a rocket hit the grille of the lead Jeep. The explosion lit the rocks towering over them. He saw the silhouettes of two men blow out on either side of the vehicle, which was tossed onto the nose of the next Jeep. Hassan narrowly missed them, skidding left and stopping next to the driver of the lead Jeep, who was lying half off the road.

The two Jeeps behind slid sideways to a stop in the road as machine gun bursts echoed from beyond the lead Jeep. Skaff was exposed to the attack. He dove from his seat to the rear of the second Jeep, between two men already returning fire with an Uzi and an M-16.

He rolled to his feet and yelled to the two back Jeeps, motioning for them to form a double barricade with their vehicles, keeping the men covered both in the front and the rear in case the attackers attempted to sandwich them in the gap. Skaff turned back, confident that his men needed no further direction. This mission called for battle-hardened veterans, and he had personally selected the nineteen men who were with him now. Every man among them had proved himself in years of combat. Some even owed their life to his cool command in battle. Some had returned the favor multiple times.

Skaff scanned the forward battle to account for the remaining eleven men, his position shielded by the lead Jeep transfixed on the grille of the second. To the left, Hassan was pulling the driver of the first Jeep to safety. The other two men from Skaff's Jeep were covering him with sporadic fire from their Uzis. Ahead, the driver of the second Jeep was placing a case of grenades handy to his partner, who had fitted his M-16 with a grenade launcher and was set up in the backseat. Skaff was standing beside the other two passengers in the second Jeep. That left the three passengers from the lead Jeep.

He spotted Saif on the right. He had been thrown clear onto the sand without apparent injury. He was crouched behind a boulder, occasionally returning fire with his Desert Eagle .50-caliber side arm. Failing to sight the other two, he shouted to the driver, who had acquired an Uzi.

"Rafik? Sayyed?"

He nodded forward. Skaff crawled over the middle of the Jeep to the hood. Sayyed was wedged between the lead Jeep and the grille of the second Jeep, most likely dead. Rafik was lying on the hood of the second Jeep. Skaff checked for a pulse. Nothing. He closed Rafik's eyes and whispered a short prayer. Skaff couldn't play favorites with his men, but this loss was harder than any other would have been. At nineteen, Rafik had already spent four years with Skaff, rarely more than fifty yards from his side. Four years of relentless, driven hate. Skaff had been Rafik's ticket for revenge. Perhaps now he had found the peace revenge had not been able to bring him.

Skaff was crawling back to get a weapon when the second rocket hit the bottom of the lead Jeep. The gas tank exploded, sending most of the shrapnel back toward the attackers. The force of the blast threw the second Jeep back five feet, knocking over the two shooters behind. The grenade launcher and the man with it fell into the front seat. The driver was standing to the side. He returned fire with the Uzi.

Skaff helped reposition the grenade launcher and crawled out of the Jeep. The two in back were already firing again. He scanned the area and then dove toward the two Jeeps in the rear. Of the eight men between the Jeeps, one had taken a round in the right shoulder but was still firing left-handed, propped against a door. Three were facing the rear but indicated they hadn't seen any action, yet. Two were covering the walls on either side with M-16s, but also hadn't seen action. The final two had grenade launchers on their M-16s. They waited until they saw several volleys of tracer bullets originating from a single location. Then they fired three seconds apart at the source. The machine gun fire stopped. Skaff slapped them on the back. Perhaps they would get out of this thing alive.

Then a rocket hit Skaff's Jeep. Hassan was behind a curtain of stone, firing with an Uzi, having propped the injured driver in a cleft in the rock. But the other two were using the Jeep for cover. One tumbled backward, clear of the Jeep. The other was knocked down as the Jeep rolled over, pinning his leg under it. Skaff ran through a volley of automatic weapons fire and pulled the first man to his feet. They raced to the Jeep, joined by Hassan, and rocked it back over. Then they dragged the injured man to safety next to the injured driver.

Skaff felt a shudder of unease ripple through the adrenaline-laced focus that always came over him in combat. If this kept up, the whole team would be shredded before they had used half their ammo. He grabbed Hassan's arm and yelled into his ear over the din.

"We have to take out that rocket launcher or we don't get out of here. Take those three and circle around." Hassan nodded and stepped away but Skaff grabbed his arm. "Take a radio."

He let go, and Hassan ran to the rear while the others laid down covering fire. Skaff used the opportunity to race to the front two Jeeps and get the four there away from the vehicles and behind the cover of the rocks. As they ran for cover, another rocket hit the top of the lead Jeep, sending fragments of the grille and fenders flying in all directions. Skaff ran through the explosion back to the rock curtain. When he fell against a boulder the injured man pointed at Skaff's leg. He looked down and saw that his left trouser leg was slashed in three places. Blood was seeping down to his boots. He looked around to see how the others had fared.

Saif seemed to have been hit in the arm by something. He was now firing the Eagle while holding his upper arm with the other hand. The other four seemed to have escaped unscathed. Skaff's radio had not survived the rocket. He nodded to the man next to him, who wielded an Uzi while he made it to the two back Jeeps, getting an Uzi and a radio. He turned it up all the way and slung it over his shoulder. Then he began firing at the source of tracers beyond the rubble of the Jeeps.

Looking for some encouragement, Skaff probed his memory. In almost three decades of fighting, he didn't recall anything quite as dire as the current circumstance. He had two confirmed dead, one unconscious, three wounded but still firing. Almost a third of the force. The numbers were bound to increase as long as that rocket launcher was working. His calculations were interrupted by Hassan's voice squawking through the pandemonium.

"We got the rocket launcher, but I think they have another on the left. And now we're pinned down, so we're going nowhere."

The last word was drowned out by a rocket blast on the rock curtain above the injured men. Skaff doubted he could get a team around the other side. Even if he did, the enemy would be expecting them. No way around. No way through. He scanned the sheer rock walls on either side. No way over. The fedayeen had chosen their positions well and appeared to have ample men, weapons, and ammo. It seemed likely that most of this team would share the fate of Rafik and Sayyed. Probably all. The thought sickened Skaff, turning the adrenaline in his veins to bile in his throat.

There was one last hope, but it might be too late. He selected another frequency on the radio and shouted over the gunfire, "*Lehafil Levanon Sanctzia. Lehafil Levanon Sanctzia.* (Activate Lebanon Sanction.)"

•

Chapter 2

Marjeyoun, Lebanon.
Thursday, 21 November 2002. 01:41.

Skaff yelled their location into the radio, threw it down and exchanged his Uzi for a grenade launcher. He joined the other two in lobbing a pattern wherever they saw muzzle flash or tracers. The fire would be silenced, sometimes for as long as a minute, but inevitably resumed. Skaff was no longer conscious of the passing of time. He had exercised his last option. All that lay ahead was a fight to the death. He banished all other thoughts from his mind and focused on tracers and the rhythm of the battle until he reached for another grenade and discovered there were none left.

He was reaching for the Uzi when a rocket blasted the rock, sending out fragments that lacerated the arms of the men on either side of him. A rocket hit the gas tank in Skaff's Jeep, and metal screamed through the air. The Jeep shielding Skaff and the other two was peppered with shrapnel. The windshield shattered, a tire blew, water ran from the radiator.

Then, over the roar of the burning gas tank, a noise erupted from behind them and snarled over their heads. A huge explosion flared beyond the front of the outcropping, followed closely by a second. Skaff looked back to see the two Israeli AH-64A Apache gunships from Metulla that had responded to his signal. The relief was so profound and sudden that he staggered back against the Jeep. They would live. His men would live. He would live to see his daughter again.

Painted a flat black, the helicopters were barely visible against the night sky. Even with a full moon, they were little more than dark spots bereft of stars, spitting out 30-mm ammo at ten rounds a second. He watched as they crept forward, strafing the Hezbollah positions, and launched a second round of Hellfire anti-armor missiles. Their night-vision headgear would allow them to see the terrorists as if it were noon.

In the flash of the blast Skaff saw a silhouette running toward them, spraying machine gun fire. Saif and Skaff both opened on it with Uzis, and the figure stumbled to the ground. After two more rounds of missiles, the 30-mm cannons fell silent and Skaff could hear the rotors of the Apaches. The pilots waited for more fire, but none came. They circled the killing zone and returned, facing the band of SLA soldiers gathering on the road between the rocks. They hovered for a second and then banked away in opposite directions, fading into the night sky.

Skaff found his radio and signaled Hassan. "Proceed forward and secure the west perimeter to the road. On your all-clear, a team will secure the east perimeter. On their all-clear, the third team will secure the road to your location."

He waited for Hassan's acknowledgement then sent the four men between the Jeeps to secure the east perimeter, telling them to wait for Hassan's signal before leaving the road. He checked on the soldier with the shoulder wound. Assured that he would be OK, Skaff gathered the force from the second Jeep and instructed them to secure the road after receiving the signals from the perimeter teams.

As the teams secured the area, Skaff gathered the injured men, assessed their wounds, and verified that Rafik and Sayyed were dead. After some intermittent gunfire, the teams declared the area secured. Skaff set up a light perimeter defense and directed the remaining men to get them out of there. They commandeered Hezbollah vehicles to replace the destroyed Jeeps.

As the men began the work of clearing the road and preparing for departure, Skaff took the time to dress the cut on his leg and indulge his contemplative nature. He added the names of Rafik and Sayyed to the long and growing list of good men he had seen die in the struggle that had defined his existence from his earliest memory.

Would it never end? Skaff thought of his daughter, Hayat, the surprise blessing God had brought at a time most of his other children were beginning families of their own. Conceived on a winter night much like this one, back when Skaff and his men could still live in their own houses, back when Israel possessed the castle. Born after the collapse of the resistance, when SLA fighters who chose to stay in Lebanon were forced underground to avoid prison. She had never seen her father in the daylight. He tried to imagine how she might think of him. Perhaps as some large and daunting but gentle creature of the night? A djinn that crept in at unpredictable times and told her stories and tickled the backs of her knees?

Two years old and already so silent and solemn. He thought of the smile he had coaxed from her only hours before as he had put her to bed and then approached the unbelievable luxury of a few hours with his wife.

Skaff didn't see any hope that he would ever live in peace or that Hayat or her children would know life free from war. If history were any indication, this struggle wouldn't end until the return of the Messiah.

"*Maranatha, Yeshua* (Come quickly, Jesus)," he whispered as he wrapped a bandage around his leg.

He watched as Saif's arm was dressed, thankful that it was nothing more serious than the slash of a passing fragment from the Jeep. Sayyed's family was not so fortunate. They would be planning a funeral that would be attended by Hezbollah in the hopes of capturing SLA militiamen too distracted by grief to remain in hiding. Rafik would have seventeen SLA soldiers at his funeral this night with no malicious Hezbollah eyes to profane it.

He had come to Skaff four years earlier after three nights of hiding in the rocky wastes near Sadaar. His story was painful, told in breathless gasps through clenched teeth. They had no running water because the Israelis had hit the pumping station. He was with Abu, a friend, returning to the house with water when he saw Hezbollah fedayeen in a circle behind his house. He stopped, standing on the ridge with the buckets stretching his arms when Abu pushed him behind a boulder. They peered down the hill toward what was in the center of the circle that interested the Muslims. Then the backs parted and Rafik saw his sister, held to the ground by her hands and feet by four men. A fifth man was rising to his feet and shouldering his rifle.

Rafik jumped to his feet, screaming, but Abu tackled him and shoved his forearm into Rafik's mouth. He struggled for several minutes, even biting Abu's arm, but the only response he got was a fierce scowl and whispered curses. Rafik finally relaxed, and Abu relented. When they looked over the boulder again, they saw four Jeeps in a circle on the road behind the house, facing outward. Men were holding Rafik's father down between them. Four ropes led from the Jeeps to his legs and arms. Rafik's mother and sister were being held against the back wall of the house. They were screaming and crying.

The men stepped away from the Jeeps and one fired his sidearm into the air. The Jeeps raced in four directions. Abu tackled Rafik again and didn't let him up for an hour. They waited until dark. Then Rafik returned to the house, put on his heavy jacket, and told his mother he was going to find Major Skaff. It took him three days on foot, moving only at night, to find the Skaff home in Marjeyoun, where Zaki fussed over him, fed him, and made it clear there was no need for discussion on the matter of where he would live. Skaff pointed out that their own son was named Rafik, which might cause confusion. She answered that if one Rafik was a blessing, two would be twice the blessing.

He lived there, one Rafik serving as mentor to the other, until the Israeli withdrawal. Then, like Skaff and the rest of these men, he lived in hiding, fighting Hezbollah, patiently but fervently killing as many as he could. But he would fight no longer.

Not for the first time, Skaff considered slipping his family across the border. Maybe he would find General Lahd and his restaurant in Tel Aviv, supplementing the excessive security force that worked there. Hayat would be able to grow up in a home that had a father more than a few hours a week. True, even this choice would not give her a life free from the terrorists. There had been several suicide bombings in Tel Aviv this year in malls and residential areas, even a shooting at a restaurant that killed three people and wounded ten times as many. But there would be better schools, medical facilities, a better life.

Even as he flirted with the idea, Major Skaff knew he would never leave Lebanon. For the past thousand years his ancestors had fought in this very place, from 1139 when European Christians had first captured Shqif Arnoun to this day when Lebanese Christians struggled to live in the land where their families had lived since before the first Crusaders. He knew he could never live anywhere else.

As he began transferring ammo and supplies from his demolished Jeep to a Hezbollah truck, his thoughts turned to Roberts, the crazy American who had somehow convinced the Israelis to let him through the fence last summer. At the advice of his wife, Skaff had sent a man to guide Roberts through the wadis to his location. He came through the wastes like a mad prophet in a Jeep, robe and white hair blowing in the wind.

He asked many questions about the life of Christians in Lebanon. As they sensed his passion and sincerity over the week he stayed, Skaff's men spent hours telling him of the schools destroyed by both Israelis and Muslims in the struggle, nonexistent medical supplies, and crumbling infrastructure. Roberts didn't take notes, but in his final conversation with Skaff he recited in detail the concerns the men had shared, down to naming wives and children and their specific needs.

That was when Skaff began to suspect that perhaps this madman could do something about their plight. But six months later he still had heard nothing from Roberts. Only God knew if anything would come of it.

Chapter 3

Los Angeles, California.
Friday, 22 November 2002. 20:00.

It wasn't that Cooper minded being in an 11,000-square-foot ballroom filled with beautiful women and their escorts. It was that on this night he preferred being out on the town with one particular woman.

He consoled himself with the thought that escorting Stevie to the Women in Show Business awards dinner was good for business and easy on the eye. He knew by the occasional glances and subdued tones as he passed that his presence nudged more than one conversation to some supposedly private difficulty he had resolved.

Although he provided services for Fortune 500 companies and multinationals, entertainment clients dominated the roster of private individuals who engaged his firm, International Research and Intelligence Group, specialists in corporate and personal security.

Stevie's excitement about her Angel of the Year award had overcome his objections. Fortunately he had accomplished his goals in the first week of his trip—hosting Tom Zhang's retirement party at the Hong Kong intelligence office and evaluating the individuals who were moved up the food chain, from the new director down to the new hire. He cut his trip short by two days and emerged from the fourteen-hour flight to push through one more evening before surrendering to fatigue and jet lag. The forty-five-minute nap in the limo from LAX to Malibu helped, as did the extended hot shower that followed. He could tell that Stevie was too preoccupied by thoughts of the awards dinner to pay attention when he answered her questions about the trip, but he kept her distracted with stories anyway until they arrived at the Huntington Ritz-Carlton in Pasadena.

They entered the ballroom to the flash of cameras. At first Cooper stayed beside Stevie as she lightly held his arm and greeted actors, producers, directors, and other luminaries in the film industry. As she gradually detached from him and became engrossed in a conversation with a producer, he mingled but kept her in sight at all times, constantly maneuvering to stay within ten feet of her. He did this unconsciously as one would instinctively scratch an itch and so naturally that the person speaking to him would never realize a part of his attention was focused on Stevie and not on the conversation.

Cooper was skillfully not answering a blunt question from a director about an actor notorious for his sexual conquests when he noticed a man wearing all white, from tie to shoes, plowing through the crowd directly toward Stevie. Cooper brought his non-answer to a close and asked the director if he would like something from the bar. He set a course designed to intersect the man before he reached Stevie. At a distance the man appeared to be Christopher Lloyd on a bad hair day, but as he drew closer Cooper noted that he was shorter and stockier.

Cooper stepped around the cluster where Stevie nodded as the producer lamented the quality of scripts she was forced to read. He noticed that as he moved to the side, the man altered his course away from Stevie and toward him. Cooper relaxed slightly and glanced at Stevie, who smiled at him and continued nodding to the producer.

The man didn't slow his pace until he came to an abrupt stop a foot away and enclosed Cooper's right hand in a two-fisted handshake.

"Matt Cooper, you're going with me to Israel next week." His voice carried as if he were used to talking to large groups without a mike. He continued to pump Cooper's arm with an interlocking grip. "We leave Wednesday morning."

Cooper gripped the man's right forearm with his left hand and forcefully extracted his right hand, stepping back to diminish the man's intrusive presence. He heard surrounding conversations falter and felt Stevie's amusement. "I believe you have the advantage of me. I didn't catch your name."

"George Roberts, Global Adventures." He produced a card with a flourish and closed the gap between them, tucking the card into Cooper's breast pocket.

"Global Ventures?"

"Global *Ad*-ventures."

Cooper discreetly edged to one side and pulled the card from his pocket. At first glance it appeared to be all white. He flipped to the other side, also blank. Then he realized the name of the company and the man were embossed on the card and overlaid with high-gloss white ink. The contact information was in silver along the bottom edge.

"And how can IRIG assist you, Mr. Roberts?"

"It's George." He stepped forward and placed a hand on Cooper's shoulder. "Wednesday noon, LAX, El Al flight 106. The ticket's booked." He patted Cooper's shoulder and turned abruptly away. Stevie laughed.

Cooper watched him depart. "Enjoy your trip, Mr. Roberts. Send me a postcard."

"You're going with me, Cooper. Get used to the idea," he called over his shoulder. "Don't forget your passport. And it's George."

Cooper shook his head. He felt Stevie's hand on his arm.

"Who was that?"

"Colonel Sanders, from the look of him. Let's sit down."

They threaded through the tables and found their name cards near the front of the room. The other six chairs were already occupied. Stevie introduced him to a studio head and his wife. Cooper introduced her to the CFO of a special effects company and her husband. Neither needed introductions to John Abbott, who currently had two movies in the top ten box office list, or his girlfriend, the co-star of one of the movies.

As dinner was served conversation drifted to wine. Cooper lamented that his source for the excellent '69 Puligny Montrachet had moved to the Virgin Islands. Abbott came to his rescue with a name. Cooper fumbled in his pockets for something to write on and came out with the white business card. He didn't recall putting it in his pocket, but it was useful. He asked around for a pen and saw George directly across from him at the next table. George smiled like he had just sold his millionth box of chicken fingers. He nodded at the card Cooper held and gave him a thumbs-up. Cooper ignored him and took the pen the CFO held out to him. Abbott scrawled on the card and Cooper pocketed it.

Stevie's award was presented early in the evening, but their presence at a front table made it impossible to slip out. As Cooper endured one excessive acceptance speech after another, the jet lag began to claim him. He rubbed his eyes and looked around, only to catch George staring at him again. George did a subdued two thumbs-up. As the speaker sat down to applause, Cooper excused himself and stepped into the hall. He wandered through the corridors and pushed a wireless headset into his ear, using the voice-recognition mode to call his favorite workaholic in operations, Marci. She answered on the first ring.

"Hi, Matt."

"Marci, you're at work at eleven on a Friday night. Do you realize how pathetic that is?"

"It's terrible, isn't it? I should be in therapy or something. But dedication like mine deserves a raise, don't you think?"

"I'll consider it as soon as you take a vacation. Do me a favor and run a check on George Roberts, Global Adventures."

As she looked up the info he found the door he was looking for. He stepped out into the cool November night onto a veranda. The garden that extended below was silvered by the full moon. He nodded to a guy who stepped out on the veranda and lighted a cigarette. *Brave soul, he could get tackled for doing that in southern California.* Marci came back on the line.

"George Roberts. Interesting guy. Former head of Jet Stream, the guys who pioneered the corporate jet travel business, retired in the '90s. He's a millionaire several times over, entrepreneur with multiple ventures, some still active. The main one is Global Adventures. It's part travel agency, part humanitarian organization, part holy-roller convention. He takes groups of Christian Zionists on trips to the Holy Land where they hit all the tourist spots and then work with local officials to provide grunt labor for medical and rebuilding projects in areas hit by the PLO. Kind of a kosher Habitat for Humanity, I guess."

"That explains the Jimmy Carter grin."

"What?"

"What else you got?"

"The comments say he's a tough cookie. His success is based on bulldozing through all obstacles. He has a reputation for being driven and highly competitive, but not ruthless. Wait. What's this? It says, 'His ambition is informed by the sensibilities of his spiritual worldview.' Where did that come from?"

"Probably Dixon's granddaughter. Graduate student. A couple of years ago we gave her a summer internship doing corporate research as a favor to Dixon."

"Oh yeah. That one."

"Thanks, Marci. Now go home."

"Aye, aye, Captain. Over and out."

On the way in, he tossed the business card into a pristine ashtray. Possibly by some trick of the light on the white ink, it seemed to flash as it came to rest on the charcoal black crystals imprinted with the Ritz-Carlton logo. He peered down at it and noticed the name and number of Abbott's vintner. *Oh yeah.* He retrieved it and dropped it back into his pocket.

The drone of self-indulgent speeches came mercifully to an end as he returned to the table. He helped Stevie with her wrap. As she said good-bye to the others, Cooper held his hand to his ear and spoke quietly.

"Alex, we'll be out in two minutes."

He used to drive to these events but found the wait for the valet service could easily hit half an hour. A New Year's Eve party at this very hotel had resulted in an hour-long wait–an hour of mind-numbing conversation with a bombshell date so vacant he could hear echoes when he whispered into her ear. The next day he had made two resolutions that remained unbroken. Never go to a party without a driver. Never go on a blind date arranged by friends in the film industry.

Stevie and Cooper wended through the other guests, past a line of the rich and famous waiting for their cars and into the open door of the limo.

"The scenic route, Alex," Cooper said, holding the door open for Stevie.

"Yes sir." Alex closed the door behind Cooper.

The first half-hour was all L.A. freeways. Stevie turned to Cooper as they left the Ritz.

"So, what was all that between you and the ice-cream suit?"

"Ms. Zorn, allow me to congratulate you on your award."

He gave her the passionate kiss of a man who has been out of the country for two weeks.

Chapter 4

They didn't speak again until they were on the Pacific Coastal Highway. Alex settled into a leisurely pace once he turned up the coast. Cooper reclined against the door, his arms wrapped around Stevie as she lay against him. They looked out the open window at a black velvet sea edged with a silver lace of surf. The brisk air tasted of the salt of sweat and sea. Cooper reflected on how Stevie had transformed his life in two short years, ending three years of hell. Unfortunately, she had not had the same effect on Nikki.

Cooper had not been successful at convincing Nikki that she wasn't responsible for her mother's death. Not a surprising conclusion for an eight-year-old when the last memory of her mother was a bitter, screaming argument and the screeching of tires on the driveway. Hours later the officers had arrived at the house to find Nikki alone with the housekeeper. They had asked for Lola, and hearing she was gone, asked for a description of the car. Then they asked the housekeeper to contact Cooper.

He had arrived from the office an hour later to hear the report of a guardrail destroyed, a mangled Porsche, and a body at the bottom of a ridge in Topanga Canyon. Cooper had told Nikki it wasn't her fault. What he hadn't told her was that he suspected it was his fault.

Based on the blood-alcohol level the autopsy revealed, the police had not looked any further for the cause of the wreck. The Porsche was his car, but he knew Lola could handle it. She had driven it many times with complete control when angry, even when drunk, on the roads that twisted through the hills and canyons along the coast. He was sure it wasn't an accident.

He assigned his best forensics team to the car when it was recovered. It took a few days of digging through the twisted metal to discover the transmitter/receiver on the steering column and the wires leading to the mechanism that locked the steering column when the key was turned off. The key was still turned to on, but the steering column was locked. The team concluded that the transmitter was used to track the location of the car. When it approached the hairpin curve, the steering lock was engaged.

Cooper didn't think it was a coincidence that at the time of the wreck he was three months into a joint investigation with the FBI into reports of mob infiltration of dockworkers, collusion with the Chinese mafia, and the smuggling of drugs and people into the country.

In his line of work, he was forced to maintain a high level of security in his personal life. When he bought the house, he had installed an electrified perimeter fence with motion-sensitive floodlights and cameras atop the existing six-foot wall, supplemented with tightly woven razor wire. On-site security personnel monitored the cameras. His neighbors had considered him paranoid. Following Lola's death he had reinforced their perceptions.

The new system allowed access based on biometrics, ranging from voice recognition at the gate to fingerprint scans for access into the house. The system controller was buried deep in the underground safe room, a command center with two-inch steel titanium sheets imbedded in the twelve-inch concrete walls. The designer of the vault doors at Fort Knox had built the single entrance into the room from the house. Retina scans and DNA signatures were required to open this door, invisible from the outside of the safe room. The other entrance, an escape tunnel leading to a door concealed in a fountain near the perimeter fence, required all four levels of biometrics to open on either end. A second security code was required to pump out the inert gas that filled the tunnel under normal conditions.

While the system brought some sense of security from outside threat, it had not healed the emotional wounds. He had gone through a succession of housekeepers and nannies, all defeated by Nikki's willfulness and self-sufficiency—and particularly by the random tantrums. But the tantrums abruptly ceased when she turned twelve, to Cooper's bewilderment and relief. She focused her energies on acting and landed a weekly show on the Disney channel. It kept her busy, and half of Malibu breathed a sigh of relief.

As for his own scars, a series of disastrous blind and double dates convinced him he was better off drowning his emotional needs in a deluge of work. He turned his energies from courting women to courting clients. He dramatically expanded the international intelligence network that was the basis of his corporate security business and acquired many high-profile clients as a result.

The increase of terrorist activity in the '90s led multinational companies to be proactive when it came to facilities management and travel, particularly in locations outside North America. IRIG was second to none in knowledge of the local environment worldwide, a fact that brought to Cooper's office those who required extreme security. As a result, the last five years had been profitable, if lonely.

The private side of his business had brought him Stevie. She had gone to the police about a stalker who was sending her notes through the mail, but when she found a fresh note on the kitchen counter in her Brentwood townhouse, she decided to transfer her security business from the public to the private sector. At a fund-raiser for battered women in 2000, she had cornered Cooper and used her considerable charms to convince him to personally oversee her security.

He did what he could at the townhouse, but the property manager wouldn't allow all the modifications he recommended. He put a detective on the stalker problem and delivered him to the police, complete with sufficient evidence to remove him for three to five years with time off for good behavior. Cooper personally visited him in jail and impressed upon him the inadvisability of pursuing his obsession once released. The stain in the inmate's coveralls as he left the conference room led Cooper to believe his advice had been effective.

In a town infested with grasping covetousness, Stevie swirled into his life with her breezy self-confidence and a disarming ambition that was more a passion to do all things well and enjoy them fully. After six months of attending to Stevie's security by escorting her to dinners, parties, night clubs, premier openings, Academy Awards functions, and bowling, Cooper convinced her that the best security was available in his Malibu fortress. She moved in Memorial Day 2001.

The transition from client to friend to lover was gradual. As he rolled strands of her black hair between his fingers, he felt rather than thought that it had gone beyond that. He had traveled this route with Lola much faster, but not this far. Despite the good years, and there were many before her slalom into alcoholism, he had held something in reserve for reasons even he didn't completely fathom. Self-preservation? Independence? Whatever the motivation, he had guarded the deep places. He was beginning to sense that contrary to his long-held conviction, perhaps it was possible to relax the final defenses. He allowed himself to toy with the idea of a soul mate, one that knows all and shares all.

Stevie broke in on his thoughts. "I do believe you're avoiding the question."

"Hmm?"

"The man in the ice-cream suit. You change the subject every time I bring him up."

"You only brought him up once."

"See? You're doing it again."

"He wants me to go to Israel on Wednesday."

"The day before Thanksgiving? What for?"

"He didn't say."

The limo pulled into the driveway. Cooper heard Alex speak into the voice-recognition system. The gate opened, and Alex drove through. When the gate was completely closed, a section of the driveway near the house began to sink, forming a ramp down to a security garage door. Alex lowered his window, placed his hand on a scanner, spoke the code, and the door began rolling into the ceiling of the garage. He pulled into the garage. Once the door closed behind them, Alex opened the limo door for Stevie. Cooper got out the other side and allowed the system to sniff him like a family dog, approving his presence.

A press of a button as he entered the den opened the drapes as *Birth of the Cool* came on over hidden speakers. Recessed spotlights threw ovals of subdued light on various items of furniture. He stood by the wall of glass and looked at the ocean, pursuing his thoughts from the drive. He noticed Stevie in the reflection of the window, bathed in yellow light, a carafe of water in her hand.

"I might go," he said without turning.

"Go where?"

"Israel."

She set the carafe down and looked at him. "You're joking."

"Maybe."

"What about Thanksgiving?"

"We'll do the turkey thing Tuesday. You can tape the ball games, and we'll watch them when I get back."

"What's in Israel?"

"High-tech business and security threats."

"Why go with the man in the ice-cream suit?"

"I hear he gets around."

Their voices had remained calm as they talked from opposite sides of the room, him to her reflection in the window, her to his back. Stevie came halfway to him and sat in an armchair. Her voice hinted at frustration.

"Matt, we were supposed to start on the business plan for the production company next week. Stan is coming down from San Francisco."

He turned to her. "I think the two of you can handle it. It's pretty straightforward. You know what you want; Stan knows how to do it."

"That's not the point. It's not my project; it's ours." Her voice was no longer calm.

"Don't overreact. You don't need me. I'll just be sitting around getting bored while Stan works his magic."

She leaned forward. "So, I'm just a checkbox on your schedule? You hook me up with Stan and check me off?"

He raised his voice. "Don't be ridiculous. That's not fair. You know contracts and spreadsheets aren't my thing."

"Oh, it's not enough that I'm boring. Now I'm also ridiculous and unfair." Now they were both shouting.

Cooper held his hands up and looked around the room for a rational person to side with him. Nikki walked in and flopped down on the couch, one leg hanging over the arm.

"What's all the hollering about?" She eyed Stevie suspiciously.

Stevie flowed back into the chair. "He's going to Israel to get himself blown up." She drank her water as if unconcerned.

Ah, that's it. The argument over the contracts was just a cover. Cooper shook his head, admitting to himself, if not to Stevie, that she had blindsided him again.

"What?" Nikki turned her wide brown eyes to Cooper. "When? Why?"

"Adventure, why else?" Stevie said before Cooper could answer. "There've been over twenty suicide bombers in Israel already this year, more than two a month. Yesterday a guy blew himself up on a city bus. Eleven people dead. Irresistible to an adrenaline junkie."

Cooper raised an eyebrow at Stevie. She was better informed than most in the crowded ballroom they had just left.

Nikki studiously ignored Stevie. "Dad, you're not really going over there, are you?"

"I'm just thinking about it." He stepped over the table in front of Nikki and sat on it. "But you know how it works, Nikki. My clients pay me to know the risks better than anyone else and tell them how to avoid them. I don't have a field office in Israel. I have several clients who do business there. Some even have subsidiaries there. A man with contacts has offered to go with me. It's good timing."

Stevie made a noise that registered her disagreement.

"But what about all the suicide bombers? You know, like *She* said." She rolled her eyes in Stevie's direction.

"I won't lie to you. Everything Stevie said is right. About the bombers, at least. I'm not admitting to the adrenaline addict part."

"As if it could be denied." Stevie got up. "Let me know when you've come to your senses. Until then, I'm busy." She left the room.

"If *She's* right, why are you going?"

"Didn't we already cover that part?"

"Dad, don't go."

"Nikki, it's what I do. It's my job. Just like being a cute little pain in the neck is your job."

"Dad, I'm not joking."

"Me, too, neither."

"Dad!"

Cooper shrugged. Nikki jumped up from the couch.

"I'm busy too." She ran from the room.

Cooper watched her go. He sat in the empty room for awhile. Then he stood up.

"Well, Matt, how about a nightcap?" He stepped to the bar. "Thanks, don't mind if I do," he said as Miles blew *Israel*. He raised a toast toward the stereo and drained the glass.

Chapter 5

Cooper looked around the table, noted that everyone was present, and nodded to Sarah, who sat to his right, notepad in her lap.

"Susan," she said.

Susan Patterson, head of Administration, cleared her throat. "Budgets are due Wednesday before the Thanksgiving break. I'm still missing a few."

She looked over her librarian glasses at Frank Perkins, head of Investigations. He suddenly developed an interest in his notebook, flipped through the pages furiously, and scribbled something. Then he looked around innocently in the silence.

He smiled at Susan. "Is it my turn?"

Dr. Hampton, head of Forensics, choked back a laugh and turned it into a cough. Susan ignored him and turned her basilisk gaze on Luis Montoya, head of Special Ops.

"Some of the budgets I have received will need revision or additional justification."

Montoya met her eyes and looked back at her coldly. The clash between Montoya and Susan was legendary. After a warning from Cooper, she had backed off from calling him extravagant and irresponsible in the meetings, but it was clear her position remained unchanged, if unspoken.

She continued. "The meetings for benefits were held last week. Everything is settled for next year. There are some questions about the company we're using for our 401(k) plan." She turned to Cooper. "I'll show you the alternatives at our Wednesday tag-up."

"It'll have to be today. I'm doing Thanksgiving with Nikki and Stevie tomorrow and getting on a plane to Israel Wednesday."

The attendees grew quiet. Those looking through notes or gazing out the window while waiting for their turn stopped and looked at Cooper.

Susan frowned. "You just got back." She flipped through her calendar. "I'll have to cancel some meetings to fit you in today."

Cooper smiled. "I'm sure you'll work it out. Let me know when, and I'll make space for you." He looked to Sarah, who was taking notes.

She checked her list and said, "Claire."

Claire Moquard, head of Undercover Operations, set her notes down on the table. "Before I report, can I inquire about this sudden trip to Israel? I don't recall it being mentioned in the last staff meeting."

Claire looked like she should have an accent. Her featureless Midwest speech always struck Cooper as incongruous with her straight black hair, large brown eyes, mahogany skin, and aura of sophistication. From the moment Dixon had introduced them a year ago, he had visualized her in a sari, a dot on her forehead, and huge gold hoops hanging from her ears. An impression he had never mentioned to her.

"Sure," Cooper said. "It's not an emergency. An opportunity came up at the last minute, and I'm taking advantage of it. I'll be establishing contacts in Jerusalem and Tel Aviv in preparation for launching a regional office."

Claire smiled and twirled a pen through her fingers like a cardsharp, her meeting idiosyncrasy. "I'd be interested in coming along. I have some family connections in Haifa that might be helpful. And I've done some undercover work there before. Could speed things up for us."

Cooper nodded and regarded her thoughtfully. It wasn't a bad suggestion, but his instincts rejected it. He always went alone on the initial trip to evaluate an area for a field office, spent time walking the cities, eating in small, family-run places off the beaten path, having a few drinks in bars and taverns, soaking up the essence of the region. It had worked well; he didn't want to change it now.

Besides, things were bad enough with Stevie. A business trip with his beautiful head of Undercover Ops was inadvisable.

"Thanks for the offer, Claire. However, I'll be traveling with a tour group for cover and want to keep my profile as low as possible. And I'm sure you've got plenty on your plate already. Let's hear your report."

As Claire smiled and referred to her notes, Cooper heard Sarah's sigh of relief. He glanced at her, but she just jotted down a heading in her notes as Claire began her report.

———

The phone was ringing when Cooper returned to his office. He looked at the clock then reluctantly picked up the receiver. "Matt."

"Coop, what's this I hear about you going to Israel?"

"Dixon, have you been talking to Stevie?" William Dixon was director of the CIA for the western U.S. and an old family friend.

"She called me right after I got your message. Wants me to talk you out of it. I told her that after thirty years I know better. May as well try to talk a dog out of howling at the moon."

"Great. So, what do you have on Roberts?"

"He checks out. Lots of activity in the Middle East. Actually, in Israel. All humanitarian work. Has contacts from ambassadors and ministers down to truck drivers and waiters, but stays out of the politics. In the States, spends his time getting resources for his trips—volunteers, supplies, and money."

"So he's legit. No connections to any agencies?"

"Not of the kind you're thinking of. We don't deal with him. Neither does the other side. Not that we haven't tried. Somebody approached him back during the Reagan years. He turned us down cold. Laughed, actually."

"I bet that went over well." Dixon just grunted. Cooper smiled. "Thanks for the info, Dixon. If you will, check up on Nikki and Stevie while I'm gone."

"I got your back, Coop. Already invited them to Thanksgiving dinner."

Sarah walked in as Cooper hung up. "Line two. George Roberts."

"Have a seat, this won't be long." Cooper pushed the speakerphone button. "Mr. Roberts, how can I help you?"

"It's George. Morning, Matt. Just calling to see if you prefer a window or aisle seat."

Cooper smiled at Sarah and looked back at the phone. "What makes you think I'm coming, Mr. Roberts? I just got back from China, it's the end of the year, and I've got lots of loose ends to tie up right here in L.A."

"Matt, I already know you'll be on the plane. Man proposes, but God disposes."

"Are you saying God told you I'm going with you?"

"God didn't tell me to ask you if you wanted to go. He told me to tell you that you're going."

"Funny, He forgot to tell me about it."

"Did He?"

There was a silence as Cooper stared at the phone, wondering how Roberts could be so certain. Sure, he had already decided to go, but how could Roberts know that? Cooper looked up. Sarah was staring at him, waiting for his answer. Roberts continued as if he were reading Cooper's thoughts.

"Matt, there's no point in playing this game. We both know you're going. Since September 11, you've been thinking you should have an office in the Middle East. I can help you collapse weeks of work into days."

Cooper didn't deny it. "Why would you do that?"

"Contacts, Matt, contacts. Because you know people with resources. Because once you see the need yourself, firsthand, I won't have to convince you to help. I won't be able to stop you. You won't be able to stop yourself."

"Roberts, you seem pretty sure of yourself."

"Not of myself, Matt. Me, I'm just an old broken-down millionaire with too much time on his hands. I'm sure of the One who holds us all in His hand. Like my big brother, I just do what our Father tells me."

"I'm not a religious man, Mr. Roberts."

"That's fine. Religion doesn't interest me much anyway. So, window or aisle?"

As much as Cooper hated to give Roberts the pleasure, it seemed silly to keep up the charade. "You can use the ticket for one of your charity cases. I've already booked a first-class seat. Aisle, if you must know."

"That's great, Matt. Emilio was disappointed when he couldn't raise the money. I'll tell him you gave him your ticket."

"Tell him whatever you want, Mr. Roberts. Just send me an itinerary for your group. I'll be making my own plans, but I need to fit them in with the group activities so I don't draw too much attention."

"Will do, Matt. And I'll get you to call me George before the trip is over."

Cooper hung up the phone and looked at Sarah.

"What a strange man," she said.

"You should see him. So, what do we have lined up for the rest of the day?"

She went through the list, closed the book, and set her face with a determined expression. Cooper recognized it. It was the one that preceded the I'm-doing-this-for-your-own-good lecture. Despite her youth, she was amazingly good at being a mother hen. Walter, Cooper's workout partner, had found it endearing when they were dating. When Cooper's administrative assistant moved back East to be with her family, Walt suggested Sarah. Cooper was doubtful. It was one thing for Walt to date a girl barely old enough to buy a drink; it was another for Cooper to rely on her to help him run IRIG. But a double date gave him a chance to meet Sarah and size her up. Cooper was impressed. The formal interview went well, and Cooper ignored his initial misgivings and gave her the chance to prove herself. Four years later he had never found a reason to regret his decision.

Walt's experience with Sarah had been different. He proposed on the fourth date, and they were married not long after Cooper hired her. But the mother-hen characteristics Walt found so endearing while they were dating began to chafe against his independence and need to be in control. By their third anniversary, it seemed to Cooper they were living in a careful and deliberate détente designed to forestall open warfare. It saddened him. As much as he liked Walt as a workout partner, he knew Sarah deserved better. But people make their own choices. All the more reason to be very careful before choosing.

Cooper took the mother hen head on. "And this would be about?"

"Was I that obvious?"

"Yes, but that's OK. Let me have it. Whatever it is, I'm sure I deserve it."

Her determined expression softened. "It's Claire."

"Oh, that."

"Yes, that," she said, her attitude returning.

"The trip."

"Yes, the trip. You saw how she tried to weasel her way into it."

"And you saw how I shut it down. I can handle myself with Claire."

"That's just what she wants you to think, Mr. C. She's after something, either you or the agency, I'm not sure which." Her eyes narrowed. "Maybe both."

"Sarah, you know I value your opinion, but you're just going to have to let this one go. Claire is the right person for the job. You saw her résumé. I doubt there's another person in the country better suited for the position."

Cooper was thankful the résumé had been enough reason to hire her. When Dixon came to him with the request that he fill the open position of director of Undercover Ops with one of his own people, Cooper resisted. Cooperation with the CIA was useful, but positions at the director level were critical. It had to be someone who could actually do the job. Claire's résumé had settled that issue. The other applicants hadn't even come close. Not that the CIA couldn't have fabricated a world-class résumé, but it checked out with every resource Cooper had to validate it. And he used everything he had.

Her first year on the job confirmed that she was as good in the position as she looked on paper. Perhaps too good, which was probably what had Sarah worried. Anybody who was paying attention would realize that director of Undercover Ops wouldn't satisfy someone of Claire's abilities. But they wouldn't know that she was CIA and had a career path ahead of her far beyond IRIG. She wasn't after Cooper's job or after Cooper, either. Her sights were set much higher. Cooper wouldn't be surprised if she took Dixon's job after he retired, which wasn't that far off. He seemed to be grooming her for the position.

"She's a use-'em-and-lose-'em type. You think you can handle her, but she's left plenty of victims on her way up, for sure. You aren't the first one she's set her sights on. Men always think they can handle it all. That's what makes it so easy for the Claires out there."

"So, how's Walt?"

Sarah flushed and gathered her book and pen. "That's not what this is about."

"Maybe not. But as much as I value your input, you should remember two things. One, men aren't the only ones who can have their perceptions colored by their own issues. And two, not every man is like Walt." He took a deep breath. "Sarah, you have done your duty. You have warned me about Claire. I will handle her. You should let it go before it affects your work."

Sarah nodded and left, eyes watering. Cooper let out a heavy sigh as he watched her go. He wished there was something he could do to ease the pain her personal life had become. The thought crossed his mind to say a prayer for her, but he shook it off. Like he told Roberts, he wasn't a religious man. To start praying now seemed hypocritical.

Instead he turned to his Rolodex and worked his way through the roster of North American field contacts, touching base and getting a feel for things before he left the country again.

Chapter 6

Safe house, Zahedan, Iran.
Tuesday, 26 November 2002. 16:00.

Ali al-Huzayfi waited in an empty room on the second story. He stood in the shade of the shutters, watching the dust filter through the elongated shadows of men as they went about their business in the late winter afternoon, dancing bits of light being swallowed in the passing darkness. No one looked up at the window, as if by ignoring it they could also deny knowledge of his presence. He knew they feared him, as they feared and revered the One to whom he reported, the One whose name was now known around the world. It was reassuring and maddening. His survival relied on the fear others felt toward him, the certainty that he held life and death in his hand and would mete out justice without regard for personal feelings. Personal feelings were weakness, and weakness was death.

The maddening part was the irrational notion in the heads of these same people that he was a regrettable but necessary evil, like a headsman or a sewage worker. He could see the thought behind the fear, and also their fear that perhaps he did see it. Did they not see that he was the very fist of Allah? He was not a necessary evil; he was an instrument of righteousness. Holiness was a terrible and exacting standard. It was the breath of the God they prayed to six times a day. He was the avenging right hand of the Prophet. In their small minds they could not see that his was a noble calling denied to all but the most elect. The very smallness that prevented them from serving also prevented them from seeing. Although he sometimes hated them for their dullness, he mostly pitied them for their fate, to tread the well-worn path of mundane existence while he served the highest calling at the will of the holy One.

As the shadows lengthened he saw them coming singly, indistinguishable from the wretches whose shadows mingled with theirs. Over the space of an hour, the five slipped through the gloom past lesser men into the doorway below. None acknowledged his presence at the window.

Ten minutes after the last arrived, Ali took the back stairs to the room where they waited at the table in the fumes of the lanterns. Their subdued conversation stopped when he entered.

Ali acknowledged their presence, sat at the head of the table, and glanced at a man in the doorway. Tea was brought in and served.

"*Assalaamu alaykum,*" he said at last.

"*Wa alaykumus salaam,*" they responded.

Al-Huzayfi looked to his right to Abdouh Makkee, his lieutenant for security and intelligence. "Makkee, what is the news?"

"The buildup of forces in Kuwait continues. The Americans have amassed fifty thousand troops and four hundred fighter jets and bombers. They have announced that the invasion plan calls for over two hundred thousand troops. The central command is setting up in Qatar."

Al-Huzayfi nodded. He was aware of the American presence in Qatar and the disruption to their activities in the Horn of Africa. "And what is said of this?"

"The UN opposes the buildup. Saddam says he has no weapons of mass destruction and the U.S. has no right to invade. War protests have been staged worldwide. Canadians are volunteering to come to Iraq as human shields."

"Your thoughts?"

"Saddam cannot win against the Americans. He saw this ten years ago. His forces are as maidens against mighty warriors. Though he use chemical or even biological weapons against them, he cannot stop them. He will be forced to abdicate."

"Don't be a fool. Saddam will never abdicate. His own people will kill him if he does. I myself will cut out his entrails if he does. He knows this. Saddam will not abdicate."

"Then he will be destroyed," Makkee said.

The man to his right, Nidal Sidi al-Suri, interrupted. "It is not so. The UN will not approve an invasion of Iraq. The Security Council has been taken care of. And Saddam has replenished the chemical agents he used against the Kurds. If the cowboy Bush moves to defy the UN and invade a sovereign land, his soldiers will meet their death in the desert and be disgraced before the world." Al-Suri leaned back in his chair and took up his tea. "Saddam will not be destroyed."

Al-Huzayfi shook his head. "It is as Makkee has said. The Americans will invade. Saddam will be destroyed. I have seen it."

The men around the table looked at one another without speaking. Al-Suri nodded doubtfully. "It will be as you say."

"The Great Satan will bruise our heel, but we will crush his head. And what of training?"

Al-Suri set down his teacup. "The matériel we moved from the Afghan training camps into Iraq before the Americans invaded has been moved to Syria. It is safe from the invasion. Most of it can be used in the Sudan. Some we have sold to

Hezbollah, some to the PLO. All is going according to plan. No unexpected losses."

Al-Huzayfi nodded and looked to the end of the table.

Afad Salim spoke up. "The infrastructure is in place to supply resistance fighters after the Americans invade Iraq. We have weapons, ammunition, and volunteers, including suicide bombers. We're still working on medical supplies."

"Transportation?"

"We have a series of safe houses and trucks for each leg. It will have to be done in piecemeal fashion."

"We use animals if we must. They will not attract attention."

"I will see to it."

"Al-Fadel?"

Khalid al-Fadel frowned. "The Americans have gained cooperation in confiscating accounts. Our operating capital has been seriously reduced. We are not yet in danger, but if the trend continues, it could affect our ability to complete the special project. It requires unusual amounts of cash."

"I will speak to the One about it. He is aware." Al-Huzayfi turned to the man at his left. "Khidamat?"

Jamal Khidamat cleared his throat and scanned the room quickly before speaking. "In the Muslim world, of course, we have the sympathy of the people—especially after Afghanistan. Europe is divided. No one will openly refuse cooperation with Bush in legal prosecution of known sympathizers, but some are resisting his push to invade Iraq. In the U.S., although there is some resistance, the popular opinion is in favor of Bush invading Iraq."

Khidamat licked his lips nervously, seemed about to say something, then leaned back into his chair. Al-Huzayfi regarded him thoughtfully.

"Come, Khidamat, there is something else you wish to say. You must speak it."

"You heard al-Fadel. We're losing valuable assets in Europe that can finance our efforts to turn the minds of the Americans and others sympathetic to our cause. Al-Suri didn't say, but I know we experienced serious losses in training when the Americans invaded Afghanistan. Salim said we have weapons and ammunition. He didn't say we have enough to field only a few hundred fighters for less than a month before we run out. Nobody will say what we all really know." As he gestured around the room, eyes looked away from him. He became angry. He leaned forward.

"We went too far. When the towers fell, my heart rejoiced but my mind spoke to me that we had awakened a sleeping giant. Most Americans can't spell Afghanistan, even fewer can point to it on a map, but they unite behind Bush to invade and overthrow the government. They talk about freedom, but submit to the Patriot Act because they think it will restrict our operations. And countries that would resist efforts to probe into their internal law enforcement are now openly cooperating with the Americans to shut down our financial network."

Khidamat spread his hands. "No man is more faithful to the One than I am, but the 9/11 attack was a mistake. It cost us a complete country"–he looked to Makkee–"many trained people who will take years to replace"–he nodded at al-Suri–"valuable infrastructure that we may never regain"–he looked to Salim–"and hundreds of millions of dollars lost"–he gestured to al-Fadel. "It did not demoralize the Americans; it galvanized them.

"Attacks that kill dozens, or even hundreds, wear down our enemies without causing them to strike back. We cannot strike a killing blow against such a large beast; we can only hope to weary it until it gives up. If the blow is too great, it will be shocked from its lethargy and strike the killing blow against us.

"The 9/11 attack made this mistake. The special project will do worse. It should be abandoned before it destroys not the Americans, but us."

The others sat in silence. Al-Huzayfi nodded. "Khidamat, you have spoken from your heart. Now I will speak from mine." He pulled a Walther PPK from his robes and shot Khidamat in the head in a single smooth motion. The body slammed back into the chair and fell against al-Fadel, who shoved it away from him. It fell to the floor.

Ali looked at the empty chair as he spoke. "The 9/11 attacks shut down the airspace of the most powerful nation in the world for almost a week." Three men rushed through the door, weapons drawn. Al-Huzayfi ignored them. "It so crippled the industry that many airlines are teetering on the brink of bankruptcy. It caused an economic depression that shows no signs of relief over a year later. The American economy is a goblet of brittle crystal balanced on the edge of a knife. One more jostle, and it will fall and shatter.

"Then the Americans will no longer care about who is training in places they can't spell or who is being tortured in places they can't pronounce or what happens to the usurpers who are squatting on the Dome of the Rock. They'll be looking at breadlines and using the Patriot Act to quell their own internal revolutions. Once their economy is in shambles, they will quit poking their nose into the business of the rest of the world and worry about their own problems."

Al-Huzayfi looked around the table. "And we, my fellow warriors, will give the goblet the final jostle. The Americans, they are fond of naming their projects. In their honor, I have named our special project. It will be called the Last Straw. It will break the back of the Americans."

Refugio Elementary School, Los Angeles, California. Tuesday, 26 November 2002. 06:30.

Emilio rinsed out two mugs, turned on the hot plate under the kettle, and shuffled out to unlock the door by the teachers' parking. Last night the unexpected cold spell had reminded him that his knees were not the same since Pork Chop Hill. In truth, few things were the same since Pork Chop Hill. He stepped out on the asphalt and walked to the chain-link fence that surrounded the playground. He looked down Wilshire Boulevard across I-110 and saw something very unusual. The cold front had swept the sky clean of smog. The sun was rising unseen behind the skyscrapers of the financial district half a mile away, creating a halo of baby blue that faded to midnight blue directly above.

He saw something that made him smile. Venus was floating just above the skyline. He spread his arms to catch the nascent warmth of the new day and closed his eyes. *Root and offspring of David, I turn to you as to a light shining in a dark place, until the day dawns and the morning star rises in my heart.*

When he opened his eyes he saw Amil walking up the driveway behind the school and felt warmed. He unlocked the gate, greeted his old friend with a soft hand on his shoulder, and walked with him into the building. Amil, the companion of his dark days. Emilio never saw him without thinking of Juanita, an edge of sorrow that tempered the joy of his presence. The two small men walked together in comfortable silence down the dim hall to the maintenance room. The kettle was just beginning to grumble. Amil sat down slowly in a metal folding chair with a wooden seat and back. It was still cool inside. He kept his sweater on.

Emilio pried the lid off the tin of teabags, dropped a bag in each mug, and carefully replaced the tin in the cabinet. Then he pulled the lid from a plastic container filled with sugar and placed the container, a spoon, and chipped saucer on the large wooden spool that served variously as a table, footstool, and workbench. When vapor hissed around the ill-fitting lid of the kettle, he turned down the heat and poured. As he set the kettle down, he heard Amil chuckling gently.

"I have a treat for you, my friend," Amil said.

Emilio set the mugs on the spool and took the sturdy wooden chair opposite Amil, who pushed a hand down into the misshapen lump that was his sweater pocket and withdrew a small box covered with odd symbols.

"My son has returned from Lebanon last night. These were made fresh yesterday in Beirut."

He opened the box. Emilio looked at the assortment of round and square pastries filled with some kind of nut mixture. He looked up at Amil.

"Baklava," Amil said.

"Ah," Emilio said.

Emilio spooned the teabag from his mug and set it on the saucer. He raised the mug to his lips, blew away the steam, and took the merest of sips. He rested the mug on his knee, allowing the warmth to seep through the ache, and selected a pastry. A square one. He bit it gingerly, gathering the flaking crust with his lips, and chewed it slowly. He nodded at Amil.

"Bueno. Many thanks to your son."

Amil nodded in reply, put three spoons of sugar in his tea, and stirred it steadily while nibbling on baklava.

Emilio moved the mug to his other knee to warm it. "He travels much, your son."

"He has much international business. Many people here desire food from the East, labels they remember, many things." He selected another piece of baklava. "But not all get it this fresh." He sipped his tea slowly.

They drank in silence. The light seeped in through the frosted window in back, gradually overtaking the single bulb hanging over the hot plate.

"Maybe I can bring you more baklava. They have this in Israel tambien?"

Amil raised his eyebrows. "You go to Israel?"

"Yes. I didn't tell you? I received a ticket from a generous benefactor. I leave tomorrow and return in December."

"It is a pity you will not see Lebanon."

"I will see it from a distance. We will build a barn in a kibbutz in the Golan Heights."

"You will go to the Holy City? To the Sepulcher? To Golgotha?"

"Yes."

Emilio saw the mist in Amil's eyes.

"Remember me in the Lord's city."

"I will, my friend. I will."

They sat in silence, sipping tea and sharing the dawn. Inside Emilio, memories, prayers, and hopes mingled with the growing light.

Eye Spy Surveillance, Burbank, California.
Tuesday, 26 November 2002. 08:30.

Bernie cranked the security bars up out of the front window displays, flipped the Closed sign to Open, and pulled the string on the neon. The Eye Spy Surveillance sign buzzed and flickered to life in the window. Then he stepped behind the counter and eased onto the stool, the blonde wood polished to a high gloss by years of sliding on and off. He preferred to be on the stool when customers were in the store since it allowed him to look them in the eye instead of in the pocket protector.

He surveyed the bank of monitors behind the counter that allowed him to see every inch of every aisle and shelf in the store from multiple angles. Check. He flipped the switch that unlocked the security bolts in the front door with a solid, satisfying clunk. He flipped it down and back up just to hear it again. Then he opened his first Diet Coke of the day, booted up the computer, and checked the spam folder before clearing it.

He opened the e-mail from missilebases.com. If he ever got enough to retire early, he was definitely going to check out an old Atlas missile silo, maybe buy one and convert it into a house. Ten years ago he wired his dad's old bomb shelter in the Pasadena house with power, cable, Internet, and phone. It was a great place for blasting away on a multi-user assault game. He could turn it all the way up and play all night with no complaints from the neighbors. The thought of actually living a couple hundred feet underground gave him a warm feeling.

He forced himself to file the e-mail and check out the Web site later. Usually he could count on a couple of free hours for e-mail before being bothered by customers. Snoops were of necessity creatures of the night. Most, anyway. There were exceptions. But today he didn't have time for e-mail or exceptions. He had one day to finish the inventory before the trip.

So, of course, one of the exceptions immediately walked in, wearing his annoyingly perpetual smile. "Bernie, how's the world treating you?"

"Same as it always does, Frank—like a red-headed stepchild. The Man said, 'In this world you will have trouble.'"

"That's why you have to stick it to the man."

Bernie tilted his head down, looked over his glasses, and locked his gaze on Perkins. "Oh, they stuck it to Him, alright."

Bernie watched his smile fade slowly. Perkins looked around the store. "So, I need some GPS tracking systems and latent print kits."

"Sure."

Bernie slipped off the stool and walked around the counter. Perkins was right behind him. He grabbed a stack of boxes. "Here." He shoved them at Perkins and walked on. Then he stopped suddenly. Perkins ran into him.

"Hey, don't crowd me." He pushed Perkins away and pulled a box from the shelf. "You need some of these."

Perkins shifted the stack of print kits under one arm and took the box. "A camera? We developed our own."

Perkins put the box back on the shelf. Bernie pulled it back off.

"Not like this one. Can't beat it for sensitivity and resolution."

"We got ours down to 0.2 lux."

"Resolution?"

"Six hundred lines."

Bernie looked up at Perkins and laughed. "The box says 1 lux, but I did some mods on it. Swapped out a chip, made a few tweaks. Negative 0.4 lux. Gives you a usable image in starlight." He could see Perkins didn't believe him. "Resolution 1,200 lines. You can blow it up to eight feet. See that?"

He pointed at a poster of a couple kissing on the Santa Monica pier. Perkins looked at it and then down at him.

"You're kidding."

Bernie delivered his most withering stare. "Nobody has ever accused me of having a sense of humor, Frank." He shoved the camera back at Perkins. "Take it and try it. If it doesn't do everything I say, bring it back." He walked to the GPS tracking systems. "How many?"

"Ten."

Bernie carried them to the register, rang it up, and ran the card.

Perkins signed the receipt. "Hey, I have some year-end money I need to burn, so the dragon lady doesn't decide I'm not using my budget and decide to shrink it for me. I'll drop by Friday and get a new shotgun mike from you."

"You'll have to get it from Merv. I'm flying to Israel tomorrow."

"That's funny. Matt's flying to Israel tomorrow too."

"Matt?"

"The boss." Perkins tapped the PO on the counter. "CEO of IRIG. Interesting coincidence."

Bernie looked over his glasses. "There are no coincidences, Frank. There are consequences. There are the inevitable results of the actions of ourselves and others. There are divine appointments. There are the seemingly random threads of our lives that form a grand tapestry that only a transcendent being can comprehend." He pushed up his glasses. "But there . . . are . . . no . . . coincidences."

Perkins smiled nervously and backed toward the door. "So I'll check with Merv, then."

Bernie watched him walk out. He waited until the sense of solitude returned to the store. Then he got back to the inventory.

Chapter 7

Hollywood, California.
Wednesday, 27 November 2002. 15:00.

Nikki found a stool behind the set and sipped the passion-guava smoothie from the commissary cart. Not a good day. Too many retakes. When she remembered her lines, Tony forgot his. And when he finally got it right, she forgot hers. Before long they were both so frustrated neither could get through a scene and John called a break.

Shouldn't have gone to LAX this morning, she thought. *That was the first mistake.* He always wanted her to go with him and see him off. He would goof around with her in the car and give her a big hug on the curb while Alex unloaded the bags. But when the door closed and Alex drove away, the limo always felt too big and empty, like the air had been sucked out. *Big, stupid car. Why take it when there's only two of us?*

The loneliness grew as they drove up the 405, down the hill into the valley, and onto the 101. The radio didn't help. The TV didn't help. The iPod didn't help. Finally she just shut everything off and looked out the window. Then the chicken Caesar salad and steamed artichokes at Stanley's when what she really wanted was a pizza, even though she knew it would just make her sleepy at the shooting.

By the time she got to the set, she was depressed. But she shook it off, like she always did, went through some exercises, and was joking around with Tony when John showed up, in a hurry like always.

But it didn't click. Everything sounded flat. The way she said the lines made them sound stupid. Then she took a closer look at the lines and decided they really were stupid, so of course they sounded stupid. But then the way everybody looked at her, she could see they thought she was the one who was stupid and were just too nice to say so. And that made her feel stupid and she forgot her lines.

Tony looked around the corner, saw her, and smiled. She tried to smile back but knew it didn't fool him, so she just sipped her drink, turned on her stool, and faced a jumble of wires. He would get the idea.

There was a nail on the floor. She set the smoothie down, picked up the nail, and bounced the head on her ankle, watching the skin turn white as she pushed down and squeezed all the blood out, then grow pink again when she pulled it away and the blood rushed back. She pushed harder, saw a larger circle of white, felt the skin pinch against the bone, pulled it away. It left a red circle. She watched it slowly fade back to pink.

She wondered about the suicide bombers. *Was that really true, or did She just make that up to scare me? And make Dad change his mind?* It was hard to tell. She'd ask Tony to look it up on the Internet. Tony liked knowing everything. It would make him feel important if she asked him for information.

But what if Dad does get blown up? What if he is in a restaurant and this guy with a crazy look in his eyes comes in and suddenly everybody knows and starts screaming and the crazy guy reaches in his coat and then . . . She turned the nail over and tried poking her ankle with the point. It made a miniature crater of white, a focused pinprick of pain that slowly faded when she pulled it away and the pink crawled back in. She didn't really want to think about that, but now that *She* said that stuff about the suicide bombers, it was hard not to. *That's probably why She said it. I won't think about it.*

She closed her eyes. *First Mom, now Dad.* She stood at the gap in a guardrail. A car floated over the edge and slowly angled down like an Olympic diver. A convertible. Behind the steering wheel long black hair and a scarf flapped in the wind like the tail of a kite. A man was in the back seat. *Dad?* He looked back at her. It was the suicide bomber. She could see his crazy eyes. She heard a noise and turned to see her Dad running toward her, reaching out for her, calling her name. Then his eyes turned crazy and he was the suicide bomber. He reached in his coat. She fell backward off the guardrail, diving toward the car, reaching for the scarf.

Nikki pushed the point harder against her ankle. The picture of the crazy man and the guardrail and the scarf and everything collapsed down into one tiny white dot in the middle of the darkness. Her ankle was the universe, and the small white dot was at the center where a new star was forming.

"Nikki, are you ready to try again?"

Nikki jumped and dropped the nail. She opened her eyes and saw a jumble of wires.

"Nikki?"

The voice came from behind her. John's voice.

"Yeah. Coming."

She looked down. A small red dot glistened on her ankle, reflecting the lights on the catwalk. It was a globe, a new world in an empty universe, the Eden where she stepped forth and gave names to her pain. She stood up, leaving the drop untouched. She thought she could feel it shining like a red tear. *Focus*, she thought.

Then she stepped out onto the set and went through her scenes perfectly.

Chapter 8

El Al flight 106, over the Atlantic.
Thursday, 28 November 2002. 01:00.

The flight attendant set a glass of Chardonnay next to the pile of papers on Cooper's tray. He dropped his pen and picked up the glass, thankful for the excuse to take a break from the paperwork Susan had handed him Monday evening when he finally left the office. *She was right about one thing. One day in the office between trips is not enough.* He held his glass up in a toast to Susan and took a sip.

And I was right when I booked my own ticket. He glanced back past the curtain to the block of seats booked by Global Adventures. He could see Emilio snoring in his aisle seat with an umbra of wispy white hair like a Latino Einstein. Emilio, who had pushed past the protesting flight attendants before they reached cruising altitude to kneel down and take Cooper's right hand in his two calloused hands, thanking him four times for providing Emilio a seat and promising that God would reward him for his great kindness. Cooper was thankful when the amused flight attendant finally escorted Emilio back to his ticketed cabin with firm instructions to observe the seat belt sign.

Even boarding had been an experience. Roberts intercepted him when he emerged from the Red Carpet club and introduced him to several of the volunteers, most notably Bernie, who appeared to be a conspiracy theory nut with a spy gadget store in Glendale. The rest appeared to be fairly normal. If going to Israel for Thanksgiving could be considered normal.

I'm going to Israel for Thanksgiving, so what does that say about me? But he had business there. Fieldwork, which was much more inviting than the paperwork he was avoiding. He shoved the papers into his portfolio and sat back to enjoy the wine and almonds the flight attendant handed him. As boring as paperwork could be, he really should be spending more time in California and less time on the road. Nikki was self-sufficient, perhaps too much so. Things would be changing, already were changing. Regardless of whether she wanted it, she would need guidance.

And then there was Stevie. Nikki and Stevie. Matt and Stevie. Stevie.

Cooper didn't consider himself a ladies' man, but neither had there ever been a shortage of women in his life. He enjoyed their company and had no doubt they had enjoyed his, but until Lola he had not felt the need to limit his choices. She blew into his office like a blustery autumn day, disrupting his comfortable, if unconventional life, slamming the shutters open and rumbling the trash cans down the sidewalk. When Lola was at a party, it lasted until dawn. And when he brought her home, she completely redecorated his apartment. He decided to marry her before he ended up with a Pomeranian or a mink farm or a new boat.

Even though his agency was only three years old, he found himself handing off jobs to the employees. His time with her bordered on obsession, even after they married. They traveled to the Caribbean and the South Pacific, infesting the beaches by day and dancing in the moonlight with tropical drinks at night.

Then came the once-in-a-lifetime chance to buy IRIG, a national agency with a sixty-year track record of success. For the next three years he focused on taking the agency international by opening offices in Japan, Hong Kong, and Taiwan. At first Lola went with him, until she got tired of seeing the sights alone.

When the Taiwan office was running on autopilot, Cooper took a breather. He knew something wasn't right. Lola spent her time at home, watching soaps, and napping by the pool. He thought about the last few years long enough to start feeling guilty. For his thirtieth birthday, he took her to Greece. She tagged along on the sightseeing, never too far from a drink. After three weeks she tired of it and refused to leave the hotel. Cooper became angry, and they quarreled. She ordered more wine from room service; he took to wandering the streets of Athens. After two weeks of aimless walks he happened across a detective agency. Before long he was involved in shoptalk with the owner and planning another expansion.

When Cooper realized he would not be able to expand the agency to Europe and break through Lola's boredom at the same time, he suggested it might be time to start a family. It took her a few days to get used to the idea, but she finally came around. Nine months after they left Greece, Nikki was born. But even Nikki failed to keep Lola's attention for long. She became one more thing for the housekeeper to keep track of. Cooper tried nannies, but none would endure Lola's drunken outbursts. By the time Nikki was five, she was cleaning up spilled drinks when Mommy passed out and helping her into bed. But by the time she was eight, even Nikki reached her limit. That's when the fights began.

But that all ended five years ago with a mangled Porsche. He hired a nanny and stepped back into the old habits—casual dating, the occasional fling, never keeping one woman too long and never bringing one home. After vanquishing all nannies and housekeepers chosen by Cooper, Nikki established her position as queen of the castle on her twelfth birthday by suggesting that she interview the next round of housekeepers. She had selected Rosa, and domestic tranquility had returned. At least for five months. Until Stevie moved in.

Nikki sulked for a few weeks but didn't return to the tantrums. Other than a few isolated blowups, the first six months were marked only by Nikki's refusal to acknowledge that Stevie existed. On Christmas she actually accepted a gift from Stevie, an iPod. The last year they had co-existed in an uneasy peace, neither encroaching on each other's perceived territory. Stevie left the management of the house to Nikki and Rosa, only making suggestions on holidays, and then with complete deference to their judgment. Nikki didn't force a showdown by challenging Stevie's claims on his time. But she had yet to say Stevie's name, referring to her only as *She* and *Her*, speaking in capital letters, even when Stevie was present.

Perhaps he could navigate this minefield indefinitely, but he wasn't sure he should. Or that he wanted to. He sensed that somehow he should negotiate something more than a nonaggression pact, something more like an alliance. He saw the need for change but not the means. It was amazing how a kid could do what no adult had ever done—make him feel inadequate.

Giving up the task as hopeless, he checked unfinished business off the agenda and moved to new business. He said nothing to Stevie of his thoughts on the drive from the banquet. He had avoided thinking them again, but they returned unbidden at the most inopportune times—in the staff meeting, waiting in line at Starbucks, while brushing his teeth. He loved her, but he had loved many women. Why was she different? What made him want to open his chest like a closet and show her the skeletons? To allow her into places he had never dreamed of taking Lola, even in their wildest and most intimate moments, before the ascent of IRIG and the disintegration of their marriage? Should he trust this feeling?

In many ways, with Stevie he felt the same elation of adrenaline he felt while in the field, the scent of danger, confidence in the intel and his skills, but an uncertainty of outcome. With Lola he had felt amazement, exhilaration, and abandonment, but never uncertainty. Never the desire to expose himself in a nakedness of the soul. Never the terrifying lack of control over the outcome.

Stevie had been attracted to him because of his strength, his ability to protect her. What would she do when she saw his inadequacies, his vulnerabilities? Would she despise him for his weakness? Would she turn the tables, step in to protect him, and undermine the very foundation of her attraction to him? Would he be giving her the weapon by which she would, with the best of intentions, destroy the relationship?

Cooper sensed that the key to the old business lay in the resolution of the new business. Although Stevie had said nothing, he could tell something was on her mind. He was beginning to suspect that the relationship could not stay as it was and survive. But he didn't know if it could move forward and survive. Perhaps it was doomed to destruction regardless of the choice he made. If so, that should take the weight of the decision off his shoulders; it didn't matter which he chose. The thought didn't bring him relief. He finished his wine and put back the seat for some sleep.

———

Isaac Cohen was waiting for them when they got through customs. Immediately his eyes locked with Cooper's, even though Cooper was camouflaged in a throng of Global Adventure volunteers. Cooper saw in an instant that Cohen was exactly the person he needed in Tel Aviv, felt it intuitively in the instantaneous communication that passed between them as strangers who knew each other without speaking a word.

And then, as quickly as it had come, the moment passed and Roberts was gathering his ducklings and trundling them to the waiting bus, while Cohen directed the loading of the luggage, double-checking with the assistant who was placing a third column of check marks to indicate the transfer to the bus, the first set marking their delivery to the L.A. baggage handlers and the second to mark their retrieval from the Tel Aviv baggage handlers.

While waiting with the other ducklings to board the bus, Cooper shoved his hands in the pockets of his leather flight jacket and strolled around in the cool of the late afternoon sun, noting the various people and vehicles and subconsciously checking for something that didn't fit. His attention was drawn to a cab driver standing next to his cab, watching the loading. Even though he was at the front of the queue, he didn't appear to be anxious to pick up a fare. In fact, when an older man approached, the cabbie asked him where he was going then jerked his head toward the next car.

Cooper looked at Cohen and noted that he also had seen the cabbie. Their eyes met again. Cohen's expression didn't change, yet Cooper knew his thoughts. The movements of the cab and its driver would not go unnoted.

As the bus jerked forward, Cooper found himself trapped in a window seat near the front by Bernie, the conspiracy nut. He began outlining his personal theory on terrorism in the

Middle East. Cooper didn't follow it too closely, focusing most of his attention on the route and the people and vehicles near the bus.

Bernie appeared to be content with a captive, if not captivated, audience. His theory proposed that the PLO was actually a rogue element of the Knights Templar that went underground in 1307 after the massacre but was perverted by a reactionary Muslim group in 1633, the year the Catholic Church forced Galileo to recant his theory of the solar system, because they thought he should credit the Arabic civilization destroyed by the Crusades as the foundation for his work. Or something like that. Bernie claimed they had passed the mission of protecting Palestine from invasion down through the centuries as part of a secret society that was reawakened when the Jews took Jerusalem in 1948.

The exposition of Bernie's theory consumed the hour drive from Tel Aviv to Jerusalem. Cooper stayed in his seat as the others filed off the bus, looking out the window at the soldiers in front of the hotel, Uzis slung over their shoulders. He caught sight of a cabbie that could have been the man he had seen in Tel Aviv, but the windows were not clean and he could not be certain, although he did see Cohen watching the cab as it passed in traffic. Cooper began to wonder who knew he was here and if Roberts was as clean as he appeared. Somebody seemed interested in their arrival, somebody unwilling to step up and introduce himself and welcome them to the Holy Land.

After they checked in, Roberts met Cooper and Cohen in the bar of the hotel, took an isolated table in a corner, and ordered coffee for the three of them.

"Matt, tomorrow is orientation," Roberts said. His voice was softer than Cooper had ever heard it, barely loud enough for him to hear without leaning forward.

"Give my regards to the speaker. I'll give it a miss," Cooper said, matching Roberts' level.

"Oh, we won't be there."

"We?" Cooper looked from Roberts to Cohen. Cohen smiled but said nothing.

"The prime minister asked me to stop by. I'd like you to tag along."

Cooper blinked a few times but otherwise did not change his expression. "The prime minister."

"Matt, we're going to give you the grand tour. First we'll talk to the PM. He likes regular updates on our work. While we're there, we may as well talk to the minister of defense and the minister of justice."

"By all means."

Roberts motioned to the approaching waiter, and they fell silent as he served the coffee and left.

Roberts stirred sugar into his coffee and tapped the spoon on the edge of the cup. "Then tomorrow night, just for fun, I propose a jaunt into Lebanon." He lifted his cup and took a sip.

Cooper set his cup down untasted. "We're flying to Beirut? I didn't see that on the itinerary."

"And you won't. Officially, we've never been there. All three times." Roberts smiled at Cooper's raised eyebrows. "I thought you might be interested. Matt, your eyes are about to be opened. After your visit with Major Skaff, your life will never be the same. I'll give you tonight to reconsider."

"No need. I'm in."

"There might be some shooting."

"No problem." Cooper took a sip of the coffee. It was strong and hot.

"I can't guarantee you'll make it back alive. And if we're caught, nobody will rescue us. We will just cease to exist."

He set the cup down. "Are you trying to scare me?"

"Matt, you have a daughter. Are you prepared to leave her without a father?"

"You made it back three times. I like the odds."

"Ever study probability, Matt? No matter how many times in a row you get heads, the next toss is still fifty-fifty."

"Do you plan on going?"

"I will go, even if you don't."

Cooper leaned back in his chair and looked at them, first at Roberts, then at Cohen. Roberts' face was serious, but his eyes were warm with concern. Cohen's face was a mask, unreadable.

"Knowing the odds, you're still going."

"Knowing the odds."

"Then why shouldn't I?"

"Matt, you're not a believer. Cohen and I have pledged our lives to this mission. If God chooses to require them of us this night, or any night, we will give them willingly, although not wantonly, in His service. Our families know this and accept the risk. We are prepared to walk into God's presence. Are you?"

Cooper leaned forward over his coffee. "I told you I'm not a religious man," he whispered fiercely. "I'm here on business, not for a tent revival. Is that what we're going across the border for?"

"No," Roberts answered calmly. "We're going to contact the head of the underground resistance and arrange the shipment of medical supplies. There is a price on his head. Last week he lost three men when his caravan was ambushed. There could be another attempt while we are there."

"Then drop all the mumbo jumbo. If you're in, I'm in. I don't need some religious liability waiver form."

Cooper sat back in his chair and picked up his coffee. Roberts didn't answer. They sat in silence for awhile, drinking their coffee. Then Cooper smiled.

"Besides, since you'll be leading the way, I figure you can run interference for me."

Chapter 9

La Guardia International Airport, New York.
Thursday, 28 November 2002. 19:00.

He walked directly to the bathroom, the one next to the secure door to the baggage handling area, without looking around. He stepped into a stall, opened the gym bag, and pulled out the coveralls with the faded company logo on the back. They were two sizes too large and fit nicely over his suit without wrinkling it. The black dress shoes were exchanged for a pair of brown steel-toed boots, well scuffed. Then the fur-lined cap with earflaps. Last, he hung the security badge around his neck.

The job had been easy to get. With outsourcing of ramp work and the squeeze for cost savings, contractors couldn't afford to be too picky about who they hired for these low-end jobs with few benefits. Security checks didn't go beyond checking the National Crime Information Center database.

He zipped up the bag, checked his watch, then called the automated flight information system with his cell phone. The 7:23 from Paris was ten minutes late. He waited in the stall fifteen minutes. One person came in while he waited. He watched the movement of the shadow across the floor from under the stall door until he heard the door close. When his watch beeped once, he left the stall, washed his hands, and stepped out to the security door. The badge unlocked the door, and he entered without incident as he had done before.

He got to gate 82 as the tug was disengaging and the walkway rolled to the side of the plane. He moved to the shadows near the door, an area not covered by the security cameras, and watched as the cargo containers rolled out on the elevator conveyors, noting when the third one was lowered to the tarmac and connected to the tug. His eyes never left it as it was towed in a line of other containers into the dock area next to a conveyor to be unloaded.

Two workers began tossing luggage from the first container onto the conveyor. He watched with satisfaction as another worker walked to the third container, reached past the canvas curtain and pulled out a black Anvil case. It was just large enough to hold a briefcase inside. He knew the worker suspected it held drugs, as it did. Half a million dollars worth of cocaine. He also knew the $1,000 the worker received for walking it to the street would guarantee no questions or attempts to look inside–that and certain assurances that had been made when the deal was made. Assurances regarding what had happened to the last worker who was curious.

He pushed a button on his cell phone as he watched the worker walk to the security door. He spoke briefly, put the phone away, and returned to the bathroom to change clothes. As he was tying the black shoes, his cell phone rang. He answered it, smiled, and returned it to his pocket. The case had been delivered to a van that pulled up curbside just as the worker stepped from the building. The final check had gone smoothly. He would be able to report that the channel was tested and ready for operation and that the product required to finance the op had been delivered.

He washed his hands, dried them carefully, and stepped out of the bathroom.

Marketplace, Jerusalem, Israel.
Friday, 29 November 2002. 10:00.

The market was crowded and noisy and smelled unfamiliar. Emilio stood tentatively at the door of a shop filled with rugs and tapestries. They looked expensive.

"Are you going in or not?" Bernie looked over his shoulder. "It's just a bunch of old rugs. What would you do with one of those?"

Emilio shook his head. Juanita had loved rugs. She always kept one next to the bed so her feet wouldn't touch the cold wooden floor in the mornings. He remembered her slender feet, so pale and smooth, even when she turned fifty. He closed his eyes. He tried to remember if the rug was still there on her side of the bed, the side to the window. A small rectangular weaving with Aztec markings. He couldn't remember.

Bernie's voice buzzed in his ear. "Just remember, if you're going to get one, don't pay the asking price. They always set them high for tourists. They expect you to bargain."

Emilio felt him leaning into his back. "So, you getting a rug or what? Want me to Jew them down for you?"

Emilio shook his head again. "Did you see a pastry shop? Back there?" He turned around.

Bernie twisted his head around and squinted. "Uh . . ."

"I must get some baklava for my friend."

Emilio turned from the rug shop with a twinge of regret and walked to a canopy on the corner. An array of cheap souvenirs crowded the tables. T-shirts with "Don't worry, bee Jewish" and "One fish, two fish, red fish, gefilte fish" on them. A kid with sunglasses sat on a stool, industrial music blaring from his headphones.

Bernie picked up a small vial. "Oh sure, water from the Jordan River."

Emilio looked at the kid, worried that Bernie might offend him. The kid smiled from behind the sunglasses. Emilio could hear the English lyrics from ten feet away. The kid wouldn't hear a word they said.

Bernie shook the bottle and squinted at it. "I bet he fills them from the kitchen sink. If it really is water." He nudged Emilio. "Things are not always what they seem, you know. Especially in a place like this."

Emilio looked at Bernie reprovingly. "We are very lucky to be here, my friend. Very lucky to be here."

Bernie looked at the stall. "Here? It's just a cheap tourist trap."

"Here, in this city where our Lord walked. Many people wish for this day but do not see it."

"Well, yeah, that. Sure." He set the vial back down.

"Juanita, she would walk to the cathedral on her knees for the chance to be here. And me, I can never thank Mr. Cooper enough. Juanita, she would like Mr. Cooper."

"Now that you mention it." Bernie looked suspiciously at the kid, grabbed Emilio's arm, and pulled him out of the stall and into the throng milling through the market. "I'd say that Mr. Cooper isn't all he seems either."

Emilio looked at Bernie with alarm. He dragged behind until Bernie let go of his arm then began looking for a pastry shop.

"Did you notice he wasn't at the orientation?" He trailed behind Emilio, who was moving slowly. "And he wasn't with the group today either." Emilio saw him jostle through the crowd to get beside him. "And he rode in first class. Don't forget that."

"He rode in first class so I could have his ticket."

"He's not one of us. That's what I'm telling you. I think he's a spy." Emilio snorted. "No, really, I'm serious. You know he works for an international detective agency. Owns it."

Emilio stopped. It took Bernie a few steps to realize he was no longer beside him. He turned back.

"Here," Emilio said.

"Here?" Bernie said.

"Yes, here." Emilio pointed. "Baklava."

Chapter 10

The drive up Highway 1 to Metulla was long and cold. Cooper leaned against the door and thought over the events of the morning. As accustomed as he was to dealing with celebrities and political figures, Cooper was surprised to find himself having tea with the prime minister less than twenty-four hours after arriving in Jerusalem. He had dealt with governments before but always with their intelligence organizations, not the executive branch.

Roberts chatted with the PM the same way he talked to everyone, as if he were an old friend. As the meeting progressed it became apparent that they really were old friends. Roberts had been running missions to Israel for over twenty years and had dealt with a succession of PMs.

After the tea was served and the small talk dwindled, the PM turned to Cooper. "And what is your interest in Israel, Mr. Cooper?"

"I am assessing security issues so as to advise and protect my corporate clients if they choose to travel or invest here." In response to the blank gaze he added, "And Mr. Roberts is educating me on some of the humanitarian concerns. I understand we will be visiting a kibbutz to rebuild a barn destroyed by a raid."

The PM smiled. "George has a way of bending the agenda to fit his plans, does he not? But this is a good thing he does." He placed his cup on the saucer and looked at Cooper as if evaluating him. "Mr. Cooper, there are many needs. The suffering does not stop at our borders. George was a major help when we opened the gate in the Good Fence."

"The good fence?" Cooper looked at Roberts, who became preoccupied with sugar and milk.

"In the 1970s, a rudimentary fence along the northern border discouraged PLO raids, attacks from Syria through Lebanon. But not only the Jews suffer from the Muslims. The Maronite Christians in Lebanon also became the targets. Mothers came to the fence with babies, sick, hurt. We had not the heart to send them away. In 1976, we opened a gate in the fence to allow aid to those in need. A hut was built; it grew into a clinic. George brought supplies from the West.

"When we created the safety zone in southern Lebanon in 1982, we were able to allow much more traffic through the gate. Fifteen hundred people passed through each day. Maronites living in poverty because of the oppression from the Muslims were allowed to take jobs in Metulla to support their families. We were able to provide more aid directly to families in southern Lebanon. George continued to help. Since the withdrawal two years ago, Hezbollah now controls southern Lebanon and the land beyond the fence. We can no longer allow traffic to pass so freely.

"However, though the gate is closed, the needs continue. The situation for the Maronites has deteriorated. Infrastructure has been destroyed in two decades of fighting and has not been repaired. Medical and educational needs grow as never before.

Many Christians with means are fleeing. Those who cannot leave are in greater danger."

The PM spread his hands. "It is ironic, is it not, that the Jews are coming to the aid of the Christians in Lebanon. Why do the millions of Christians in your land not help? George is the angel of mercy to these people, but he is only one man. Where are the others?"

Roberts placed his cup on the side table. "Mr. Prime Minister, thank you for your time. I'm sure Matt will help take the message back."

The PM stood up, as did Roberts. Cooper scrambled to his feet. The PM and Roberts shook hands.

"George, thank you for all your help. Please see me again before you leave. Mr. Cooper," he said, taking Cooper's hand, "may your stay here be successful. It is a pity you cannot see the needs in Lebanon for yourself."

Cooper looked to Roberts and back to the PM. He got the clear impression the PM knew of their trip. "Yes sir. Thank you for your time. I will think on what you said."

Cooper shot an inquiring look at Roberts on the way out of the office but got no response. After a meeting with the minister of justice and lunch with the defense minister, they returned to the hotel for a travel bag, slipped past the room where the volunteers were in the midst of orientation, and met Cohen at the service entrance. He was at the wheel of an old Peugeot in need of bodywork. However, when they got on the highway, it was clear the car had maintained a close relationship with a good mechanic. And the armor plating underneath and on the sides had been done well. It hardly showed.

The car didn't look out of place in front of the Arazim Hotel in Metulla. There were few recent model cars on the streets. When he stepped into the lobby, Cooper felt as if he had stepped into a 1950s spy movie. It was cluttered with couches, chairs, potted plants, and Persian rugs. A fire roared in a gigantic fireplace, and a system of fans run by one very long belt spun slowly, distributing the warmth.

A dark man in a darker suit greeted them from behind a broad wooden counter polished to a glossy shine. He took keys from a board on the wall and checked a set of cubbyholes for messages. He handed an envelope to Roberts along with the keys and rang for a bellboy. They agreed to meet at eight in the lobby for dinner.

Cooper dismissed the bellboy with a tip and looked out over the city. It was a hodgepodge of old buildings and recent construction. The snowy peak of Mt. Hermon loomed behind the town. A kilometer down the road were the Good Fence and the Fatma Gate.

Behind that fence men plotted the extermination of the Jews, planning raids to kill soldiers, businessmen, shopkeepers, janitors, mothers, children—anyone they thought shouldn't be here.

Cooper tried to imagine what it would be like to live in the shadow of a fence like this one, a barrier erected to restrain death from overflowing into the daily routine. Cooper thought of the bellboy who dropped the lone duffle bag on the bed and smiled as he accepted the tip. The fence was built before he was born. He had never known life without the fence. He woke up this morning, showered, and brushed his teeth in the shadow of the fence. He walked to work in the shadow of the fence, smiled at customers, carried their bags, loaded and unloaded luggage, gathered a few shekels in tips. In a few hours he would walk home and eat supper in the shadow of the fence—the fence he hoped would keep men from murdering him in his bed tonight. Tomorrow and probably every day of his life, he would do it again, all in the shadow of the fence.

The fence PLO terrorists compromised with a custom ladder to the west in March, causing a traffic jam on the highway by sniping cars. They then walked through the traffic, tossing grenades into open windows and finishing off the wounded with shots to the head.

It was a wonder they weren't all insane.

At eight, Cooper, Roberts, and Cohen were escorted to a private room in the back of the restaurant. It contained a table, eight chairs, and a sideboard with a pitcher of water. There was no conversation as the meal of fish and chicken with pita bread was brought in, their plates filled, and the serving dishes placed on the sideboard. After the door closed, Roberts took the goblet at the place setting next to him and turned it upside down on the table. Immediately a door at the back of the room opened and a stocky man with a large mustache entered the room.

"Don't be alarmed, Matt," Roberts said in response to Cooper standing and facing the intruder. "This is our guest, Major Said Skaff. Major Skaff, meet Matthew Cooper."

Skaff nodded to Cooper, righted the goblet, and took the seat next to Roberts. Cohen poured water into the goblet.

Roberts stood and served Skaff. "Any troubles getting across?"

"None," Skaff said.

Even with the single word, Cooper could tell he had a strong accent. He was very curious to know how Skaff had crossed, through some special arrangement with the officials or some more covert means, but knew better than to ask. From here on out it was a need-to-know basis, and he didn't need to know. Questions would only strain the relationship.

Roberts took his seat, and after a quick prayer, they ate.

"Major Skaff, I appreciate you coming on such short notice and at risk to yourself. In addition to arranging for delivery of the items we discussed in May, I'd like to propose a slight change." Roberts paused to take a bite of a falafel. "I'd like to bring Matt across. I'd like him to see how things are."

Skaff stopped and looked at Roberts in disbelief. He glanced at Cooper and then back to Roberts. He put down his fork.

"No, it cannot be done." He looked at Cooper with suspicion. "Why do you ask such a thing?"

Cooper wasn't sure if Skaff was asking him or Roberts. He opened his mouth to answer, but Roberts cut in.

"I asked Matt to come on this trip because I know he has a purpose here. He will be the instrument to bring much good to your people."

"This is not a small thing you ask. It cannot be done lightly or without strong purpose."

"I do not ask it lightly. In fact, it wasn't even my idea. God has shown me that Matt will play a key role. I don't know what it is or when or where, but I know he is supposed to be here now and that he must be in Lebanon tomorrow. I don't know why."

Skaff looked at Roberts thoughtfully. Then he turned and scrutinized Cooper. He studied him without comment for several minutes. At first Cooper looked back but eventually resumed eating. After a few minutes an expression of surprise crept across Skaff's face. He turned back to Roberts.

"But he is not a believer!"

Cooper set down his fork and looked at Skaff in amazement. Roberts smiled.

"Yes, Major. I won't ask how you came to know that, but you are right. Matt is not a believer. But he is still a weapon in God's hand. But you must make this decision for yourself. Ask God yourself. We will abide by your decision."

The meal proceeded in silence. When he was finished, Skaff took a final drink of water and pushed his plate away.

"He will come. We will leave an hour before sunrise. Meet me behind the tailor's shop on Shein Kin. Bring nothing, no passports or identification."

Then he disappeared through the back door.

———

Five hours later Cooper, Roberts, and Cohen were waiting behind the shop. Cooper was shivering in his leather flight jacket. Roberts and Cohen didn't seem to mind the cold. The portion of the sky visible between the buildings was washed out from the lights at the fence. Even in the night it made its presence felt.

Suddenly Cooper became aware that Skaff was standing next to him. He didn't know how long he had been there.

"He comes. Only him," Skaff said quietly.

"Good morning, Major," Roberts whispered. "Are you sure? I wanted to arrange the final logistics for the shipments."

"Someone will visit you at the hotel today, and it will be done. Only he will cross."

"OK. In that case, I think I'll put in a few more hours against the jet lag. When shall we see our friend again?"

"Tonight before midnight."

Skaff touched Cooper on the shoulder, and they disappeared into the shadows in the alley. At the end of the street they stepped into a darkened building and donned robes and head coverings. Then they walked through the darkness to the fence and, after a brief conference with the commanding officer, through the checkpoint. The commander handed Skaff a burlap sack and slapped him on the shoulder as they crossed.

On the other side they climbed into an unmarked brown Jeep and drove away from the glare of the fence into the waning darkness. By the time the sun edged over the horizon, they had gone fifteen kilometers on unmarked roads and were somewhere between Qlaia'a and Marjeyoun. To Cooper it looked like sunrise in the badlands.

Skaff reached in the back seat, dragged the sack across, and dropped it in Cooper's lap without explanation. Cooper looked at him.

"Open inside," Skaff said.

Cooper opened the sack. He pulled out a large silver Coleman thermos. Paper cups rested in the bottom of the sack. He looked at Skaff.

"Cousin in America. You know, Philadelphia." He smiled, the first Cooper had seen. "Israelis fill it when I come."

Cooper shook his head and poured them each some coffee. It was still hot, almost too hot to drink, and very strong. It was a delicate dance to enjoy the coffee without wearing it, but at least it kept his hands warm.

In the pale dawn light Skaff pointed out a water pumping station. "Hezbollah bombed it three years. Never fixed. Carry water by hand." Three kilometers later he pointed out a power substation. "Israelis shelled four years. From the shqif, the . . . the castle." He nodded to the ridge two kilometers distant where the ruins of Castle Beaufort glowed in the waxing morning light. "Never fixed. Use wood, lantern."

As the sun came up they sipped coffee and toured the devastated countryside, Skaff pointing out homes, schools, hospitals, and shops in varying stages of destruction. Some were still in use despite the fact that they were half rubble and threatening to collapse in a slight wind or even a strong sneeze. With each item, the weight of the damaged infrastructure pressed down on Cooper. He asked fewer questions.

Along the streets and in the doorways of buildings Cooper saw children of all ages, many with missing limbs. "Landmines," Skaff said. Others had rambling scars running down backs or legs. Some had fresh wounds in need of treatment. He could tell that some would succumb to infection or disease if not treated soon. He thought of Nikki and felt a deep gratitude for all he had. A whispered prayer of thanks escaped his lips before he was aware of what he was saying. He looked at Skaff and flushed, but Skaff had not heard him over the noise of the Jeep. Any lingering sense of hypocrisy he felt faded as he looked at another child with little future and less hope.

Then as Skaff turned the Jeep in a cul-de-sac, Cooper saw a girl maybe four years old peek out from an open doorway. She wore a white cotton robe that stopped a few inches above her bare feet, which were dusted with the pale sand of the road. Jet black hair hung down the side of her face in ringlets. She smiled shyly. Cooper smiled back. As they passed, she moved out of the door to watch them go and Cooper saw the other side of her face. The left eye was gone, a raw, red socket in its place. Her ear was melted into an angry red-white mass of scar tissue, the hair burned away on the left side of her head. She waved at him as they pulled away. He waved back numbly, too shocked to wipe away the tears.

He didn't speak for an hour.

Chapter 11

Marjeyoun, Lebanon.
Saturday, 30 November 2002. 11:20.

Eventually Skaff stopped at a shop, left Cooper in the running Jeep, and ran inside. He came out a minute later with their lunch wrapped in newspapers. He drove to a deserted wadi where they ate a simple lunch of beef wrapped in pita bread.

After ten minutes of silence, Skaff spoke. "You have family?"

"A daughter."

"Wife?"

"She died five years ago."

"I give you my regret," Skaff said.

"Thank you," Cooper answered, touched by the sincerity in Skaff's voice.

After some silence, Skaff spoke again. "This daughter, she is how big?" He held his hand up about waist high.

"She's thirteen."

"Thirteen," Skaff said. Then he smiled. "Ah, thirteen."

Cooper smiled back. "Oh, so you know, do you? You have children?"

"My son, he is fourteen. Others are . . . gone." Cooper couldn't tell if he meant they were dead or merely grown and had their own families.

"So you do know. Thirteen must be the same everywhere."

Skaff looked doubtful. "Rafik, he desires to fight. But he must protect the home. It is not the . . . the glory he desires, but he knows it is his place."

Cooper thought on this and then asked, "No daughters?"

Skaff's eyes softened, and he smiled slightly. "Hayat. She is two." He held his hand above the ground. Cooper nodded and smiled. Skaff nodded back. "She is the glory of my old age."

"Old age? You can't be much over fifty."

"Forty-five. But that is old here. Many die young."

"The glory of your old age, huh? She must be something else. Too bad I can't see her."

Skaff looked at him for a long time. "Yes," he said at last. "That is too bad."

He stood up, dusted off his hands, and crumpled the newspapers into the back of the Jeep. He turned to Cooper.

"Now you wear this and go in the back. Down where nobody see you." He held up a black scarf. "Over your eyes. Like this." He put the scarf around his eyes.

"You want to blindfold me?" Cooper stood up.

"We go to my men. But only I know the way." He held the scarf out to Cooper.

Cooper hesitated. He had no reason to suspect Skaff, but he disliked placing himself completely at his mercy. Then he felt a calm. It suddenly seemed like the right thing to do. He shrugged, surprised at his own willingness. "OK." He laughed and stepped forward, took the scarf, wrapped it around his head and tied it in the back.

"No," Skaff said, "no good. Like this." He untied the scarf, wrapped it around Cooper's head three times in overlapping layers, so that it covered from the top of his head past his nose, then tied it in the back. "Now you come here."

Skaff led him to the Jeep and helped him lay down in the back, then covered him with a tarp. With all the jolting that followed, Cooper assumed they had not returned to the road but had instead continued up the wadi, but the turns and bumps all blurred together after thirty minutes. When they finally came to a stop, he had no idea which direction they had taken.

When Skaff liberated him from the Jeep and the scarf, Cooper saw they were in the elbow of a large wadi, a narrow crevasse dug deep. He followed Skaff up a steep trail that switched back and forth. After sixty feet of climbing, the trail leveled out onto a wide shelf. A cave stretched back from the ledge.

A dozen men were scattered about, cleaning weapons, preparing munitions. When they saw Cooper they looked to Skaff for explanation. He rattled off something Cooper didn't understand, and they seemed satisfied if not entirely comfortable with his presence. Skaff introduced him to each, one at a time. Some didn't speak English and merely nodded.

They sat in a circle, and the men ate cold rations while Skaff unfolded a paper on the table. It appeared to be a map of a small compound. Cooper could see markings for what appeared to be fences, roads, and buildings but couldn't read the words. He looked on as Skaff began talking in Arabic and pointing to areas on the map, indicating the approach, the direction of attack, and the roles the various men would play. Cooper deciphered as much as he could, looking over the simple map. After some discussion, one guy glanced in Cooper's direction and asked a question. Skaff shook his head.

Skaff folded the map, pointed to Cooper, and said something to the guy who had asked the question. In broken English, the guy began telling Cooper the story of how he came to be fighting in the resistance. Each soldier in turn told his story. For those who didn't speak English, Skaff translated. Each story was enough to break a heart. Taken together, they were overwhelming. Cooper fought back the tears, but when those telling their own stories began weeping, he could no longer contain his tears. He listened and wept with them. He saw Skaff looking at him with a steady and reflective gaze. He turned away.

Cooper was amazed that each soldier ended his story thanking God for His provision and protection. It seemed to Cooper that God had forgotten these people—had abandoned them long ago.

Why weren't they blaming Him instead of thanking Him? After all, it was the fact that they were Christians that had caused them all this trouble in the first place. He started to ask but found he couldn't form the question in a way that wouldn't sound like a profanity. In all his years of investigations and intelligence work, he had never seen such a hopeless situation. But to see not a flickering flame but a burning fire of hope among the hopeless brought to his mind the little girl waving and smiling with the half of her face that still worked. He turned away and walked to the mouth of the cave, torn between brokenness and anger.

Such deep suffering wrapped in even deeper faith was alien to him. He couldn't explain it. He had rejected the religion of his parents as irrelevant, a crutch to justify their own failures. And in California, faith was a fashion statement. Anybody could cobble together a patchwork quilt of ideas, beliefs, and theories and build their own religion to fit their weaknesses. But these people . . .

He glanced back at them. They were warriors. Theirs was not a religion of convenience or excuses. They might be suffering because of it, but they also had a hope that transcended the suffering because of this faith. What would it be like to have faith with a ferocity that approached violence? To believe something that strongly? He couldn't imagine it.

After some sleep in the back of the cave, they climbed down to the Jeep as the sun was setting. Skaff stowed Cooper in the back and drove for a long time. When he stopped and threw back the tarp, the fading sunset allowed Cooper to see the wadi walls and scrubby bushes surrounding the Jeep. Skaff signaled for silence and motioned for him to follow. They walked a kilometer as the darkness fell, skirting buildings and avoiding roads. Then they darted across a dirt road, through a ravine, and to the back of a house. Cooper smelled wood smoke and cooking meat.

Skaff let out a low whistle and was answered from the darkness of the doorway. They both entered, and the door closed behind them. Cooper heard a rough embrace and some whispered words. Then a blanket was pushed aside from a doorway, and light filtered into the hall where they stood.

Skaff was standing with his arm around a lanky boy almost as tall as he was. He ushered them all into the room and a woman let the blanket fall back into place.

"This is Rafik, my son," Skaff said, standing behind with his hands on the boy's shoulders. The boy nodded. "This is Zaki, my wife," he continued, placing his hand on the small of her back. She nodded. "They do not speak the good English. And there," he pointed to another doorway where little fingers clutched the edge of the blanket and one eye peeked out, "is Hayat." Skaff knelt down. "Hayat," he said softly. He held out his hands and whispered in Arabic. Slowly the girl inched from behind the blanket. Then she ran to Skaff and buried herself in him.

Cooper smiled. "I can see why you call her the glory of your old age. She's beautiful."

———

They sat in a semicircle around the fire and ate. Zaki asked tentative questions of Skaff, who translated. Cooper answered, describing life in California. Zaki and Rafik showed signs of amazement and sometimes disbelief at the answers. Cooper was not surprised. After only a day in southern Lebanon, much of it sounded incredible to him as well. Grocery stores that covered several acres and malls the size of a small city where kids spent ten years of Skaff's wages on a pair of basketball shoes even though they didn't play basketball. And gyms where machines monitored your vital signs while you climbed moving stairs and listened to your iPod and watched one of the five hundred cable TV stations, so you wouldn't gain weight when you spent the rest of the night eating pizza and watching more TV until you passed out. It sounded absurd while holed up in a crumbling adobe house with all the doors and windows blacked out to make it appear abandoned.

She asked questions about his family. Rafik showed even more interest when he talked about Nikki, arguing with Skaff when he told them she was on a TV program. At that point he evidently decided Cooper was making it all up, although Cooper could see that he wanted it to be true.

After the meal, the others disappeared behind the blankets. Skaff and Cooper sat watching the fire and drinking tea. Cooper began asking questions. Why the constant fighting? Why not just accept that there were Muslims, Christians, and Jews all living in close proximity and be done with it?

Skaff shook his head. "You come from the different world. America began with the idea of freedom. Religious freedom.

Here, it has never been so. A thousand years ago Crusaders came through, killed many Muslims. Then Muslims came back, killed many Christians. Then the Christians again. And so it has gone for hundreds of years. Sunni Muslims come to kill Shiite Muslims. Chalcedon Christians come to kill Maronite Christians. My people live here from before the beginning. They convert. My family is Christian for over eight hundred years."

"But after a thousand years of fighting, don't you think it is clear that nobody is going to win?"

"After World War II something must be done with all the Jews left over from the Holocaust. In 1948, the UN made the nation of Israel. They say, 'We will put them here.' Never since A.D. 70 when Titus destroys the temple is there a place Jews can call their country. The Arabs have Palestine fourteen hundred years. They don't want the Jews, so they fight. But the Jews win. Then all the Arabs agree to attack the Jews. Lebanon, Syria, Jordan, Iraq, Saudi Arabia, Egypt. They all attack. Six on one. Six very big on one very small.

"But it is very hard thing to kill Jews. Babylon can't do it. Persia can't do it. Rome can't do it. Germany can't do it. Now all the Arabs try, but can't do it, either. But they will never stop trying."

He gestured to the world outside the blankets. "Iran, Syria give Hezbollah ten thousand rockets, some go sixty kilometers, reach Haifa. Nasrallah, the Hezbollah leader, this year he says he supports America trying to bring Jews back to Israel to rebuild their temple over the Al-Aqsa Mosque."

Cooper raised his eyebrows. "He does? That's surprising."

"Why does he say this? He says to newspaper, 'If they all gather in Israel, it will save us the trouble of hunting them down all over the world.' They will never stop until every Jew they can reach is dead. Even if UN gives all land back to Arabs, they still fight. And not only Jews, Christians also."

Skaff stared into the dying embers. "They will never stop, and so we must never stop. To stop is to die." He looked at Cooper. "But it is the same for you."

"What do you mean?"

"It is not just here. The Muslims take the fight all over the world. Europe, Asia, Africa, Russia. Even to New York City. They want Jews out of Palestine. They want U.S. out of Middle East. But they already spread to the South Pacific. They do not lie down peacefully if we give them what they ask. They will reach for more."

Skaff looked at his watch. "It is time. I must get you to the gate, and I have much work tonight." He stood and stomped his feet, shaking the feeling back into his legs.

Cooper stood next to him. "What work is that?"

"Night mission."

"Does this have anything to do with the talk in the cave today?"

Skaff looked at him in silence for awhile. "Do you know the three Israeli soldiers kidnapped from Shaaba Farms?" Cooper shook his head. "Two years ago Hezbollah attacked Shaaba Farms, Golan Heights, Mt. Hermon. Twenty kilometers." He pointed to the southeast. "No word, nothing, two years. Now we hear word they are in Bekaa Valley. Sixty kilometers." He pointed north. "We meet Israelis there at 3:00 a.m. Them in helicopters. Us in Jeeps."

"I'd like to go."

"No, I cannot take you. George is waiting for you."

"He can wait a little longer then. You said this is my fight too. I'd rather fight them here than wait for them to come to Malibu. Besides . . ." He looked around the room, out past the blankets to the day that was finishing. "I'd like to do my part. I've seen what has happened here. I want to do more than look and listen."

"You know how to use a machine gun?"

Cooper laughed. "Yes. I went to a commando school in Central America in the '80s. Never thought I'd actually use it outside of training. We trained on a lot of unusual weapons." He looked at Skaff. "Unusual in the U.S., that is."

"Have you been in a battle?"

"I've been in a few fire fights. Gangs, mafia, automatic weapons."

"Have you killed a man?"

"Yes, I pulled the trigger when I had to. I know I'm not trained in this sort of thing. I'm not asking to lead the attack. I can follow orders. I'm not looking to be a hero; I just want to see it for myself. And if I can help bring those three boys back . . ."

Skaff closed his eyes for ten seconds. When he opened them, he smiled. "Let's go."

Chapter 12

Somewhere in the Bekaa Valley.
Sunday, 1 December 2002. 03:00.

The Israeli Defense Force rolled in on time. Cooper heard them and looked to the west from the cover of the small wadi where they had hidden the Jeeps. In the light of a fingernail moon, the Yas'ur 2000 was practically invisible until the moment it touched down, dropping from the two-hundred-foot cruising altitude used to evade radar detection. He was startled at first to see the Lebanese markings on the side and looked at Skaff with concern, but received no acknowledgment. He looked back at the chopper. Men started dropping out the door while it was still six feet above the ground. Half a dozen men were out before it settled, and the remaining half dozen were out in the next five seconds. The chopper took off, continuing east and banking to the north, as if it were a Lebanese patrol ship.

A brief signal from Skaff's flashlight brought the Israelis to the ravine, where terse greetings were exchanged. Cooper stepped out of the Jeep, noting that many of the Lebanese and Israelis seemed to know one another. Skaff greeted the lead officer and introduced him as Captain Eshkol.

"Mr. Cooper, I heard you were in Lebanon." Cooper looked at Skaff, who shrugged. Eshkol paid no attention. "The major assures me you understand your role in this mission and will pose no problems."

"I'm fully briefed and understand the plan of attack. Don't let my presence be a distraction."

Eshkol nodded and turned to Skaff. "Major, I heard of your loss over the radio as we left the ship. Are you still intent on participating in the raid?"

Skaff nodded without a word, his jaw tightening.

Eshkol placed a hand briefly on Skaff's shoulder. "There are no words at such a time. But none of us here are untouched by our own personal sorrows. We all carry the scars of each other's wounds. I will count on you to keep your head clear. Let me know if you cannot do so."

Eshkol turned to the group without waiting for a response from Skaff. The men had formed a circle around the Jeep— twelve Israelis, nine Lebanese, and Cooper. Eshkol summarized the highlights of the raid a final time. An equipment check followed. All communications gear, night-vision goggles, and weapons were verified operational and ready. Cooper pulled the slide back on the Desert Eagle and pushed it into his waistband at the small of his back. He expected to have more use for the mini-Uzi. He flipped the safety off, draped the strap across his shoulder, checked his headset with Skaff, strapped the assault knife to his ankle, and donned his night-vision goggles.

Then they scattered to the Jeeps, the twelve IDF in three Jeeps, the nine Lebanese and Cooper in the remaining two. Cooper rode shotgun next to Skaff, three Lebanese soldiers in the back, for the silent five-kilometer ride from the meet point to the camp, thinking over the last four hours.

The drive up from Marjeyoun had been slow and tedious, topping out at perhaps 20 kph. They had applied Hezbollah markings to the five Jeeps in a ravine north of Marjeyoun, and then left, two men to a jeep, at ten-minute intervals, each team with a unique route, sometimes overlapping the routes of others on the network of back roads and tracks that crisscrossed the desert. They traveled with their headlights off, using night-vision goggles to navigate.

Skaff and Cooper were the last to leave. Few words were spoken. Twice they had seen the approaching lights of a Hezbollah night patrol and pulled off into a ravine, cutting the engine and waiting in the darkness until it rolled slowly past. The undercurrent of adrenaline increased as they approached their destination. Then the call came over the radio.

Skaff had flinched at the squawk, barely audible over the jostling of the Jeep, and pulled off the trail behind a rise before acknowledging the transmission. He left the engine running. Cooper didn't follow the exchange in Arabic, but sensed a fundamental change in Skaff as it progressed. His tone, initially curt, became more deliberate, as if challenging something he knew could not be true. His final comments were soft, as if spoken in a cathedral. He replaced the radio and walked away from the road, stumbling through the sand.

Cooper got out of the Jeep but didn't follow. Skaff's manner didn't invite questions. He waited, hearing Skaff speak into the darkness, the words sometimes sounding like an argument, sometimes like a prayer. Skaff threw his arms open, spoke loudly, and then dropped to one knee, leaning with both arms on the other leg. Cooper looked around, nervous at the sudden sound, then back at Skaff. He scooped up a handful of sand, held it up to the sliver of moon and let it drizzle from his fist as if from an hourglass. He stayed there for a long time, right hand held up to the sky, palm open, staring into the moon and whispering. Then he fell silent for a longer time. Finally his arm dropped to his side. He brushed his hand on his leg and stood up.

Cooper watched him return. He got back in as Skaff walked around the Jeep without comment, backed out from behind the rise, and returned to the road.

After a few kilometers, Skaff spoke softly over the noise of the engine.

"Two hours after we left the house, Hezbollah fedayeen attacked. Rafik was cut with machine guns." Skaff drew a line along his gut with his right hand. "He lived only so long to tell what happened. Zaki and Hayat are dead."

Skaff drove on, staring into the night. Cooper stared, speechless. Rafik. Brave, daring Rafik. He had found the glory of death protecting his family. Had died with the knowledge that he had failed, had lived long enough to tell the story of his own failure. Cooper could not imagine a fate more laden with despair. Zaki, a jewel that teased Cooper's mind toward Stevie, a comparison he had resisted since the evening meal. Both dark, determined, and beautiful. And Hayat. Cooper refused to think of Hayat. He swore at the blackness that surrounded them. If he allowed himself to think of Hayat, his heart would break.

Skaff made no sign that he knew Cooper was in the Jeep with him. He drove through the night, watching for signs of Hezbollah with the night-vision goggles. No further words passed between them, even after they joined the other four Jeeps at the meet point, guided by the transmitter a Mossad agent had planted the night before. Skaff had briefly broken his silence when the Israelis joined them and the introductions were made. The silence returned as they drove to the camp.

According to Skaff, the Israelis had drilled for days on an exact model of the camp. Some of Skaff's own men had first-hand knowledge of the location based on past reconnaissance. The Jeeps drew to a stop behind an outcropping of rocks. Eshkol led them three hundred meters to a rise that looked over a compound matching the map Cooper had seen the previous afternoon. Only twelve hours ago. A lifetime ago.

Eshkol pulled the team together for a last briefing. "The choppers have a fix on the bodies in the compound. Five on level one of alpha building." He pointed to an Israeli, and four others stepped next to him. "Four on level two of alpha building." He pointed to another Israeli, and four more stepped next to him. "The grouping suggests all are unfriendlies."

He turned to Skaff. "We show four bodies in beta building. Grouping suggests unfriendlies." He addressed the group at large. "The available intel does not suggest clear indication that the package is here to be picked up. We will go in regardless. Take care, we may find them yet. Remember, we need a talker, but don't take any chances. We have fifteen minutes from initial contact until response from the next camp. We will extract ten minutes after initial contact."

He nodded, and the men resolved into attack teams. D-time was set for three minutes, forty seconds, and the teams dissolved into the darkness.

There were no sentries. When the IDF hit the front and back doors of alpha building, Eshkol signaled the extraction team on the ship. The Yas'ur 2000 would be escorted by two Apache choppers, just like the insertion flight. The F-16s patrolling the coast would provide added backup in case things heated up.

The ground floor team burst through the front door. One remained by the front door. The remaining four crossed the large front room in two seconds. One stopped in the hall, the final three splitting off into the back rooms. Two men were in the first room, obviously unfriendlies in that they were unguarded and unrestrained. The IDF soldier targeted the one on the left with a short burst from the nine-millimeter Magal and closed on the second as a possible capture. The sight of the body rolling and an arm reaching under the pillow caused a change of plans.

In the second room a form rolled from the bed on the right, coming up with an assault weapon and getting a few bursts off into the wall before he was silenced. His roommate threw back the covers but didn't even get his feet on the floor before he too was dead.

The third IDF soldier burst into an empty room and looked around at the vacant beds, dazed. He checked a closet, then stepped to the door and looked to the backup in the hall. Both were startled when the bathroom door at the end of the hall slammed open and a form emerged with handgun blazing. They returned fire and the fifth resident of the first floor staggered back into the bathroom, dead.

On the second floor, it got rough. The rush through the back door up the stairs necessarily took longer. At the first room one IDF soldier kicked the door open and dropped to the floor as a second rolled through the opening and several feet beyond. Automatic gunfire peppered the empty doorway and the second soldier targeted the black shape behind the muzzle blast. In the deafening silence that followed, the first soldier burst into the room and overpowered the groggy form in the second bed. The second soldier pressed the barrel of an Uzi to his neck and all resistance ceased.

The next two IDF soldiers took no chances. A kick of the door and a flash-bang grenade was answered by wild, unfocused automatic weapons fire. A fragmentation grenade followed, and the nine occupants of alpha building were accounted for. Ninety seconds had passed since the assault had begun.

Eshkol and his lieutenant acknowledged the all-clear and entered the building for search and assessment.

Chapter 13

Somewhere in the Bekaa Valley.
Sunday, 1 December 2002. 03:22.

Cooper took his position at the front right corner of beta building as directed, mini-Uzi ready. Skaff was on the left corner, so that they each had sight down one side of the building and both commanded the front door. Five Lebanese soldiers maintained positions at points around the compound in the event of unexpected backup from unknown outlying sentries or patrols. The three Lebanese with personal knowledge of the camp took the front door of beta building. When D-time hit, they entered, one soldier remaining just inside the door for cover as the other two hit the targets.

Cooper heard a confusion of automatic fire from inside the building then silence. He looked to Skaff for a signal then heard a shout in the headset from one of the Lebanese on the perimeter. He turned. From the back of the building he saw two figures running toward him, AK-47s swinging up to firing position. With his night-vision goggles they were as plain as if they were jogging on the beach.

He realized they were too far away for the mini-Uzi, which was inaccurate beyond short distances. He tossed the Uzi over his shoulder on the strap and dropped to one knee, pulling the Desert Eagle from the small of his back.

The approaching figures fired rounds at him while running. Cooper ignored the wild spray of bullets kicking dust up around him and sighted on the lead figure. A single pull of the trigger sent it staggering to the ground. The second figure came into range, halting abruptly and firing frantically. Cooper sighted and fired. The figure went down. A few additional shots fired with greater precision and less urgency satisfied Cooper, and he rose to his feet. Skaff raced around the side of the building and confirmed the kills.

The three Lebanese emerged from the building and confirmed two kills inside. The four unfriendlies in beta building were accounted for. Skaff sent two of the soldiers out for a recon of the area, kept one at the door of beta building, and nodded to Cooper. They both entered the building. Cooper looked around the room they had entered. Skaff flipped up his night-vision goggles, turned on a flashlight, and began searching the room. An open door in the back revealed two bodies on the floor, weapons kicked to the wall. Cooper removed his goggles, flicked on his flashlight, and stepped into the next room, a small space with a table, two chairs, and a closet.

He opened the closet and a figure lunged out into the glare of the light, sending him staggering back across the room. He hit the table and rolled over it. The flashlight tumbled to the floor but didn't go out. The attacker followed him, grabbed a chair and swung it down. Cooper rolled to his knees and the chair splintered on the floor next to him. He shot his right leg out and spun around, catching the attacker at the ankles and sending him crashing to the floor. Instantly Cooper was on him, left knee in his groin, left hand clutched at his throat. He reached up to Cooper's face, but Cooper leaned forward, cutting off his air. Hands clawed frantically at Cooper's face. Cooper drew his right leg up and pinned an arm to the floor with his knee.

He looked into the man's face. It was contorted with a hate that exceeded its fight for breath. Cooper saw Zaki dead, Hayat dead, Rafik spitting blood while he told the tale of his failure, his guts ripped out by AK-47 rounds, saw the hand that pulled the trigger. Cooper groped along his right leg, found the assault knife, pulled it from the scabbard, and buried it in the man's belly. He watched as the eyes grew wide, the silent scream aborted by lack of oxygen. He turned the knife and ripped it to one side, then the other, paying in kind for Rafik's wounds. Then Cooper snagged the man's hair in a fist with the left hand and dragged the knife across his neck slowly with the right, watching with satisfaction as his last breaths were sucked through the gash in his throat.

It wasn't until he saw the red dot of the laser sight from Skaff's Barak 45 play across the man's face that he realized someone had entered the room. He slid to the side, wiped his knife clean on the shirt of the dead terrorist and stood to face Skaff. They looked at each other in the dim glow of the flashlights. Cooper realized Skaff had probably made it to the doorway by the time he had pinned the terrorist, had watched the slow butchering, had seen his face as he had done it. He searched Skaff's face for a reaction but found nothing but a silent question. He retrieved his flashlight and focused it on the closet.

Inside, a lead trapdoor revealed stone steps that led down to a dungeon, a lead-lined room invisible to the heat sensors of the reconnaissance flyovers. Skaff descended first, followed by Cooper. A row of five cages, three feet square and five feet tall, lined a back wall. Skaff found a light switch and stepped toward a pile of papers on a table by some file cabinets. Cooper walked to the cages. The smell of human waste indicated they had been occupied recently. Blood and feces were smeared on the floor and the bottom of the bars. He turned away as the signal for extraction came over the headset.

Skaff closed a file drawer and killed the light. They climbed the steps, closed the trapdoor and the closet door. The Jeeps were waiting at the gate of the compound. Eshkol climbed behind the wheel of one.

"The recon team found a large ammo dump. We'll have the Apaches take it out."

He jerked his head to the back of the Jeep. Cooper saw a body, hands duct-taped behind his back, a shirt taped over his head.

"It wasn't a total loss. We got a talker. No time to get much out of him, but he said our boys were here yesterday. We'll take him home and have longer conversations, perhaps find out where they were taken last night. But right now, we're about to have some company. The alarm was raised faster than we expected." He looked at Skaff. "We'd appreciate a lift to the extraction point before you head back south. It's going to be close."

The IDF team was distributed across three Jeeps. Skaff and Cooper joined Eshkol in his Jeep. The remaining Lebanese took the last two Jeeps and headed south.

The race to the extraction point was quite different from the cautious drive to the camp. Eshkol navigated the rugged trail barely discernible through the night-vision goggles at a bone-jarring pace, followed by the other two Jeeps. Cooper looked to the north and saw the headlights of two Jeeps a few kilometers away, bouncing toward them. There was no sign of the chopper.

The IDF team began bailing from the Jeeps as they slowed. Eshkol threw the Jeep into neutral, pulled the hand brake, and

jumped to the sand. Skaff jumped behind the wheel as the Israelis in the back grabbed the hostage and took cover behind a
low rise. The IDF team formed a scattered line of defense facing the oncoming Jeeps using available ground cover.

Skaff led the other two Jeeps in a wide arc that placed them
in a flanking position to the Hezbollah Jeeps, which were now
only five hundred meters away. In the night-vision goggles
Cooper saw a terrorist struggle to his feet in the back of the
lead Jeep, dragging a rocket launcher to his shoulder.

Then he heard the sound of the Yas'ur 2000, and suddenly
it was on the ground between the Jeeps and the IDF team.
Two Apache gunships raced past it and fired missiles. The lead
Hezbollah Jeep was hit dead center as the terrorist got control
of the rocket launcher. The rocket careened into the desert,
where it exploded harmlessly. Random automatic weapons
fire came from the back Jeep before missiles from the second
Apache hit it. By the time the shrapnel had settled, the IDF
team was aboard the chopper and it was pulling away. Eshkol
hung on the door and saluted. Cooper saluted back as Skaff
whipped the Jeep around and began the race to beat the sun
to Marjeyoun. Minutes later a huge fireball behind them announced the destruction of the ammo dump.

An hour before sunrise, Skaff swung the Jeep off the road
and climbed a rise. He stopped at the top and looked over
the dark land west toward the sea. Cooper thought he recognized the cluster of buildings below as the place he had
shared his last meal with Skaff's family. Skaff walked to the
front of the Jeep, spread his arms, and spoke loudly in another language. Then, to Cooper's surprise, he began speaking in English.

"O Lord, turn Your wrath from the land and its inhabit-
ants. Put an end to trouble and sedition, banish from it war,
plunder, hunger, and plague. Have pity on us in our misfor-

tunes. Console those of us who are sick. Help us in our weakness. Deliver us from oppression and exile. Grant eternal rest to our dead. Allow us to live in peace in this world that we may glorify You."

He turned and faced Cooper, the features on his face barely discernible in the weakening darkness. "Matthew, hate does not defeat the oppressor. Yes, we fight. We fight to live. But we embrace hate, we die."

Cooper shook his head. "How can you not hate them after what they've done?"

"The enemy must not defeat me. If he brings hate in my heart, I have lost and he has won. Flee from hate as from a powerful lion. Do not follow the enemy into hate."

"But you kill them."

"I kill them if I must. I do not hesitate. But not to pleasure in it. I pray that God have mercy on their souls."

Cooper felt his face burn and was grateful for the darkness to hide his confusion. He could not tell if it was shame or anger he felt, or both. "How is that possible? It doesn't seem right. Or even natural."

"I have no family but God. I have no home but God. Like my brother, the Christ, I have no place to lay my head. Like my brother, the Christ, I will not hate the persecutor. This is a hard thing. I do not say it lightly, but I say yes to the Christ." His voice cracked. "Though He slay me, yet will I serve Him. *Maranatha, Yeshua. Maranatha.*"

Skaff slumped over the hood of the Jeep, the radiator still pinging as it cooled in the night air, and wept, his face buried in his upper arms, his forearms raised over his head, his fingers clutching at the back of his head. Cooper stood by uneasily as he heard Skaff muttering incomprehensibly, occasionally picking out the names of his family in the deluge of whispered pleadings.

Then, as the light crept back into the world and the outlines of things became visible, Skaff straightened himself, wiped his face on the sleeves of his shirt, and returned to the Jeep.

"We must get you back across the Good Fence before dawn."

Cooper sat down next to this man he could not fathom and allowed himself to be escorted back to his life.

Chapter 14

Safe house, Zahedan, Iran.
Tuesday, 3 December 2002. 17:00.

Although the wall had been cleaned, repaired, and re-painted, the outline of bloodstains was still visible on the empty chair. When al-Huzayfi entered the room, he could see them avoiding the sight of the chair as they would if unexpectedly encountering a woman without her burka. He stood at the door in silence to allow the tension to build then sat down at the head of the table.

"*Assalaamu alaykum,*" he said.

"*Wa alaykumus salaam,*" they responded.

Tea was served, and al-Huzayfi looked to Makkee. "Tell me of this raid in the Bekaa Valley." Ali knew Makkee had heard of the raid only an hour ago.

Makkee seemed to recoil internally from the shock but spoke without hesitation. "The raid. Camp Lam. A training camp closed for the winter. Israeli helicopters and SLA ground forces were involved. Probably looking for hostages, but they had been moved two days before. Only a handful of men there, all junior. All dead now, except the outlier sentry who made the report."

"Supplies?"

"Destroyed."

"Documents?"

"There were few documents at the camp. Nothing serious, just training manuals and such. No specific information." He shrugged his shoulders nervously. "It is mainly used for storage during the winter. Not active work."

"Yet one wonders how they learned of its location. We must review our security and perhaps interview the camp leaders. Al-Suri, how does this affect our training?"

Makkee said, "It shall be done," as al-Suri cleared his throat.

"We have several months to rebuild a facility at a suitable location. However, we must replenish the supplies or reduce the roster for spring training. Camp Lam was one of our primary ammunition dumps. Most of the training there is done for Hezbollah and the PLO. Perhaps we could get advance payments from them to restore the supplies." He looked at al-Fadel.

Al-Fadel shook his head. "Most of the matériel there was provided by Hezbollah and the PLO in preparation for the spring training."

"We could suggest that our investigations indicate it was a security breach from their ranks that caused the raid, therefore they must bear the cost of replacing the ammunition," al-Suri said.

"You shall be the one to deliver the message and collect the payment," al-Fadel responded. "Do not neglect to give them a receipt."

"Salim, how does this affect Last Straw?" al-Huzayfi asked.

"It doesn't. Camp Lam was used as a facility for an initial planning summit a year ago, but it does not provide the type of training we require for this project. Last Straw is primarily a matter of secure shipping, placement, and timing."

"Timing. That is the point. Makkee, can you help us with this timing?"

Makkee had relaxed as al-Huzayfi's attention moved on. He leaned forward at the table and peered down at a stack of papers. "Timing." He flipped over a few sheets.

"The Americans. When will they invade?"

"Our best guesses show late February. They have deployed a carrier group." He found the paper he was looking for. "The *Truman.*" He looked up. "The *Harry Truman* has been deployed to the Gulf. And General Franks is in Qatar, observing war games. There are no significant increases in troops or matériel. They are well under one hundred thousand, and they need twice that to invade. Even if they started tomorrow, it would take them over a month to be ready. We have at least two months, more likely three."

"February. Salim, how is this timing?"

"February is close. March would be better."

"February."

Salim nodded. "February."

Chapter 15

Los Angeles, California.
Wednesday, 11 December 2002. 10:15.

The 800 number said El Al flight 105 was delayed, which suited Stevie, since she was just passing the wreck by the Lincoln Street tunnel that had traffic backed up to Topanga Canyon. The extra hour she allotted to pick up a GPS international map module for his mobile phone was spent reading the two dozen bumper stickers on the van in front of her and reviewing the meeting with Stan. She wanted to discuss the options for structuring the production company with Matt before finalizing the incorporation papers.

The radio provided details on the snowstorm that had brought New York City to a standstill. Thanks to a disaster in 1993—a showdown with a black slope in Vail—she was in L.A., driving her XKS Jaguar Champion with the top down and not worrying about the storm shutting down the Nutcracker before Christmas. *Funny how what seems like a tragedy at the time looks like a blessing years later,* she thought.

It hadn't been easy. Selling the place in Manhattan, moving to L.A., taking temp work and counting pennies, wondering if the break would ever come. Then, just as she was estimating the cost to move back to Seattle, a call came that changed everything. The last four years had brought the kind of parts that not only challenged her but also opened the possibilities to move past acting into producing and maybe one day, directing.

The stalker's note on her kitchen counter had been a shock. Matt had simply been the best solution to a problem. At first. She wasn't prepared for the enthusiasm he brought to the solution. He was at her side practically every time she left the house. She couldn't even shake him by announcing she was going bowling, although she hadn't been bowling for two decades, not since her father died. Instead he showed up at her door with his own bowling shoes, still in the box with the laces in a plastic bag, and a monogrammed ball, the dust from the etching still evident. Too stubborn to admit she was bluffing, she went bowling.

On the lanes it became evident he had never held a bowling ball in his life, although he maintained the charade with constant chatter about bowling leagues and tournament trophies. While she slowly racked up a perfect 300, he threw a couple dozen gutter balls and ended up with a score that would have won the Master's in Augusta. When he stepped past the line, slipped on the lane, and rolled into the gutter with his ball, they laughed, gave it up, and had a chocolate shake at the snack bar. It was the night she suspected she had found more than a security escort.

With her star on the rise, it would have been easy to write Matt off as another wannabe, one of those who lurk on the fringe of the movie business, enthralled with the glamour but without the skills or breaks to play a primary role. In one of her earliest lessons in human nature Hollywood style, she learned that the most surprising people would abase themselves to get next to fame–top attorneys, CEOs of multinational corporations. Talented people with remarkable careers were just as susceptible to the bug as the suburban housewife reading *People* under the hair dryer. The only difference being their money, which allowed them to push through the other wannabes with their faces pressed to the glass and become the wannabe with access. They would talk diffidently about the roles they had played in college or at the Santa Barbara community theater or of the screenplay idea they would get down on paper as soon as the pace eased up a bit.

When Matt responded to her plea for help with an enthusiasm exceeding that of the stalker, her first reaction was to be thankful that she had discovered early that he was a closet wannabe. She appreciated him when she needed his services; she humored him when she didn't. But after the bowling night, she realized she had misjudged his disease. He wasn't smitten by her fame. He was smitten by her. Not Stephanie Zorn, but simply Stevie.

At first it scared her. NYC had provided a few painful lessons in keeping up her guard. Hollywood seemed less cynical, but even here it didn't take long for the ulterior motives to begin showing through the frayed fabric of the first few relationships. The old lessons in setting boundaries were reinforced. She appraised suitors with the jaundiced eye of a pawnbroker accustomed to dubious assurances of authenticity. As a result, she had remained free from opportunistic alliances but increasingly aware that when she should have been most fulfilled, she was in fact alone and lonely in the middle of a crowd. She longed for someone to share her life with but grew in the conviction that such relationships simply didn't exist in Hollywood. Before she left Seattle for NYC, she had already decided that she would find some way to balance career and children. A life without children wasn't an option. In the lonely nights while she ate blueberry yogurt and read scripts, she began to suspect that there was no way to have a real life to go along with her success and fame—that perhaps she would have to move back to Seattle after all.

So when it became apparent that she might have actually received what she wished for, it scared her. Matt didn't want her for what she could do for him; he wanted her. Just her. Was practically desperate for her. The impossible was sitting across from her, sipping a chocolate shake, unlacing those ridiculous bowling shoes and fast-talking the soda jerk, trying to unload a green bowling ball in mint condition with MC etched on the side, offering to throw in the monogrammed bag free. It was like going out to the parking lot and finding a unicorn where you had parked your Mercedes. Such things didn't exist in this town. For weeks the debate raged internally while she tested him for authenticity, each trial becoming more ridiculous until their dates began to look less like a relationship and more like a bad romantic comedy. When, in the midst of it all, he asked her to move into his Malibu fortress, she was undone. She lowered the drawbridge and flew the white flag.

It was all she had dreamed of. He was patient, loving, mature, sensible, sexy, exciting.

And, yet . . .

He gave so much, but he held something back. She had lowered her guard and erased the boundaries. But she could sense that for all his need and even devotion, he still maintained a layer of defense buried deep around some ancient ruin. It took months, but she gradually began to make out the outline of the barricade. At first she wondered if he held back because she had not received Nikki's approval. Perhaps Nikki's reaction had created misgivings. Then she wondered if some casual comment had been misconstrued, if he might be nursing a slight grudge. Or just boredom. As she learned more of his past, she wondered if it was a lingering wound from his first marriage. Now she just wondered. Speculations came in hordes. Answers came not at all.

It was all the more puzzling because in public and private he valued her with an unfashionable old-school deference that was irresistible. As they circulated through the shark tank of Hollywood social events, she could see that the other women, young and old, noticed how Matt treated her. She would see a woman look at her with envy and Matt with longing. A woman with Oscars at home in the closet and a headliner heartthrob on her arm. She would watch as Matt fended off the predators, some calculating and clever, some clumsy and coarse, and wonder how long it would take before one found the secret to his defenses and slipped into the place that seemed closed to her.

As she whipped into the parking structure, walked past the ticket agents, flashed the security badge Matt had given her, and rushed through security to the gate, the uniforms and weapons caused her to consider that it might not be a leonine climber that took Matt from her. It could be a bullet or a suicide bomber. She looked through the crowd waiting for the outbound flight and saw the plane taxi in. She hung back, relying on the Dodgers cap and Oakleys as camouflage.

Matt was the third one off the plane. She resisted the urge to wave. He spotted her immediately, smiled, and pushed through the crowd to her. The reunion caused more than one person to smile. When Stevie had reassembled her disguise, she hooked her arm in his and walked him out of the international terminal and back to the car.

"How was Israel?"

"Stevie, it was . . ."

He stopped and looked at her. She stopped and looked back. He was changed. It wasn't just the sunburn that was already beginning to peel. There was something in his eyes, something he seemed to have trouble putting into words.

"Yes?"

"I don't know. I had no idea. You have no idea. I . . . I don't know how to describe it. I'm worn out, but I'm rested."

She pulled on his arm and dragged him forward. "At least you didn't get yourself blown up." She looked at him obliquely. "But you did get a burn. Snow-skiing on Mt. Hermon?"

He smiled. "I spent most of last week at a kibbutz, rebuilding a barn."

She frowned. "A barn. Is IRIG diversifying into international construction contracts?"

He laughed. "How did you guess? I'm hoping to beat out Haliburton to rebuild Iraq."

"Iraq needs rebuilding?"

"It will in a year or so. Got to build my referral clients now."

They reached the baggage claim area. Stevie turned toward the carousels, but Matt pulled her toward the door. "No need. My stuff is with the group. George will have it delivered."

"George?"

"You know, the ice-cream suit."

She stiffened. The guy gave her the creeps the moment she saw him. Every morning Matt was gone she had cursed the ice-cream-suit man while doing her workout. "First-name basis these days? Did you have time to do any IRIG work while you were there? What about your connections and starting an office?"

"It's under control. George hooked me up with the perfect guy on the first day. By the third day I had developed connections a lot deeper than I had hoped for the entire trip."

She relaxed. "Good, so that's out of the way."

"There's still a lot of work to be done. Have to review and approve office space, interview and hire staff, circulate with the brass, both commercial and government. They're almost indistinguishable over there."

Stevie stopped next to the car with the remote in her hand. "You're going back?"

"Of course," Matt said. "A remote office can't be created from scratch in one trip."

"Maybe it could if you weren't spending your time pounding nails with Habitat for Hebrews. This trip could have been done in three days, I bet."

Matt stood by the passenger door and smiled at her over the top of the car. She pushed the button and got in. He slid in next to her and pulled the door closed.

"If I had gone on my own, it would have taken me six months to develop the contacts that I made in a few days. I'm willing to trade that for a few days pounding nails. I'm five months ahead of schedule because of George." He yawned. "And also exhausted."

She pulled out of the garage, paid for parking, and drove out Century to the 405 without comment. Matt put on his shades. She didn't talk again until they had passed Wilshire Boulevard.

"It's the timing, Matt. We set aside the end of the year to get the production company going. It's almost Christmas, and there's lots of work to be done, decisions to be made. Shooting for my next project begins January in Morocco. If this isn't done before I leave, it will be summer before we can wrap it up."

Matt held up three fingers. "On my honor I pledge I will not set foot out of California until the end of the year." He dropped his hand on her shoulder. "What do you have lined up for today?"

"You," she said.

He smiled. "Is Nikki at the studio today?"

She nodded. His smile grew. He ran his hand up her neck, making a fist in the thick black hair on the back of her head. She leaned her head back and her eyes closed.

"That's more like it," he said.

She opened her eyes to watch the road as he massaged the back of her neck. His hand dropped back down to her shoulder.

"Stevie, there are things happening out there we know nothing about. I know you think George is a nut case. Heck, I thought he was a nut case. I still think he might be. But there are things I should tell you about. Things that happened."

Stevie turned her head, set her chin on the back of his hand, and examined him. She reached across and pushed his sunglasses up onto his forehead. He squinted back at her. She wondered if something had really happened. Something that would break down the walls she had been unable to breach. Was it really happening? Did she dare to hope?

She knocked his shades back down over his eyes. He smiled. Something told her to be careful. Something else told her to follow her heart. She changed lanes and coasted into the valley.

Chapter 16

Malibu, California.
Friday, 13 December 2002. 18:00.

Cooper scowled at the mirror, getting his tie centered for the Christmas party. Thankfully, Stevie was downstairs somewhere, wrestling with the catering company or the string quartet or something. The moment they had arrived home from the IRIG party, she stormed off into the kitchen. Cooper shook his head and did a last-minute inspection of the parking attendants and the additional security, verifying they understood the procedures to prevent breaches of security during the confusion of guests arriving and departing. Then he went up to change clothes.

In an hour the first few would begin to trickle in. The guest list had taken weeks to perfect. They both had friends and business associates in the entertainment industry. Cooper also had contacts in law enforcement, government, and commerce. Stevie had connections in the philanthropic community. While going over last-minute additions on Thursday, Cooper had withdrawn Roberts, admitting that he came on a little too strong. However, during the party Cooper planned to work selected individuals for help with the cause.

He gave up on the tie and looked for his shoehorn. At least Claire wouldn't be at this party. Although everyone else at the status meeting had been satisfied with the summary Cooper provided on the Israel trip, a summary that omitted the raid on the camp, Claire had interrogated him, asking extremely detailed questions. He had answered her questions directly and succinctly, ignoring Sarah's meaningful looks. However, later in his office, as Sarah went over details for getting Roberts the most urgent supplies, Cooper could not deny that Claire seemed unusually and unnecessarily interested in his Middle Eastern activities.

As a result he had been preoccupied when Stevie arrived at noon for the IRIG Christmas party, greeting her distractedly and leaving her to get a drink and mingle on her own—something he realized too late. A few hours had passed, the year-end speech had been made, gifts and awards distributed, hors d'oeuvres and drinks consumed. When he finally got a glass of Pinot Noir and tracked her down, she looked at him coldly and continued her conversation with Perkins on the symbiotic relationship between meditation and exercise.

Then he felt a hand on his shoulder and turned to see Claire holding a martini. He stepped back to allow her hand to drop away. She looked him over without comment for a few seconds and took another sip. It was obviously not her first martini of the afternoon.

"I think the work at the kibbutz was good medicine," she said. "You're trimmer, and the tan looks good on you. You were a little pale after the China trip."

Behind him, Cooper heard Stevie's conversation falter. He smiled at Claire, but said nothing.

"But all work, no play, Matt. You know the drill. You need to cut loose a little. When's the next Israel trip?"

"January."

"I tell you what. I'll be in Paris next month. I'll fly down on the weekend, show you some of the hotter spots in Tel Aviv."

She took a sip of her drink, her big brown eyes unblinking as she watched him over the rim of the glass. Cooper shook his head. The conversation behind him had stopped.

Claire pushed her black hair back behind her ear with her free hand. "Or I know of a nice cabin in the Golan Heights. Great views, hot tub, lots of privacy." She took some ice from her drink and twirled it slowly between her lips.

Cooper heard Sarah clear her throat loudly halfway across the room and caught her I-told-you-so glare. Then he felt Stevie's hand on his back.

"Matt, dear, I don't believe you've introduced me to your friend." He felt her fingernails through his coat, tracing a line down his spine. Her eyes never left Claire.

"Stevie, this is Claire Moquard, head of Undercover Operations."

"Undercover? So I gathered. Moquard. What kind of name is that?"

Claire looked at Stevie without expression. "Persian."

Stevie nodded. "Head of Undercover." She looked Claire over slowly, at the business suit with skirt a bit too short to be completely convincing, the long, slender legs in dark hose, the three-inch heels. Her gaze worked back up to Claire's eyes. "I'd guess you've been under a lot of different covers in your time, haven't you, to make it up to head?" She sipped her Shiraz and wrapped her fingers over Cooper's shoulder, the same one Claire's hand had rested on a few seconds before. "Matt, you have the right person for the job. She's so obviously experienced."

Claire's blank look turned hard. She sipped her martini slowly, turned away pointedly, and looked at Cooper. "What a charming playmate you've found, Matt. When do you think you'll have her declawed?"

Stevie shoved her wine toward Perkins, who took it clumsily, spilling it on his white shirt. "Not soon enough to save you," she said, stepping toward Claire, who stood her ground.

Cooper stepped between them and turned toward Stevie. "Hold on, Stevie," he began, but she pushed at him. He stepped backward to keep his balance and ran into Claire. Her martini spilled over both of them; his wine spilled on Stevie. Dr. Hampton appeared, put his arm around Claire, and led her away toward the bathroom. Cooper put his free arm around Stevie and handed his drink to Perkins, who struggled to hold the three glasses he had accumulated.

"Stevie, let it go. She just had too much to drink, that's all. She doesn't mean anything by it."

"Sure," Stevie said, pushing Cooper away and reaching for a cocktail napkin on a nearby tray. "Just business as usual, propositioning the boss. What exactly did she do to get the promotion?"

Cooper held his arms out, palms up. "Submitted the best résumé IRIG has ever seen. She's the best in the business at what she does."

"I'll bet." She tossed the napkin back on the tray.

He stepped toward her, reaching for her shoulder. "It's just a misunderstanding. I'll have a talk with her Monday."

"Great. A private conference, no doubt. Maybe she'll get promoted to VP." She pushed him away and walked past him. "I'll be in the car."

Cooper watched her go then lifted his hand to his ear. "Alex, Stevie's on the way down. I'll be there soon."

Knowing conversation would be impossible on the drive to Malibu, he brought paperwork. Stevie was in the front with Alex. He sat in the back, stared at the untouched papers, and thought over the last two days. The glow of the reunion after his return from Israel had lasted through the afternoon and into the evening. As they lay in bed that night, he told her of the things he had seen in Israel and Lebanon. But when he came to the deepest thing, he choked. The depth of feeling that was awakened while eating a meal with Skaff's family in the flickering light of the hearth fire, surrounded by blackout curtains and blankets, was the same passion that had fueled his rage at the terrorist training camp.

To tell her of one without telling her of the other would be a lie. To tell her of neither would be protecting her. Did she really want to know what he had done in the throes of that passion—of the blood on his hands, the violence and blackness in his soul? Would she understand, feel in her heart the same outrage and thirst for justice? Or would she feel revulsion, or worse, pity?

So he had stopped, his sentence dying out into silence, and lay there. He could feel Stevie next to him, knowing there was more and wanting to be part of it. He could feel the confusion of pride and shame in his chest, the curse of the avenging angel dispensing justice and craving redemption. Could she relieve this ache? To risk it was to risk all. He could not gamble what he could not stand to lose.

He remained silent and felt Stevie's confusion, frustration, and unspoken pain as she curled up against him. All he could do was hold her tighter and wish he believed in something strongly enough to pray.

There had not been much time for conversation since. Cooper spent the rest of the week catching up after the trip, and before he knew it, there was the Christmas party. He gave himself one last look in the mirror and headed downstairs for a drink before the crowd arrived.

———

Nikki heard Dad go down the stairs. She would wait until the party was peaking, when she could slip in unnoticed, allow him to see her at the party, mingling. Then she would come back up.

She plugged the iPod into the Bose base station, picked a playlist with the new Destiny's Child album in it, and experimented with her makeup, trying to hide the circles under her eyes.

The dreams were more frequent now, almost every night. They had been gone for a long time, but not long after *She* moved in they started again. Every other month or so at first, then every month, and then every week. And ever since Dad went to Israel, the crazy suicide bomber joined the cast.

But it wasn't just at night. Even in the day, when the pressure got too high, at school or the studio or wherever, she would feel the dread descend. A feeling like something terrible just happened, like any minute someone would come in and tell her the news that would end her world. She felt it worst when she saw someone in uniform. She refused to look at the security guys when they went to the studio, would put in her earbuds and pretend not to hear their greetings through Alex's window on her way in.

And if she closed her eyes, they were there. The car, the scarf, Dad, the bomber, the cops. Flashing lights and sirens. Then she remembered the nail, how the pain gave her something else to focus on. She began wearing stud earrings, pushing one into the palm of her hand when it got too bad. She had heard of girls using a knife, but she had to be careful about creating scabs and scars that the camera would pick up at the studio.

When she had poked a couple of holes in her palm, she realized a pin would leave a smaller hole, easier to heal, so she kept a safety pin in a small vial of rubbing alcohol. She used places where the skin was thin, like the elbow or ankle, or places not visible, like the bottom of her foot, or sometimes her hip through her clothes. The pin caused a sharp, focused point of pain, not excruciating but intense enough to prevent her from thinking of anything else. Especially *them*.

When she thought about it, which she tried not to do, she realized there was something not good about it. But she didn't know any other way to stop the thoughts. Fight fire with fire and pain with pain, right? Besides, she wasn't going to do anything stupid like drugs. That was for losers. The focus she achieved actually helped her do better on the set and at school, so it was a good thing. At least partly, anyway.

She assessed the makeup job in the mirror. It looked natural. *Besides*, she thought as she pushed the makeup into a drawer, *Dad's too busy and even if he wasn't, what could he do? And I'm sure not going to tell Her.*

She poked her head out the door. Sounded like the party was rocking. Time to circulate among the old folks and be pleasant for half an hour. She walked to the landing and looked across the crowd, tight little groups of slightly tipsy adults talking a little too loudly, *The Holly and the Ivy* from the string quartet. Dad was near the piano. She spotted Uncle Will and threaded her way through the clusters of conversations, greeting those she knew along the way and smiling at the others.

She eased into Uncle Will's circle and slipped her arm into his. He looked down, smiled, hugged her, and introduced her to the group. She was fielding questions about the TV series when Dad stepped up.

"I see you made your fashionably late entrance, as usual," he said.

Uncle Will laughed the laugh that made Nikki think of a grandfather. "Now, Coop, you can't expect a bright little girl like this to want to spend her time hanging around ancient fossils like us, can you?"

"Evidently not."

Nikki smiled and looked self-consciously around the small circle of people. Most seemed to be in their late twenties and early thirties, very fit, dressed to walk the ramp at the next fashion show, and entirely too happy for a normal person.

Uncle Will put his arm around her. "Nikki, didn't you get any slots on the guest list?"

"I didn't ask for any."

"You mean to tell me you don't have any friends?"

"I have friends. I just didn't ask if they could come to the party. Dad only got back Wednesday, and by then it was too late. Everyone had plans."

"Then we'll plan in advance. You round up a half dozen of your friends, and we'll do a skiing weekend at my place in Vail in February."

Nikki looked up, eyes wide. "Really?" He nodded. She looked up at Dad. "Can I?"

Dad looked at Uncle Will. "Dixon, do I get any slots on the guest list?"

"Only two, Coop—you and the lady of your choice. This will be a young people's trip, not an old fogy trip."

"By February, I'm sure I'll need a break. Why not?"

Nikki pulled Dad down to her face. "Thanks, Dad." She gave him a kiss. Uncle Will cleared his throat. "Oh, and thank you, Uncle Will." She kissed the cheek he offered. "I'm going to get some eggnog."

She could feel Dad looking at her as she walked away. Looking like he wanted to ask her something but wasn't quite sure what to ask.

Chapter 17

Baltimore, Maryland.
Friday, 20 December 2002. 12:25.

As he did every day, he pulled a stool next to the window of the office that overlooked the container yard and opened his lunch. He set the apple aside for later, unwrapped the corned-beef sandwich, smoothed the paper out, and set the sandwich in the center. To the left he placed the baby carrots parallel to each other and perpendicular to the edge of the paper, like a row of the intermodal containers visible out the window. The wheat crackers were divided into two equal stacks and set behind the sandwich. Noting that one was slightly higher, he took a cracker from the taller stack and ate it. He pulled the teabag from the mug and held it over the top right corner of the paper, watching it slowly spin until it was aligned with the edge then dropping it down. He watched the small puddle of tea that oozed out, smiling with approval when it stopped a few millimeters from the edge of the paper.

Satisfied that everything was as it should be, he checked his watch. Twelve twenty-eight. He scanned the matrix of containers, counted five down and seven across from the far corner. He leaned back to his desk, opened a drawer, pulled out binoculars, checked the container again, nodded, and set the binoculars to his left. Container number TEX2409147.

He began eating his lunch, one bite of sandwich, one carrot, one cracker, one sip of the tea, casually glancing over the yard as he chewed. Parker's head poked in the door, asked for Dotson. He shrugged and Parker left. He turned back to the yard and noted the security guard walking through the containers with a briefcase. He picked up the binoculars and watched the progress of the worker, reaching for the next carrot.

He knew that TEX2409147 had been scanned with VACIS as part of a random check, but he had not been concerned. There was nothing about its contents or its point of origin that would have raised suspicion. With more than twenty thousand containers coming into the U.S. each day, there simply wasn't time to check them all. Only about five percent were inspected, and most of those were just scanned. A full search would take five agents and three hours, an event unlikely to happen unless something very suspicious was found. And there was nothing suspicious about container number TEX2409147.

As he took a sip of tea, the guard reached the container, set the briefcase down, broke the seal, opened the door, picked up the briefcase, and disappeared inside. Less than a minute later the guard stepped out with the briefcase, set it down, closed the door, replaced the seal, picked up the briefcase, and walked back toward the office building.

He put the binoculars back in the desk drawer and made a call on his cell as he watched the guard's progress through the yard. He smiled, realizing that the guard assumed these shipments were drugs, even though the question had never been asked. And the assumption had been correct for the first five shipments. But now the channel was proven, and the time had come to use it for its highest purpose. He wondered if the guard had noticed the difference in the weight of the briefcase. Perhaps. He knew the man well, although the man didn't know he existed or that he was watching. He knew the man would not risk the $2,000 payment to ask his handler questions or open the briefcase.

He rolled up the teabag in the sandwich paper and threw it away. As he picked up the apple, the confirmation call came in on his cell. Package received. He didn't know the next step in the plan, when it would happen, or who would execute it. But he was confident it would go as planned. He set down the phone and took a bite of the apple.

Los Angeles, California.
Friday, 20 December 2002. 18:25.

Emilio sat on the edge of the couch, a cup of tea balanced on his left knee, a plate of Christmas treats balanced on his right. A small Christmas tree stood on a table in the corner. A small fire crackled in the fireplace. Amil listened with glistening eyes as Emilio told stories of the Holy Land, describing the people and the sounds and the smells and the colors. Amil's wife listened from the doorway of the kitchen, shaking her head every time Emilio asked her to come sit with them.

"I don't know how they live up there so close to the border with raids and bombings and shootings."

Amil smiled. "We are not without these things here in L.A., but we still stay."

Emilio shook his head. "It feels different there. There is a tension, even in the very land. As I helped measure wood for the new barn, I could feel it. The force of their will, coming from the east and the north. Even when there are no bombs, you can feel them." He set the plate of cookies on the coffee table. "You know how the Proverbs say a foolish son brings his father to calamity and a quarrelsome wife is like a dripping faucet?" He smiled an apology at Amil's wife. "It's like that. You know as long as you stay there you will never be free of it. Even Mr. Cooper, he could feel it too. I saw him, how he looked at things."

Amil's response was interrupted by the front door opening. A tall, dark, handsome man stepped in and closed the door firmly behind him. He turned and smiled politely. Amil stood.

"Emilio, this is my son, Basil." He turned to his son. "Emilio is my good friend down at the school. I have spoken of him."

Basil smiled and reached over the coffee table. Emilio set the teacup down, stood, and took his hand. "I'm very pleased to meet you. Thank you for the baklava we enjoyed last month."

Amil gestured to a chair. "Come, join us. Emilio is telling us of his trip to Israel. He went with Mr. Roberts."

"Is that so?" Basil asked. "Tell me of this Mr. Roberts." He shrugged out of his coat and sat opposite Emilio.

"He takes groups of volunteers to rebuild homes destroyed by the PLO."

"Is he paid by the Israelis?"

"No, he provides the materials from donations. The workers pay their own travel expenses."

Basil nodded. "A very noble gesture. I should like to meet this Mr. Roberts some day."

"Perhaps you could go on one of the trips."

"No, I don't think so. I can't afford to have a stamp for Israel on my passport. I could experience difficulty at immigration for my business trips. Some of my vendors are not friends of the Jews." He smiled. "You can understand. They feel they have suffered at the hands of the Israelis."

"Yes. I have heard that the burglar feels he suffers from the bite of the dog."

Basil's smile froze and faded slowly. "Yes, I suppose he does." He looked at Emilio with greater interest. "You seem an unlikely friend of the Jews. How does an Hispanic come to have such a passion for the Hebrew children?"

"They are God's chosen people."

"Perhaps. Then, given everything they've suffered, perhaps they'd prefer God chose someone else for awhile."

Chapter 18

Outside Rabat, Morocco.
Wednesday, 1 January 2003. 07:22.

Stevie sat under the canopy, sipped tea, nibbled fruit, and looked across the empty expanse of sand. She didn't recall ever being awake on New Year's Day before noon, but jet lag woke her up hours ago. Shooting would begin tomorrow. The schedule for today was recovery. She wrapped her sweater tighter against the cool morning air and warmed her hands on the teacup.

She thought about Matt in Tel Aviv. The only consolation was that suicide bombers seemed to frequent restaurants and nightclubs and public transportation. He would spend most of his time in office buildings looking for a good location.

The holidays had been rough going, a mixed bag of intimacy and tension. In stolen moments of laziness amid the holiday madness, he told her of the Israelis, the kibbutz, the children, the unquenchable flame of hope that seemed to be reborn within the new generation in a land of violence and history. Hoping it was more than wishful thinking, she felt that Matt was beginning to open slowly, like a late-blooming flower. Then there were the other times, when she could sense a vague shape looming in the shadows behind his eyes. When she would look deeper, he would turn away. And always the unspoken point of contention, the uneasy alliance between her needs and his, between her career and his.

And Nikki. She could see that Nikki's delicately balanced life was on the brink of collapse. They coexisted like bordering nations both dependent on the same natural resources. Neither could risk the conflict that would arise from an attempt at dominance. She accepted it and played her part in the awkward dance. But she wasn't blind. Nikki was young enough to suffer from the delusion that she could somehow control the forces within her through diversion and denial. Stevie knew better. She also knew that someone would have to be there when the sky fell. Because it would. It was inevitable. And if Matt weren't there and Nikki wouldn't let Stevie be there then . . .

She was rescued from her speculations by another early riser. Paula dropped into the camp chair next to her. She had the supporting female role, the comic relief. When she met her before the trip, Stevie was surprised to learn that her larger-than-life screen presence followed her off the screen. She was tall and bouncy and loud. Stevie didn't know which was more startling, the flaming red hair or the booming machine-gun laugh that cut through anything, even the heavy machinery moving the set into place.

Paula took a gulp of coffee and looked across the desert. "There's nothing like morning. Fresh start, clean slate. I don't understand people who don't like morning. Who doesn't like a second chance?"

Stevie was annoyed by Paula's overbearing cheerfulness at such an early hour. "I guess it's easy to like morning if you're a morning person."

"Yes, you're probably right," Paula said. She dropped a Bible on the folding table, causing a landslide in the pyramid of fruit. "Still, David said, 'Your mercies are new every morning.'"

Oh great, Stevie thought. *One of those.* "So, you're saying the Bible is written for morning people."

"Not necessarily. My home group leader picked out a verse just for me. I have it marked right here. Proverbs 27:14." She flipped to the middle of the Bible. "'If a man loudly blesses his neighbor early in the morning, it will be taken as a curse.'"

Her machine-gun laugh rolled out across the desert, probably causing heart attacks in lizards warming themselves in the morning sun. Stevie had visions of desert animals scurrying for cover for miles around.

"Does it really say that?" Stevie asked.

"Sure." Paula pushed the Bible to her. "Right there."

Stevie read it and smiled. "It does. I didn't know the Bible has stuff like that in it. I thought it was a bunch of 'thou shalts' and 'thou shalt nots.'"

"It has that stuff too, and a lot more. You might be surprised."

"Oh, here's one for Matt," Stevie said. "'The prudent see danger and take refuge, but the simple keep going and suffer for it.'" She looked at Paula. "He's in Tel Aviv, even though I begged him not to go."

Paula looked at Stevie. "That's one thing about the Bible. It's easy to find something in it that the other guy needs to hear. It's a little harder to look in it like a mirror and see what it shows me about myself."

Stevie felt her face turning red. She opened her mouth to respond but couldn't think of anything to say. Paula was right, after all. She didn't look in it to find wisdom for herself.

Paula ignored Stevie's embarrassment. "Like that verse about the loud greeting. When I read that, I knew God was talking straight to me. I could read all the verses in the Bible about rising early to pray or to praise the Lord and think how all those night people need to change. But it's not my job to change everybody else. I'm responsible for the wisdom God shows me, and following it. And God was telling me right there that I need to be more understanding of people who aren't like me."

Stevie was surprised. "I've never heard that the Bible says God wants us to try to understand those who are different. I'm always hearing preachers saying God's going to wipe out Disneyland because of the gays or that September 11 was God's punishment on America for abortion and homosexuality or things like that. Somebody should tell those preachers they have it wrong."

"Stevie, you keep talking about what other people need to hear. You can't fix everybody else. That's between them and God. Each of us, you, me, Russell, Mark," she nodded back at the trailers, "Matt and even those preachers you're talking about—all any of us can do is let God show us our own hearts, let Him change us. I have to decide for myself if I'm going to humble myself and learn at His feet. I can't make you do it. And it's not my job to make you do it. That's your job and your decision."

Stevie didn't say anything. She looked into the distance. She knew that Matt needed to change, no matter what Paula said. For Nikki's sake, if nothing else, but also for Stevie's sake and even for his own sake. How would "learning at God's feet" change anything? Yet she couldn't shake the nagging feeling that Paula might be right.

She looked down at the verse about the loud greeting in the morning. The next one said, "A quarrelsome wife is like a constant dripping on a rainy day; restraining her is like restraining the wind or grasping oil with the hand."

She felt her face turning red again, and her eyes flinched away. Was God trying to talk to her, trying to teach her wisdom? But she wasn't a quarrelsome wife. She wasn't even a wife, for that matter. She forced herself to read it again. Did she have the nerve to look in this mirror and see what she might see? To see what God might see? It was a strange concept, trying to see what God saw. She had never considered it. What did God see when He looked at her?

She closed her eyes and asked the question again. *What does God see when He looks at me?* The question changed in her mind. *What do You see when You look at me?* She blushed again at the presumption of intimacy in the wording. But almost immediately she sensed a word in her mind. *Wife.*

She reacted immediately. *No!* she thought. Her head jerked up, and her eyes opened. She saw Paula looking at her. Had she said it out loud? She got up awkwardly from the canvas chair and walked out from under the canopy into the morning sun and let it warm her. With her back to Paula and her face to the sun, she closed her eyes and asked again.

What do You see when You look at me? She sensed the word *wife* again, but this time she didn't react or open her eyes and it was immediately followed by a second word: *beloved.*

She gasped. She felt the moisture rise suddenly to her closed eyes and overflow. She stood in the warmth of the sun for a long time, not thinking, just feeling. Experiencing the unexpected answer to a bold and presumptuous question.

After a long time she opened her eyes and turned around. Paula's head was bowed over the open Bible, her lips moving without sound. Stevie stepped back under the canopy.

"So," she said, "what exactly is a home group leader?"

Paula looked up with tears in her eyes and smiled.

Chapter 19

Cooper warmed his hands on the coffee cup and scanned the cafe for Alexia. She was late, as usual. He was impatient, which was unusual. He normally enjoyed lounging in the Figlmuller, people-watching with half his brain while processing issues with the other half. He did his best thinking when his conscious mind was distracted. On a normal visit, Alexia could be as late as she liked or not even show up at all.

But this was not a normal visit. January in Vienna was nice for skiing, but not for business. He did the European checkup tour in the spring, when he would have a few meetings with directors and field agents, a quick visit with the administrator, a few dinners with local officials, coffee with Alexia, and then on to the next office.

Today he had left an office full of people following leads on the phone, poking colored pins in maps, taking status phone calls from field agents, keying it into the database, updating it on the whiteboards, and generally running around in frantic chaos. He had several items he had to attend to personally. Alexia was the first and most important, but she wasn't the only item on his list.

Yesterday, after he got the call from Dixon but before he checked out of the Tel Aviv Sheraton, he had called her and asked her to meet him today. He knew that regardless of what he found in Vienna, Alexia would have the best street intel for the passport problem.

He had just returned to his room from a day of touring possible field office locations with Cohen. He was enjoying a glass of wine on the Sheraton's balcony while watching the moonlight play across the waves of the Mediterranean when he heard Dixon's ring tone on the KL-7 encrypted cell phone. The phone had new technology, unbreakable with current cracking tools, and was normally restricted to government agents. It was a perk Cooper had received for connecting the NSA with the geek who developed the algorithm. Before he picked it up he was already mentally reviewing his travel plans. Dixon didn't call him on this phone unless it was urgent.

"Sorry to call you after midnight, Coop. You need a few minutes to clear your head?"

"Dixon, you still at the office? I thought you'd be at happy hour by now."

"I'm giving the freeway time to clear. Look, how long will it take you to get to Vienna?"

"I could be there tomorrow if I had to."

"Start packing. I've been working this all day, and the official channels are taking too long. I have a feeling about this one, and it's not the feeling you get when you hear your rich uncle died. I need some back-channel work."

"I'm your man."

"Twenty hours ago we got a call from MI5 at Heathrow. The Brits grab a Saudi national on a routine random passport check. He's booked for a New York flight and flashes a Portuguese passport. The only problem is the number doesn't show up on the Interpol issue list. They contact the Portuguese and discover that four months ago fifteen hundred issue-ready passports were stolen from the Portuguese embassy in Vienna. The geniuses were planning on reporting it to Interpol any month, now, when they get around to pulling their heads out. Not only that, but they can't seem to remember the serial numbers of the stolen passports. So far we've talked to three different people and have three different sets of numbers, none of which include the confiscated passport.

"The Brits put the Saudi through the ringer and finally break him. He's just a mule, a test case to try the passports. Somebody gave him a week vacation to New York and a passport. Or so he says. If he's telling the truth, they were watching the circus at Heathrow and are working on Plan B."

"You can be sure of that."

"If he's not telling the truth, no telling how many terrorists already came across on these bogus passports. I've spent the day flattering and abusing officials all over Europe, but nobody's in any particular hurry."

"And you have a feeling."

"Yep."

"Did you tell them that?" Cooper smiled. He heard Dixon chuckle.

"I forgot to mention it. Could you tell them about it when you get to Vienna tomorrow?"

"Will do. But just one thing, Dixon."

"What's that?"

"Don't think you can keep me in Vienna to get out of making good on that ski trip. I'll be in Vail next month, passports or no passports. If I'm not, Nikki will make the grilling the Brits gave the Saudi look like an Oprah interview."

"Then you better get cracking."

As soon as he hung up, Cooper booked the first flight to Vienna and checked his watch. Almost 1:00 a.m.—nearly midnight in Vienna. She would still be up. He called Alexia and, over the noise of nightclub music, arranged the meeting at the Figlmuller cafe for the afternoon.

He debated with himself about the next call then decided Mario would forgive him. As director of the Staatspolizei, the secret service branch of the Austrian Federal Police, Mario was responsible for counterterrorism and counterintelligence—a good guy to have on your side in this business. And at dinner last April, Mario had said to let him know if he needed anything.

Mario was definitely not awake when he answered the phone, but after a few seconds he figured out who Cooper was and why he called. He already knew about the case and wasn't getting much traction from the Portuguese embassy, which made him suspect it might be an inside job. He welcomed Cooper to the case and promised to have a copy of all the relevant documents at the IRIG field office by the time he arrived the next day.

———

Alexia dropped into the chair opposite Cooper and shot a withering look at him over her sunglasses before she pushed them back up.

"Do you realize what time it is?"

"You agreed to the time."

"That was last night. Anything was possible last night."

"Coffee?"

"You have to ask?"

Cooper signaled the waiter. "Sorry to disturb your beauty rest, Lex, but I'm on a schedule today and dinner is booked. What have you heard about the passports stolen from the Portuguese embassy last September?"

Alexia slumped back in the chair and lit a cigarette. "That's old news, dear. I thought you were going to ask about the nukes."

"The nukes?"

"You haven't heard about the nukes? You're getting rusty, Matthew. Need to get out more."

"From the looks of it, you might need to get out less. You're what—twenty-three?"

"Twenty-two."

"You're putting on some pretty heavy miles. You can't party all night like you did when you were eighteen. You need to learn to pace yourself or you'll be no use to me."

"You're starting to sound like Uncle Dimitri."

"Your uncle is a wise man. So what about the nukes?"

"I thought you wanted to know about the passports."

"Take your pick."

"The nukes are more exciting. Everybody knows the clerk at the embassy has a weakness for old wines and young men. Not sure if it was blackmail or a payoff. Probably both. Doesn't matter."

"The clerk?"

"Marcelino somebody. Short. Fat. Bad dancer."

"And the nukes?"

"Uncle Dimitri says the Syrians bought eleven of the old briefcase nukes from before the breakup. Some of his old cronies in the Ukraine have a stash of ninety, and they finally found some buyers with cash."

"Ninety?"

"About. Maybe more, maybe less. Maybe it was nineteen. Nobody's sure how many there are. Either way, they sold eleven. They're set for caviar for the next few years."

"To the Syrians?"

"Syrians or Iranians. Either way, they'll end up in the same place. Al-Qaeda or something like it. Uncle Dimitri thinks they'll use them on Israel . . . if they work. They're pretty old, and these things need regular maintenance."

"Eleven? That's a lot just for Israel."

"They're only one kiloton. They can level maybe five hundred meters, damage out to a kilometer or so. Of course the radiation would go out a lot farther. Even if you used all of them, you couldn't destroy all of Tel Aviv. But you could make it unlivable for a long time. Kill maybe a million, maybe half right away."

"You know more about nuclear devices than the average twenty-two-year-old."

She waved her hand. "Markov. He likes to impress me by reciting statistics."

"Does he still want to take you to Cuba?"

"He never shuts up about it."

"You should go. It's a lot warmer. And I could use a good contact, well connected, for when Castro finally buys the farm."

"Cuba is no good. No nightlife. Not like they say it was before Castro. Communists don't have good clubs."

"Don't tell that to Uncle Dimitri."

"He doesn't know a nightclub from a billy club. He thinks a party is two women and three bottles of vodka."

Cooper called Sarah from the cab on the way back to the field office, trying to catch her before 8:00 a.m. and the rush of the day in California. After getting the status for ongoing investigations and the aid to Lebanon, he heard Sarah clear her throat. It sounded like the long-distance version of the Look. He braced himself.

"Mr. C. You know Claire is in Paris."

"Yes. Why?"

"She's been using the VPN to connect to the intranet."

"That's what it's there for."

"Yes, but that's not all. Mark in Operations sent me a log of file access activity. He noticed she had unusually long sessions and searched through a lot of folders, like she was looking for something."

"I do that when I can't find something."

"She spent a long time looking through the project folders for Israel. She downloaded entire directories."

Cooper stared out the window of the cab and the shop fronts. "Israel." As head of Undercover Ops, Claire had access to most of the network. She certainly could justify access to information on field offices. But why Israel? Why now?

"Just thought you might want to know, Mr. C."

"Thanks, Sarah. Keep me posted if anything else unusual turns up. And thank Mark for me."

The next call was from the private conference room to Dixon on the KL-7 phone. Dixon answered on the first ring.

"Coop, what you got?"

"Sounds like the passport thing was an inside job. I'll have more for you by Monday."

"That's quick work."

"The invoice is already on the way. But we have more problems on our hands than a few stolen passports."

"I wouldn't call fifteen hundred passports a few."

"I'll trade you fifteen hundred stolen passports for eleven stolen briefcase nukes." Cooper told him the story, referring to Alexia as Boris.

"How reliable is this contact?"

"Very. He's directly connected to the hard-line Soviets from before the breakup. Kremlin, KGB. Everything he's said before has always checked out. Remember the XTC connection to Lithuania we cracked last year?"

"Vividly. Look, Coop, I'm fighting the many-headed beast we call L.A. rush hour. When I get in the office, I'll get the authorization for you to track this all the way to the source."

Cooper was printing out the list of informants to be contacted for the investigation when Mario called.

"Matt, is your television on?"

Cooper glanced across the office. "Yes, but the sound is down."

"Turn it up and switch to seven. I'm headed over for the status meeting. Be there in ten."

Cooper caught the end of the newscast.

". . . an obscure militant Muslim faction, but didn't give details. The statement on Aljazeera TV simply said that the U.S. must withdraw from the Middle East immediately or they would bring the violence to the infidel oppressors. Officials say that Harkat-ul-Jihad al-Islami is not known to be linked with or based in any specific country and no members have been identified by name. It is believed to be one of the many splinter groups aligned with al-Qaeda. The U.S. Homeland Security reports it takes all threats seriously but has not raised the alert status as a result of the statement."

Cooper gathered the information he needed for his meeting with Mario and strode to the main conference room, oblivious to the greetings in the hallway. He was thinking of something Major Skaff had said during their brief meeting in Metulla two days before. He reminded Cooper of the dungeon they had discovered in the camp raid. Of the filing cabinets. Cooper remembered the cages more vividly, but recalled Skaff had searched the cabinets before the signal to withdraw, had taken some documents as he left. Skaff had read through the documents several times. He found some references to a special project designed to strike at the heart of the Great Satan with the fire of Armageddon. At first he had suspected the documents referred to the 9/11 attack. Then he found a reference to the 9/11 attack in the same document, indicating that it was the initial blow, but not the final one. The information was interesting, but Cooper had considered it outside his scope of operation, a matter for Homeland Security.

But that was before he had talked to Alexia. Before he had heard the threats from Harkat-ul-Jihad al-Islami.

Cooper was in the conference room when Mario arrived. He handed Cooper a Telex with the text of the statement. Cooper skimmed it and handed it back.

"What do you think this means—'bring the violence to the infidel oppressors'?"

"Ah, yes. HuJI. Small but violent. It could be anything from mailing anthrax to the president to sabotaging nuclear power plants. Who knows?"

"'Bring the violence' sounds like something more dramatic than anthrax in the mail. Sounds like suicide bombers."

"Could be."

"Maybe even nuclear. A dirty bomb, perhaps."

Mario looked at Cooper without comment. "There have been threats of nuclear attacks before. A month after the WTC attack, there was a threat of a ten-kiloton nuclear bomb in New York."

"Yes," Mario conceded. "The 'American Hiroshima' chatter from early 2001 gave it credibility. The threat of a nuclear bomb somewhere in New York City, small enough to fit in an ordinary panel van, similar in power to the one exploded over Hiroshima, caused panic at the highest levels. Obviously no such bomb or any evidence that it had entered the U.S. was ever found."

"On the other hand, nobody ever denied that such a bomb could have been smuggled in."

"True."

Cooper let the silence hang for awhile. "What do we know about HuJI?"

"Very little. We only have a few names we can link with the group. Last year on December 1, American troops found the body of a Jamal Khidamat in some ruins outside of Rebate Jali in the devil's triangle where Afghanistan, Pakistan, and Iran meet. He had been shot in the head several days before. Khidamat was a Saudi citizen with a history of assisting pro-Islamic propaganda efforts. That leaves us with one other name, Khalid al-Fadel, an international financier, Syrian with Iranian connections. His whereabouts are not known at present, but he travels frequently through the Middle and Far East as well as Europe. He appears to deal with multiple groups, brokering matériel and services between them, establishing money laundering channels for the drug revenues that finance their operations, skimming."

Cooper nodded. "Hopefully they won't be our problem. So, about the passports." He provided Mario with a summary of the progress that had been made on the various fronts, including the information from Boris. Then they left for dinner at Figlmuller's.

Chapter 20

Paris, France.
Monday, 6 January 2003, 05:43.

Luck favors the prepared, mon ami," Delfort said, running his fingers lightly over his thinning brown hair. "We are ready for every eventuality."

Cooper nodded at the lead officer at the Charles de Gaulle station of the French National Police. The room was dim, illuminated only by the light coming through the one-way glass. He could see that Delfort was not happy about him being there, but was making the best of it after receiving a few phone calls.

"As you can see, we have the man, but we have not been able to get much out of him."

Cooper flipped through the Portuguese passport and tossed it on the table. A weekend of pressure on the embassy and some private sessions with Marcelino in his jail cell had yielded a solid list of numbers by Sunday morning. Sunday night Fahad al-Fulani passed through Charles de Gaulle customs with one of the stolen passports. Mario picked up the report, and Cooper was on a chartered flight out of Vienna to Paris an hour later.

Cooper looked through the one-way glass at a gray-suited man, sitting at a table in a small, brightly lit room, smoking a cigarette. He looked tired and bored.

"Doesn't seem worried for a guy passing a stolen passport."

"Perhaps he has done such things before."

"Perhaps he could be persuaded to talk with the right motivation."

Delfort's disapproving look was instantaneous and prolonged. "This is France, monsieur. We are not cowboys of the Old West."

Cooper held his gaze for a few seconds. "You did talk to him."

"Of course we talked to him."

Cooper looked at the man again. He glanced in their direction, sighed, and took another drag on the cigarette. Cooper turned back to Delfort. "What did he say?"

"Businessman from Lisbon, importing fabric from India, looking for channels in Europe." Delfort nodded to the portfolio on the side table. Cooper flipped through it, noting the cloth samples. High quality.

"And the passport?"

"Moved to Lisbon last year from Saudi Arabia. Applied for citizenship. The address checks out. On paper, at least. Haven't had time to get a man there."

The door opened, and another officer stepped in. He glanced at Cooper and turned to Delfort. "You should see this, sir."

He turned to the stack of gear in the corner and put a DVD into a player. The screen showed video monitors indicating flight departures. The man in the gray suit who looked a lot like al-Fulani walked up to the monitors, set down an oversized salesman's sample case, and studied the listings, consulting an itinerary in his hand. A maintenance cart rolled into view, passed the monitors, and stopped at a trash can.

"Watch the briefcase."

The maintenance guy knelt down, pulled a plastic trash bag from a stack on the lower level of the cart, and shook it open. Without looking, he reached for the attaché case, pushed it onto the cart under the stack of bags, pulled out an identical case, and set it next to the man in the gray suit. Then he stood, changed the trash bags, and moved on.

Cooper looked across the room. The case was open on the side table, next to the fabric samples. Delfort rummaged through it, digging through file folders, a pair of reading glasses, some keys.

"The question is, which is the real case and which is the decoy?"

"Maybe they're both real," Cooper said. Delfort frowned at him. "It could be an exchange. One has merchandise or information, one has the payment."

"Jean, take this downtown to Forensics and see what they can find." Delfort handed the case to the other officer. "What do we know of the worker?"

"They're contacting the personnel manager of the contractor right now. We should be able to identify him within the hour."

After a shower, change of clothes, and a quick coffee and croissant, Cooper found Delfort's office. He looked up from a stack of papers as Cooper walked in.

"Your luck holds, mon ami," he said, waving Cooper to a chair. "The case had a false bottom. A quarter of a million U.S. We are having further conversations with al-Fulani. He does not look so bored now." He smiled at Cooper, a quick spasm of his lips that didn't touch the rest of his face. "The worker is Abu Doha, hired in August 1999. His shift ends at noon."

"I'd like to be with the surveillance team."

"It is not customary."

"OK. I'd like to be with the surveillance team."

"It will require approval."

"OK. I'd like to be with the surveillance team."

"I see that you are insistent. I shall inquire."

Cooper sat in the back of an unmarked Peugeot, waiting for Doha to come out of the grocer's shop on Rue Fourcroy. Agents on foot had followed him from CDG to the RER terminal where he took the B-line into the city. He got out at Gare du Nord and walked the tunnel to the Blue Line, Porte Dauphine. They stayed with him when he surfaced again at Avenue Des Ternes and strolled to Rue Fourcroy. Text messages from Cooper's Blackberry kept the IRIG field office informed of his own location as well as that of Doha. The field office relayed the information via radio to Newton, IRIG's best surveillance operative in Paris. Newton was on a BMW F 650 and maintained a position within two blocks of Cooper without ever being in line-of-sight.

When Doha went into the grocer's, Cooper transmitted their location and instructed Newton to watch the back. As the driver cracked the window and lighted a cigarette, Cooper received a message. Doha had left by the back door. Cooper got out and stuck his head in the window.

"This may be awhile. I'll be in there." He nodded to the cafe next door. "If you need to leave and I'm not back, go ahead. I'll find my way."

The driver looked at the agent in the passenger seat. He shrugged. Cooper stepped inside the door of the cafe, pulled out a small radio, and put in the earpiece. A waiter looked up. Cooper smiled and nodded. The waiter frowned and turned back to the counter.

Cooper adjusted the radio and slipped it into his coat pocket. "Newton, what do you have?"

"I'm on him. He just walked past me while I was checking the pressure in my tires."

"You need backup?"

"Nope. Johann is playing tag with me. I can give you play-by-play status if you want."

"I'll be on the line. Just give exception reports."

"Got it."

Cooper stepped into the room, found a table, and ordered espresso. He looked out the window. The agents were still there, smoking, talking, and occasionally glancing at the door. Newton came over the earpiece.

"This guy is a regular backdoor man. He did the cut-through in a tobacco shop and then hopped a bus. Johann has him."

Outside, the agent began to look restless. He kept glancing at the grocer's door then at the cafe door. After a few minutes he disappeared into the grocer's, came back out, looked both directions, then came into the cafe. He spotted Cooper and pushed past the waiter, who scowled and grumbled something unintelligible.

"He's gone."

Cooper jumped to his feet, knocking his chair back. "Gone? You let him get away?"

The waiter frowned at Cooper and turned his back on them.

"He didn't come out the front," he answered, his face expressionless.

"You didn't cover the back?"

"There was no reason for him to suspect he was being followed. Why would he use the back door?"

"Maybe because he's one of the bad guys? Forget it. You lost him, and I've wasted a flight from Vienna and a day of work." He sat back down.

"We are returning."

"Give Delfort my regards."

Cooper picked up his coffee. The agent stood for a few seconds, indecisive, then turned and strode out of the cafe. The waiter mumbled a few words in his direction, squinted at Cooper, and continued wiping down the counter. Cooper got back on the radio.

"Status."

"I'm following the bus northeast. We just passed Victor Hugo. Johann's gone ahead on the route. I'll signal him when the target exits the bus."

Cooper signaled the waiter, who reluctantly wandered to the table. He ordered a sandwich. He was enjoying a dessert port when Newton came on the radio.

"We've run him to ground. He's just gone into a detached house on Rue Des Moines. Number 17."

Chapter 21

The house was set back from the street, surrounded by a stone wall and a garden. It was not the house of an airport maintenance worker. It was an upper-middle-class house in a stable neighborhood, the kind of neighborhood that was deserted during the workday. A place where no one would notice a workman walking in at 2:00 p.m. or leaving at midnight.

Doha entered on foot at 14:03. At 15:51 a utility van verified the presence of a surveillance camera at the back door. At 17:23 a plainclothes agent walking a very inquisitive dog verified the location of two surveillance cameras in front, one at the garage and one at the front door. At 20:57 a BMW turned down the street, opened the gate remotely and entered the garage, just as the moon was setting. At 23:11 Doha left on foot. The sentry at the corner of Rue Nollet reported that he turned east, presumably headed to work. Newton and Johann would verify it, and Delfort would have a friendly conversation with him later.

Inside the van, Cooper waited with the strike team from RAID, the Reaction, Assistance, Intervention, and Dissuasion unit of the French National Police. Herbert, the lead agent, went over the floor plans, pointing out the field of view of the cameras and where the front and rear entrance teams would be positioned prior to the power cut.

Around sundown Cooper got a call on his cell. Stevie had just heard word of the suicide bombing in Tel Aviv that happened the day before. The news reported that seven foreign nationals had been killed, and she immediately suspected he was one of them. He reassured her that he was safe, but didn't tell her he was no longer in Tel Aviv.

At 03:33 the back door of the van opened and the team slipped out. Heat imaging indicated there were only two people inside in separate rooms, both apparently asleep. They had opted for silent entry with a signal for a hard entry if an alarm were tripped. Six men lined up at the stone wall, the lead man by the driveway. Two other men took positions on the back corner of the house. The tech team followed them, stopping at the utility connection.

Cooper and Herbert waited in the van. When all teams checked in, Herbert gave the signal. The tech team cut the phone and power lines. The front team was at the door in three seconds, through the lock in another ten. The tech team was right behind. The alarm panel was just inside the door. A flip of a screwdriver popped the front panel off and a jumper was inserted between the red and green wires well before the forty-five-second limit when the alarm would sound. If any other safe houses were wired into their security, they would see a normal disarm signal. The techie gave a nod in the light of the flashlight.

The teams flipped down their night-vision goggles and crept down the hall, guns drawn. Now that the moon had set, the darkness inside the house was complete. The terrorists would not be able to see them at all. The lead man stopped at the first door, pointed to three men and nodded to the door, indicating they would take the room as arranged. They nodded. He took the two remaining men and crept to the next door. He moved where everyone could see him, held up three fingers, and did a silent countdown. When he held up a closed fist, two men silently entered each room—one with a Glock 19, the other with a tranquilizer gun. A third man remained outside each door.

In the first room, the eyes of the terrorist blinked open when a hand was placed over his mouth. He tensed and seemed to realize instantly that the cold hard thing against his temple was the barrel of a gun. A voice whispered, "We will wait, quietly, until we hear from my buddy next door." The glove was pressed against his nose; his breath whistled in and out quickly in the silence.

There was a noise, the faint sound of voices on a radio barely audible, then the voice again. "OK. Now I will move my hand and we will turn on the lamp and nobody does anything funny and nobody loses their head." The gun pressed into his temple. He nodded.

In the van, Cooper and Herbert got the signal that the house was secured. They left the van, entered the house, locked the door, and closed all the curtains. Then they turned on some lights. The terrorists, looking sullen and silly in their pajamas, were pushed into chairs in the parlor. Herbert fired a few questions at them, but it was quickly apparent that they wouldn't talk. He radioed the forensic team waiting a few blocks away. They arrived and began dissecting the house.

Cooper strolled through the rooms. The house appeared to have been furnished from a mail-order catalog—utilitarian, nondescript, devoid of character. Then he found the wine cellar.

Wine was prohibited in Islam, but sleepers had to fit into the culture. In France a wine cellar was to be expected, but this was an extraordinarily fine collection. Perhaps it came with the house, or perhaps it was stocked as an investment. Cooper walked through the racks, browsing. True to local preference, they had favored the reds. But even the whites represented vineyards of quality, including the renowned Chassagne Montrachet Grand Cru. He stopped in disbelief when he saw an 1832 Chassagne Montrachet that appeared to be in mint condition. He walked past an assortment of Puligny Montrachet starting with the 2000 vintage and a variety of the five years before that, a 2001 Pouilly Fuisse with a mixture of five-year-old bottles and an assortment of Meursault and Clos Vougeots.

But the whites with their excellent taste were overshadowed with the rows of France's best reds, starting with the renowned Bordeaux. There were rows of Cabernet Sauvignon 2000 to 1997, Premier grand crus, Chateau Lafite Rothschild, Chateau Latour, and Chateau Margaux. Someone spent a lot of time building this collection. They also provided for celebration with Cristal and Dom Perignon champagne.

Cooper was looking through the Chilean wines when he heard footsteps on the stairs. Through the racks he saw a short guy with dark hair inch down the steps, eyes fixed on a device in his hands. It was Jack, the lead on the Hazmat team.

Jack looked back up the stairs. "Yeah, this is it." He walked down to the floor and stood, staring at his gear. "Charles, come check this out."

A tall guy with blond hair and a barrel gut thumped down the stairs. "Jackpot!" He smiled at the wealth of wine. "I love France, I don't care what you say."

"No, not the wine, the meter."

Charles looked at the meter and whistled. "It's hot, alright. But look around. These bottles have been here for years."

Cooper stepped out from the racks. "Maybe. Maybe not."

Jack hollered and dropped the meter. Charles cursed and caught it by the strap before it hit the floor.

"Sorry." Cooper looked at the meter and back up at the men. "Radiation?" They both nodded. "Down here?"

"Not much," Jack said. "But more than there should be in the average suburban Paris home."

Cooper scanned the room, ignored the rows of freestanding racks in the middle, and began examining the racks that lined the walls. The bottles all had a uniform coating of dust, obviously undisturbed for some time. The shelves were flush to the walls with no evidence of hidden compartments behind them and reached to within an inch of the ceiling. He looked at the floor. The bottom shelf was flush with the floor. He looked again. Almost.

He got on his knees and pressed his fingers under the bottom shelf of the first rack. There was a slight gap. He ran his hand to the right along the length. Nothing. He moved to the next rack. Halfway down he felt a vertical metal rod. He followed it down. It extended to a rounded base on the floor.

He stood and moved to the right end of the rack. There was a three-inch gap between it and the third rack. Cooper peered through the gloom into the gap. A faint line extended from floor to ceiling, barely visible. He stepped back and pushed firmly on the edge of the rack. Nothing happened. He reached to the back of the rack, wedged his fingers between it and the wall and pulled firmly. The crack widened slightly, the section of wall behind the rack pulling away from the next. He pulled harder, with no effect.

He stood back and looked at the rack for awhile then at Jack and Charles, who stared at him wordlessly. He snapped his fingers, reached into the gap, and ran his fingers along the edge of the vertical plank. Nothing. He stepped to the left side, ran his hand down the plank, and found what he was looking for. He pressed the button and pushed against the rack. It pivoted on the center, the wall behind it moving with the rack. When the left edge moved past the back of the wall next to it, it stopped. Cooper pushed harder, but it didn't budge.

He moved to the right end of the rack, which was jutting out into the aisle. Behind he could see a small room. He pushed on the end of the rack and it slid forward, the entire rack disappearing into the space behind the first rack. At his feet was a track set into the floor along which the rack rolled back into the space behind the wall. Before him was an opening into a small room filled with filing cabinets and crates.

Cooper looked to Charles, nodding at the meter in his hand. Charles lurched forward and checked the meter. He looked back at Cooper and nodded. Cooper pushed the button on the earpiece.

"Herbert, this is Matt. We found something in the wine cellar."

Cooper walked into the secret room. The first thing he noticed was eight large silver briefcases. He checked one, but it was locked. He tried a filing cabinet. Inside the first drawer he found six boxes, each containing fifty Portuguese passports.

Herbert stepped up behind him. "Well, well. Merry Christmas, Cooper."

"You're a little late."

"Not me. I'm Greek Orthodox. The twelve days of Christmas ended today." He opened the second drawer. There were six more boxes. "I'd say Doha has been naughty. I'll have to call St. Nick."

He reached for his cell phone, but Cooper stopped him.

"What do you make of those?"

Herbert looked at the briefcases. "What of them?"

"Jack's little box says they're hot."

Herbert grunted. He scanned the room and stepped to Charles. "Don't let anyone else down here. And the reading on your meter is now privileged information. Record it and stow it."

———

Several hours later Cooper checked into his hotel. After a hot shower, a three-hour nap, another hot shower, and a large breakfast, he picked up the KL-7 phone. Dixon answered on the first ring.

"Coop, you got two minutes before the commercials are over and Letterman comes back on."

"That's ninety seconds more than I need."

"Shoot."

"Remember the eleven bogies?"

"Like I can think of anything else."

"We just found eight."

"Where are the other three?"

"Dixon, I just pulled eight one-kiloton nuclear bombs out of the hands of al-Qaeda and you're asking about the other three?"

"The four million people you just saved thank you. The 1.5 million people who will be killed by the other three are asking for equal time."

"Did you hear the announcement from Harkat-ul-Jihad al-Islami? The one about bringing the violence to the oppressors?"

"Of course."

"I think that's what these nukes were meant for. And I think the other three are on the way to the oppressors."

"Why do I get the feeling you're not talking about Israel?"

"Because Israel didn't invade Afghanistan last year. Because Israel isn't the one building up troops and war machines in the Gulf right now and knocking on Iraq's door."

"I'm sure you have a point."

"If you want me to find the other three, I will start looking in the U.S., not Europe or the Middle East, because I think these passports have been in use since the day they were stolen. And I think these nukes have been here for almost as long and some have been distributed. I'm going to need cross-agency cooperation, logistical support, and nobody second-guessing me. I need a blank check."

"That's going to take a hall pass from the principal."

"Then get me a hall pass."

"I'll call you tomorrow. Letterman's back."

Cooper hung up and called Cohen. After a lengthy discussion on the options for office space and other logistics, Cooper changed the subject.

"Isaac, when is the last time you heard from the Lone Ranger?"

"Not since you left."

"I'll have Sarah send you an e-mail update on the stuff we're sending him. In the meantime, I need whatever information he can provide on activity targeted to U.S. soil. If he comes across something, we need to know immediately. We can't wait for the next meeting. Set something up."

"It will be done."

The call back from Dixon came at midnight, while Cooper was preparing for an early morning checkout and the flight back to Vienna.

Dixon spoke without greeting or preamble. "It's done."

"Meaning?"

"You got the impossible. Can't think how it happened, but you got it. Finding half the passports and eight of the nukes in less than a week helped. I'm holding an executive order mandating cooperation from the FBI, CIA, and Homeland Security; a project staff; and budget. You even got Watford, for crying out loud. But a signature from the president is one thing. Getting these guys to play nice with each other is another. But this paper says it's your rodeo."

"Great. I'll be back by the end of the week. Let's do lunch on Friday and get a game plan together."

"Done. Now go to bed."

Chapter 22

Ali al-Huzayfi could barely contain his rage. He knew that anger was dangerous for a man in his position. Acting out of passion was the path to death. But there were limits even to his endurance and self-control. Yes, he was known for rash, violent acts. He cultivated the image. But as he and the One knew, his violent acts were not rash, but painstakingly calculated. Even the execution of Khidamat, staged to look like an impulsive reaction to a challenge to his authority, had been planned weeks before. It was obvious that the man had lost his nerve, had become unduly influenced by the opinions of the West. He was worse than useless; he was a tool of the enemy. So al-Huzayfi goaded him into going too far and then performed his execution in such a manner as to reinforce the fear that was the foundation of his power.

But there were things that were truly unendurable. And the utter incompetence that cost him two-thirds of his nuclear weapons—weapons that had taken a decade and millions of dollars to acquire—was unendurable.

For al-Fulani to travel on a Portuguese passport four days

after Hassan was detained was stupidity worthy of death, a sentence that would be carried out before he left his jail cell. For Doha to return to the safe house after al-Fulani was detained was unthinkable. He would share al-Fulani's fate.

These decisions were simple and obvious. But they were too remote—orders given then carried out by others. He longed to kill something himself with his bare hands. If it were possible, he would have the two idiots sprung from jail and smuggled to Iran simply to cut them open himself.

Al-Huzayfi took three deep breaths, recited a prayer, and strode down the steps to the meeting room.

"*Assalaamu alaykum,*" he said as he entered the room.

"*Wa alaykumus salaam,*" they responded.

He stood at the head of the table. They knew. He could see it in their faces. They knew what had happened only twelve hours ago. They knew his rage. Even Abu Aidid, Khidamat's replacement, knew. He dispensed with the preliminaries.

"Who among you will answer?" There was silence. "Well?"

Al-Suri spoke. "Answer what, Emir?"

It was a term normally applied only to the One. He ignored the obvious attempt at flattery. "Answer for the loss of $20 million and the bulk of the blow of Last Straw?"

"How then shall we answer? Those responsible are in the hands of the French. Their deaths shall be as soon and as painful as we can arrange."

"And the idiot who commanded them, who selected them, who assured us they could do what must be done? Shall not he be held accountable?"

In the ensuing silence the eyes in the room moved gradually from al-Huzayfi to al-Suri, who looked calmly back at his leader.

"Yes, we can do so. But there remains the question of who selected the next superior, and the one above. If we follow this trail back far enough, we will come to Makkee." He nodded to his left. Makkee shot a murderous look at him then looked at al-Huzayfi nervously. "And, of course, you selected Makkee," al-Suri concluded. He sat without expression, watching al-Huzayfi.

"And the One selected me." Al-Huzayfi scowled at al-Suri. "Do you question him?"

"I merely come to serve you, and through you, the One, and through him, Allah."

Al-Huzayfi stared at al-Suri for a long time. "I shall remember it," he said at last. "What do we know of what happened?"

Makkee cleared his throat, gave al-Suri a final hostile glance, and turned to al-Huzayfi. "There is a report that an American civilian was present for the raid. He arrived in Paris early the morning before and left early morning the next day. The same American has also been seen in Tel Aviv and Metulla."

Al-Huzayfi narrowed his eyes at Makkee. "Who is this American?"

"His name is Matthew Cooper. He came to Israel in the party of the madman George Roberts last month. He was in Metulla the day before the raid on Camp Lam and the day after. We have no knowledge of his location on the night of the Camp Lam raid, but we do know he was on the raid last night."

"CIA?"

"Not that we can tell."

"What then?"

"It appears he is a security consultant from Los Angeles, California."

"Why was he in Paris?"

"This is not known."

"We must know more about him. We must know everything about him. He must have no further effect on our operations."

"It will be done."

"Salim, what of the remnants of Last Straw?"

Salim smiled nervously. "Of the remaining devices, two are in place, two are in transit. All shall be in place within eight weeks."

"Six weeks. The Americans have announced their intention to have over two hundred thousand troops and two carrier groups to the Gulf in the next month. And the sleepers?"

"There are many that touch parts of the plan, but only one operative per city knows the time and place. All others are expendable without risk of compromise to Last Straw."

Al-Huzayfi closed his eyes. He willed the rage to recede. It would be OK. Two million dead wasn't six, but the physical devastation would cripple the devils for decades. The emotional devastation would last for centuries. He opened his eyes and smiled.

Those in the room did not appear relieved.

———

Al-Sidal was preoccupied as he took a circuitous route from the meeting, through a bazaar and several shops, to his car waiting a kilometer away. He merged in and out of crowds, timing his step through doorways so that he would be screened by others, staying inside random lengths of time, exiting sometimes from the door that he had entered, sometimes from another. In some shops he arranged for delivery of mundane household purchases. In others he just looked, sometimes asking questions of the owner.

All this he did without thinking, so natural had the routine become after twenty years. His mind was focused on al-Huzayfi. The meeting was disturbing. He always considered the man's control of his own passions to be marginal. The arbitrary execution of Khidamat was a perfect example. Certainly he had outlived his usefulness, but the matter should have been handled far differently. Loyalty was a force much stronger than fear, the glue that should be used to bind Harkat-ul-Jihad al-Islami together. Khidamat should have been disposed of by their enemies, his death used to bring those that remained closer in the shared threat.

And then today, for al-Huzayfi to practically demand a sacrificial victim. The man was clearly insane. It was only a matter of time before he self-destructed. There was no question. The only issue remaining was how to avoid becoming collateral damage.

Al-Sidal argued with a clerk about a watch, pushed it back across the counter, and left the shop in a group of customers. Perhaps he should mention it to the One next month when they met. Or perhaps not. He was concerned for the good of HuJI, but it would be easy for al-Huzayfi to make it appear otherwise. The One had little patience with internecine struggles. A reputation for self-interest was fatal.

He melted from the street between two buildings, through an alley filled with refuse and into another street, doubling back. At least the One kept their private meetings and his alternate assignment a secret. If al-Huzayfi knew that al-Sidal was in direct contact with Saddam, the madman would probably execute him at the next meeting. The One had been wise to bypass Makkee, the obvious liaison with Saddam as head of security and intelligence, and instead use al-Sidal, head of training, one not expected to be negotiating acquisitions of chemical weapons from Iraq or nuclear weapons from the

Ukrainians. Besides, if Makkee didn't have the guts to stand up to al-Huzayfi, how could he bargain with Saddam, a man who seemed even more intent on his own annihilation? No question, al-Sidal knew he was the right man for the job, fortunately in the wrong position, which effectively masked his activities from the others.

The loss of the eight briefcases was unfortunate. Although he could not admit it to anyone, he resented al-Huzayfi's rage over the incident. If al-Sidal, the one who spent eighteen months in exhausting negotiations to acquire the bombs, could remain rational while managing the fallout from the disaster, then who was al-Huzayfi to take it so personally, to grant himself the indulgence of a tantrum? But no one could know of the role he played. The One had made that clear. In addition, the secrecy was required for his own self-preservation. Because not even the One knew of the deal he cut with the old KGB officer.

In a heavily guarded villa, a fire in the gigantic hearth keeping the raging Ukrainian winter at bay, the aging spy, knowing al-Sidal was under pressure to acquire all of the twenty weapons available, had explained that eight had already been picked up by Chechen rebels above the market price of $1 million each. But, if al-Sidal would commit the entire $20 million to the purchase of the remaining twelve, he would guarantee they would not go to the Chechens. Al-Sidal saw the scam for what it was and countered with an offer to split the $8 million the old man planned to skim. Six months later the One had a dozen briefcase nuclear bombs and al-Sidal had $4 million in a bank account on the Isle of Man, where no questions were asked and none answered.

His car pulled to the curb next to him at the arranged spot— the middle of the block on a busy street. He slipped into the backseat, and the driver pulled away without a word. Protection from al-Huzayfi's self-immolation was imperative. For the first time al-Sidal considered the possibility of an exit strategy. Four million dollars was not enough for a safe exit, but it was a start. The loss of the weapons might have a silver lining. Perhaps he could arrange to resume negotiations to replace the weapons and increase his exit fund. Perhaps even establish contacts to transition to Europe, outside the fallout of al-Huzayfi's meltdown.

He smiled a small, cold smile and leaned back in his seat. A little patience, a little skill, a little planning. He was the right man for the job.

Chapter 23

Vienna, Austria.
Wednesday, 8 January 2003. 13:03.

Cooper took a window seat near the door at the Grafin am Naschmarkt at Linke Wienzeile to watch for Alexia. He asked for the wine list. No need to start ordering the feast he had planned for her. It might be an hour before she showed up.

He started reviewing the field office resources in major U.S. cities, figuring how to juggle people to supplement the teams for the efforts in New York and D.C., the most likely targets. With only three bombs, they could target at most three cities. Would they spread out the targets as on 9/11 or concentrate their destructive power into one high-profile target? Cooper expected that like before, they would allocate their weapons to the most visible icons of American power, Wall Street and Pennsylvania Avenue.

Relocating field teams was more difficult than redirecting focus in the central office. The primary value of a field agent rested in his intimate knowledge of his territory. Shifting him to a different city placed him at a disadvantage. He must defer to the local lead. While Cooper picked employees based on their ability to work as a team, he was aware that the qualities of independence and improvisation that made for a good field agent could also make it difficult for him to take a subservient position. Matching locations and personalities would take careful planning.

But the challenges of integrating IRIG resources was minor compared to the challenge of crafting an effective operation from a patchwork quilt of various local, federal, and international agencies, most of whom were noted for their inability to work and play well with each other. Cooper had led cross-agency operations before with mixed success but never on this scale.

A flash of red outside the window caught his eye. Alexia was walking past the window through the courtyard of vacant, snow-covered tables toward the front door, her red coat flapping around her ankles. Even though she was wearing sunglasses, he imagined that he could see her squinting in the weak afternoon sunlight. He smiled. As she cleared the window a motorcycle came into view. A large black figure on a Kawasaki Ninja ZX-10R weaved erratically through the traffic, crossed three lanes, and turned toward the cafe. As it jumped the curb the figure split into two. What had looked like a large man was actually two slender men spooned together. They were both wearing black masks. He saw Alexia look back at the bike, saw the bike turn left down the sidewalk in front of the cafe, saw the arm of the figure on the back swing up a mini-Uzi.

Cooper grabbed the table and flipped it over against the window, diving behind it. Beyond the edge of the table he saw Alexia lunging through the door. Then he saw the glass explode into the cafe, heard the rounds punching holes in the wainscoting along the front, sweeping toward his table, felt a burst of pain in his left arm. The firing continued for several seconds, spraying the area near the door. Then the noise ended with the racing of the motorcycle engine and they were gone.

The silence that followed resolved into screams and sirens. Cooper rolled to his hands and knees and struggled to his feet, using the edge of the table for leverage. His jacket had a hole in it. He could feel blood seeping down his upper arm. He kicked the chairs aside and crunched glass under his feet as he ran to the door.

Alexia lay on the threshold in a pool of blood. He dropped to his knees and felt for a pulse. It was there, faint but steady. A police car screeched to a stop in front of the cafe and two officers jumped out, guns ready. He held up his good hand and called out.

"Two men on a Kawasaki Ninja dressed in black. Second man armed with a mini-Uzi. We need an ambulance." He dropped his hand to Alexia and placed it gently on her forehead. "She's still alive."

Rabat, Morocco.
Wednesday, 8 January 2003. 21:44.

The bar was almost empty when they arrived, but between cast and crew, it was now full. After three days they finally nailed the kidnapping scene, and the relief was so great Russell had suggested a trek to Rabat for a celebration. Stevie thought a long hot shower and even longer sleep was a better idea, but Russell's enthusiasm swept her along with the rest.

She sipped a Shiraz and listened to Mark and Paula comparing cases of food poisoning incurred while shooting on location. As this was her first foreign shoot, she had no war stories and no plans to acquire any on this trip. The mild case from a family trip to Mexico during high school had been enough for her. Since then, her philosophy for dining out, whether in the U.S. or abroad, was Take No Chances.

"The first day I was afraid I might die," Mark said. "The second day I was afraid I might not."

Paula's laugh boomed through the bar, the machine-gun laugh that had left the entire outdoor set in stunned silence the first day of shooting. After a week, Stevie still wasn't used to it. She looked around the room, noticed the bartender staring at Paula with his mouth open. She smiled and then noticed the TV above the bar. A twenty-four-hour satellite news station was showing an ambulance backed up to a cafe with police and EMTs running around. The marquee scrolled something about a drive-by shooting in Vienna. Then she was standing next to the booth, her hand to her mouth.

It was Matt. Matt helping load a gurney into the ambulance. His face and clothes were smeared with blood.

She waved a hand at the bartender. "Turn it up. Turn it up." He looked at her blankly. She looked back up at the TV. They had moved on to another story. She turned around. Mark and Paula were staring at her. "Matt. That was Matt. In Vienna. What's he doing in Vienna?" They looked back, uncomprehending.

Stevie dug her mobile phone from her purse and strode outside the bar into the cool evening. He answered on the third ring.

"Stevie, how's Morocco?"

"The shooting's going well. We're ahead of schedule. Did I wake you up? It's after eleven in Tel Aviv, right?"

The long pause angered her, but she didn't speak.

"Something came up. Dixon asked me to help out on a case in Vienna. I'm having a late dinner before packing."

"What kind of case?"

"You know I can't talk about business, especially over the phone. But I'm flying out tomorrow. I should be having dinner with Nikki tomorrow night. Or at least a midnight snack."

"So you solved the case OK. No problems?"

"We made some great breakthroughs, but we've also run into some problems. I'm going to be pretty busy for the next few months."

"Problems? Like being shot with a machine gun? Minor stuff like that?"

She heard a long exhale and wondered how he would spin it. Would he laugh it off? Get angry? Get logical? All she knew is that he had been shot and she had to find it out from a bar TV.

"Stevie, you are incredible. I'm not even going to ask how you heard about the shooting. I didn't want to worry you about it while you were filming. But I'm fine. I got hit in the arm, but it was a clean hit, and I was out of the hospital in a few hours. Don't even need the pain pills they gave me."

She remembered the verse about the complaining wife. Maybe it did fit her. But this was crazy. Somebody had to talk to Matt, and nobody else around seemed to be willing or able to speak sense to him. Maybe God had put her here to do the thing nobody else would do.

"Matt, what are you doing? This is not a Godfather movie; it's our life. You're the CEO of a security firm, not Serpico or James Bond. How can you put yourself at risk like this? What about Nikki? What about me?" She felt like it needed to be said, but she also felt selfish saying it. Something she hadn't felt before during their arguments.

"Remember the part where I'm flying back to L.A. in a few hours? This is why I didn't call you. I didn't want you to get distracted. You can't do what you need to if you're worrying about me. I'm fine. I'll be fine."

She bit her lip, pulled the phone away, and shook her head. She didn't want to have to push him to tell her. She wanted him to do it on his own. But she had to know. She put the phone to her ear.

"Who were they after?"

"What?"

"The shooters. Who were they after? Why that cafe? Why that time?"

"It's hard to know. There were a lot of people there. Could have been any of them."

"Did they shoot up the whole cafe, try to take everyone out?"

"Not exactly. They hit the front." She heard the grudging respect in his voice. She was on the right track to the thing she feared and the thing he didn't want to say.

"Where you were sitting."

"Yes, I was in the front. Look," his voice grew hushed, "I know where you're going with this. Was I the target? Yes, that is possible. However, I was meeting an informant. He was late. I sat there for an hour. They arrived right when he was entering the door. He's in ICU and may not make it. I'd say he was the target."

"Maybe."

"You're a tough sell."

"Yeah, I am. You're going back right away?"

"Yep."

"And staying?"

"This project will keep me busy stateside for several months. Isaac will have to get things going on his own."

"I'm thinking a lot farther out than several months."

"You always do."

"And you need to start. I need you, Matt." Tears sprang to her eyes. She blinked them away. "You may not realize that, but I do. And Nikki needs you even more. She's already lost one parent. I know she seems very together and in control, and you probably think there's nothing to worry about. But let me tell you, she's hanging on by her fingernails right now."

"Nikki? What has she told you?"

"Nothing. Absolutely nothing. Like always. But I can tell. She's not the only one in that house who has lost a parent."

"I . . . well . . . are you sure? What exactly do you mean?"

"I mean that you may be able to handle the risks you choose to expose yourself to, but that doesn't mean the women in your life can. And most especially Nikki. One day five years ago she watched her mother drive off and never come back. It was just a normal day in a normal life with normal risks. And ever since then, she's wondered when she will watch you drive off and never come back. It will take years of stability and security for her to escape that sense of vulnerability. But you're not offering her stability and security. You're offering her suicide bombers and drive-by shootings and pictures of yourself on satellite TV covered in blood. Let's just hope she hasn't developed a taste for twenty-four-hour news channels in the past ten hours."

The silence on the line lasted for several seconds. She waited. There was no question that he needed to hear this. No matter what Proverbs said, she wasn't going to let him back away from this issue.

"I don't know what to say," he responded at last. "You're probably right. I don't know how I haven't seen that before. But there are some things that just go with the territory."

"Perhaps you should consider a career change."

"But that's not all of it. Right now I have to do this thing."

"This thing? Is it more important than your own daughter?"

"I know it's hard to believe, but it might actually end up being more important than anything I've done in my life. You'll just have to believe me, Stevie. I can't explain it right now for lots of reasons."

"I don't know if I can believe that. And even if I can, I know I can't understand it."

"I don't blame you. I wouldn't either if I didn't know what I know. What I can't say right now."

Stevie wiped the tears from her face. "It's getting a little chilly out here. I'm going back inside. You can go back to your dinner. And you get home immediately, you understand me?"

"Yes. I love you, Stevie."

"I love you, Matt. Don't get yourself killed."

Chapter 24

Nikki skimmed through the menu. Knish-knish? Nosh? It was like a Dr. Seuss diner.

Her dad was squinting at his menu. "This place is a legend in Tel Aviv. When they come to L.A., they stop here. A guy in Israel told me about it."

"Great." She was happy to spend time with Dad, but did it have to be in such a weird place? An all-night Jewish diner in Van Nuys at 9:30 p.m.? She abandoned the menu. "Do they have pizza?"

"There's a bagel pizza." He looked up and saw her face. "Pizza burger? Hmm." He scanned the menu again. "Try the Reuben sandwich."

She looked back at the menu. "Knockwurst. Do I like knockwurst?"

"Try it. If you don't like it, we'll get something else. A patty melt or something."

"OK. But this doesn't count for my birthday meal."

He smiled and ordered. She looked at her purse sitting on the table by the salt, pepper, and ketchup. She moved it down on the seat next to her.

First the call Wednesday afternoon, Dad asking how she was, if she missed him, how she was doing. Now him insisting that she meet him at the airport and the late dinner at Solleys.

How was she doing? It was a logical question, but she couldn't answer it. The truth was, she didn't know how she was doing. When he was home for awhile, she didn't want him to leave; but when he was gone for awhile, she was almost afraid for him to come home. Opening up her world to let him back in would upset the delicate balance she had achieved, the fortress of self-defense with openings only at the places where she needed to interact with her world at school, at the studio, at the mall.

When he left, it took her days to quell the random panic attacks. Only focusing on physical pain worked, but with her schedule, it was hard to find a private place or time. The safety pin was small enough to conceal in her hand, so she could use it even in class. Eventually she could focus on her busy life, forget about Dad and everything else, and shut out the dread.

At least during the day. Nothing stopped the dreams. And the pin was becoming less effective. After awhile she began to see that it was such a little prick, after all. Not really serious pain. She really had to concentrate on it, and even then sometimes the images would intrude, overwhelming the pinprick like a wave washing down a sand castle.

After Christmas she bought a pack of razor blades from a hardware store, the single-edged kind for box cutters. Back in her room she pulled one out and looked at it for hours, arguing with herself. She didn't use it, but even now she could feel it next to her in her purse. It distracted her, seemed like it was calling to her. She shoved her purse further into the corner of the booth and pushed her sweater on top of it.

The waitress brought his iced tea and her Diet Coke and left. Dad pushed the glass aside and reached across the table, taking her fingers in his and rolling them back and forth with his thumb.

"So, how's my little dove?"

She smiled. "We're working on the February scripts. Tony is getting his tonsils out, so we're taking a break next week."

"How's school?"

She sighed. "Boring. I get tired of busy work."

"You'll need to work ahead so we can take that week off to go to Vail."

"Yeah."

They sat in silence for awhile, her leaning forward and sipping through the straw, him staring down at her smooth, slender fingers curled over his. He could cover two of her fingers with just his thumb.

"Nikki," he said to her fingers, "do you sometimes wish I did something else?"

"What do you mean?"

"I mean," he looked into her eyes, "do you wish I was a lawyer or a producer or a mechanic?"

She couldn't tell what it was that was in his eyes. Hurt? Fear? Regret? Whatever it was, it scared her. She pulled her hand back suddenly then acted like she was just pushing back her hair. She took her drink in both hands and leaned back in the booth.

"No."

"You aren't worried about me? Worried I might not come back?"

Why was he talking about this? Didn't he realize he was cracking open armor that she had carefully put into place? Or was he serious? Was he really considering changing jobs? She looked at him carefully.

"What would you do?"

"About what?"

"If you had a different job."

He blew out his cheeks and leaned back. "I don't know. I was just wondering. I remember back at Thanksgiving, you got upset about me going to Israel."

"Yeah." Or maybe he wasn't serious. "But you came back OK."

"But you worried, didn't you?"

"Don't be dumb, Dad. If I went to Israel, wouldn't you worry?"

"Sure. But it's not the same."

She just looked at him. Not the same. Probably not. He was always in control. He probably didn't wake up in a sweat, looking around the room for suicide bombers and cars going over the edge. He didn't have to look for something to blur out the dread that would snowball into wide-eyed panic if it wasn't headed off with something. Like a pin. Like a razor blade. She shifted uncomfortably, edged away from the purse, and glanced at him before looking away.

"Nikki."

She heard his voice. It was soft, pleading. She looked back at him.

"You would tell me if you were worried, wouldn't you?"

"Like Thanksgiving, you mean?" That one hit home. She could see it. *I'm worried*, she thought. *I have nightmares about you hugging suicide bombers, turning into terrorists.* "What are you going to do, sell IRIG?"

The look on his face. It was like she told him both legs would have to be amputated.

"Is that what you want?"

"What I want?" The fear and panic surged, turning into anger. "What does it matter what I want? You go to dangerous places. It's what you do. I stay at home. It's what I do."

He reached a hand across the table. She gripped the Coke tighter in both hands and sucked on the straw. It gurgled at the bottom of the glass.

"Nikki, it's a lot more complicated than that."

You have no idea.

"Maybe I'll think about backing off field work, working more at the executive level. But not right now."

"Then why ask?"

"There's this . . . thing that could put a lot of people in danger. I've put a major crack in the plans of the bad guys, but it's not over. I can't walk away from it right now."

As quickly as it had come, the anger faded, leaving behind fatigue and resignation. "Dad, there are always going to be bad guys." *He'll never walk away. I have to realize that and deal with it, even if he can't.*

"Just give me a few months. Hey, maybe after you're done shooting the season, we can take a break and go to Hawaii like we used to. You can do your school work in the mornings, and we'll hit the beaches in the afternoons." He smiled. "Wind surf on the windward side, jet-ski at Koko Marina, snorkel at Hanauma Bay, the whole thing."

He was trying, even if he didn't really understand. Couldn't understand. She shrugged. "Hawaii sounds nice."

The food arrived. The Reuben was a gigantic pyramid of deli meat sandwiched between rye, sauerkraut, and Swiss. It was almost as tall as her head. She looked at it in shock. He chuckled. She picked it up with both hands and held it next to her face. It reached from her chin to her eyes. Laughing, Dad held a fork out to her. She set it back down and tried a tentative bite. It was interesting in an I-hope-my-friends-don't-see-me-eating-this kind of way.

He took a bite of his Monte Cristo and growled appreciatively. He washed it down with some tea. "Have you ever talked to Stevie about how you feel?"

"Dad."

"Have you ever talked to Stevie at all?"

"Dad."

"I'm serious. You should give her a chance. You might find out you have more in common than you think."

"Dad, will you quit? I'm not going to talk to *Her.*"

"Because?"

Nikki set down her fork. "Look, I know *She* is your girlfriend. If you have to have a girlfriend, at least it's not Barbra Streisand. So, OK. I'm happy for you. Just don't drag me into it."

"She likes you, you know."

"Dad, spare me. I'm eating."

She picked up her fork and stuffed her mouth, chewing with bloated cheeks. He looked at her, picked up his sandwich, and crammed it into his mouth. He looked like a chipmunk. She snorted and he began laughing, trying to keep everything in his mouth.

She forgot all about the razor blade. Almost.

Chapter 25

IRIG offices, Los Angeles, California.
Monday, 13 January 2003. 09:00.

Cooper pressed the stop button on the VCR and turned to face the directors. "This statement by Harkat-ul-Jihad al-Islami was broadcast on Aljazeera TV ten days ago. The Feds are taking this threat seriously and have asked for our help. In one hour, the FBI, CIA, and Homeland Security will be here."

Looks were exchanged around the room. It was Cooper's first day back in the office since the Christmas holidays. They were most likely expecting a typical Monday status meeting and a trip report from Israel. Susan Patterson reluctantly closed her folder and pushed it aside, obviously annoyed. Frank Perkins leaned forward, eyebrows raised. Luis Montoya didn't change his position, back in his chair, elbows on the armrests, fingers splayed and touching. Dr. Hampton waited expectantly. Claire Moquard, dressed as always in something that took professional office attire a daring step toward evening dress, placed her elbows on the polished conference table and leaned her chin on her fists. Sarah waited, notepad in hand.

"Susan, this meeting will be completely operational, so your presence is not required. I will meet with you this afternoon to get status."

Susan nodded, gathered her notes, and left immediately. Cooper turned to Sarah.

"Sarah, I don't want any notes taken except for action items. Written records will be kept to a minimum, tagged top secret. The utmost security will be observed on every aspect of this project." He looked around the room to verify that all understood.

"I am going to say a word in this meeting that will not be said outside of this room." He paused. "Nuclear."

The electricity in the room was palpable. Cooper saw that Claire's nostrils flared.

"We have information that a group acquired eleven brief-case nuclear bombs from the former Soviets. Last week we recovered eight of these bombs. Three remain unaccounted for. The Feds believe, and I agree, that the statement we just watched is connected with the nukes. The Feds will determine which cities are targeted. We will provide assistance with logistics in the targeted cities to find the bad guys and bring them in. Outside this room, we are looking for bombs planted by terrorists. Just bombs."

"And if we find the nukes?" Claire asked.

"The Feds will handle it from there. Frank, you'll need to pull together a list of our informants for major U.S. cities and notes on gang-related cases. Bruce, your lab will be used to evaluate any evidence we acquire. Luis, your teams will be providing support for any doors we have to kick in."

"And me?" Claire asked.

"You will be the liaison between IRIG undercover operatives and the Feds. We want as little direct contact between them as possible. But you know what you need to do." He scanned the room. "See you back here in one hour."

"New York and Chicago," Dixon said.

The room had been silent while everyone arrived and more chairs were brought in. Now there was an undercurrent of murmured comments among the two dozen people scattered around the room.

"What about D.C.?" Cooper called from his chair. A few nodded in agreement.

"D.C. is an obvious target. We will do some work there. But all the chatter has been focused on New York and Chicago, so we will concentrate our initial efforts on those cities. If D.C. shows up on the chatter, we will increase our efforts."

"With all respect, sir," Claire said, "I think you should add L.A. and San Francisco to the list. And maybe Atlanta."

"We expect at most three targets."

"But we don't know which three. The question is, What are they targeting? Financial centers? Then San Francisco should be included. Communications centers? Then D.C., the Bay Area, and Dallas should be included, with some attention to Kansas City and Atlanta. High-profile government? Then obviously D.C. should be included. Population density? Then L.A., San Francisco, and New York are the top three."

"Exactly," Dixon said. "You have just demonstrated that whatever metric we choose gives us a different list of cities. We can try to guess their strategy by looking at past hits, which focus on symbols of American power and strength. But the process of natural selection eliminates terrorists that do the expected. Like capitalism, terrorism succeeds by doing the unexpected,

by redefining itself, by breaking with fashion and becoming in-
novative. So we can try to second-guess them, or we can listen
to what they talk about."

"And if their Darwinian adjustment is to intentionally talk
about one thing while planning another?"

The room was quiet as Dixon and Claire stared at each
other. Cooper suppressed a smile, happy to see someone else
on the business end of Claire's pointed questioning. At the
same time, he wondered at the wisdom of her putting her real
boss on the spot in front of the top men in the top security and
law enforcement agencies in the nation. Didn't seem the most
obvious career-enhancing move.

"We have filters in place to account for misdirection."

Claire sat back in her chair. Her expression indicated neither acceptance nor rejection of this explanation. Dixon ignored her.

"All briefings and status meetings will take place in this
room. Coop has set up a war room at the end of the hall. Now
let me tell you what we are up against.

"Six years ago, General Alexander Lebed, national security
advisor to Boris Yeltsin, told us that the USSR could not account for 84 of the 132 one-kiloton suitcase nuclear devices
they had developed during the cold war. Later, on *60 Minutes*, he said that over 100 out of 250 suitcase nukes were unaccounted for. In the spin storm that followed, Moscow said
variously that the devices never existed in the first place; that
if they did exist, they had been destroyed; and that all nuclear
devices were secure.

"Unlike the U.S., the USSR didn't serialize all their weapons, so there is no way to tell how many they had or of what
type. In addition, many didn't have any safeguards to prevent
malicious detonation. And even when they began adding safe-

guards, they were so simple that it would be a trivial matter to bypass them in a few days or a few weeks.

"Our intelligence indicates that HuJI acquired eleven of these devices. This data went from rumor to fact when, with the help of IRIG, we recovered eight of them in a raid on a safe house in Paris. Two were deteriorated past the point of being operational. Six were fully functional. We must assume that the remaining three are fully operational.

"It's been over half a century since the only time nuclear weapons were used in war and over a decade since the end of the cold war. I'm the only person in this room who was alive when Little Boy and Fat Man were detonated. They were twelve- and twenty-two-kiloton weapons, respectively. We're looking at smaller weapons, one kiloton. In case that sounds small to you, consider that the bomb that killed 168 people and destroyed the Murrah Federal Building in Oklahoma City eight years ago was estimated to be equivalent to 2.5 tons of TNT. One kiloton is four hundred times more deadly, equivalent to 1,000 tons of TNT.

"In a package like this."

Dixon set a silver briefcase on the conference table.

"This is the shell of one of the inoperable devices recovered in Paris. If this were the real thing and were detonated right here in Van Nuys, most of the buildings up to a half-mile away would collapse. Anyone in that radius in direct contact with the blast would receive second- and third-degree burns on exposed skin. Half would be exposed to lethal doses of radiation; the rest, life-threatening doses. In a densely populated area like this, a quarter of a million people would die immediately. Within twenty-four hours the death toll would rise to half a million, as those with serious injuries failed to receive medical attention in time."

He rested his hand on the briefcase. "And they have three of them." He paused to let the information sink in, then nodded at Cooper and sat down.

Cooper walked to the front of the room.

"Morning, folks. Let me give you some more good news. We have reason to believe all three of the devices are already in the U.S. They may be en route to their destination, they may be in a safe house awaiting deployment to their final position, or they may already be in place.

"In addition, there is reason to believe that during the cold war the Soviet Union smuggled briefcase nuclear devices into the United States through diplomatic dispatches, which are immune from inspection, and were never removed. The KGB could have sold these devices to HuJI, saving them the trouble of smuggling them in. It could be that the chatter is merely a diversion to direct our energies to the entry points, while they position a device that is already in the country. They might even allow us to capture a device on the border to lull us into a sense of false security then deploy a device that is already in the country.

"Our experience shows us that they look for a triple bang, striking high-profile targets that are centers of finance, transportation, and communications. Significant casualties are a given with such targets. The high-chatter areas fit this profile. If they strike in the next few weeks, and there's no reason to think they will delay, a harsh winter will increase the death toll.

"We hope to recover the devices before they are actually deployed. Finding a safe house will be easier than locating the device once it is in place. They do produce a detectable amount of radiation, but a sensor must be within ten meters with no obstructions to pick it up. Otherwise, the radiation they emit is indistinguishable from the background radiation present in most cities in things like granite and fresh asphalt. So our best bet is finding the people who will lead us to the bombs."

Cooper motioned to a stack of documents.

"Based on al-Qaeda training manuals recovered from raids on training camps, we know what to look for. Those of you experienced in tracking down criminals might expect them to hole up in low-income high-traffic areas where they can blend in with those of similar ethnic backgrounds. The reality is counterintuitive. They look for houses or ground floor apartments in newly developed areas where there is high mobility and people do not know each other. Older areas of town are more stable. People know their neighbors, and strangers are easily identified. And low-income areas tend to have more paid informers. Ground-floor housing offers more options for escape, from tunnels to secret passageways into adjacent buildings. They avoid secluded or isolated locations since they are more easily placed under surveillance.

"You should focus on areas that match this profile. We will have full stations set up for Chicago and New York. There will be two more stations to cover multiple likely targets with smaller teams. This will allow us to react quickly if the chatter picks up in another location. We hope this will reveal the third location quickly."

Cooper nodded to a man sitting at the table. "Bob Watford of the Justice Department has requested that all available agents in Chicago and New York be put on working the watch lists for terrorist activity. Over the past fifteen months the bureau has compiled a list of those involved with terrorists or sympathetic to them and a field integration file for each name on the list, containing federal ID number, date of birth, green card data, dates of entry, and fingerprints where available.

"The first order of business for the teams in the target cities is to scrub these lists, updating contact information and passing

it on to the interviewing teams for scheduling. We will inter-
rogate as many as we can locate. I've asked Bob to send a top
agent to each city to expedite the process. We have thousands
of people to visit and little time. We're focusing on the sleeper
profile—loner, works hard, keeps to himself, no friends, goes to
the mosque, devout. And anybody walking around with a large
briefcase."

Chapter 26

Climax, Saskatchewan, Canada.
Wednesday, 15 January 2003. 17:00.

He checked his heart-rate monitor. Holding steady at 107. Good. Remember to breathe. In through the nose for a two count, out through the mouth for a one count, in rhythm with the skis. One hour into the run, he had got past the burn. Now he was on the plateau. Too bad he had to stop for the fence. It would throw him off for awhile.

He had waited two weeks for the weather to lay a fresh layer of snow down. The package had been in the basement stash, right where the drugs had been on previous runs. He didn't know who put it there. Didn't want to know. It was nice to get a quiet night in the Climax house, finish off Oliver North's *Mission Compromised* with a pot of tea and a fire. Then a late breakfast and a little work. Percy, his business partner, would be pleasantly surprised when he returned from his midweek getaway with the Logan audit wrapped up.

Sunset was right on schedule, his pace dead-on with his regular routine. He timed the border crossing for the gloom of twilight, that between-time when it was neither day nor night and things were not what they seemed. The horizontal lines of the fence resolved out of the gray of dusk into distinct lines of silver. It took a few minutes to get out of the skis, take off the pack, get everything across the fence, and back into his stride.

As he pushed off, he checked the monitor. Down to 73. Should level off at 107 in fifteen minutes or so. He'd just have to climb the curve again, push back to the plateau. Then two more hours and Turner, Montana, where his Range Rover was waiting.

He thought of the cargo in the pack. *What would Abu think?* He glanced up at the first stars, thinking that Abu was probably smiling like he had when he drove the Mercedes de-livery van into the lobby of the American marine barracks in Beirut–when he delivered six tons of TNT and death to 241 Americans. That was twenty years ago. The Sunday morning he was awakened in the little Phoenix apartment by the screams of his mother.

He had finally got her calmed down with some tea and some Valium from the neighbors. But she refused to sleep until he promised her he would not go back to the Golan, would not join his father in the PLO, would not become a suicide bomber. A promise he had not intended to keep. He was counting the days until, like Abu, he would return to the homeland and con-tinue the fight.

Even back then at age fifteen he could see that Mother had been seduced by the luxury of America, had become compla-cent. How could she–one of the five million Arabs exiled by the Jews, run out of their homes, pushed into refugee camps and hovels and makeshift settlements that were razed ran-domly when the IDF decided there might be a PLO member nearby–turn a blind eye? He had pitied her for her distress, but he also despised her for her weakness. He vowed that he would be worthy of Abu's sacrifice.

He found it ironic that he was, at this moment, fulfilling his vow and keeping his promise. He had not gone back to the Golan. He had gone to Montana. He did not join his father in the PLO, he had joined Harkat-ul-Jihad al-Islami as a sleeper. And he had no intention of becoming a suicide bomber. He would be at his office in Billings when the bomb was detonated. So he had kept his promise. And, true to his vow, he was proving worthy of Abu's sacrifice. He would reap a thousand-fold the harvest of Abu's labors.

He would always think of Abu as he was the day he got on the plane. Down at the ranch in Wyoming he had the picture Mother had snapped of the two of them in the Phoenix airport, him at seven, his arm around Abu's waist; Abu, eighteen, arm resting on his shoulder. And the smile. The smile one marine had reported as Abu had crashed the fence and barreled past. He would always remember the smile.

He checked the monitor. Back up to 103. Breathe. Back to the Rover. He'd be in Billings by midnight. This weekend he would take the pack to the ranch, where it would stay until another unknown person picked it up for an unknown destination. Perhaps Denver or Kansas City. Maybe even Chicago.

He smiled. Percy needed a break. Maybe he would take him down to the ranch for some hunting this weekend.

Outside Rabat, Morocco.
Tuesday, 14 January 2003. 05:42.

Stevie sat cross-legged in the camp chair, wrapped in a blanket and facing the spot where the sun would appear. Next to her, Paula huddled under the lantern and read aloud softly from the Psalms. Stevie was surprised that Paula could do anything softly, but even she seemed subdued by the predawn hush. Or maybe it was what she was reading.

In the initial days after her arrival, Stevie found herself up at dawn, unable to force her internal clock to the local time zone. Paula was always there, smiling and welcoming the day with a vigor Stevie found annoying at first. The results of that encounter threw Stevie off balance. She was surprised to find herself firing questions directly at God. Stevie, the self-reliant, get-it-done-yourself girl. The one who learned early that she couldn't count on others to be there. Not even the ones required by law, custom, or genetics to come through. They moved away, they died, they sank into an alcoholic lassitude, they curled inward into a cocoon of denial and obsession. They failed.

Her family had failed. Her friends had failed. God had failed. Probably because He wasn't there to start with. So why did she walk into the desert, face the morning sun, and ask Him a question? It was Paula's doing. She was talking to Paula and the next thing she knew, she was talking at God. And then the startling thing, the event without precedent: he talked back. She had asked a question without the expectation that it would be answered or even that someone was there to answer it. The ultimate rhetorical question. The answer, even the possibility that there would be an answer, derailed the orderly little boxcars in the train of her life.

But beyond the fact of the answer, there was the content of the answer. It was more overwhelming still. Beloved. Could it be so? And if it was so, could she believe the unbelievable truth? She had felt the hint of it, and she was undone. The next day as she wandered in the gloom before dawn, she asked again. Having tasted of the well, now she wanted to drink deeply. Paula had been there, reading again. Stevie asked a few cautious questions. Paula gave a few simple answers. She read from the middle of the Bible, a part she said was the Psalms.

It was like poetry. It was hard to believe that it was written thousands of years ago by a shepherd who later became a king, but that's what Paula said after she closed the book. It sounded like some prince-and-the-pauper story. Stevie nodded politely but hardly heard the explanation. Instead she was listening to the words reverberate inside her like an echo of the message she had sensed the day before. It was like recalling a dream and feeling the imprint of the emotions linger into the waking hours. She sensed the words were the gateway into the place of answers. She came back the next day, still sleepless from jet lag, and Paula was there again.

But a week later, after she had adjusted to local time, she still found herself waking up just before dawn and returning to the canopy and the table and the lantern and Paula and the book. When their dawn meetings were eclipsed by the shooting schedule, which started with the first available light and lasted until the last usable ray vanished, Stevie surprised herself and Paula by suggesting they move the sessions up an hour instead of dropping them.

Each morning Paula opened the book to the middle and read from the Psalms and Stevie let it wash over her. She heard this shepherd-king speak her life, the pleadings of a young girl for a father who took his life in a moment with a gun and a mother who took her life over three decades with a bottle. He didn't write those things, exactly, but she could hear it in his desperate pleading for God to rescue him from his enemies. From the way they echoed in her heart, she knew the words came from the same place in his heart, like a piece that fit in two different puzzles.

Then they came to number twenty-three. The words were familiar to her mind. She had heard them before, maybe at a funeral or something. But even more, they were familiar to her heart. It was a shepherd speaking of his own shepherd, of how he was tended and protected and comforted by the same one who had said, "Beloved."

I shall not want. I will fear no evil. My cup runs over. Goodness and mercy will follow me all my life.

Paula fell silent. Stevie barely noticed. She leaned forward and read it to herself. Forever, it said. She didn't know she wanted a shepherd, but she was beginning to think it would be nice. She spent most of her life being her own shepherd. At first it was survival, then success. But now it felt like it all was just a grasping greediness to hoard against the inevitable famine, against the slow and painful pangs of deprivation and decline and desperation. Could she really lie down in green pastures? Could her soul be restored? In her experience you lost your soul in the struggle to buy the green pasture that you never had the time to lie down in or you would lose it to the next sheep. If only it could be like the shepherd said.

"I know what you're thinking," Paula said.

Stevie flinched at the sound. She looked at Paula, feeling guilty. Then she realized she was being silly. There was no way Paula could know what she was thinking.

Paula continued without waiting for a question. "You're thinking it's too good to be true." Stevie stared at her. "But you're wishing it were true."

"How . . ."

"He told me. He said, 'Tell her it's true. Tell her there is a shepherd.'"

"He?"

"God." Stevie's eyes narrowed, and Paula laughed. "Oh, don't worry. I'm not hearing voices. I was just sitting here, listening to my mind and my heart and it just came in, like a thought."

Paula squinted at her. It seemed to Stevie that she was looking for something, some kind of sign.

"I think you know what I mean," Paula said. "I think He spoke to you on New Year's Day. You've just been scared to believe it or to say anything. Afraid it might be nerves or jet lag or fatigue or wishful thinking or indigestion or any of a dozen other things. But He told you something that day."

Stevie's eyes narrowed. She turned her head slightly, like a half protestation, and looked at Paula with apprehension.

"That's the other thing He told me. He didn't tell me what it was He said to you. He just said to tell you that the thing you heard on New Year's Day, it's true too."

That's when Stevie started crying. Slow, silent tears. It could be true. It might be true. As she closed her eyes and the tears crept down her face, she realized it was true.

The Lord is my shepherd, she thought. *I shall not want.* Then she shuddered. *But what about Matt?* Then she felt the words wash over her. *Though you walk through the valley of the shadow of death, I am with you. Matt is not your shepherd. I am your shepherd.* She nodded fearfully, wanting to trust. *But what about my career? The production company?* The words came again. *I prepare a table for you. Your cup runs over. You are not your shepherd. I am your shepherd.* She nodded again, beginning to relax her grip on the arms of the camp chair. *The Lord is my shepherd. I shall not want.* It was true. It was gloriously and impossibly and unbelievably true.

She opened her eyes and looked into Paula's tear-brimmed eyes. She smiled a timid, trembling smile.

"The Lord is my shepherd," Stevie whispered.

"Oh, honey," Paula whispered back. "He's my shepherd too."

Paula reached out and took Stevie's hands and squeezed them. Then, to Stevie's surprise, she got up, pulled Stevie to her feet, and hugged her so hard Stevie had to struggle for breath. It felt awkward at first, but then it felt comforting, like a homecoming. Stevie hugged her back and they stood hugging and crying and laughing and feeling much more euphoria than was proper that early in the day.

Chapter 27

War room, IRIG offices, Burbank, California.
Wednesday, 15 January 10:20.

Cooper poured another cup of coffee and pointed the carafe at the door where Dixon was walking in. Dixon shook his head. Most of the light in the room came from computer screens and the track lighting over the maps. The people sat in gloom, studying the chatter that poured in from around North America—video feeds from surveillance teams, audio feeds of tapped phones and rooms, profiles of suspects, news stories, e-mails, Web sites. All were evaluated, summarized, and entered into the growing database on each suspected site. The two large Chicago and New York stations dominated each end of the room. The two multi-site stations were in the center. Language experts familiar with specific cells helped sift between disinformation and legitimate intelligence. Experience had validated the direct connection between chatter and likelihood of an incident.

Cooper noticed Claire was at the New York station. She leaned over a screen with the intensity that marked everything she did, her straight black hair hiding her face. She seemed oblivious to the pencil twirling through the fingers of her right hand. Many of her operatives were the sources for the information coming in. She had good reason to be engrossed in the case, but Cooper couldn't shake the unease he felt watching her. She had been on the case before she was supposed to be. He wondered if the project helped legitimize an inappropriate interest, providing a cover for another agenda—an agenda that was not in the interest of IRIG or the country.

He met Dixon at the Chicago station. An FBI agent motioned him over.

"We think Oak Park fits the profile for Chicago. Central location, middle-class area with lots of recent development, very mobile population. Just north of the Eisenhower Expressway, here." He pointed to the map.

Cooper looked at the map. "I'd expect some activity in the north." It had been a decade since he had worked a case in Chicago. Very likely much was changed. He looked behind the FBI agent to Dixon, who nodded. "Great." Cooper looked at the agent. "Let's get a team trolling through the area and develop a list of locations that fit the profile."

He looked through the information that had been added to the database in the last twenty-four hours. Many of the teams hadn't been home since Monday when the project started. The scrubbed list was significantly shorter.

He moved to the New York station and stood there for a few minutes behind Claire, scanning the screens. She saw his reflection in a monitor and jerked around, the pencil shooting from her fingers, past Cooper's ear and into the next station. A CIA agent frowned at her and pushed it aside with his foot. Claire shrugged. Cooper sat down next to her.

"Anything new?"

"My guys identified several likelies. We brought in a few for questioning, but we can't get much out of them without leaning on them, and with the Feebs there, we can't really lean that hard." She glanced at the next station and lowered her voice. "They like to go by the book. If you let me work with my guys, I think we can make more progress."

Cooper shook his head. "Can't do it. It's bad enough that Dixon has such high visibility and CIA is working the stations. If the FBI finds out the CIA is financing most of the project, they'll have a fit. With the Patriot Act and executive orders, things are a little more flexible when working terrorism angles domestically, but we can't use them for routine questioning of informants. If we find a device, well, that's different."

Claire nodded impatiently. "Word is spreading fast. We have a solid list, but it's starting to unravel. The illegals are fading before we can get to them."

Cooper sat down, leaned back with his hands behind his head, and looked at the wall maps. Claire turned back to her screen and continued working through reports from the field. After a few minutes Cooper leaned forward.

"Maybe we're doing this backward. Instead of looking for likelies, maybe we should look for friendlies. Muslims who enjoy the freedom they have in the U.S. Muslims who are just as disgusted by the militant Islamic fundamentalists as we are."

Claire considered the suggestion. "That's not the way they've always done it. Might get some resistance."

Matt leaned forward. "Get Abe on the phone."

She dialed his cell number and put it on speaker. Abe Wilcox, the Justice Department agent sent to New York, answered on the first ring.

"Abe, Matt Cooper here. I hear the list is getting shorter."

"Yeah. The ones we do get aren't exactly happy to talk to us. Great Satan and all that."

"I'm sure it's tough going. What if we try something different?"

"If it works, I'm all for it."

"Instead of bringing in Muslims who hate the U.S., let's try talking to some who like the U.S., who enjoy the freedom and opportunity they've found here. The ones who don't want to be lumped in with the extremists on the jihad bandwagon."

There was silence on the line. Claire smirked.

"It's worth a shot," Wilcox said.

Claire stared at the phone. Cooper smiled.

"They might be willing to help, might report suspicious activity," Cooper said. "Target moderate mosques instead of the conservative ones, perhaps Islamic studies in the universities. Do a little footwork and push through. Most of the time the breakthrough comes from the place you least expect." Cooper wished he could get there on the streets and get the vibe on the scene. It always led him to the solution. "My guess is your guys are more experienced at working with suspects and hostile subjects than sympathetic ones."

"You friends with Miss Cleo?"

"Let's just say this isn't my first rodeo. They're going to have to take the clothes hanger out of their coats before they put them on for a change. Loosen up, direct the conversation to family and goals, do a lot of listening to irrelevant information. If they do it right, something will eventually bubble to the top."

"I'll try it." He sounded doubtful.

"Try it more than once. Give it forty-eight hours at least. It takes awhile to get the rhythm. It's a change-up pitch."

Chapter 28

Department of Middle Eastern and Islamic Studies, New York University, Greenwich Village, New York. Friday, 17 January 2003. 09:36.

Most of the students rushed in at the last minute, but Amira always arrived early. For them it was just another class, another book to read, another paper to write, another test to take. For her it was another world, a journey with the thrill of a forbidden pleasure. As she transferred from the bus to the Staten Island ferry to the Manhattan subway, she felt like a spy, certain nobody could guess that the Muslim woman in the scarf was headed to Greenwich Village. And like a spy, she surreptitiously watched the other passengers, speculating about where they were going or maybe what they were running from. What secrets did they carry as they swayed with the motion of the train? What hidden desire or wasting remorse or silent satisfaction lay behind the impassive masks that froze their faces as they stepped through the doors?

She knew about secrets. In Pakistan, sequestered safely within the walls that protected the house from the outside world, she had burned with unspoken longing. While life in Islamabad was not life under the Taliban, Esam had ideas about what was proper for women in general and his wife in particular. He entrusted to her the running of the household and provided servants enough to ensure she need not go to the market herself. She heard that in Europe and America women moved freely among the men, working along with them, discussing, learning, expressing their ideas, discovering new things, creating new things. She initiated conversations with Esam, but nothing interested him outside his business and politics, and he considered a conversation with a woman on these topics a waste of time.

Amira envied her sister who had married a more progressive husband. She fed her yearning for art and knowledge through books and magazines and afternoon teas to discuss the lectures and university classes her sister attended. On such a starvation diet of culture Amira survived. Then one day in 1995 Esam decided he could no longer stand the charade of Pakistan's national politics and the effects on his business. He moved his family to America, settling on Staten Island near an uncle.

But the protection of a Muslim community held no guarantee of immunity from the insidious influences of American culture. They could no longer afford a small army of servants to insulate themselves from the outside world. Amira did her own shopping. To be out on the streets, flowing with the river of humanity on the sidewalks, even if most of them were Muslims, was a luxury beyond her imagination before coming to America. As she waited at the light, she peered into the taxis, hoping to see someone startling. Usually it was just the driver, probably a Pakistani himself.

First it was lecture night at the mosque with a schedule of guest speakers, then a series of classical concerts, then a retrospective film festival featuring 1940s movies set in the Middle East. For five years she dragged Esam to event after event until he begged for mercy. He agreed to the courses in the Department of Middle Eastern and Islamic Studies at NYU in exchange for quiet nights at home. Twice a week she embarked on the covert mission to Greenwich Village disguised as the Muslim woman that she was, drank tea in the break room, ingested with silent gratitude every syllable of knowledge she was offered, and returned home to Staten Island.

She looked over her notes for her ten o'clock class and sipped her tea. A man she hadn't seen before came in, got coffee, and sat at the only other table. Her pulse quickened. Nobody came in here; she was always alone for her tea. Now a stranger, a young African American in a black suit and close-cropped hair was sitting three feet from her. She glanced at him nervously. He was looking at her book. He caught her glance and smiled. She looked quickly away.

"*Israel: Fact through Fiction.* That sounds like an interesting course. Are you from Israel?"

She flinched and reflexively shook her head without looking at him. She did not talk to strange men. She rarely talked to any men, even those she knew. Only Esam. The silence grew. He waited as if he had just spoken, as if it were natural that a pause of several minutes followed a simple question. Just on the edge of her vision she could see his black fingers in an arc around the Styrofoam cup. Her eyes moved slowly to his hand—slender fingers, the undersides a dark pink, a gold band on his ring finger.

"So you're not from Israel," he said, as if she had answered him.

She shook her head. She had come to Greenwich Village in search of knowledge and adventure. Today adventure walked in and sat next to her, but she couldn't bring herself to speak. She scolded herself for her foolishness.

"Pakistan," she whispered. She glanced at him again. His eyebrows were raised.

"You're from Pakistan, but you're taking this class?"

She nodded.

"I admire that, wanting to learn about other cultures." He pointed to the book under her notes. "Yizhar. Is that a good book? Do you like his writing?"

She looked down at her tea and nodded slowly. She sipped the tea. It had cooled too much. She set the cup down and stared at her own fingers around it.

"They don't feel like they should feel, don't think like they should think," she said hesitantly. From the corner of her eye she saw him nodding. Emboldened, she continued. "They have their own thoughts, but it is not permitted. They must do what is expected."

"The characters, you mean."

"Yes." She looked at him. His eyes were gray. She did not know black men had gray eyes. She realized she was staring and looked away. "The characters. That is their struggle, their fate."

"I know the feeling. How about you?"

He was looking at her. She could feel it. She looked back at him, into his gray eyes. "Yes," she said quietly. "This is a feeling I know."

"Pardon me for asking, but you are a Muslim, are you not?"

"Yes."

"All this stuff about Iraq, what do you think about that?"

"Saddam is a butcher." She spoke without thinking, without considering the awkwardness or the inappropriateness, just letting the thoughts flow out as they came to her mind, as if she were speaking to a woman. It felt indecent and right at the same time. She enjoyed the feeling. "He is not Muslim, he is not human, he is animal."

"You don't object to the United States invading a Muslim nation? What about Afghanistan?"

A man asking her opinion. It was absurd. She was answering. It was exhilarating. She inhaled slowly, tasting the dry heated air as though it were a rare, intoxicating fruit. A forbidden fruit. She allowed her thoughts to align themselves amid the chaos of fear and fulfillment in her mind.

"They say they follow the true Islam. True Muslims do not help murderers kill innocent people. True Muslims are peaceful. They would not be invaded if they followed the Prophet, may His name be praised."

"What about the Al-Farouq Mosque, right here in New York, over in Brooklyn? The guys behind the first WTC attempt met there to do their planning."

The thoughts came, but they shocked her. She was unable to say them, but she must say them. She must not turn back from this moment. If she betrayed it, it might never come again. She checked the doorway, making sure they were alone, and spoke softly.

"Islam does not permit killing innocent people. Murder of women and babies does not honor Allah. They are worse than infidels."

The man followed her gaze to the empty doorway and turned back to her. "A thought that is not expected, right? Not permitted?"

He understands, she thought. *He agrees*. She said nothing. She looked back down but could feel him studying her.

"Have you said this thought before?"

She hadn't said it before. She had thought it many times. But women did not say such things, did not express opinions on such topics, did not criticize the soldiers of Allah. This man had somehow drawn it out of her, created the space where the thought was born into words. She said nothing, fearing that perhaps in her elation she transgressed. Perhaps she was wrong. Perhaps to be silent was not betrayal. Perhaps it was betrayal to speak.

"I didn't think so." He lowered his voice. "You have trusted me by telling me this thought. I will trust you by telling you something you can't tell anyone else. Then we will be bound together by our mutual trust and our secrets." He paused. "Do you understand?"

She nodded, afraid to hear his secret.

"I work for the government. We suspect that another attack is planned. I am looking for someone who might have seen something unusual, something that might not seem important, but could help us prevent another tragedy, one worse than September 11."

She looked at him, at the empty doorway, and back to him. Could this be true? Would the government come to a break room and talk to strangers to find terrorists? It seemed improbable. But if not, then what was his goal? The alternatives all seemed even more unlikely. A spy from the mosque? A sex fiend?

He leaned across his small table, looked into her eyes. "Have you seen any strangers in your neighborhood or at your mosque? Anyone with a bulky briefcase or suitcase?"

A briefcase? How did he know?

He must have seen it in her eyes, the sudden shock. He spoke quickly, with greater intensity.

"You have seen something, haven't you? It might be nothing at all, or it might be something very important. If you tell me, we can check it out. If it is nothing, then no harm is done. But if it is what we are looking for, thousands of lives will be saved."

He looked at her, waiting. She wasn't sure.

"Please trust me," he said.

Of course she wanted to prevent a disaster if she could, but it wasn't her place to talk to foreigners about her own people. It wasn't permitted. Then, in a moment, she knew she would tell him.

"Yes, I have seen something. Last week, Saturday, a man came to the mosque, a stranger. He had much luggage. After, I saw him go into a building on my block, on the next corner."

"Do you know his name?" She didn't. "What building did he go into?"

"Apartments."

"Do you know the address?"

"No. Only it is on my street on the corner."

"Corner of what streets?"

"Copley and Elm."

The man pulled out a notepad, drew a cross and labeled one line Copley, the other Elm. He drew an arrow and wrote an *N* above it. "This is north, toward Manhattan. Which corner?" She pointed. He wrote an *X*. "What kind of luggage?"

"He had a suitcase and a large briefcase, as you said."

She saw the reaction. It frightened her. "They're going to blow something up, aren't they?" she whispered. "They're going to try it again."

"Not if you help us. I need to know the address and the exact apartment where this man is."

"I don't know it." How would she know the apartment of this strange man? It was an absurd question.

"But you can find out. Here." He pulled a card from his breast pocket. "My name is Chris Johnson. You can reach me at that number any time of the day or night. How can I contact you?"

She shook her head. He could not call her. For Esam to discover this conversation took place was worse than any disaster she could think of. She took the card.

"I might call you. If . . ." She dropped her cup into the trash and picked up her books. "But I am late to class." She looked out the door, saw that the hall was empty, and rushed out.

Chapter 29

**916 Copley, Apartment 5, Staten Island, New York.
Sunday, 19 January 2003. 09:13.**

His name was Sami Nasir. That was all they got out of him.
Cooper pulled Wilcox aside and spoke softly. "This is
not the place, and he is not the guy." He looked at the oversize
silver briefcase. It held two dozen cans of garbanzo beans. He
looked around at the apartment. No pictures, no personal effects, very little furniture. Dirty clothes were piled in a corner
of the bedroom. The closet had two shirts and one pair of
slacks. The suitcase held socks, T-shirts, and underwear. He
nodded at Nasir. "I think he was a decoy—a trial run to see if
anybody was watching. But he might know the real guy and
the real place."

Wilcox nodded. "We'll take him in and sweat it out of him."
He stepped to the team and began giving directions.

Cooper didn't respond. He wasn't going to play it that way.
He looked at Nasir, who was still disoriented. Not surprising.
Five minutes ago he had been sound asleep. Now he was sitting in a kitchen chair in a T-shirt and boxers, handcuffed and
surrounded by men with automatic weapons.

Things had gone surprisingly well considering that two days

ago there were no leads. Wilcox had called him a few hours after he heard from Johnson. First he had sent an agent to the city for the building plans and another to the phone company for names and apartment numbers for all phones in the building. Then he met Johnson at the site for an initial reconnaissance. They found that the apartment building shared walls with a corner deli and a law office. The double front door was locked. An intercom with eighteen buttons and nametags allowed tenants to buzz visitors in. All the ground floor nametags had Middle Eastern names. The back of the building had a single fire door that opened into a small paved loading area bordered with trash bins. Each apartment had one set of windows on the back wall. A fire escape zigzagged across the back of the building.

Wilcox called Cooper from the alley. By midnight Cooper was in New York.

He found they had made the most of a difficult surveillance situation. Wilcox placed a car across the alley in the back of a loading zone for a furniture store. A remote camera with joystick control broadcast video and audio to a van on the street at the front of apartments. It wasn't enough, but it was a start. They needed to know which apartment. Going door to door might be a good way to sell Girl Scout cookies, but it didn't work for capturing terrorists. The assault team had to be inside and in control before the people inside knew it had happened.

The surveillance team recorded the traffic in and out of the building, researching the license plates of any cars. If a taxi dropped off a passenger, it was stopped two blocks away and questioned about the fare and the location of the pickup. They made no attempt to tap the phones. A request to tap the entire first floor would only result in a good laugh for the judge.

Saturday, Cooper worked from the New York IRIG office and called for status every two hours. Dixon called him just as he was finishing his lunch—a pastrami on rye with fresh chips.

"Coop, I hear you're in New York."

"I flew out yesterday afternoon. Wilcox found a talker."

"I hate it when the Feebs catch a break like that."

"I'll take them any way I can get them."

"What was that? Are they tearing down your building?"

"Sorry." Cooper brushed away crumbs. "Just finishing off lunch. Potato chips."

"I would return the favor, but this cantaloupe isn't co-operating. Look, while you're over there, you should touch base with my boss. This is an unusual multi-agency operation with high stakes. He's following things closely. I think it would ease his mind and, more important, keep him off my back if he met you."

Cooper grimaced. He needed a distraction like he needed an appendectomy. "You want me to fly down to D.C.? We're in the middle of a thing, here. It could pop at any minute."

"No problem. He's just finishing up a conference in New York. He flies back to D.C. tomorrow, so he could meet you today."

"Can he come here? I don't want to leave the command center in case we get a break."

"The mountain shall come to Mohammed."

An hour later Cooper heard a discrete cough. He looked up from his paperwork. An agent was standing at the door of the office, a tall man in his fifties standing behind him. Cooper stood and nodded at the agent, who promptly disappeared. He walked around the desk and held out his hand.

"Matt Cooper, CEO of IRIG."

The man stepped forward and shook his hand. He was slender with gray streaks in his sideburns. "Lester Watson, assistant director of Intelligence over Covert Operations."

"And Dixon's boss."

"Yes, I have that honor." He smiled. "It's a mixed blessing, I assure you."

Cooper motioned him to a chair and sat back down behind his desk. Watson had an air of almost European sophistication about him that Cooper didn't associate with agency men, not even the ones at the top.

Watson sat down. "I've been reading up on you. Very impressive."

"Thanks. Just trying to make a living."

"I'd say you're doing considerably more than that. Took a small regional agency international in three years. Formed liaisons with government law enforcement and counterterrorism agencies all over the world. Not business as usual for a farm boy from Muscatine, Iowa."

Cooper nodded, masking his surprise. The man was thorough and discrete. It was a compliment but perhaps also a warning. Watson was watching this one closely, as Dixon had said, and he was letting Cooper know.

"I was concerned when this rather unconventional operation was forced on me down the food chain. But then I read the report of your work in Vienna and Paris. How did you accomplish so much in so little time?"

"I have the best of both worlds. Due to my liaisons I have access to information and assistance from people like you without being limited to operating by your rules."

Watson smiled. "I'm glad we have the benefit of your network and freedom. Hopefully, you can make as quick work of it here as you did in Europe." He looked at the stack of papers in front of Cooper. "Are you here on other IRIG business, or have you already located a target?" he asked, stirring as if preparing to leave.

"We have a possible suspect. Narrowed it down to a building, but no name. Based on the strength of the intel I decided it was best to be on-site in case of a breakthrough. Right now it's mainly wait and see." He gestured to his desktop. "And catch up on paperwork."

Watson stood. "I am painfully familiar with that aspect of the job. I won't keep you from your work. Thank you for taking the time to visit with me. I suspect Bill is getting tired of me breathing down his neck, but this is a high-profile case being followed at the highest levels and we can't afford any missteps."

Cooper showed him out and returned to his work. He could see why Dixon made his request. Listening to lectures from Watson could get tiring very quickly. He worked through the afternoon and went to the hotel early to combat the jet lag with some sleep.

He was awakened at 1:00 a.m. Sunday by Wilcox. Johnson's contact had called with a name and apartment number. Sami Nasir, apartment 5 in the back of the building. Fifteen minutes later Cooper was sipping coffee at the command center in Bayonne, New Jersey, scanning the blueprints and floor plan for apartment 5 as the supervisors trickled in. Everyone was alert, fueled by coffee and adrenaline. As they discussed tactics, Wilcox woke up a judge to get the search warrant going. The surveillance team was informed of the target and instructed to provide status every fifteen minutes.

The primary goal was to recover the bomb if it was indeed in the apartment. Taking the suspect alive was a very high secondary goal. If he were killed, the trail would end. The two lead agents would subdue him while he was still in bed. If he broke free, they would use a Taser instead of firearms. Deadly force would be used only as a last resort.

They had a plan and a team by sunrise. Cooper dispatched a van with a heat sensor to scan the back of apartment 5. An hour later the report indicated one body horizontal in what appeared to be a bedroom. It was a forty-five-minute drive to the apartment. They used a code two approach, no sirens, only red lights that were extinguished two blocks from the target.

The van parked at the end of the alley. Cooper and Wilcox pulled up behind it. After a last check, Cooper followed the entry team up the alley. They wore KEVLAR vests and helmets with cameras that were monitored at the command post. The techs opened the fire door without incident, and the team moved to the apartment door five feet away. The leader pushed a pinhole camera under the door. The apartment was quiet, lit only by a sliver of light coming through the bedroom door from the back window. It appeared that the suspect was still asleep.

On the signal the battering ram hit the door and the lead agents were in the bedroom in two seconds. Nasir barely had time to raise up on one elbow before the agents had him on his stomach and his hands behind his back. The agents behind them were scanning for any trip wires or devices set to detonate in case of a raid.

Within minutes it was apparent that there was no bomb in the apartment. The forensic team entered and began a thorough search. The assault team loaded Nasir into the backseat of an unmarked car and left.

Cooper and Wilcox followed the car containing Nasir. As they swung off 278 onto 440, Cooper broke the silence.

"Abe, I'd like to talk to Nasir first."

Wilcox drove in silence. Cooper waited.

"It's not procedure, but this whole operation isn't procedure," Wilcox said. "I might take some heat for it, but I'm willing to play along. You were right about the change in tactics on the front end." He looked at Cooper. "But I want to be in the room."

"As an observer."

"Right. You take your shot. I'll give you a few hours. If you're not getting anywhere, my boys take over."

"It might take more than a few hours."

They followed the lead car into a secured underground parking structure. They joined the two FBI agents escorting Nasir at the elevator. The five of them rode to the third floor together.

Chapter 30

Federal facility, Bayonne, New Jersey.
Sunday, 19 January 2003. 09:38.

The room was small with four solid walls, no one-way glass with people watching. It contained a table and two chairs. Nasir sat in the chair with his back to the door. His hands were on the table, handcuffed together. He was looking at his hands. Cooper pulled out the empty chair and sat down. He looked up at Wilcox, who was standing by the door.

"Can you take those things off?" He pointed to the handcuffs.

Wilcox hesitated then removed them. Nasir rubbed his wrists but said nothing. He didn't look up.

Cooper looked at Nasir. He was pushing fifty if he wasn't past it. The baby-blue coveralls were too long for him, but not loose. He had the look of a man who had seen rugged years but not recently. At one time he had been short and stocky instead of short and dumpy. Cooper could see resignation in his face even without eye contact. Nasir knew the risks and had already accepted the consequences. He looked like a man preparing for death. Determination, a steeling of the resolve, some regret, but no fear.

"I could use a little something," Cooper said. "How about you, Sami? Coffee? Tea?" There was no response. Cooper looked at Wilcox. "Abe, could you have them bring two cups of hot water and two teabags? And sugar, not sweetener. And if there are any pastries or anything around, we could use some of those too."

Wilcox stepped to the door and spoke to someone outside without leaving the room. Cooper looked at Nasir and smiled.

"Sami, my name is Matt Cooper. I'm a businessman. I'm not a cop, not a federal agent, not a soldier. Now Abe over there, he's a federal agent. But he's promised to let me do the talking, so you don't have to worry about him." Cooper smiled. Nasir made no response.

"I don't have a lot of time. I have to get home in time for my daughter's party. She turned fourteen last week, but we didn't have time for a party. She won't let me put it off again. You know how teenagers are. You've already been through it, haven't you?"

He saw Nasir shift in his chair, his eyes harden, his jaw clench. Perhaps that was the right direction. "Do you have children?" The jaw muscles bulged again. He could feel the tension, the muscles flexing under the coveralls. He sensed that he would do better by forming a rapport with Nasir rather than pushing him until he broke.

An agent came in with a tray. Cooper waited while he transferred two cups, two teabags, a spoon, a handful of sugar packets, and two bagels to the table. Cooper thanked him. When the door closed he looked at Nasir.

"I was hoping for Krispy Kreme. You would figure here in the middle of all this law enforcement you could get a donut."

Nasir snorted. Matt pushed the sugar to his side of the table.

"I got those for you. I don't take sugar, but I figured you do and not the fake kind, either. Am I right?"

Nasir nodded. It looked like an automatic response.

Good, Cooper thought. *He's lowered his defenses, even if he doesn't realize it.*

Nasir took a teabag, moving with stiff formality, tore the package open and dropped it in the water. Then he stirred in three packages of sugar.

"Sami, I think that despite our differences we understand each other pretty well. Me, I'm trying to protect my home and my family. You understand that, I'm sure." Cooper saw a slight nod. "And you're putting your life on the line for a cause you believe in enough to die for." A larger nod. "At some levels I can understand that. I've done the same thing."

Nasir made eye contact. Cooper saw suspicion and curiosity.

"Yes, it's true. I've risked my life, even been shot, while fighting for something I believe in. We are both men of action. When we see what must be done, we do it. I think we understand each other."

He saw it in the eyes. It was so slight Wilcox probably didn't notice from his perch by the door, the hardness fading as Nasir accepted the truth of his words.

"So, I'll ask you some questions, straight up, no tricks. You answer me the same way and maybe we can work this out. It might just be a misunderstanding."

Nasir nodded and sipped his tea.

"How long have you been in the U.S.?"

"I came in Safar, six months before Ramadan."

"Six months before Ramadan. April, then."

Nasir shrugged. "If you say so."

"In April you came to New York?" A nod. "From where?"

"Afghanistan."

"But your passport is Pakistani."

"I have lived in many places. Saudi Arabia, Pakistan, Afghanistan. My father bought a factory on the Gomal River when I was eleven. Making tea pots." He held up his cardboard cup.

Cooper smiled and nodded. He held up his own cup and sipped his tea. Nasir began talking of his early life in Saudi Arabia in his grandfather's house. He talked about the move to Pakistan and the factory. Cooper kept him going with occasional questions, all focused on his early life. He made no attempt to turn the conversation to the arrest or the briefcase. After awhile Nasir fell silent, thinking back on his childhood. Wilcox shuffled restlessly in the background. Cooper waited.

"But when I was young, I quarreled with my father and joined the Mujahadeen to free Afghanistan from the Soviet Union. You know how the youth are." He almost smiled. "Allah granted us favor, and we chased the Russian dogs from our land. I went home and began helping with the factory."

He told of his marriage, arranged by his father, of his children, two boys and a girl, of how his father retired, how he took over at the factory. Then he fell silent again. Cooper waited, but Nasir didn't resume. Instead, a sadness seemed to seep through him. Cooper broke the silence.

"And you came to the U.S. almost a year ago. What have you been doing since you arrived?"

"I work delivering bread to restaurants. I go to the mosque. I read the Qur'an."

"Friends? Do you spend time visiting with anyone?"

Nasir shook his head. "I greet my brothers at the mosque. We talk some. Many of the brothers, they come to America, they change. I do not wish to speak with them."

"And your family. Did they come with you?"

Nasir's jaw clenched again. "I came alone." He set the cup down and looked away.

Again this hardness at the mention of family. Cooper chose to keep the conversation flowing. He changed subjects.

"So you are one of the Afghan Alumni?"

Nasir looked at him, puzzled.

"You spent the '80s in Afghanistan? Fighting the Soviets?" A nod. "Did you meet bin Laden?"

"Yes. He is a very devout man. A warrior for Allah."

"You knew him? You spent time with him?"

"Yes. We moved frequently, but often I would be in the same camp. We fought together. It is difficult to keep al-Salat, the daily prayers, when fighting with the resistance. Osama bin Laden never failed to keep al-Salat. Even in a battle with the Soviet infidels I have seen him stop for 'Asr, the middle prayer. He is a great man in his devotion to Allah. He will not rest until the infidel is erased from the land of Allah's people."

Cooper noted that the hard glint in Nasir's eye at the mention of his family almost turned to a sparkle as he spoke of bin Laden. He thought of Johnson's report on his conversation with the woman at NYU.

"You say bin Laden is a holy man, great in his devotion to Allah, but he kills innocent people."

"Infidels are not innocent."

"Women and children?"

"He is devout, the most devout man I have known."

"And he slaughters children like they are nothing but goats. How can that be holy?"

"He defends our lands from the infidels who profane the name of Allah."

"He defends your lands by murdering the most defenseless among us?"

Nasir protested; Cooper responded. It went back and forth like a tennis match, Nasir enumerating bin Laden's virtues as a spiritual leader, Cooper reciting his villainy as a bloodthirsty monster. When it became apparent that Nasir was uncomfortable with the thought of bin Laden as a murderer, Cooper decided to take a break. He checked his watch and discovered it was mid-afternoon. They had been talking for over four hours.

He asked Wilcox to get lunch for Nasir and found a quiet spot for a quick phone call. Then he got lunch for himself, a sandwich brought in from a nearby deli. He was finishing the chips when Wilcox walked in. He sat across the table.

"I don't think you're getting anywhere with this Osama's-a-bad-guy-no-he's-not thing. I'm going to let my boys have a crack at him."

"Give me one more hour. Johnson's on his way with the secret weapon."

"Secret weapon?"

Cooper smiled. "You'll see. If it doesn't work, I'll go back to California and leave it to your boys."

An agent walked in. "You Cooper?"

Cooper held out his hand for the large envelope. He opened it and handed a stack of 8-by-10-inch glossies to Wilcox. He shuffled through them and looked at Cooper.

"Muslim attacks on women and children. Nasir seems to be suffering from denial about the guys he works with. It's time for him to face it head-on."

Chapter 31

Back in the interrogation room Cooper walked to the table and dropped the pictures in front of Nasir. He glanced at the top one and looked at Cooper, waiting for an explanation.

"This is the handiwork of your holy man."

Nasir looked down at the top photo. He didn't touch it.

"Go ahead. Look at them all."

Nasir didn't move. Still standing, Cooper leaned across the table and grabbed the photos. As he spoke he slapped them down one at a time like a blackjack dealer in Vegas.

"Two months ago, on November 21, 2002, Nael Abu Hilail put on his belt, just like you did this morning. The difference was, his belt was much larger and deadlier. He left his house knowing he would not return. Then he got on a Number 20 Egged bus in Jerusalem. It was full of people, including children going to school."

These were not photos that appeared in newspapers. They were from IDF files, clinical and graphic. Nasir looked away.

"He waited. At 7:10 the bus stopped on Mexico Street in Kiryat Menachem, a stop where other school children were waiting for the bus. Then he did what he came to do."

He slapped down another photo. Nasir flinched, but didn't look at the picture of part of a body—what remained of a boy who was not yet a teen and never would be.

Cooper's voice grew louder. "In the name of Allah and purifying the sacred places from the stench of the infidels, he killed school children. Five women and four children died in the attack."

He slapped down pictures of sickening gore, one after another. Twisted metal, smoke, debris. A torso hanging over the side of what was left of the bus. Body parts, children and adults with heads broken and bloody. Slapped them down viciously with the flat of his hand, the sound bouncing off the hard walls of the small room like the report of a rifle. Nasir continued to look into the corner.

He was practically shouting now. "Blew them to pieces. He was called a hero, a great warrior of the faith. His father said, 'Our religion says we are proud of him until the day of resurrection.' His religion. For his religion he killed her. And him." More pictures slapped down. "Look at them. They died for your holy war."

Nasir looked obliquely at the row of photos. His face was a mask. Cooper dropped another picture on the table. It showed a woman in her thirties, dead from gunshot wounds. He lowered his voice until it was barely audible.

"On November 10, 2002, in Kibbutz Metzer, Ravital Ocha-yon told her two boys a bedtime story. Matan was five; Noam was four. Then she tucked them in. A gunman kicked in the front door and broke into the bedroom. She threw herself between the gunman and the children."

Cooper placed two more pictures on the table. Pictures of two young boys, dead from gunshot wounds.

"He shot her and the children at point blank range," he whispered. "Then he left and killed two more people, Yitzak

Dori and Tirza Damari." He placed the pictures on the table. "Hamas praised the attack."

Cooper leaned over the table, his hands pressed against the photos littering the top. "Your holy man, Osama bin Laden," he shouted, "devout man of Allah, has said that the fate of Israel is the same as the fate of the Soviets in Afghanistan. He makes this possible." He slammed his hand on the pictures. "He trains these people like he trained you."

He stood glaring at Nasir for several seconds. Then he sat slowly and leaned on his elbows across the table, looking directly into Nasir's face. "But I don't think you're really one of them," he said quietly. "Not one of the butchers. You know that Islam does not sanction the killing of innocent women and children."

Nasir stared at the photos. Sometime during the tirade the mask had melted. He looked at the two boys. His eyes were brimming.

"Sami," Cooper said. "I think we understand each other. We are men of action, but we are not butchers. We would not willingly participate in something that would result in the death of innocent women and children. Millions of women and children."

Nasir raised his head. He looked at Cooper.

"Sami, the plan is to kill millions of Americans. Is that what you signed up to do? Do you want to multiply this," he gestured to the photos, "by hundreds of thousands?"

Nasir shook his head. A tear broke free and crept down his cheek. "The Americans will back down. They will take their tanks and planes and ships and leave. And there will be no need to follow through."

"Look at these pictures. Do you really think that they will bring a bomb here and leave it unexploded? Sami, you know the American government can't meet the demands of terrorists. We will never follow a policy of appeasement." He looked steadily in Nasir's eyes. "They will follow through, and millions of innocent people will die a death more horrible than the ones in these pictures."

Nasir looked down at the two boys, bloody in the beds. He whispered two words so low Cooper couldn't hear them.

"Two years ago, near my home in Pakistan, the government captured al-Qaeda fighters. They were taking them to a prison. Something happened, a fight, a gun battle. Many escaped to the mountains. The Pakistani soldiers went from house to house. I was not home, there was a mistake, my father threatened the soldiers. They . . . they . . ." He shook his head, looked down, then leaned his head into his hands. "My father, my wife, my children . . ."

He pushed the pictures away. Cooper scooped them up and handed them to Wilcox.

"Sami, I'm sorry to hear about your family. It is a pain that no one should have to endure. I can't even imagine how it must feel. If I were to lose Nikki and Stevie . . ." He allowed himself to consider the unthinkable, the agony Nasir had endured. He felt the moisture rising to his eyes. It was simply unimaginable.

"What did you do?" he asked.

Nasir looked up, seemed to see something in Cooper's eyes that comforted him.

"I returned to Afghanistan, to the Durante training camp, to Osama. I left everything behind. I joined my brothers and their fight. Osama sent me to America, to New York, told me to start a new life and wait for the word to come. When I saw the towers fall, when the time came and the thing was done, the blow was struck without me. I knew nothing. I thought he forgot me. But then a man visits me last year. He says I will carry something important, something that will change things forever. Something that will drive the Americans from our land

and our holy places. He said the Americans will run like frightened chickens to save the four cities."

Cooper jerked up in his chair. He heard Wilcox gasp behind him. "Four? Did you say four cities?"

Wilcox came to the table. "What?" He looked at Nasir. "How do you know it is four?"

"He said there would be four cities, one for each of the four holy months—Dhu al-Qada, Dhu al-Hijja, Muharram, and Rajab."

Cooper looked at Wilcox. "Four." He looked back at Nasir. "So, this man. What happened next?"

"I waited many months. Then one day he brings me a silver suitcase. I am to bring it to a certain house and stay there for one month. Then I can return home. I am not to open the suitcase." He shook his head. "Beans. I bring beans. I lose my family. I give my life to fight the infidel, and I am given beans. Beans will bring the Americans to their knees." He laughed bitterly and shook his head.

Chapter 32

Safe house, Zahedan, Iran.
Tuesday, 21 January 2003. 17:00.

Sami Nasir is in custody. Can any of you explain how this happened?"

The room was silent. Al-Huzayfi let the question hang for a full minute, careful to maintain an appearance of calm. He had heard rumors that his passion placed the mission at risk. He knew that the One realized this was nonsense, but the suggestion had been made that he temper the image they had developed together. That perhaps some members of the team might become concerned about his stability and attempt to introduce change that would truly destabilize the organization. He had adjusted accordingly, for the good of HuJI. His position was incidental; it was the mission that was important.

"This was not a random raid. They knew who he was, what he was." He turned to Makkee. "Has our inside contact turned?"

"No!" He shook his head forcefully. "We have no reason to believe that to be so."

"When was our last communication with the Stallion?"

"Last month."

"Before Paris. Before New York."

"Yes."

"I am not convinced."

"Sir, you know the background of the contact as well as I do. While some losses must be accepted to maintain cover, there has never been a reason to question the loyalty or commitment of the Stallion."

"Can you define 'acceptable losses'? We have already lost two-thirds of our nuclear arsenal, hundreds of passports, and now a sleeper in New York, a comrade of the One. Does this fit in the realm of acceptable losses?" Al-Huzayfi took a breath, pulled back the edge and volume that had crept into his voice. He resumed calmly. "If the Stallion has not turned, then how do you explain the fact that Nasir is in a New York jail right now?"

Aidid cleared his throat. "We have information that this Cooper is managing a large investigation, pooling his resources with the U.S. government. He is bypassing the channels they normally use."

Al-Huzayfi narrowed his eyes at Aidid, evaluating his tone. Was he pushing him, attempting to nudge him into an emotional outburst? This new one was still an unknown factor. But it was clear he was not the fool Khidamat was. He would bear watching. He turned to Makkee.

"Why did you not report this?"

Makkee looked wearily at Aidid and sighed, then to al-Huzayfi. "It is not confirmed. I do not distract this meeting with rumor and speculation. We have been watching Cooper. When we have something of substance, I will report it. A lot of suits have been in and out of his offices in California. Some we know. And he was in New York this weekend. But we have not directly connected him to the apprehension of Nasir."

"If your men had not blundered, Cooper would be dead and we would still have Nasir."

"Perhaps, but it is not confirmed that he is responsible at this time."

"I want a file on Cooper. Photos, addresses, family, everything. Today."

Makkee pulled a folder from a briefcase and placed it in front of al-Huzayfi. Al-Huzayfi was startled for a second, but then opened the folder and picked up a photo and smiled. "Mr. Cooper, prepare to die an infidel's death." He flipped through the papers. "Is there enough here to do what must be done without exposing more of our organization?"

"He has returned to L.A. It would be best for us if we take him in another location, preferably outside the U.S."

"I want him dead in two weeks whether he travels or not. It should appear that he has died of the random violence that infects America or due to his own excesses. Have you found a vulnerable spot in his organization that can be used?"

"There is a possibility, but it is very high risk. It could lead to questions we don't want asked. It could even compromise the Stallion."

"The Stallion doesn't appear to be helping us in any other way. Perhaps the best use of the Stallion is to remove this obstruction, even with high risk. I want no more delays or losses due to Cooper."

"As you say, it shall be done."

"Now for the recovery." He closed the folder and looked at Salim. "Have we activated the backup sleeper?"

"He has been briefed and has already deployed the device to an alternate location unknown to Nasir. I regret that we have lost a loyal man, but Last Straw will not be affected."

"And the devices?"

"All are in country. The last two are on schedule for positioning."

"So not all the news is bad. We make progress. And the Americans?"

Makkee opened another folder. "Two carrier groups are now in the Gulf. Three more are scheduled for deployment. Troops are approaching ninety thousand. Twice that expected to be deployed in two weeks."

"So they approach their doom. And we can strike before they do? In February?"

Makkee nodded slowly. "It can be done in February if necessary. March will be better for the optimum placement."

"We will lead them, take this preemptive warfare to their homeland. We will give them a deadline and let them embrace their fate."

He would bring this dream to fruition. And in the euphoria of the aftermath, he would find the snakes spreading the rumors about him and kill them personally.

Nidal Sidi al-Suri sat in his kitchen, alone and in the dark, reviewing the meeting. It was clear al-Huzayfi was no longer in control of the operation. They lost several men in Paris and now Nasir. Not to mention the eight bombs and the passports. The success of the mission was no longer certain. Although he preferred that Last Straw, as al-Huzayfi ridiculously called it, would conclude in triumph, al-Suri couldn't deny that failure might solve his problem. As head of training, he would not be held responsible. Salim and al-Huzayfi would bear the brunt of the failure.

This Cooper character could be useful after all. If he survived, al-Suri would continue to mention him at the meetings, pushing al-Huzayfi's hatred for the man to greater heights. He was certain that some ill-advised and impulsive reaction would result. A reaction that would further jeopardize al-Huzayfi's tenuous control of himself and the organization. A meltdown was inevitable. And the One would have a stable, trusted lieutenant available to step into the vacuum created by al-Huzayfi's self-destruction. A man proven through years of successful completion of covert operations and negotiations.

All that was required was to wait, occasionally stir the pot, and guard against any stray bullets. The light in the kitchen suddenly came on. His wife was startled to see him sitting at the table, smiling. She screamed. He stood to calm her.

"Everything is alright, my dear. Everything will be alright."

Hollywood, California.
Tuesday, 28 January 2003. 10:20.

Several hours until shooting began. Homework all done. Nothing to do but sit and think. It was not a good idea. Dad had dropped her off on the way to the Van Nuys airport. She knew he was staying in the country, but that didn't seem to make a difference. Eyes closed or open, the thoughts played themselves out like movie reels.

Nikki joggled the knob on the bathroom door for the fifth time. It was locked, just like the other four times. She put the toilet seat down and sat. She looked at her purse, which was sitting on the edge of the sink.

The pin was useless. She found that out during his trip to New York. *She* was gone, which shouldn't matter, but it did.

While *She* was around, Nikki could focus on the resentment that crowded out the demons. But with *Her* out of the country, Nikki found it hard to keep her anger alive. As it faded, the images slipped in to take its place.

She could see the outline of the razor blade through the purse, like she had X-ray vision. Then, against the backdrop of the designer bag, a movie played. The car, the guardrail, the fluttering scarf, the yawning blackness of the canyon . . .

Her arm jerked up by itself and snatched at the purse. It fell. She stared at the junk scattered across the floor like pieces from different puzzles. Nothing matched. Then she saw the edge of the blade, a triangle of gleaming metal poking from the mouth of the purse. It became a single tooth in the smile of the suicide bomber, his eyes crazy and deep like the yawning blackness of the canyon . . .

She fell to her knees and clawed at the face. A sharp slash of pain spiked through her eyes like the flash of a camera. She blinked and looked down. Blood oozed up from an inch-long slice in her index finger. She watched it, wet and glistening, until it broke free and dripped onto the white tile floor. She watched a second drop, then a third roll over the edge of her finger and hurtle to the floor. The pain faded and the fourth drop became a convertible plunging into the yawning blackness of the canyon . . .

She squeezed the cut between her thumb and middle finger, rolling it back and forth. The pain surged back up, drawing all attention to itself. The canyon receded, the bathroom receded, the studio receded, the world receded. It shrank down to a white dot in the center of a TV screen when the power is cut. A white slash tore across the blackness of the screen like the Milky Way in a desert night. As she rolled the cut between her fingers, the Milky Way undulated through heat shimmers.

She had no idea how long it had been. She began to see the bathroom again, as if she were opening her eyes, but she realized they had never been shut. She looked at her hand. Her fingers were slippery with smeared blood. The tile was spattered with dozens of drops, and blood was drizzled like a strawberry sauce on a dessert at Maitre D'.

With her other hand she tore off a wad of toilet paper and wiped up the blood. She flushed it and rinsed her hand in the sink. As she pushed her junk back into the purse, she came across the vial of alcohol, the one with the safety pin in it. She sat back down on the toilet, poured some alcohol onto a pad of toilet paper, and squeezed it against the cut. She closed her eyes and fireworks lit up the night sky.

When the first application of alcohol evaporated, she soaked the pad and squeezed again. Time must have passed, or maybe it just stood still. Then she was fishing a Band-Aid from her purse and wrapping her finger tightly, so that a steady undercurrent of pain pulsed from it like a radio beacon.

She felt a slight sense of euphoria, like she had done a double-espresso shot at Starbucks. She felt calm and confident. She checked her watch. Only half an hour until she was supposed to be on the set. She checked to make sure all traces of blood were gone from the bathroom and from herself. Next time the cut would be intentional, not accidental, and the location not as visible.

She looked at herself in the mirror, smiled, and unlocked the door.

Chapter 33

Elmhurst, Illinois.
Tuesday, 28 January 2003. 13:20.

The IRIG Gulfstream was diverted to O'Hare because of weather. Morse, the pilot, notified Cooper when they began descending from thirty-one thousand feet. He shoved papers into his briefcase and looked at the cloud cover as it rushed past. It would be a few minutes before he would be able to glimpse the city draped in winter gray. After a week of following developments from the IRIG headquarters, he was impatient to be on the ground and immersed in the activity of fieldwork. And he was very curious to get a look at this Christian army Perkins had recruited.

He thought back on the Monday briefing where Perkins explained the rapid progress over the weekend. The previous Thursday Perkins was complaining to his source for surveillance gear about the delays due to lack of field agents. When the source found out they were tracking suspected terrorist activity, he became agitated and began explaining a convoluted conspiracy theory about the Knights Templar and Galileo. That was when Cooper interrupted.

"Bernie? Bernie is our supplier for gadgets?"

Perkins stopped midsentence, his mouth open. He closed it then opened it again. "You know Bernie?"

"Boy, do I know Bernie. And how exactly is he helping?"

"It seems he is part of this international group of religious busybodies who do everything from rebuilding homes in Israel to providing local information related to the Middle East for a national newsletter."

"Global Adventures."

"Yeah," Perkins said. "So, he asked what kind of intel we needed and by that evening he had four dozen people on the street taking notes on the traffic in and out of mosques. Which is where we got this lead. Volunteers in their own cars, bikes, motorcycles, cell phones. Little old ladies, geeks, Boy Scouts. Unbelievable, really."

Claire stopped twirling her pencil and thumped it on the conference room table. "We're using amateurs and born-again wannabes on this investigation now? Does IRIG really want to go down this road?"

Cooper listened, nodding slowly. "Let's hear the lead."

"Yesterday afternoon a young Middle Eastern guy arrives at a Bridgeview mosque in a taxi dressed like he just came from an OPEC summit. Gets out with a suitcase and a large brief-case. Twenty minutes later the same guy comes out with the cases, but he looks like everybody else on the street. He gets into a car in the mosque parking lot with an older guy and they drive to an Oak Park apartment complex. After fifteen minutes inside the old guy comes out and drives off."

"Is he still there?" Perkins nodded. "Tell me about the apartment."

"Ground floor, no windows in adjacent buildings over-looking the entrance, which is in back, not facing the street."

Matt looked at Claire. "I'd say score one for the Christian army. After a week of being stalled, we have a lead worth flying out for."

"Onward Christian soldiers," Susan said. Cooper frowned at her. "It's a song. A hymn."

Of course Claire would be upset. George's army had scored where her undercover network and informants had failed. Cooper turned back to Perkins.

"Let's put the soldiers back on the mosques and start twenty-four-hour surveillance on this apartment. Set up a command post with the locals, the Feds, and our guys. We'll let the Feds get the court orders for taps and electronic monitoring. We need building plans, photos of all elevations, including aerial." He turned to Sarah. "When we're done here, get Dixon on the phone. I'll need his help to get the Nuclear Emergency Support Team on-site. I'll fly out tomorrow morning."

As they touched down Cooper smiled. It would be a long time before Claire got over this one. He carried his briefcase and luggage down the steps. The driver stowed them in the trunk of the Town Car and took I-294 to a command center based in Elmhurst. The building was owned by the Chicago Police Academy. It was ten miles from the safe house and twenty from downtown, well out of the blast zone if the wheels came off.

In the conference room he found the local FBI lead, Roger Morgan; the liaison for the Chicago police and county group, Lt. Elias Johanna; the NEST team commander, Dr. Bradley McKinney; and the Chicago IRIG lead, Mike Sullivan. A full city map dominated the far wall, next to a photomontage of the blocks surrounding the apartment complex. Cooper took the coffee Sully offered him and flipped through the surveillance log. Morgan walked to the map.

"They chose wisely. They're in this building, apartment 6 on the back corner. None of the surrounding properties have windows facing the back of the complex. Each apartment has a separate outside entrance. You can see the walkway from the parking lot, but not the door. There is a rear entrance on an interior walkway that's only visible from the corridor. The best we can do is watch the front walk and the points where the corridors open to the parking lot." He pointed to them on the map. "They've been covered since we took over from the Bible thumpers about twenty-four hours ago." His expression left no doubt about his thoughts on that subject. "Four Middle Eastern men have entered during that time; two have exited. At 0430 we sent a van through the parking lot. Heat-imaging showed two people inside."

McKinney coughed. "And no nuclear emissions beyond background levels."

"Is that conclusive?" Cooper asked.

"Not at all. If the container is properly shielded, we would have to open it to get a reading. It might be there; it might not." McKinney shrugged.

Cooper regarded him for a moment. "These devices, can they be detonated casually or does it take some effort?"

Johanna dropped his chair from its balance against the wall with a thump and leaned forward on his forearms. "You mean, if we hit the place, could they fry us?"

"Us and about 100,000 other folks. Worst-case scenario."

They all looked at McKinney. He winced. "It is possible to arm it to be detonated instantly with a remote device. It would be suicide, of course."

"Suicide bombers are not unheard of in this crowd," Morgan said.

McKinney nodded. "True."

Cooper shook his head. "The mission is bigger than simply detonating a nuclear device as soon as possible. It is targeted for a specific time in a specific type of location. Downtown, not Oak Park. If they arm it now, it could blow earlier than they want and in the wrong place. That would be a failure, or at least not their first choice." He walked to the picture of the apartment and studied it. "They have to balance the risk. Arm it now in case of capture and risk premature detonation in the wrong place or arm it at the target and risk capture with no detonation."

Johanna asked, "What do we know about this guy? We have a profile on him?"

Cooper shook his head, still facing the photo. "No, but it doesn't matter. He's just the courier. Somebody else is calling the shots. He's the one we have to figure."

"So, what do we know about that guy?"

Cooper turned to the table. "Nothing."

"Nothing?"

"There is very little data on Harkat-ul-Jihad al-Islami. We knew about two guys, but one was assassinated, probably by his own men or a rival gang. We know about Khalid al-Fadel, the finance guy behind it, but he's not running the show."

"So, you're saying we have to guess what might be in the mind of somebody we know nothing about, some Mr. X terrorist guy behind door number one, Ali bin Dover or whatever?"

Cooper looked Johanna in the eyes. "That's what I'm saying."

"And based on this guess, I'm going to risk my men and the lives of a couple hundred thousand citizens?"

"You catch on pretty quick," Morgan said.

Johanna stood up. "Just like a Feeb—shoot first, ask questions later. If you think I'm going to take that kind of risk based on a guess, you're crazy. I say we keep surveillance and take him down if he moves with something big enough to qualify."

"You're taking the risk either way," Morgan said.

"What is that supposed to mean?"

"If you don't hit the place, you're betting that he won't blow it there, either intentionally or accidentally. Inaction is a decision. But it's still nothing more than a guess."

Cooper stepped to the table. "If that briefcase is what we think it is, he's going to blow it. It's just a question of when and where. You want to sit outside and watch his car while he pushes the button?"

"Hard data," Johanna said. "We need hard data, not mushy guesses. I can't make decisions based on vague speculations."

"Not a problem," Morgan said. "You won't be making the decision, anyway."

Cooper interrupted Johanna's outburst. "Sully, I want to see the place and talk to some of the volunteers. I need a better sense of things before I make the call."

Sully nodded and pulled a cell phone from his pocket. As Cooper followed Sully to the garage he heard Johanna's voice booming down the hall. "Him? A civilian is making this decision? You're all crazy." He couldn't make out Morgan's reply.

Oak Park, Illinois.
Tuesday, 28 January 2003. 15:12.

In Sully's BMW, the steady drone of facts and opinion on the news station provided a background for Cooper's thoughts. As they turned onto Eisenhower Expressway, he considered the mind behind this scheme. Perhaps it was bin Laden himself, but Cooper suspected it was someone who either reported to or was associated with him. Ruthless and violent was a given, but also perceptive and calculating. Someone able to command the respect, or at least obedience, of other violent men and bend them to his will. A man who might walk on the edge of a cliff but knew exactly how far he could lean without falling. A man who wanted too much and was able to get it. Such a man would push those around him to their limits and beyond. He would expect precision. He would settle for nothing less than a perfect statement, maximum death, maximum destruction. He would not risk a premature detonation. It would look like a sloppy failure, and this man would not accept it.

Sully took the Harlem Avenue exit, went north half a mile, and turned right.

"That's it."

Cooper looked it over as Sully drove through the parking lot, around the back, and out the front. If the guys who wrote the al-Qaeda training manual had included pictures, this place would have been in the book. Nice cars in the lot, nice landscaping. People busy making payments on the Audi and the component home theater system with plasma display; people who had no idea who lived in the next apartment. He noted the operatives in place: in front the lady walking her dog, little puffs of breath coming from both their mouths; in back the cable TV van by the pedestal; on the east side the red-nosed jogger in bulky warm-ups and knit cap stretching before the run.

"It fits the profile."

Knowing Cooper's style, Sully pulled into the parking lot of the mini-market across the street—a diminutive grocery-convenience store with plenty of traffic and parked cars. A perfect observation point. He parked, turned off the car, but left the radio on the news station. Cooper listened to the talk show for awhile and allowed the substratum of conversation to drown out the traffic noises around the car. Then he gradually pushed it to the back of his mind and narrowed his focus on a single building across the street, then to a single apartment, then to a single window, then to a single pane in the window. Now the radio was like a curtain of noise that shielded him from other distractions. He cleared his mind of everything except the pane of glass. Then, very slowly he let the details of the case rise like flotsam from his subconscious, inspecting each as it bobbed to the surface, considering connections, discarding conclusions, accepting others. After half an hour of silence, he turned to Sully.

"How do you read it?"

Sully turned down the radio. "What?"

"Do we wait, or do we go in?"

"I give it at most two days. These guys aren't going to sit on this thing and hatch it. They're going to plant it somewhere and grow a mushroom."

"This is the place. We move in twenty-four hours if they don't move first. How about the taps?"

"Nothing of importance. We got the phone in the place and pay phones in a two-block radius."

"Have there been any gaps in surveillance since the case arrived?"

"Since the Feds picked it up, it's been constant at all angles. Before then the volunteers didn't have complete coverage."

"It's time to step it up. He's going to move the case if he hasn't done so already. He'll either take a taxi or, more likely, have a driver who doesn't know what the cargo is. We need a four-man team on the ground and a chopper."

Sully started the car and pulled out of the parking lot. He contacted the command center on a secure line and relayed the decision. He scheduled two-hour intervals for briefing in the conference room with a secure conference line for those in the field. Then he drove through River Forest as Cooper checked in with the IRIG war room to get briefings on the other locations.

As Cooper finished the last call, Sully circled by Concordia University and headed south to Denny's. He pulled up to the left of a maroon LTD old enough to vote. "Roff," he said.

Cooper looked out his window. Large blotches of gray primer covered the driver's door and front fender of the LTD. Mud-caked ice encrusted the wheel wells. The hood and trunk had a severe case of rain measles mixed with cat prints. A bulky silhouette moved behind the grimy window, and the door cracked open like the port of a space capsule after reentry. The squeal of dry hinges was audible over the news program. A set of fingers like sausages plopped over the top of the doorframe. Below the door a large suede desert boot, splayed open at the top, laces hanging down, scraped the asphalt. Using the door and the headrest of the driver's seat for support, Roff pushed himself upright and squinted at the sky as if it had insulted him.

He was wearing a green hunting cap squeezed onto his head. Large ears and black hair in need of a trim pushed the earflaps out like fledgling wings. A thick black moustache rested atop his lip. A red muffler wrapped his neck and hung down the front of a plaid flannel shirt. He edged out of the car and slammed the door, dusting potato chip crumbs from the pleats of capacious tweed trousers.

Cooper turned to Sully. "Roff?"

"He's the afternoon lead for the volunteers."

Sully got out of the car. Cooper shook his head, Claire's words echoing his own misgivings at recruiting amateurs, and religious ones at that. He joined the others at the back of the car. Roff was only five feet eight and packed into the flannel shirt like a wanton sausage. Cooper figured he weighed 250 if he weighed an ounce.

Sully gestured to Cooper. "Roff, this is my boss, Matt Cooper."

Roff pivoted. "Mr. Cooper, it is a great pleasure to meet you." He took Cooper's right hand in both of his own and squeezed like he was trying to stop a bleeding wound. "I want to take this moment to thank you personally for your commitment to America and our freedom. You are indeed a patriot and a citizen worthy of commendation."

Cooper looked to Sully, who smiled, and back to Roff, squinting as he tried to figure him out. Under the visor of the hunting cap Roff's eyes shone with intelligence, conviction, and sincerity. Cooper knew instantly that whatever else this man might be, he was as genuine as a silver certificate.

"Thanks for your help." He extracted his hand from the double-fisted grip with some difficulty. "I say we go try out the Grand Slam."

Chapter 34

Oak Park, Illinois.
Tuesday, 28 January 2003. 15:58.

The late-afternoon crowd was sparse. They got a booth in a corner well away from other diners, placed their order, and waited for the waitress to leave. Then Roff, his hunting cap still screwed onto his head, fixed his unnerving blue eyes on Cooper.

"On January 23 at 1300 hours I received a call from Bernie Whiteman regarding the need to monitor the city for possible terrorist activity. I organized a team of fifty volunteers. We assigned thirty-five for daylight and fifteen for night surveillance, according to work schedules and other responsibilities. We targeted locations of high Muslim activity, particularly mosques. As there are over fifty mosques in the greater Chicago area, we focused on known conservative or fundamentalist locations."

Cooper was startled by the succinct, direct style at such variance to Roff's previous comments. He seemed to be reciting from a written report.

"There were several items of interest over the weekend, but I will focus on the events that led to our current situation. On January 26, Myrtle Crepsbach was on duty at a mosque that has been outspoken in its support of Hamas, including raising

funds for the legal defense of a known terrorist. At 1420 hours
a young man of obvious Middle Eastern descent arrived via
taxi. He was wearing a black suit, white shirt, black tie, black
overcoat, and dark sunglasses. He removed a suitcase and a
large briefcase from the taxi, tipped the driver, and entered the
mosque via a side door.

"At 1440 hours the same gentleman emerged from the
mosque carrying the suitcase and briefcase. His appearance
was dramatically altered. He was wearing a heavy cable knit
sweater, muffler, jeans, and a wool cap. An older man, also
of Middle Eastern descent, dressed in a conservative suit and
overcoat, accompanied him. The older gentleman directed the
younger to a black Lincoln Town Car, license RB4983, where
they placed the cases. Myrtle followed them to the Oak Park
apartment complex you now have under surveillance. They arrived at 1512 hours, and both went inside with the cases. At
1527 hours the older gentleman emerged without the cases and
returned to the mosque. The younger man remained inside. On
January 27 at 1145 hours agents of one or more unnamed government agencies assumed surveillance of the subject and we
returned our resources to their previous schedules."

Roff stopped abruptly, took a sip of his coffee, and looked
at the IRIG men. Cooper smiled. Roff had delivered the entire
report without referring to notes or pausing to remember details. Volunteer or not, religious or not, he was more efficient
than many of the field agents for IRIG. Perhaps Perkins had
stumbled on something after all. But it wouldn't do for Claire
to meet Roff. Cooper would never hear the end of it.

"Nice report. Have you done this before?"

"No."

"Do you have a job?"

"I regret to divulge that I am practically unemployable. My
digestive system exists in a delicate balance with the outer world

and my inner landscape, a balance that can't always be maintained. I suffer from a particularly troublesome pyloric valve that closes up at the slightest discomfiting circumstance. I am forced to lie supine for hours on end. The agony can sometimes be relieved by ingesting Dr. Nutt and the occasional cheese dip."

"But you organized and successfully managed a large-scale surveillance operation at a moment's notice. You appear to have a photographic memory."

Roff nodded demurely. "I merely employ what meager gifts the Creator has bestowed upon me. You will find all the members of our little society have special abilities. We are the living stones that make up the temple, the many members of the body, each contributing to the welfare of the whole, as the apostle wrote."

"As you know, you have been an incredible help to our investigation. Surely we can do something for you."

Roff shook his head. "I understand that you have provided assistance to Mr. Roberts in obtaining funds and supplies for our work." Cooper nodded. "That is all the reward we desire."

"Well, thank you, then."

"Oh, no sir, thank you." Roff looked up and rubbed his hands together. "Ah, here it comes."

Cooper looked over his shoulder. The waitress was approaching with a plate full of hot dogs.

"It is indeed a shame," Roff sighed, "that Dr. Nutt is not available at this establishment."

Elmhurst, Illinois.
Tuesday, 28 January 2003. 19:35.

Cooper was hanging the last of his clothes in his room at the Marriott when the call came. Five more men were in apartment 6. The first arrived an hour after sunset, the rest over the next fifteen minutes. The agents tried to get a laser listening device in place, but no suitable point for positioning it was found. A large gathering seemed to indicate an attempt to place the device. Some would be used as decoys to defeat any possible surveillance. It was standard practice, so Cooper wasn't concerned that their team had been spotted.

Cooper contacted Sully on a secure channel on the radio and ordered an extra chopper, a team to place tracking devices on the cars, and more men on the scene to cover each suspect as he left. He also pointed out that a large operation was easy to detect, so the men on the ground shouldn't take any chances. They should fall back and ask for air backup rather than risk being made.

Then he ordered takeout from the restaurant and returned to the command center. He worked through his notes, taking regular updates from Sully. The men emerged around nine, all empty-handed. Three tracking devices had been put in place. The other two cars were too conspicuous to approach without some kind of diversion, which had been deemed inadvisable as it might raise suspicions. The ground teams focused on the two cars without tracking devices. All five cars drove to residences. The courier never left the apartment.

They now had surveillance running on six locations, targeted most heavily on apartment 6, the suspected location of the bomb. At midnight, Cooper returned to his hotel with instructions to be notified if anything happened.

Nothing happened.

Oak Park, Illinois.
Thursday, 30 January 2003. 04:08.

The apartment complex was eerily quiet three hours before sunrise. And very cold. The wind blew in from the lake, dropping the temperature below zero. Cooper shivered inside the armor that all the team members wore, his preferred Glock 23 with laser sight in his gloved hand. He had a .380 as backup, but doubted that he would need either. One guy inside, likely asleep. The entry team would have him subdued in seconds.

The decision was made at sundown, unanimous with the exception of Johanna, who just shook his head and muttered, "Hard data, hard data." All depended on total surprise, lightning execution, and disabling the occupants before they could trigger anything. They needed this guy alive. There were three other bombs to find.

The signal came. The entry team went in. Cooper was inside within five seconds. He saw beams from the laser sights and flashlights zigzagging across the walls as the teams stormed each room. He heard one "clear" after another as they worked down the hallway. Thirty seconds after the door was opened they were all standing in the kitchen.

"Light's off, no one home," Morgan said. He flipped on the light.

A map of Chicago was spread over the kitchen table. Papers with notes in Arabic lay on top of the map. Six teacups were on the counter with varying levels of cold tea in them. The anchor agents were still at the front and back doors.

"Check all the rooms again with the lights on," Morgan said. "And be careful. You don't want a trapped animal jumping out of a closet with a knife when you're not looking."

Cooper sat down at the table and looked at the map. A circle was drawn around downtown Chicago, from Division to Roosevelt and Lake Michigan to the Kennedy Expressway. Something like five square miles. It didn't tell him anything he didn't already know.

Morgan came back in. "The place is clean. No briefcase, no bad guy."

Cooper stood up. "When did we get the heat imaging?"

"An hour ago. There was a body in the first bedroom."

"Then he just evaporates. We have guys on every exit, but nobody saw him go out."

"You got it."

"But that's not the only mystery. Why now? What woke him up at 3:00 a.m.? It's like he knew we were coming."

"Maybe he just got lucky."

"Maybe. But I get suspicious when the bad guys get lucky."

"You think he had some help?"

Cooper looked across the kitchen at the phone on the wall. "How about the taps. Any calls?"

"None. But he could have a cell phone."

Cooper's phone vibrated. He snatched it from his hip. "Matt."

"What happened?"

It was Claire. Cooper's eyes narrowed. "Meaning?"

"I was following the status in the IRIG war room. They say we hit an empty house."

"Looks like it."

"I thought we had it locked down."

"We're working on it. You got any ideas?"

"Is this the work of your Christian Army?"

"Sully and the Feds took over three days ago. Our target has been here ever since. You know that."

"I don't like it."

"You think I do? We have plenty of questions. If you have some answers, let me know. Maybe you should be calling your informants instead of me. Bye."

Morgan raised an eyebrow. Cooper shook his head.

"Let's get NEST in here," Cooper said. "Maybe they can find something."

Eighteen hours later Cooper had some answers. NEST reported zero radiation, but the forensic team discovered a built-in bookcase that swung away from the wall to reveal a passage to apartment 7 on the opposite corner of the building with a front door facing the street. It was empty, although the apartment manager said it was rented to a Canadian couple with two children. When he tried to contact them, he came up blank. A conversation with Roff confirmed that a family had been seen entering and leaving apartment 7 on occasion, but they seemed to have vanished along with the suspect.

On the flight back to California, Cooper went over the raid again in his mind. Everybody on the case had been involved in the decision. Ten hours before they hit the apartment, not only did the command center in Chicago and the assault team know, but also everyone in the war room at IRIG headquarters. The guy was there at 3:00 a.m. He was gone by four. Something stank.

Cooper picked up the secure phone wired into the communications system on the Gulfstream. The call was answered on the second ring.

"Talk to me."

"Twink, it's Matt."

"I know that. Let me have it. I got about ten seconds before they find me." Cooper heard the sound of automatic gunfire over the phone.

"Who is it this time?"

"The Romanians. They're new, but they learn fast." Shouting, followed by two explosions. "That should hold them off."

"This might take more than ten seconds. Can't you pause it or something?"

"Matt, I can't pause people. They keep coming, no matter what I'm doing. Hey! Watch it! It's me, you idiot!" The automatic fire became frantic. Unintelligible words were muttered between the blasts, then a large explosion. "Great."

"Twink?"

"My own guy just blew me up. So, what have you got?"

"I need the full spread on this one. Claire Moquard."

"Spell that."

Cooper spelled it and gave him phone numbers and addresses.

"Full spread?" Twink asked. "How far back?"

"Let's take the bills back three months. No, make that six. From here, all numbers incoming and outgoing and full recording. Daily reports. Call me immediately if something unusual pops up."

"Got it."

Cooper hung up. If Claire was up to something, he would know within twenty-four hours.

Chapter 35

Van Nuys, California.
Friday, 7 February 2003. 10:49.

Cooper's frustration was increasing. Things had gone well at first. Four days after forming the task force they had their first tip and within the week the raid in New York and a talker with solid intel. The next week they had another suspect and another raid. But since then things had stalled. They came up empty in Chicago and, although the chatter remained steady, leads had dried up. A week passed with nothing solid to work on. It was maddening.

Grasping for something to drown out the chaos in his head, he reviewed the daily phone logs from Twink, ending with the new one that arrived this morning. As head of undercover ops, Claire had contacts and informants all over the world. Any one of them could be her link to al-Qaeda or HuJI. Twink's report noted the numbers she called frequently and the ones that were unique. Matt cross-referenced the overseas numbers against IRIG records. All were legit. He did the same for the other numbers.

When he saw the first report last Saturday, two numbers bothered him—numbers that were called frequently. A week later, they still bothered him. One was an equestrian center somewhere off Mulholland Drive near Topanga State Park. He didn't remember Claire mentioning an interest in horses. He made inquiries, discovered she regularly went riding and was one of their more accomplished clients. It had been a minor revelation, a seemingly harmless secret compartment of her life. But it was also an excellent place to meet a contact, riding in the hills alone.

The other troublesome number was the cell phone of one Karim Bactar, an Egyptian national. Cooper looked over the log of all recorded conversations between Claire and Bactar—arrangements for dates, cutesy sweet-talk that Twink summarized on the report with obvious disgust. Cooper didn't see anything new, but he still didn't like it. He grabbed his sweater and briefcase and walked to the outer office.

"Sarah, I have some errands. I'm available via cell if anything comes up."

Her look told him she could feel the tension emanating from his office all morning. "It'll work out, Mr. C."

He squeezed a smile out. "Of course it will. I just need some distance. But if anything breaks, I need to know immediately."

She nodded. "And you should pick up something nice for Stevie while you're out. You're probably driving her crazy too."

His smile was genuine now. Sarah was always watching out for him, protecting him from himself in his dealings with women. "'Too'?"

She swatted at him with the papers she was filing. "Just get out of here, Mr. C."

The sun had warmed the air enough. He put the top down and pointed the nose of the Jaguar at Woodland Hills and the equestrian center. Once on the road he pushed a button on the steering wheel, said "Twink," and waited for the call to be connected.

After several rings a voice mumbled over the stereo.

"Matt, are you crazy?"

"Why is your phone on?"

There was a pause, the sound of things being knocked around. "It's not even noon, yet, man."

"I was going to leave a voice mail."

"Oh, that's a good idea. I'll hang up."

"Twink, you're already awake. I have a quick question."

"What makes you think I'm awake?"

"The phone calls to Karim Bactar."

"I don't know anybody named Karen Packard."

"No, Twink. The phone calls between Claire and Karim. You wrote summaries of the tapes."

"Oh. Those phone calls. Thanks a lot for bringing that up. I haven't even had breakfast, man."

"So you remember what I'm talking about?"

"It was disgusting. Worse than a Disney teen-romance movie."

"Could it have been code?"

There was silence.

"Twink, you still awake?"

"Yeah, I'm thinking, man. Code. I don't think so. Did you see the duration of those calls? Code is usually succinct. A few special phrases with a certain meaning placed in a context where they seem innocent. This stuff goes on forever. Besides, they see each other in person plenty. Three or four nights last week. She could just tell him in person, not in code over the phone."

"OK. Thanks for the info. Go back to sleep."

"Fat chance."

He found the stables backed up against the hills of Topanga Park. He wandered around, looking at the corral and riding circle and the stables until a woman noticed him. She was dressed like a ranch hand from a Doris Day movie.

"What can I do for you?" Cooper wasn't fooled by the smile. She kept a solid stance and a strong grip on the curry brush.

"My daughter's birthday is coming up, and she's been talking about riding lessons. Do you do that sort of thing?"

"Not on purpose. We provide stables, break-in services, practice space for competition, that kind of thing."

Cooper looked past her to the stables. "I think a friend of my sister-in-law comes here. That's where I heard the name." The woman just looked at him. "I think her name is Claire something. Dark hair." No response. "Since I'm here, mind if I look around?"

"This is a working stable, not a tourist attraction."

"Of course. I was just thinking the next time I see Claire, I'd have something to talk about." He stood there. She stood there. "Something to tell my daughter, anyway."

She sighed and shrugged. "Look around. Don't touch anything." She turned to go, stopped, and turned back. "And if you get bit or kicked, I'm not paying a red cent."

"Got it."

He put his hands in his pockets and strolled into the gloom of the stables, enveloped in the aroma of manure, straw, and horse. After a minute he noticed he had a shadow. A Hispanic guy in his twenties watched him from a dozen yards away, moving with him as he walked through, peering into the stalls.

After a few stabs at conversation, Cooper found a topic of interest–the women of all ages drawn to horses. The young man spoke in heavily accented English, going through the roster of attractive female clients. By guiding the conversation Cooper learned that Claire rode alone, usually for an hour or less. No other clients had visits that consistently coincided with hers. Cooper suggested that she might be meeting a lover out in the hills, but the man rejected the notion as ridiculous. He was impressed with her appearance, but also with her apparent dedication to riding.

Cooper waved at the woman as he left. She ignored him. It didn't seem like Claire was using the riding club as a front for meeting her contact, but he wouldn't know for sure without following her on a ride, something he wouldn't be doing any time soon.

Van Nuys, California.
Friday, 14 February 2003. 09:23.

The status meeting degenerated into a freewheeling brainstorming session. Cooper watched in silence, wishing for some solid bit of information he could work with. On Monday, Montreal had appeared in the chatter. Throughout the week, references to Montreal increased, sparking a debate at the IRIG office. Claire argued that the Chicago raid came up empty because the suspect was scouting for a location, not planting a device. The device was on the way to Montreal or already there. She argued they should focus on Montreal and intercept it before it crossed the border.

Cooper argued that all devices were almost certainly in country by now and that the Montreal chatter was unrelated to the nukes. Dixon argued both sides, playing devil's advocate against whoever seemed to have the most compelling position at the time.

Cooper's position was as much wishful thinking as it was conviction. Working with the FBI, CIA, and Homeland Security was enough trouble. He didn't relish adding the Canadian authorities to the mix. The Montreal IRIG office was working all angles from likelies to friendlies, but nothing surfaced beyond the chatter.

As he listened to the debate, Cooper had the uneasy sense that things were spiraling out of his control. In the absence of real data, the theories and suggestions became increasingly absurd. He needed an objective view, input from outside the self-referential perspective the case had assumed. He jotted a name on his notepad, wrestled the meeting to a messy and inconclusive close, and returned to his office.

Five minutes later he was speaking to Patrick Guenon, Royal Mounted Police agent assigned to Interpol in Montreal. They spent a few minutes catching up on the years since they met in Paris where Guenon worked with Interpol.

Guenon's specialty was drugs. As al-Qaeda developed the drug trade to finance terrorism, Guenon had developed an extensive network in Europe to track the movement of men, money, and merchandise. The IRIG office in Paris benefited from the fruits of his network, even after he finally obtained a transfer to his native Montreal where he duplicated his success in Canada. The IRIG Canadian offices focused more on corporate security and travel. As a result, the men rarely talked since Guenon's move.

Cooper steered the conversation to his current problem, describing the threat without mentioning the nuclear aspects. Before Cooper asked, Guenon offered to see what he could pull from his informants. The call ended with a standing dinner date should they ever find themselves in the same city. Cooper felt a slight sense of relief.

Van Nuys, California.
Monday, 24 February 2003. 22:10.

As soon as they were clear of the airport, Cooper asked Kelly to start the coffee when they began the descent. The he reclined his seat in the IRIG Gulfstream, hoping for at least three hours of rest on the five-hour flight to Montreal. As Cooper had hoped, Guenon's network was efficient. In less than a week he had verified that there was a heightened sense of expectation and dread in the Muslim community. Informants whispered that the word on the street was something big was going to happen. Opinions were varied and vague about what might happen, but they all agreed that it would be tragic.

As the week progressed the IRIG network singled out some suspects and a safe house. Cooper allowed Claire to convert him to her viewpoint without revealing his alternate source of information. In Friday's status meeting with the task force, he capitulated and agreed to fly out Monday for a Tuesday morning raid. He was confident he could tie up any loose ends before the weekend and the promised ski trip to Vail, where Stevie would join them straight from Morocco.

As the jet reached cruising altitude, a call startled him out of his slow descent into sleep. Increased activity at the safe house indicated that the time frame for the raid should be moved up. Cooper agreed that the raid should happen before he landed. With some difficulty he finally drifted into a fitful sleep, dreaming of his reunion with Stevie.

Montreal, Quebec, Canada.
Tuesday, 25 February 2003. 06:10.

Kelly woke him on the approach to Montreal-Trudeau. A few splashes of cold water helped to clear his mind as they taxied to the Starlink Aviation hanger where Guenon had a Benz with heavily tinted windows running.

Guenon's greeting was subdued. On the half-hour drive to the safe house on Toupin Boulevard, he briefed Cooper. They had one suspect in custody, apprehended in the process of destroying documents. They recovered maps of Washington, D.C.; New York; and Chicago. The man in custody didn't respond to direct questions, instead answering with long political and religious monologues in a style reminiscent of bin Laden videos. He announced that he expected to be killed, but that Allah would guarantee their success and reward him in the next life.

It was not a story designed to increase Cooper's satisfaction with the progress of the case. Another dead end, but this time with a taunting flunky to twist the knife of failure in his gut. An increasing sense of gloom settled over him as they approached the safe house. They parked across the street from the front door just after 7:00 a.m. Guenon got out, but Cooper looked at the house without moving. It was on a corner at the end of a set of row houses—narrow three-story buildings lined up like dominoes. The sight of it inexplicably filled him with dread.

He watched Guenon start across the street and then look back at him. With a conscious effort Cooper pushed the door open and climbed out of the car. He looked at the agent across the street on the front steps, then at the SWAT team loading a double-parked van around the corner. The site seemed to be secured, but the sense of dread increased. Cooper suddenly became alarmed, conscious of an unseen threat. He scanned the street corners and doorways. Nothing. The sense of danger increased. He responded by dropping to one knee on the side of the car. As he did so, fragments of pavement exploded a few feet in front of him, accompanied by the twang of a ricocheting bullet. A second bullet slammed into the fender of the armored Mercedes as the agent on the front steps raised an M-16 and fired at a third-story window in the house behind Cooper. Guenon dove for cover next to Cooper behind the car.

The SWAT team responded immediately. The window took hundreds of rounds. The four men hit the front door with a staggered entry while two circled to the back. Cooper stayed next to Guenon, listening as the SWAT team cleared each room and floor on their way to the top. In less than a minute an agent called out from the window. Cooper and Guenon stood up. The agent leaned out the window, avoiding the shards of glass jutting from the frame. He held a thumb up then drew his hand across his throat to indicate the shooter was dead.

Cooper looked at Guenon. "Is there anything in there I need to see?" He nodded to the safe house.

"You're bleeding."

"What?"

Guenon pointed. Cooper raised his hand to his ear. It came back red and wet. Now that he saw the blood, the pain registered. Guenon wiped his neck and gently daubed at his ear with a handkerchief and offered it to Cooper. He took it and held it to his ear.

"Looks like it took a small bite from the edge," Guenon said. "It should stop bleeding soon if you keep pressure on it."

"You get the maps. I'm going to get a look at the sniper."

Cooper hollered to the SWAT team that he was coming in and raced up the stairs to the third floor, past rooms that looked like set pieces from the 1940s. The dead man was a Caucasian with short black hair, dressed in brown and black. He wouldn't stand out in a crowd.

The agent pointed out a briefcase customized to accommodate a disassembled rifle. Taped to the lid was a photograph of

Cooper taken with a telephoto lens from a distance. He looked at it closely. The entrance of a building was visible in the background. He could just make out the corner of a logo. It was a picture of him outside the IRIG offices in Van Nuys.

Cooper felt a wave of nausea and recognized it as the effect of adrenaline with nowhere to go. He took several deep breaths and looked around the room. Three members of the SWAT team were in the room. They were all staring at the photo. Almost in unison they looked at him. The lead agent looked away uncomfortably when Cooper met his gaze. Cooper recognized the look—pity mixed with reluctance to empathize too closely with the marked man. To acknowledge Cooper's vulnerability was to be forced to admit his own mortality. And once that happened, how could he do what must be done the next time? For his own survival he must maintain the illusion of invincibility, at least in his own mind. The others also looked away awkwardly. Cooper walked from the room without speaking.

Guenon had the car running. They sped to the airport. Cooper shuffled through the maps with his left hand. They were like the map recovered in Chicago. A large section of downtown was circled on each. He set them aside. Guenon glanced over at him.

"So, did you get a good look at him?"

"Yeah. He looked a lot like you, only not so ugly."

Guenon chuckled.

"Patrick, who knew about this raid? On your side, I mean."

Guenon drove in silence for a minute. "My department, the SWAT team, the communications group. Just a few groups, but a lot of people between them all. And you?"

"Same on my end, only worse."

Cooper thought for awhile. He didn't like what he thought about.

"You were out in the open, in the middle of the street. He had a clear shot at you," Cooper said.

"Yes, it is true."

Chapter 36

Montreal, Quebec, Canada.
Tuesday, 25 February 2003. 08:22.

After Kelly fussed over his ear, applied first aid, and brought him a clean shirt, she offered him his typical healthy California menu, an avocado and spinach salad with seared ahi and fresh fruit. He decided to take his life into his hands again and opted for a New York strip, rare, with fresh horseradish.

Then he looked out the window and considered his plight. Ever since New York the terrorists were one step ahead of him. And then, suddenly Montreal pops up on the chatter. A safe house with nothing of importance in it and a man with a rifle across the street. A man with his picture. The Montreal chatter was obviously bait to lure him into the sights of an assassin. There was no longer any doubt that he was targeted, not the investigation.

He recalled that as soon as Montreal popped up, Claire insisted they pick it up and run with it. It was time to learn more about Claire and her new friend, Bactar. However, given Claire's propensity for perusing IRIG servers, it was clear it must be a back-channel inquiry. Although it was 6:00

a.m. in California, he didn't hesitate to pick up the phone. There were still people in L.A. who owed him favors.

Joe answered as if he had been waiting by the phone for his call. Cooper set a noon meeting at the farmers market on Los Feliz.

He took his time with the steak, savoring each chunk, and finished up with a raspberry sorbet. He checked his watch and signaled Kelly for some coffee as he called the IRIG HR department, the group that handled classified employment background checks. He asked for a complete check on Karim Bactar, rush priority, back channel, which meant it was for Cooper's eyes only and came to him on his secure e-mail.

They touched down in Van Nuys at 10:00 a.m., where Alex was waiting with the car. A few minutes later Cooper walked past Sarah into his office. She followed him.

"I thought you would be out the rest of the week." She stepped closer. "What happened to your ear?"

"We came up empty. But I was thinking on the flight back. Susan's been bugging me about getting the annual evaluations done. They're supposed to be finished before the end of the quarter, and it's almost March." He sat down behind his desk. "I'll need the complete personnel files for all the directors. I'd like to get started before lunch."

"And the ear?"

"Cut myself shaving."

"Since when do you shave your ears?"

"Uh . . . full moon?"

Sarah opened her mouth then evidently changed her mind. She closed her mouth and shook her head.

"Sure, Mr. C." She walked out the door as Dixon walked in.

"Coop, how many lives do you have left? You're probably working on your third cat."

"Close the door and hold your voice down."

Dixon closed the door, walked to the desk, and leaned over, squinting at Cooper's ear. "Doesn't look like much. Must have been a budget sniper."

"I knew you would take it hard. If it makes you feel any better, he caught me while I was ducking. My left ear was about at the place where my heart was a fraction of a second earlier."

Dixon smiled. "It restores my faith in the bad guys. I was starting to worry that they were slipping." The smile faded and he leaned forward, elbows on knees. "Matt, this is the second attempt in two months. The move from drive-by to sniper means they're getting serious. It's time for you to pull back from the field and focus on managing from here. The investigation can't afford to lose you."

Cooper smiled. He didn't remember the last time Dixon had used his first name. "The investigation can't afford to lose me?"

"OK. I'd hate to lose you too. And I'm sure Stevie and Nikki have similar feelings on the subject."

"There's no need to worry them with it."

"You go home with a chunk missing from your ear and you think they won't notice? Coop, they're women. They'll notice if one hair in your eyebrow is out of place."

"Pulling out of the field is not protection from an assassination attempt. They can hit me walking into the front door of IRIG as easily as they can in Montreal."

"But you don't use the front door."

"The point is that I'm equally vulnerable whether I manage the case from here or I get my hands dirty in the target cities. We don't gain anything by restricting my movements, and we lose a lot. I can't move this thing forward by holing up in the war room and listening to conference calls. I don't work that way. I have to be on the ground, talking to the field agents and suspects, walking through the safe houses. It's how I work. You know that."

Dixon dropped back in his chair. "Yeah, I know that. I'm just getting nervous. Third time pays for all, and I think you've about exhausted your budget of extra lives."

They sat in silence. Dixon stared out the picture window over Van Nuys. Cooper studied him. It would be nice to get his perspective on the leak, but a sense of caution held his tongue. Claire was his best bet, but the leak could be anywhere. Best to keep the mole hunt completely in the back channel.

Dixon sighed and repositioned himself in the chair. "But we still have a problem. Somebody's been talking out of school. And it seems you're their favorite subject."

"He had my picture, Will. The sniper had a photo of me in his briefcase."

"Who knew you were going to Montreal?"

"Practically everyone, if you think about it. There are at least half a dozen agencies and organizations involved in this thing, not counting the Canadian groups that got pulled in once we crossed the border."

The intercom buzzed and Sarah's voice said, "Mr. C, I have those files."

Cooper leaned forward and pushed the button. "Thanks, Sarah. I'll pick them up in a bit." He leaned back in his chair and looked at Dixon. "You, for example. How many people in your group knew about it?"

Dixon looked at the corner of the room as he did some calculations. "I'd say at least a dozen, from field agents up to my boss. And since we crossed the border, maybe Watson's boss. Shoot, maybe even the president."

"And we all know what a chatterbox he is," Cooper said.

"You have a good point, though. In the interest of inter-agency cooperation, there are dozens of people in the loop on this operation. If I can't keep you out of the field, let's at least agree to tighten up communications to a need-to-know level. It might slow us down, but it should increase our security. And your schedule or location will not be disclosed unless abso-lutely necessary. You should use your cell phone for all incom-ing and outgoing calls to make it more difficult for anyone to know your location through low-tech means."

"Good ideas. Can you get the ball rolling? I have to stop by the doctor's office for a tetanus shot. Never know where those bullets have been."

After Dixon left, Cooper retrieved the files from Sarah, cop-ied Claire's photo, addresses, and phone numbers, placed them in an envelope with the little info he had about Bactar, and then locked the files in his filing cabinet.

At noon, Cooper walked through the aisles of the farmers market, past booths of produce from the valley, to a cantina with tables scattered under a canopy. Joe sat alone at a table near the trailer, putting away a plate of huevos rancheros. He had a fork in one hand, a bottle of hot sauce in the other. He al-ternated between the two. Cooper dragged a plastic chair back from the table and dropped into it.

Joe looked up and smiled. He wore his hair cropped close to his head, a lime green madras shirt, and black slacks. He was built like a linebacker for the Raiders. As an enforcer for Nick Licata, he had taken out his share of runners. Although he had left the Mafia long ago, he still knew people who knew people. He could get close enough to Bactar to know what flavor of gum he chewed.

"You need a plate of these." Joe waved a fork over his plate.

He leaned back and called over his shoulder to the trailer. "Estelle, bring Matt a plate."

Cooper shook his head. "I can't stay long enough to eat, but I will take a cup of coffee."

Joe hollered the order back to Estelle and turned to Cooper. "So, what is the need, my friend?"

"I need to know what these two do. Where they go, who they talk to. Twenty-four seven." He pushed an envelope across the table. "She's a professional. She'll pick up an ordinary tail with her eyes closed. Don't know about him, but take no chances. He might be as well."

Joe nodded and took another bite of eggs. Estelle set a cardboard cup in front of Cooper without comment and disappeared into the trailer.

"I'd like a daily report, 7:00 a.m., on my cell."

Joe nodded again. Cooper sipped the coffee. It was bitter and blistering hot. He set the cup on the table.

"I'll owe you for this one."

Joe pulled a cloth napkin from his lap and wiped his face. "My friend, do not even mention it. I do this for you, but I will still owe you."

Cooper stood and held out his hand. Joe stood, took the hand with his right and leaned toward Cooper, throwing his left arm around him and hugging him. Cooper walked back through the market to his car, smiling at the vagaries of fate that put an ex-Mafia enforcer and a detective on the same page.

———

Just before 5:00 p.m. a secure e-mail arrived in Cooper's inbox, announced by a red circle with *MCS* in the center on his monitor. It was the background report on Bactar. He was a thirty-five-year-old legal resident from Egypt, in the U.S. since 1995. He had moved through several start-ups in Silicon Valley, working his way up from software systems design to systems architect to director before taking a position as chief technical officer for an L.A. company that provided embedded operating systems and control software for aerospace applications, both military and civilian. He was enthusiastically single, moving through the Southern California club scene with the grace of a predator in its natural habitat. He had no criminal record, not even a parking ticket, and he had a 780 credit score with no visible financial problems.

Cooper recognized many of the haunts that Bactar liked to frequent, the places he and Lola practically lived before Nikki arrived. Places like the Buffalo Club on Olympic, the Firefly on Ventura in Studio City, and the Sky Bar on Hollywood. Bactar didn't appear to be dangerous, at least not to Cooper. Given his proclivities, he might be dangerous to Claire's emotional health, but she could give as good as she got in that arena.

Outside Rabat, Morocco.
Wednesday, 26 February 2003. 05:26.

Stevie sat in the dark, cross-legged in the camp chair, enveloped in a blanket. Paula would be here soon. For the final time they would watch the dawn together. She was struggling with a confusion of thoughts and feelings. Before leaving her trailer, she had looked in the mirror, examining her face for signs of the change. Nothing. The new Stevie looked just like the old

Stevie. Matt would meet her in the Denver airport in two days and never know the difference.

She pulled the blanket closer, suddenly uncertain at the thought of meeting Matt. Her perspective had changed. Would it change their relationship? Or would the momentum of the relationship change her perspective? Maybe after a few weeks in California she would morph back to the same old Stevie. Or maybe after just a few days.

Had she really changed that much? Sometimes she felt radically different; other times she didn't feel different at all. Then she thought back to the first day of the year and knew she was changed. *Beloved.* Whenever she listened, she could hear it reverberate into the empty places, the places that had been hollowed out by the losses in her life. The places that had never been filled, not by career or awards or money or even Matt. Until New Year's Day. She realized with relief that if she ever doubted, all she need do was ask the question, *What do you see when you look at me?* Always the same incredible and irresistible response.

It was that response that drove her back to their predawn meetings every day, where she sat and listened as Paula read echoes of her own desperate cries in the words of the shepherd-king and the one answer to them all. As the certainty of the answer soaked into her soul, Stevie found herself wanting to give something back. She wanted to change, to make herself pleasing to the one who loved her so relentlessly.

And she found that Paula was right. It wasn't easy to gaze into the mirror and see the truth about herself. How could he love what she saw? And how difficult it was to change those unlovely ways. But as relentless as he was in his pursuit of her, she resolved to be that relentless in her pursuit of becoming pleasing to him.

An approaching lantern roused her from her reverie. She stirred and heard a gasp.

"Oh, honey! You startled me. I almost dropped the lantern." Paula hung it on the hook in the center of the canopy. "What are you doing sitting out here in the dark? Aren't you frozen?"

Stevie unfolded out of the camp chair and groaned. "I guess I am."

Paula watched her. "How long have you been out here?"

"I don't know. Awhile."

"Couldn't sleep?" Stevie shook her head. "Are you worried about going back?" Stevie shrugged. "That's OK, honey. You've been through some big changes in the past few weeks, but it's all happened in the desert. Going back to the old life can be a challenge."

"It's been hard, but I've made some changes I like. But what happens when I get back? Can I keep the old reactions from coming back?"

"You can't do it by yourself. No such thing as a Lone Ranger Christian. You need a support group."

"Like a twelve-step program?"

Paula's machine-gun laugh blasted the sun over the horizon. As the first rays of dawn flashed into the canopy, she sat down in the other camp chair. "Sort of like that. It's called a church."

Stevie shook her head. "I don't think I'm ready to go to a church. Maybe I'm still a little prejudiced, but I think going into a church would give me the creeps. All those people having expectations and looking down on you."

Paula laughed again. "You've been going to the wrong churches then. But you can take it slowly, one step at a time. First try out a small group."

"A small group of what?"

"Other believers. They usually meet one night a week in someone's home. We can find one close to the studios or close to home or wherever is convenient. "

"Define small."

"A half-dozen people or so. Other people a lot like you—being real, no expectations."

Stevie watched the sunrise. Maybe she would try it.

Malibu, California.
Wednesday, 26 February 2003. 07:00.

At precisely 7:00 a.m. Cooper's cell phone rang as he sat in the corner at Starbucks. It was Joe.

"We picked up Claire when she left work. She didn't go home. She went to 2024 Coldwater Canyon just inside the Beverly Hills city limits. This place is owned by Karim Bactar, who bought the house two years ago. She arrived at the residence at 6:34 p.m. and was inside until 9:20 p.m. when she left with Bactar in a silver Porsche Carrera belonging to Bactar. They were dressed for the clubs. They went to dinner at the Buffalo Club. At 11:50 p.m. they arrived at the Sky Bar and remained there until 3:00 a.m. I sent some guys inside. Their conversation was inconsequential.

"They were very friendly. The staff of the Sky Bar has seen Bactar there often, never the same woman two nights in a row, but all are hot in the estimation of the bouncer. We followed them to Bactar's house. Claire left at 6:45 a.m. dressed for work and appears to be en route to IRIG."

Cooper said, "Acknowledge. Continue the project," and hung up the phone. Like the riding club, the bar scene in itself was not a threat, but it could offer protective cover for clandestine meetings. Claire was still at the top of the list.

At the office he opened the secure e-mail first. It contained additional information on Bactar from national and overseas sources, including Interpol. No known connections to criminal or terrorist organizations. The deeper they dug, the more Bactar appeared to be just what he seemed—a playboy working his way through the trendy female population.

Chapter 37

Stevie walked into the den with a mug of hot chocolate. Will sat in an armchair with his stockinged feet on the huge misshapen slab of polished pine he called his coffee table and swirled cognac in a glass. Matt was sprawled at one end of the overstuffed couch that had a view of Eagle's Nest during the day. Now only the snow-laden branches of a few fir trees were visible and the edge of the light spilling out the window. She took the other end of the couch, leaning against the arm, and tucked her feet under her. She cradled the mug, took a sip, and looked at Will.

"Will, after what happened in Montreal, don't you think it's time for Matt to back off?"

"Even if I wanted to pull him off this thing, you think I could?" Will shook his head. "Stevie, if you succeed in stopping Coop from doing something he wants to do, I'll hire you immediately."

Matt snorted and took another sip of Kona coffee.

Stevie frowned. She had noticed his ear in the Denver airport on the walk from the commercial flight to the IRIG jet.

She failed to contain her initial outburst when she heard the story. But then she remembered what God had told her in Morocco. Matt was not her shepherd. And she remembered what Paula had told her. She couldn't change Matt; only Matt, or maybe only God, could do that. So she shut up, but it didn't seem right. She argued silently with God the entire flight from Denver to Eagle airport. She could tell Matt was disappointed and frustrated at the quiet treatment, but it took all her strength to keep from blurting out a litany of reasons why he should back off the case.

On the drive from the airport to the cabin, she tried to distract herself by telling Matt about the Morocco trip, but after awhile it seemed pointless, and she fell silent. Then she saw Nikki and her friends in the cabin and knew she had to speak her mind. Matt may not be her shepherd, but he certainly was responsible to provide a home for his daughter and not even God could argue against that one. She took a shower and warned God about what she was going to do. She hoped to get Will on her side and make Matt see sense. His response wasn't helpful.

She glanced at the girls splayed around the roaring fire at the other end of the room, running their fingers along maps of the slopes and arguing over which to try first in the morning. She lowered her voice.

"But Will, this is the second time he's been targeted. And this time there's no question. They were going for him. And if he hadn't ducked on a hunch, they would have succeeded. You can't tell me that you don't think he needs to back off."

"Nope. I agree with you. He should stick to the office and stay away from windows. I'm just saying my opinion is irrelevant. Coop's going to do what he decides to do." He took a sip of cognac. "But I have to admit, as long as he's on the case, I'm not complaining. We're making progress. Not fast enough, though."

"What is so important that it's worth Matt's life? He won't tell me anything."

"Of course not. He may be stubborn, but he's not stupid."

Matt snorted again. Then he was scrambling for the remote. He pointed it at the sixty-inch projection TV at the end of the room opposite the fireplace and turned off the mute. Stevie turned to see what had caught his interest.

". . . the splinter al-Qaeda group that six weeks ago demanded the U.S. get out of the Middle East or suffer unspecified violence. Today on Aljazeera TV, Harkat-ul-Jihad al-Islami demanded that the U.S. pull all troops out of the Middle East by March 15 or suffer direct attacks on U.S. cities. The statement said that the attack on September 11, 2001, was a small payment on a debt of blood the U.S. owes the Muslim world. They claim U.S. sanctions and military actions have caused the death of four million Muslims and if the U.S. does not in good faith begin withdrawal of all forces by March 15, they will collect the balance of the debt in a single day. The U.S. Homeland Security reports it takes all threats seriously but has not raised the alert status as a result of the statement."

The talking head moved on to a story about the buildup of troops in the Middle East, and Matt muted the TV. He glanced back at the girls. Stevie followed his gaze. They were still huddled around the maps, giggling and ignoring the adults. She looked back at Matt and Will and noted the glance that passed between them.

"That has something to do with it, doesn't it?" They looked uncomfortably around the room, avoiding her eyes and each other's. "Hey, I may be stubborn, but I'm not stupid."

Will looked at her and smiled. "No wonder you make such a good pair. It's like a matched set." His face got serious. "Stevie, you can guess all you want, but you know we can't talk about this."

She stared back and forth between them. Of course they couldn't discuss details of a secret investigation, but Matt's life was in danger. There had to be some way to discuss it, to make sense of it. She pointed back at the TV.

"She said four million in a single day. They took out two one-hundred-story office buildings and only killed three thousand." Stevie did the math. "How can they take out over five hundred one-hundred-story office buildings in a single day?" She looked at Matt, willing him to answer. "They can't do that with conventional weapons, can they?" She saw his eyebrows creep up slightly. She turned to Will. "Are you saying they have nuclear weapons?"

It suddenly felt quiet. She turned and looked past Matt. The girls had stopped talking and were looking over their shoulders at her. She must have raised her voice without realizing it.

She flashed a big smile at them. "So, have you decided which slopes to try tomorrow? I could show you which one I wrecked my knee on."

Nikki rolled her eyes and turned back to the maps without comment. The other girls followed her lead. Stevie turned back to the men and lowered her voice.

"They can't have nuclear weapons. Where would they get them?"

After a silence, Will said, "Stevie, we can't answer your questions. You're just torturing yourself."

"At least answer one question. Could they kill four million people in one day with conventional weapons?"

Matt shook his head. "It would be almost impossible."

"So . . ." She fell silent and stared out the window into the blackness. Not this. She wasn't ready for this. *Though I walk through the valley of the shadow of death*, she thought. *Help me. Be my shepherd.* "So . . ." She looked over at the girls, at

Nikki. *Thou art with me.* Tears welled up, blurring her vision. "So," she whispered, "that's what's so important."

How could she fight the needs of four million people? It wasn't fair. Why couldn't somebody else save them? *I will fear no evil. No evil.* Couldn't somebody else be the sacrificial lamb? Why Matt? *The Lord is my shepherd. Matt is not my shepherd.* She kept reciting the words in her mind, willing herself to believe it and for her feelings to follow.

But it all made sense now—what he had to do, but couldn't say. The thing that would cause him to leave his daughter, even when he knew she needed him to stay, needed him to spend the years it would take to teach her heart to not fear tomorrow. The thing that would cause him to ignore her pleading that he stop for her sake, for their sake. That would cause him to stare down the barrel of a sniper's rifle, to walk away from those he loved and into the crossfire of centuries of hate and violence. *The Lord is my shepherd. Remember. The Lord is my shepherd.*

It was too much to ask. How could this be dropped in her lap? She wasn't ready for this. It was too soon, too much. She stood. She wouldn't fight it, but neither could she sit there and act like it was OK. Matt reached for her, but she pushed his hand away and climbed from the sunken living room to the bottom of the stairs. She stopped and looked back. Will was staring down into his cognac. Matt looked like an illustration of an apology but said nothing. Nikki looked over her shoulder and saw her standing there. Her forehead wrinkled in confusion. Stevie felt her gaze all the way up until she was out of sight.

Cooper watched her go up. She deserved the truth, even if it did hurt her worse than a lie. Not that she would be fooled with a lie or stop until she knew the truth. And she knew she had found it. He could see as it washed over her like a wave, sweeping her out to sea. She had seen that it was the answer that could not be questioned, could not be gainsaid or side-stepped. It was the answer that leered back like the skull on a jar of poison.

Dixon's KL-7 phone brought Cooper out of his trance. Dixon pulled on his shoes and coat, grabbed a cigar, and stepped out onto the deck. Cooper walked over to the girls.

"What's the verdict?"

"All the bunny slopes are on the front side. Plus, Suzanne says she knows a really cute instructor."

"He won't know what hit him."

They giggled and turned back to the brochures. Cooper stood looking at them, soaking up the life, freedom, and inno-cence into the void that Stevie's look had opened in his chest. As much as he hated what it was doing to Stevie and Nikki, they were precisely the reason he had to do it. Stevie finally knew it. He hoped Nikki never had to face that demon. Better for her to resent him for his neglect than for her to realize she was the reason for his choice. Better for her to lay it at his door than at her own.

Dixon came back in and tossed his coat on the couch.

"Let's warm up that coffee."

He walked into the kitchen. Cooper followed with his mug. Dixon poured a refill, got out a mug for himself, and topped them both off with Bailey's.

"About thirty miles north of Minot, North Dakota," he said quietly, "a Lidar satellite detected the presence of a large mass of aerosols consistent with a nuclear explosion. We got the boys on it. About a quarter mile of Highway 5 is completely gone. There's a crater big enough to play rugby in, and it's hotter than a two-dollar pistol at a crap game."

Cooper just stared at him, watching his mouth move. Until now, tracking the devices had been a cat-and-mouse game. The stakes were real and they were high, but abstract. Just a silver briefcase and a stack of statistics. Until now.

Dixon blew on his coffee and took a sip. He grimaced and blew on it again. "Looks like they got careless and we got lucky. I'm betting it was en route to Chicago. We can shift the Chicago team to D.C. It hasn't been on the chatter, but it's a logical target and you found a D.C. map in Montreal."

"Montreal was a setup. We can't trust any information we got there."

"With the Chicago bomb gone, it's a better use of our resources to focus on D.C."

"Assuming that was the only device available for Chicago. They might have a backup, one of the old KGB boxes."

"Perhaps. It's your call, Coop. You're the one with the paper from the president. But my gut tells me the smart money is on D.C."

Cooper set his coffee down, leaned against the kitchen counter, and rubbed his eyes with the heels of his hands. "You're right. The smart money is on D.C. I'll set up a conference call for tomorrow morning while the girls are on the slopes, and we can brief the teams. I'm just worried about Stevie. I don't know how much more of this she can take."

He picked up his coffee and leaned his elbows on the island, facing Dixon. "She's figured it out, Dixon. She knows what we're up against, and that's going to wear her down. They finished the location shooting, but she still has the studio work, and together the strain could break her. She'll probably let something slip, and then Nikki will figure it out. She's smarter than both of us put together. Once word of the nuke by Minot gets out . . ."

Dixon waved his hand. "They're already on it. NASA is reporting a meteor impact in a remote area of North Dakota in the middle of a bunch of farmland. No injuries. Can probably pick it up on the news if we get back to the den. They've got the radar tracking data and everything. Of course they've blocked it off because sometimes meteorites release radiation and toxic gases. So everybody will see exactly what they expect to see, a Hazmat team cleaning up a meteor crater. One of the trucks hauling out the toxic soil will haul in an actual meteor from our collection in Roswell, and everybody's happy."

Cooper sipped his coffee, doubtful but willing to be convinced. "So, what about March 15? That's only two weeks away. You think it's a real date?"

"I wouldn't be surprised if they set a date and then pulled the trigger two days early."

Chapter 38

Vail, Colorado.
Saturday, 1 March 2003. 07:22.

Nikki wrapped herself in a thick robe and slipped out of the room. The other girls would sleep for an hour or so. She envied them that. Her restless sleep had been populated with the familiar cast of people she loved morphing into killers and reaching for her. For the last three hours she had listened to the breathing and movements of the other girls, afraid to go back to sleep. She considered taking the razor to the bathroom, but the possibility of discovery was too great. Finally she heard Dad sneezing like he did in the morning.

She searched the cabin without finding him. Then she thought to look out the dining room door. He was partially obscured by the corner of the kitchen, but she could see his back wrapped in a blanket. He was probably having a cup of coffee and looking down the slopes to the town below. There was a layer of fresh snow on the deck railing, but the deck, tables, and chairs were swept clean. Probably Rosa.

She turned to the kitchen and smelled coffee. Rosa smiled and asked if she wanted some hot chocolate. Nikki nodded and went to exchange her fuzzy slippers for snow boots. She retrieved the mug from Rosa, wrapped a blanket from the cedar chest around her shoulders, and pushed the door open.

Dad turned at the sound and smiled. She knew she looked goofy in pajamas, a robe, a blanket, and snow boots, but she didn't care. She gave him a sleepy smile that faded as she rounded the corner. *She* was there, wrapped in another blanket, reading a book. *She* looked up and smiled. Nikki looked away and took the chair farthest from *Her* and closest to Dad.

"You're up early," he said. "Where are your friends?"

"They're still asleep."

"Their snoring wake you up?"

"Dad." Sometimes he could be ridiculous. But the picture of Sabrina snoring flashed into her mind, and she couldn't suppress a laugh. She tried to turn it into a cough, but she could see Dad wasn't fooled.

"That's why I'm up," he said. "Stevie woke me up with her snoring."

Nikki didn't look at *Her*, but from the corner of her eye she saw *Her* give Dad a look. It wasn't a killer look, only a six or seven, but high enough to tell her they weren't exactly getting along. She noted it, not sure if that was good or bad. She would analyze it later.

Nikki sipped her hot chocolate. "When do the slopes open?"

"Nine. I have a meeting this morning, video conference, but I'll join you for lunch at the lodge."

"Dad, you promised." This weekend was supposed to be work-free, just them. It was bad enough *She* was here, but to have to compete with videoconferences too . . .

"Something happened last night. We'll just have a quick meeting to get the team to change directions, and then I'll come up to the slopes and watch you fall down."

Something happened? She darted a look at *Her*, remembering the fight. *She* was upset about something, and as much as she hated to admit it, when *She* was upset, it was usually something worth getting upset about. There was something bigger than a conference call going on.

Nikki looked at Dad with suspicion. "You're going somewhere, aren't you?"

"No, nothing like that. There's just been a change in plan. We're dropping one city from surveillance and adding a new one. There's not enough information in the new city to make a move in the next few days. Monday we'll all go home together."

She wasn't convinced. She couldn't count the times that unchangeable plans changed because new information came out of nowhere. She felt her eyes being drawn to Dad's left ear, to the little missing half-moon that made it look like a mouse had been nibbling on it. In her dreams she saw that ear, saw the missing place grow until it consumed his ear and then his face and his head. She pulled her eyes away from the ear to his eyes. He looked at her, searching her eyes. He knew there was something; she could see that. He was trying to figure out what it was.

She looked away, down the valley at the snow-covered roofs of houses down the ridge, to the village with the gray slush ruts powdered over with a fresh coating of white. From the corner of her eye she saw a movement. She glanced at *Her*. *She* was wiping away a tear. Nikki frowned. That was all wrong. *She* never cried. *She* got angry, a silent angry or a focused, determined angry, but *She* never cried.

Nikki turned back to Dad for an explanation. He hadn't seen the tear. He looked back at her.

"What?"

"There's something else. It's not just a conference call."

"Of course there are other things. There always are. But for this weekend it's just the conference call."

"Promise?" She didn't attempt to hide the skepticism.

"Promise."

Nikki looked back at *Her*. *She* looked up.

"He means it, Nikki. Even if things change later, he means it right now. He's doing his best. We just have to do the same."

Nikki looked at *Her* in shock. Something was seriously wrong. *She* had never taken his side before. Had never given up. And it was clear this was a declaration of defeat. *She* was giving up. It was unthinkable. She looked at Dad. He seemed as shocked as she was. How was she to interpret this unexpected change if he didn't even understand it? It made no sense. But no matter what *She* did, Nikki swore that she would never give up. And who did *She* think *She* was, trying to smooth things over and make it better? She stood up and spoke to no one in particular.

"I was raised to think a promise means something. I was raised to keep my promises. And I expect others to keep their promises too."

She wrapped the blanket around herself and shuffled back into the cabin.

———

Cooper set the VMC-1 on the coffee table in front of the couch. The portable videoconferencing system fit in a small briefcase and included a fifteen-inch color LED monitor, keyboard, and ports for various communication links. Cooper connected the KL-7 and picked up the joystick that allowed him to navigate menus and also zoom and pan the local camera built into the case above the monitor and the remote camera in the IRIG conference room. In the picture-in-picture thumbnail he could see himself and Dixon sitting next to him on the couch.

He selected the menu option to dial into the Van Nuys conference room through the secured satellite conference system. The call connected, and they had a view of the IRIG staff and law enforcement liaisons seated around the conference table. It was a small group, just Claire, Perkins, and Montoya from IRIG, Watford for the FBI, and Gilberts for Homeland Security. In California it was before nine on a Saturday. Most were dressed casually and were surrounded by various evidences of breakfast on the go. Cooper leaned forward, elbows on knees.

"By now you should all know about the meteorite in North Dakota." He saw nods around the room. "Dixon thinks we should shift the Chicago team to D.C. I agree. Objections? OK. Perkins, you take the lead in transitioning the team, swapping out the regional experts, and getting the database adjusted."

Perkins set down his coffee and made some notes. "Got it." Even on the small screen the told-you-so look on Claire's face was obvious. Cooper ignored it.

"Then there's the other bit of news. We now have a deadline—March 15. Anybody not aware of this development?"

Perkins leaned back in his chair. "The ides of March. We're on it."

A cell phone played "The Macarena" loudly, and Perkins jumped like he'd been electrocuted. The rest of the room looked at him with expressions varying from amusement to annoyance. Perkins looked around apologetically and glanced at the display. He looked up at the camera.

"Matt, it's Isaac. It's like 1:00 a.m. over there. He might have some info that would change our plans."

"Take it," Cooper said.

Perkins said, "Hello," on his way out of the room.

"Good. Now let's forget March 15 and remember March 12. Dixon thinks HuJI could set a deadline and then push up the schedule to catch us with our pants down. I agree. In addition, March 15 is a Saturday. The most likely strike time is midweek in a business district."

Claire stopped twirling the pencil through her fingers and slapped it down on the conference table.

"Matt, I'm going to D.C. I can get a red-eye out tonight."

"What can you do in D.C. that you can't do from California?"

"Come on, Matt. You know being on-site makes a big difference. It's the way you work yourself."

Cooper hesitated. Last year he wouldn't have given it a second thought, but the past months caused him to examine everything Claire did for sinister interpretations.

Claire continued. "With the timetable moved up, we have to expedite our investigation. I can cut a week from the process by being there myself to eliminate delays and speed bumps, bypass dead ends, and focus on the critical leads."

Before Cooper could respond, Dixon said, "Good idea."

Perkins came back in. "Matt, you have to hear this. Isaac just heard from the Lone Ranger. They hit a safe house near Baria a few hours ago. Among the things they recovered were plans for an operation in New York and Washington, D.C. They included phone numbers, so we might be able to target safe houses and accelerate our schedule."

Cooper saw Claire pull out her cell phone. She would be in D.C. before dawn.

"Great. Track down those numbers and let me know the plan. I have a lunch date I can't break, but I'll keep my phone on."

They signed off, and Cooper looked at Dixon.

"You know they can do a raid without you," Dixon said.

"Of course, but you heard Claire. I'm a field agent masquerading as a CEO. I have to get my hands dirty or I lose my connection with the pulse of the operation. This is no time for detachment. If we get a lead, I'll have to be there." He disconnected his phone, snapped the VMC-1 shut, and stood up. "Besides, this will all be over in two weeks and I'll take a nice long vacation."

"Sure you will."

Chapter 39

North America, 34,000 feet.
Sunday, 2 March 2003. 03:20.

He was crossing the Mississippi when Perkins called him. The teams were in place, and they wanted to hit immediately. Cooper agreed. By the time he got to the site, it would be daylight.

He had delayed his departure as long as possible, perhaps too long. Lunch had gone well. The time on the slopes seemed to clear Nikki's resentment. Stevie was quiet, which was uncharacteristic. She seemed to accept the situation with some degree of understanding short of resignation. He was thankful that he didn't have to spend the lunch on the defensive. He had set the phone to vibrate so they wouldn't be interrupted.

It went off while he was suiting up for the slopes. The New York numbers were disconnected, and the addresses most recently connected to the accounts were vacant apartments. They had better luck with the D.C. numbers. They matched two houses in Fairfax County in northern Virginia, one of the top counties for issuing green cards to Middle Eastern immigrants. Consultation with local FBI offices indicated both houses were on their watch list.

Cooper agreed that both should be hit as soon as possible. He knew it would take several hours to set things in motion, so he resolved to spend the afternoon with Stevie and Nikki on the bunny slopes before breaking his promise and leaving Saturday night. It was a time memories are made of. They skied and fell and laughed and rolled down the hills and took pictures and drank hot chocolate by the fire in the lodge.

He waited until they got to the cabin to break the news. Stevie just nodded like she knew it was coming. Nikki's response was more demonstrative. Dinner passed in uncomfortable silence, and Nikki disappeared with her friends into the bedroom they shared. Dixon diplomatically holed up in the study with a book on medieval siege engines.

Cooper found Stevie in the bedroom. She was curled up in an armchair, a comforter draped over her legs. She was reading. He walked up behind her, rubbed her shoulders, and looked into her lap.

"A Bible?" He stepped to the bed and sat down facing her. "Since when did you get religious?"

She turned back a page and read aloud. "The Lord is my shepherd. I shall not want." She looked at him. Her eyes were red but dry. "Have you ever heard that before?" she asked, her eyes searching his face.

He was puzzled. Religion had never been a topic of interest to her. "Sure. Psalm 23."

She looked surprised. "How did you know that?"

"My parents made me go to church until I was sixteen. We had to memorize it."

"Do you believe it?"

The question annoyed him. "That the Lord is my shepherd?"

"That God loves and cares for you like a shepherd does for his sheep."

"No."

She looked back at the open page. "Even though I walk through the valley of the shadow of death, I will fear no evil, for you are with me." She looked back at him. "You're walking into the valley. Aren't you afraid?"

"No," he said quickly. He hoped she would drop the conversation. Normally he would just tell her he wasn't interested and change the subject, but she was already upset about the D.C. trip. He didn't want to make matters worse.

"Why not?"

"Because I know what I'm doing. I don't need some good-luck charm like a verse or a St. Christopher medal or something to give me confidence. I have training and experience. That's what keeps me safe in the face of death, not some divine protection, angels hovering around me and all that."

He realized he was pacing by the bed and ranting. He clamped his mouth shut and sat down on the bed. She was probably upset now. He didn't know why she was suddenly religious, but if she was, going on a tirade about it wasn't likely to reduce the tension between them. She had no way of knowing this was a hot button for him. They had never discussed it before.

"What about the bullet?" She glanced at his ear. "You don't think God protected you from death?"

"No," he said, forcing his voice to say calm. "It was instinct, a sixth sense. It's probably part training, part experience, part something intangible, like a special talent. Like having perfect pitch or a good eye for photography or being able to do math in your head or something like that."

She sat silent for awhile. "Why did you quit going to church?"

"I didn't see the point. It seemed to me that most of it was wishful thinking or finding excuses for your own failures. Like my dad . . ." He stopped suddenly. He didn't mean to get into this.

"What about your dad?"

"Oh, nothing. It doesn't matter." He walked to the closet and pulled out the small suitcase.

"It matters to me. You never talk about your parents. Why not?"

First the religion thing, now the family thing. It was not the conversation he wanted. He tossed the bag on the bed irritably. "Because there's no point in talking about them. That's the past. No need to dig it up."

"Are they dead?" she asked quietly.

"No," he snapped back then regretted it. "Not as far as I know," he said more calmly.

"As far as you know? When was the last time you talked to them?"

"When I left home."

"When you were eighteen?"

"Yeah." He paced between the dresser and the bed, dropping clothes into the suitcase. He was zipping it closed before she spoke again.

"So what is the connection between religion and your dad?"

He breathed a heavy sigh, pulled the suitcase from the bed, and set it firmly on the floor. Why couldn't she let it go? "Look, do we really have to talk about this? I'm leaving in a few hours, and I'd rather spend the time on more pleasant topics."

"It's important to me."

A meter somewhere in his head redlined. "It's important to you to know that my dad was a failure who ran his own business into the ground through incompetence and misman-agement and then had the nerve to excuse it by saying it was God's will that he fail? Who lost job after job when he didn't follow through when the boss was counting on him because he was too busy with fifteen different church committees and called it religious persecution? Who accused his wife of being rebellious and strong-willed when she tried to get him to see sense? Who drove away everyone who loved him by telling them what failures they were when all the time his own life was a complete disaster?" He jerked the suitcase up from the floor. "That's important to you?"

"Of course," she said, her eyes brimming. "If it shaped you, it's important to me."

He was breathing heavily through his nose. He set the suitcase back down and tried to calm down. "I left when I was eighteen, and I never looked back. I made my own way instead of rubbing the Bible and waiting for a genie to pop out and grant my wishes. You're no different. You didn't let circumstances control your destiny. You didn't wait around for life to get better. You made it happen." He waved his hand at the Bible in her lap. "I don't know why you think you need to pick up a crutch when you're doing just fine. But if you want to, go ahead. Just don't expect me to join you."

Stevie wiped the tears from her face with the comforter. "What about Major Skaff?"

He frowned at her, confused. "What about him?"

"I remember how you talked about him a few months ago. Do you think he needed a crutch?"

The irritation crept back in. "I don't know what I said about the major. It's beside the point. Do your thing if you have to." He picked up the suitcase and turned to the door.

"Do you mind if I pray for you?"

"Whatever," he said over his shoulder and walked to the door. "I'm going to work out some details with Dixon and head to the airport."

On the drive to the Eagle airport, he thought about the conversation. He wasn't pleased about how he had handled it, but there was no time to fix it. He needed to be in D.C. before morning.

———

As they began the descent from cruising altitude, Cooper got the report on the raids. The targets were apartments in Muslim neighborhoods two miles apart. The first held a recent immigrant, a devout Muslim from Syria who was very cooperative. He had only been in the country a few days. He went to the mosque where the imam connected him with temporary housing. The two men who lived there left the day before after cleaning out a bunch of papers. He didn't remember their names. He would be detained for further questioning and perhaps a polygraph. He could be a decoy working with the suspects, but most likely was simply a man looking for a place to stay.

The second apartment was more interesting. They found an empty apartment—completely empty, with the exception of a wall phone in the kitchen. A piece of paper was taped to the phone. It had a phone number on it. A reverse lookup in the 911 database gave the address of an apartment one block down the street. When they entered that apartment, they found papers and clothes scattered about. Once the apartment was secured, they began knocking on doors and questioning the residents. Most were asleep when the raid took place, but one man was up, rocking a colicky baby. He reported hearing footsteps running through the hall and a man yelling, "Get out now. They're coming." He carried his baby to the front window and looked out. He saw two Middle Eastern men carrying suitcases run out into the street and climb into a cab with a Middle Eastern driver.

The apartment showed evidence of an evacuation inter-rupted. Documents were scattered, but most were generic in nature, al-Qaeda training manuals and such. It would take days to process all the documents to see if anything of significance had been overlooked. The initial scan didn't reveal references to a specific attack or weapons. As they followed the leads, these might surface, but a lot of footwork lay ahead.

When he landed, Cooper went directly to the D.C. IRIG office. Claire was there, just back from the second location. He motioned her into the conference room, closed the door, and sat on the conference table.

"What happened?" he asked quietly.

She dropped into a chair and leaned one elbow on the table. "We were made. Somehow."

"Did the surveillance teams blow it?"

"Not that I saw. I got here at 2100 hours yesterday and was on-site on Youngblood Street within twenty minutes. The raid went down at 0430, over seven hours later. If they blew it before I got there, why did they wait until a few minutes before to clear out?"

"Maybe they were still destroying evidence."

She shook her head slowly. "That's cutting it close. I would say they left at the last minute because they found out at the last minute."

"Maybe they had someone watching the empty apartment and the raid tipped them off."

"No. We realized afterward that we saw the suspects go by in the cab a few minutes before the signal to go in. We didn't realize it at the time. They were just a couple of Middle Eastern guys in a cab."

"Were you with the surveillance team the entire seven hours?" She nodded. "You never saw anyone leave, not even for a few seconds?" She shook her head. "So you're certain that nobody there contacted the suspects?"

Claire leaned forward. "You think the surveillance team tipped them off?"

"What's your explanation?"

"The surveillance team is local. They haven't been in on any other raids. There's been a series of close calls. Obviously the problem isn't with the local teams. It's higher up."

"Agreed."

She looked at him in silence for a long time. "You have some ideas, don't you?"

"I suspect everybody," he said deadpan. "Occupational hazard."

Her eyes hardened. "What's your plan?"

"I'm open to suggestions."

She leaned back in her chair. "It's not for me to say. That's up to the person in charge."

"Let's say you're the person in charge."

"Hypothetically?"

"Yeah, hypothetically. What do you do?"

"Hypothetically I would be suspicious after Chicago; I would take action after Montreal."

"What kind of action?"

"I would get phone records on my primary suspects, wire taps, background checks, assign surveillance." She looked at him steadily without blinking. "I would wake up with them in the morning, take them to work, go out with them at night, put them to bed. And I would do it all back channel."

"Sounds like a good idea."

"And I would narrow the pool by tightening up security and communications and reducing exposure to ancillary organizations."

Cooper nodded without comment.

"Hypothetically."

"Right, hypothetically."

Chapter 40

North America, 32,000 feet.
Monday, 3 March 2003. 06:20.

Cooper pushed the files aside and looked out the window. Now that they were above the cloud cover, he could see the effects of the sun climbing behind the jet, the soft-edged undulations extended in all directions, highlighted in rose tints.

He couldn't keep his mind on the financials he was supposed to review. After the initial success in New York, to be confounded in three consecutive raids was not only frustrating, it was disturbing. The empty apartment in Chicago was inconclusive. They were operating the night before, as if unaware of the surveillance. The lone occupant of the house disappeared sometime during the hour before they hit. It was possible he had detected the activity and slipped out. Or not. There was enough to prompt some investigation on Claire, which had led nowhere.

The sniper in Montreal moved the issue from speculation to certainty. He was waiting for Cooper. But a lot of people knew about Montreal—FBI, CIA, Homeland Security, the counterterrorism branch of the Royal Mounted Police, IRIG. And not just the principals. Dozens of support personnel were in the loop. Finding the source of the leak for that raid could take months.

Hence the decision to keep the D.C. raid very tight. The report of the Muslim Paul Revere running up the stairs with the news of the raid indicated that the leak was deep within the organization. But where?

The lead on Bactar had looked promising, but if he were working for HuJI, his cover was incredibly convincing. Cooper didn't figure Bactar as the Scarlet Pimpernel of Islamic Jihad. More likely he was just what he seemed, the son of a wealthy oil sheik doing his best to eradicate his father's considerable fortune in the most amusing manner possible. No point wasting time chasing that wild goose.

But the conclusion that Bactar was not a threat didn't eliminate Claire from the list of suspects. She did have connections to the Middle East. Cooper's investigations showed that her family left Iran during the madness following WWI and wandered through Europe for several decades before settling in New York just before Pearl Harbor was bombed. Her grandfather tried to enlist but was denied. Her father fought in the Korean War and was an advisor for the Vietnam War. One brother worked for the American embassy in Paris, another fought in the Gulf War. It was a family history wrapped in the stars and stripes, beyond suspicion. Which is exactly why Cooper was suspicious.

She still had family back in Iran. Who better to recruit for deep infiltration than the ambitious daughter of a general who had spent a lifetime competing with her brothers for attention and respect? She had the connections; she had the motivation; she had the cover. And as Cooper had seen in the game she played at the Christmas party and her romps with Bactar, she didn't seem to be overly encumbered with scruples.

But the investigations, as exhaustive as they were, came up blank. She would have to be pretty good to escape detection. But it was clear that whoever the leak was, he was good, so a clean report so far meant little. She remained his primary suspect.

But there were others. The entire IRIG executive staff, with the exception of Susan, had operational knowledge of all the raids. That included Claire, Montoya, Perkins, and Dr. Hampton. The other three officers were a longer shot, having no known associations with the Middle East, but things had reached the point that long shots must be considered as well. He would have to dig deeper and wider.

Which brought him to Dixon. As the primary liaison for all government teams, he knew everything as well. Dixon as the leak was inconceivable to Cooper. He had known the man for fourteen years, had worked with him in the office and the field, had placed his life in Dixon's hands countless times. Vacations together, scuba diving in the Caribbean, trout fishing in Wyoming, skiing in Colorado, wine tours of the French countryside and Napa Valley. He knew the man as well as he knew himself, if not better. His background exceeded even Claire's family for God, country, and apple pie.

A dedicated Catholic from the American heartland, Dixon attended Notre Dame, majoring in international relations, studying Russian, Arabic, and Hebrew with plans for a diplomatic career in the Middle East. He was an ROTC officer and, after discussions about Ia Drang with his family over Christmas 1965, volunteered for Vietnam. Based on his college career he was recruited by intelligence and worked on special ops. The CIA picked him up during his first tour, and he was established in D.C. before the war ended. His language skills drew him to a position as a Russian specialist during the cold war. His rise through the ranks was rapid.

Cooper was setting up his Berlin office in November 1989 when the wall fell. He met Dixon in a West Berlin bar as they toasted the death knell of the Soviet Union. The rapport had been immediate, and they got together as often as their travel permitted, which was quite frequent when Dixon became the western U.S. director for the CIA in 1996–the year before Lola died. He had helped Cooper pick up the pieces, had become Nikki's unofficial godfather, and, more recently, told Cooper he was an idiot if he didn't marry Stevie immediately.

Dixon was family. Cooper felt guilty putting him on the suspect list, even in his mind. He forced himself to consider the possibility. His position in the CIA gave him access to a wealth of information of great value to the terrorists. It also gave him the ability to influence events. But Cooper kept coming back to motivation. What could possibly motivate Dixon to betray his heritage? If something had happened, Cooper felt certain it must be a recent event. He knew Dixon's background as well as anyone. What more could Cooper hope to find that he didn't already know or that the CIA had overlooked? He forced himself to investigate the possibility, however remote he thought it might be.

He gladly left that subject to consider Watford, the lead contact for the FBI, and Gilberts, the contact for Homeland Security. He knew almost nothing about them. Then there was the D.C. team. Unlike earlier raids, in D.C. the information had been limited to IRIG, the Feds, and the D.C. contacts. Which meant the D.C. teams had knowledge of all three raids. That included perhaps two dozen people. There was a total of somewhere around thirty people to check out. But who would check them out? The agencies that would normally perform the investigations were themselves suspect. Perhaps he would get Dixon involved in investigating the others while he dug deeper on Dixon.

Cooper looked out the window. Through the occasional break in the clouds he could see broad stretches of flat land. Could be anywhere from Ohio to Colorado. He checked his watch. Probably Kansas. He got up and walked back to the service area. Kelly looked up from her magazine.

"Can I fix you something? Coffee? A glass of wine?"

"I'll get it myself. I need to stretch my legs."

She smiled and turned back to her magazine. He poured some coffee and stood in the back, looking out the window. He would be at the office before noon. Monday. Nikki would probably be late, depending on how it went at the studio. Stevie still had the studio work to do on her current project. Probably would be working late also.

He couldn't decide if that was good or bad. He had no interest in continuing the religion conversation, although he couldn't help wonder why a self-reliant woman like Stevie suddenly found a need for religion. But he had the feeling that sooner or later the conversation would turn around and bite him. Better to avoid it completely. He turned away from the window and these dead-end thoughts and returned to his seat.

He found his thoughts returning to Montreal and the sound of a bullet grazing his ear. One week today. Being a target for gunfire was not a new experience for him. He had been hit more than once. In the past he had shaken it off and gone on. He rarely thought of it. But this was different, more personal. He had the unnerving sense that the man with the picture had whispered his name as he pulled the trigger.

Cooper shook his head. It was foolishness and he knew it, but still the feeling of a personal malevolence persisted. He was rethinking the shooting in Vienna. Alexia took the worst hits, but perhaps that was only because she was at the beginning of the arc of fire as they swept the front of the building. From the moment he saw her on the floor of the restaurant he was certain she was the target, that she had been careless somewhere along the way. Montreal changed things.

Somewhere on the other end of a long chain of connections, a man was making decisions, directing resources, issuing orders. In Chicago he had delved into the mind of the man on the other side as an academic exercise in an attempt to assess the risks of the raid. He considered the motivations and characteristics of his opponent in an abstract fashion but didn't give flesh to the personality he created in his mind.

Until Montreal. It was as though the monster was born of the fragment of flesh torn from his ear. Cooper's imagination had breathed life into that pinch of dust, and now he faced an opponent who was no longer an abstraction. A real person bent on his personal destruction. Someone who seemed to know him by name.

Then I'll give him a name, Cooper thought. *Something he would find insulting. A nice Jewish name. Berkowitz.*

He attempted to picture Berkowitz. He thought of Osama bin Laden with less hair and more meat on his bones. He would probably never see this man, but he would defeat him all the same. He would find the mole in the organization, and that would lead him to Berkowitz.

Giving up all pretense of getting anything else done, he pushed the financials into his briefcase and looked out the window as the Rockies came into view.

Chapter 41

Safe house, Zahedan, Iran.
Tuesday, 4 March 2003. 17:00.

When al-Huzayfi walked into the room, al-Suri smiled inside. Cooper had survived the sniper through some inexplicable miracle. Worse yet, the sniper was dead. Granted, due to the quick action of the mole, the one who was known by the ridiculous name of Stallion, no one important was captured at the Chicago, Montreal, and D.C. raids. Yet more reason to smile. He was in the unique position of having something to celebrate regardless of how things turned out.

Al-Huzayfi departed from normal procedure and spoke to the head of security and intelligence first. "Makkee, what of the Egyptian?"

Al-Suri was gratified to see al-Huzayfi unsettled to the point of disrupting his obsession with protocol. The Egyptian had one use only—to remove the annoyance called Cooper. But only desperation would cause him to attempt to use the Egyptian, a useless man—one better to kill than to recruit.

Makkee shook his head. "I am afraid he is not a suitable tool for our purposes."

"He is Muslim. Has he no respect for jihad?"

"He is hardly Muslim. He is more decadent than most Westerners."

"If he cannot be persuaded to help us through devotion to Allah, then perhaps he can be persuaded by appealing to the gods he worships. Wealth, prestige, or even his own personal safety. Every man worships something, even if it is only himself. Find his god, reveal to him how he may serve this god by removing Cooper."

"As you say," Makkee said.

"What of the Americans? We have given the March 15 deadline. Will they strike before then?"

"They could strike at any moment. There are 220,000 troops in the theater, five carriers already here, and a sixth, the *Nimitz*, left San Diego yesterday." Makkee recited the information without referring to notes. "B-2 stealth bombers have been moved from Missouri to Britain and Diego Garcia."

"We must strike first. One week. All must be in place by Monday." Al-Huzayfi turned to his right.

"Salim, can you review with me the agreed plan for arming the devices used in Last Straw?"

Salim shifted uncomfortably. This puzzled al-Suri. It was a simple question, one any of those present could answer, even Aidid the newcomer.

"The plan was to arm the devices after deployment at the final location."

Was? Al-Suri looked at Salim. Why did he speak in the past tense?

"Then perhaps you can explain how one came to be detonated on a remote highway in South Dakota, annihilating a half-mile of useless farmland instead of a half-million people?"

Al-Suri could see that he was not the only one stunned by this news. When did this happen?

Salim could not have been more miserable if he had been staked out in the desert at noon. He gained time by sipping tea, setting his cup down slowly.

"I cannot say for certain. Yusuf has assured me that it was not armed when he placed it at the drop point in Wyoming. Unfortunately, the men who picked it up are not available to explain themselves."

"Have you created a network of incompetents? How can Last Straw succeed if every third person in the chain is an idiot?"

Salim had no answer.

Al-Suri broke the silence. "Perhaps it is this Cooper. Salim has been with us for years, and this sort of thing has not plagued us until Cooper became involved. Perhaps he is smarter than the government planning we have dealt with up to now." He paused to let the idea permeate. Then he released the shaft. "Perhaps he is smarter than our own planning."

The effects were immediate. Al-Huzayfi sputtered for a brief moment before he visibly clamped down his reaction. When he finally spoke, it was through clenched teeth and a controlled rage.

"Cooper is an annoyance. He escaped the sniper through sheer luck, perhaps through a bargain with Satan. But he is no match for my plans. He is no match for me."

"Perhaps. But he seems to be doing quite well. He escaped your assassins in Vienna and Montreal. He caused considerable damage to our organization and holdings in Paris and New York. He evidently has learned enough to anticipate the plan we have in place. He seems to be everywhere he needs to be, and only through the reaction of the Stallion are we able to prevent complete failure. At present it is the Stallion who has saved this operation, not the plan."

Al-Huzayfi leaned forward. "If Salim's idiots cannot deal with this horsefly, I will do it myself."

Al-Suri raised his eyebrows. "Your reach has indeed become long if you can strike Cooper from the comfort of your chair."

Though he made no movement and no comment, hatred and fury seethed from al-Huzayfi. It was as if the oxygen were sucked from the room. No one breathed. His left hand quivered briefly.

"Cooper shall drink the bitter lees of my judgment. Do not mistake me, al-Suri." "We wish you every success, Emir. We will rejoice with you over the death of this infidel."

Without another word, al-Huzayfi stood and strode from the room.

Calabasas, California.
Wednesday, 5 March 2003. 13:20.

Bernie took the Mulholland Drive exit off the 101, a half-dozen cars behind the black Audi. The guy didn't suspect a thing, he was sure of that. He had been very careful, never getting closer than five cars.

The guy had been in the store before, and Bernie hadn't liked the looks of him then. But now, after everything that happened in Chicago and D.C., Bernie was looking at every customer through a different lens. Roff told him what they were looking for in Chicago, and this guy had the look. Affluent, assured, assimilated. Up to something, no question. Buying surveillance gear and devices to control things remotely. He would find out what it was, and then this Basil guy wouldn't look so smug.

Good thing Merv was in today. Made it easier to disappear for a few hours, or even a few days if he had to. Merv needed the hours. The way he went through girlfriends, he might even need a third job. So when this guy Basil walked out the front door, Bernie watched him go to his car, told Merv he'd be out for a few hours, and went out the back to his white unmarked panel van. If he had to, he'd call Merv on his cell at six and tell him to close up.

The light changed, and Bernie followed the Audi left, past the shopping center to Valmar. Things got a little tougher when they turned right again and started going up the hill. Lots of turns and short little streets with cul-de-sacs. Where people with money lived.

Jesus, don't let him lose me, Bernie whispered. He kept his distance when he could. When the Audi rounded a corner he punched the gas then lagged back once he caught sight of it. A mile up the hill Basil turned right onto a short street. Bernie slowed and saw the garage door open on the house on the corner. He rolled past as Basil pulled into the garage and then scanned the curbs. He saw what he was looking for in the rearview mirror—a cable company pedestal. It was on the wide street catty-corner from the driveway.

Bernie went down the next street, pulled to the curb, put on the parking brake, went to the back, and opened the doors. He flipped through a stack of magnetic decals, past the carpet cleaners and the septic tank services and found one for the cable company. He returned to the wider street and parked next to the pedestal, pulled a cap on to match the decals, walked to the back of the van, and climbed in.

He sat down in a swivel chair and powered up a bank of equipment. Hard drives whirred to life, lights began blinking, beeps indicated the successful conclusion of power-on-self-test cycles, and a series of monitors flickered to life. One booted to a Linux command prompt, another to an X Window System console. A set of four smaller monitors showed views from four external cameras. The top corners of the van had been inset to accommodate the cameras, and white cloth corners were snapped into place over them. From a distance of ten feet they were indistinguishable from the body of the van, but the gauze allowed each camera an unobstructed view for 180 degrees. Laser listening devices enabled line-of-sight audio surveillance to any location viewable by the cameras. All were remote controlled by a switchable joystick on the console in the van.

Bernie positioned his cameras, started the tape rolling, and pulled his fourth Diet Coke from the cooler. He was used to waiting. Basil wouldn't know what hit him.

Chapter 42

Malibu, California.
Sunday, 9 March 2003. 04:00.

Cooper picked up the phone on the second ring, completely awake.

"Cooper," he said quietly. He looked at Stevie. She was still asleep. He slipped out of the room.

"Matt, this is Claire."

"Has there been a break? Did we get a line on the third city?" He went downstairs to the living room.

"No. It's something else." There was a silence. Cooper waited. "I'm calling from the Santa Monica police station. I've been charged with murder."

"Murder?" It wasn't easy to surprise Cooper, but she succeeded. "Who? How?"

"Well . . ."

"Never mind. What do you need me to do?"

"Call Bernstein. Get him down here. And I wouldn't mind if you came down yourself."

Cooper had earned some brownie points through the years. On the way down he called the judge and a bondsman and convinced both that Claire was not a flight risk and that he would personally accompany her for her court date. Bernstein was waiting for him in the parking lot. They went in together. Bernstein disappeared into the inner sanctum to rescue his client. Cooper waited.

The sun was just coming up when Claire, Bernstein, and the bondsman emerged. There were circles under her large brown eyes. A dress that looked like a large tie-dyed T-shirt and probably cost several hundred dollars hung on her frame like a drop cloth thrown over a dining room chair. There were several rusty brown splotches across the front.

The bondsman nodded to Cooper and left. Bernstein told Claire to call him if she needed anything and hugged her. Cooper saw the muscles in Claire's arms flex as she hugged him tightly. Bernstein shook Cooper's hand and whispered, "Take care of her." Cooper nodded and watched him walk out.

He turned to Claire. A Claire he had never seen. He wondered if anyone had seen this Claire. Certainly not since she was in junior high. The fortress of self-assurance had crumbled. The defiant challenge that had seemed a part of her eye color was gone, replaced by confusion and the hint of an apology.

Cooper did something he would have thought unimaginable only minutes before. He stood beside her, put his arm around her shoulders, and escorted her to the Jaguar. She climbed in like it was a hiding place. Cooper started the car.

"Where to?"

She sat in silence, staring out the windshield. He waited. She didn't speak.

"How about you come out to our place?" he said, surprising himself.

She was startled out of her trance. She looked at him blankly.

"You don't look like you're ready to be alone."

The blank look faded slowly, replaced with a more familiar caution. "What about . . . your girlfriend?"

Only then did Cooper realize the problems his invitation posed. There was certainly no warm spot in Stevie's heart for Claire. The house in Malibu might not be the haven he had envisioned. Still, as he looked at Claire, laid bare and defenseless, he could not imagine any response other than his own instinct to provide sanctuary.

He put the car in gear and pulled out onto Main heading south. "Maybe you should tell me what happened."

Claire shuddered. She took a deep breath and let it out. "I've been seeing this guy, an Egyptian. Karim. Last night we were supposed to go to the Sky but we had a fight. It was pretty loud. I slammed the door and left rather loudly in my car. Had a few drinks in a few places, no place where anybody would know me. They mellowed me out, and I went back to Karim's place. Around midnight." Her hand rose to her face. She rubbed her eyes.

Cooper drove past Ocean Park and pulled into the Starbucks off Main. "You stay here." He went in and stood in line. Bactar was dead. What did that mean? He cursed his luck. After a week he had cancelled the surveillance on Claire, just two days ago. It seemed a waste of time once it was apparent that Bactar wasn't connected to the case. Or at least, didn't seem to be. Now Cooper wasn't so sure. He didn't believe in coincidence. He picked up a grande Americano and a triple espresso and returned to the car. Neither spoke as he drove down to the beach. They found a bench, wrapped their hands around the cups, and waited for the morning sun to warm their backs.

"I take it you didn't find Karim the same way you left him."

Claire shook her head. "The door was open. All the lights were on. He didn't answer when I called out. I found him in the bedroom handcuffed to the bed. A pillowcase was stuffed in his mouth. There was . . ." Her voice broke. She shivered. Cooper waited. She finally found her voice. "There was a lot of blood. I don't remember much after that. I think I screamed. There were some neighbors and then the police."

"The neighbors remembered the argument. And you had blood on you."

"There was a knife. I must have picked it up because I remember the police taking it from me."

"That's awkward."

A laugh burst out of Claire. A smile flitted across her face. "You would think I would know better. I mean, I do know better." She shook her head slowly, looking out across the placid ocean. "But it was different. I don't know how to describe it. It was like . . ." She turned to Cooper. "It was like I wasn't there. Or maybe like I was somebody else. More like that, like I was somebody else watching me. Somebody who could only watch but couldn't change anything." She leaned back on the bench. "I guess you never know until it happens." She sipped her espresso. "You think you know. But you don't."

Cooper stood slowly and took a few steps toward the water. He watched the gentle swells pulse in and out. It was hard to reconcile this Claire with the calculating climber he knew. And even harder to see her as a mole helping arrange the death of millions of innocents. It could be an act. He turned and looked at her on the bench. She didn't appear to realize he was no longer next to her. She stared at the horizon as if she could see Tokyo.

He would never have predicted she would come undone in any circumstance. Evidently she was just as surprised about her reaction as he was. The old Claire was easy to picture as a partner with the terrorists. And up to now, everything had happened with the old Claire in operation. The past was not changed. The old Claire might still be the one. But what about the new Claire? If she really was the mole, this murder might change things. Assuming she didn't kill Bactar.

There was too much uncertainty. He needed to reduce the unknowns. Maybe Joe could uncover some dirt on the murder. And sequestering Claire in Malibu wasn't a bad idea. No matter what happened, he would insist that she take a leave of absence until this was cleared up, which would take months. Having her at his house for the next few days would make it easier to keep track of her movements. At least until March 15. After then it might not matter.

But what about Stevie? It was a big house, but probably not big enough for the two of them. He walked back up to the bench.

"I was serious. You need some space to recover without having to worry about things like meals and laundry. We have a guest wing. Rosa will make sure you have whatever you need. You wouldn't have to see anyone if you didn't want to."

"We just have one week to find the nukes. I can't disappear now."

Cooper shook his head. "No matter where you go, I'm going to insist you take a leave of absence until you're cleared. I can't have someone charged with murder on the executive staff, actively involved in investigations."

Claire bristled. "I haven't been indicted yet."

Cooper smiled inwardly. The old Claire wasn't far below the surface. "True. And if they don't indict you, we'll welcome you back with open arms. But not until everything is settled."

"But this has nothing to do with the nukes."

"I'm not talking about the nukes. I'm talking about the executive team of the largest security consultant agency in the world. I won't have even the hint of suspicion about IRIG. It's not an option. And I suspect your real boss will say the same about the agency."

"You're crazy. Saturday is just six days away. We can't afford to lose any resources."

"True. But that doesn't change anything." He sat next to her. "Claire," he said softly.

The old Claire looked at him, defiant, challenging.

He continued in the same quiet voice. "I'm sorry this happened, and not just because it's costing me my head of undercover operations at the time I need her most. I'm sorry you lost Karim. I'm sorry you had to go through this. And I'm sorry I have to put you on forced leave. But that doesn't change what happened. At least let me give you a retreat from the madness for a few days."

The defiance slowly crumbled as Claire seemed to recall what had happened a few hours before. "What about . . ."

"Stevie? Let's get back in the car. I'll call her, and we'll settle it right now. If it doesn't work out, I'll take you home."

"My car is still back at . . ."

"Don't worry about your car. Alex will take care of it."

———

As unexpected as Claire's transformation was, it didn't compare to the shock of Stevie's response. She answered the phone and told him he was missing a beautiful morning on the deck. He briefly explained the situation, and she told him she would have Rosa get the guest room ready. He began to wonder if he had dropped into a parallel universe without noticing.

Stevie met them at the front door. Cooper stepped aside to let Claire enter first, but she hesitated, looking at Stevie as if uncertain of her welcome. Stevie stepped across the threshold and wrapped her arms around Claire. Cooper could see that Claire was shocked. She tensed, her arms at her sides. Then she seemed to melt. Her body quivered, she drew in a ragged breath, and a tear rolled down her cheek. Her arms moved up as if of their own volition and her hands clutched at Stevie's white cotton blouse, bunching it up in her fists. Whatever reserve she had displayed since leaving the police station dissolved, and she practically collapsed into Stevie's arms, clinging to her as to a fragment from the wreckage of her life.

He watched until the wave seemed to pass then ushered them both inside. Stevie led Claire to the guest wing, and Cooper went into the kitchen. He was picking through a bowl of sliced fresh fruit on the island when Stevie returned.

"I got her into a hot bath and pulled the blackout curtains in the bedroom. She'll probably sleep for most of the day."

Cooper looked at her as if seeing her for the first time.

"What?" she asked.

"I wasn't sure if I was doing the right thing bringing her here."

She studied him. "Why?"

"Well, after the Christmas party, it just seemed like it might not be a good idea."

"Oh, that." She was silent for a moment. "A lot has changed since the Christmas party. For everybody, not just Claire."

He pushed a large chunk of cantaloupe into his mouth and grunted. He wasn't going to get suckered into the religion discussion that easily. He felt her studying him and turned to look at her. She seemed to want to say something. Instead, she turned to the stove.

"You want some tea?"

He swallowed the cantaloupe. "No, I just had some coffee."

He watched her as she moved around the kitchen. She filled the kettle with water and flicked on the burner. She got out a cup and a tin of PG Tips. Then she turned back to him.

"Matt, about the religion thing."

He looked at her without comment.

"It's not really about religion. It's more about . . ." She looked around the room, searching for the right words. "It's more like coming home."

"I thought your family were atheists." *Oops, I meant to stay out of it.*

"They are. That's not what I mean. It feels like coming home. Not to the home I really had. At least, not after . . ." She shook her head. "What I mean is that it feels like going back to the home that should have been. Where you are known and accepted and loved."

"And everybody knows your name."

She turned back to the stove and checked the kettle. "I know you're not interested," she said, keeping her back to him. "I'm not going to try to talk you into anything. I just wanted to tell you how it felt for me. I'm not saying you have to feel the same way."

He felt cheap and mean. Why did he have to ridicule it? He could tell it was important to her. He wanted to share the experience with her, but he refused to be hypocritical, especially about this. As far as the known-and-accepted thing, that could only go so far. If he were truly known, he was certain he would not be accepted, not by Stevie, not by anyone. He knew the beast that lay within himself, the Jekyll-Hyde schizophrenic that could slice up a man and enjoy watching him die. There was no homecoming for him.

Chapter 43

Manuel's, East Los Angeles, California.
Monday, 10 March 2003. 13:40.

"Relax," Cooper said. "Roberts gives it two thumbs up." He pulled a chair of tubular steel and cracked red vinyl back from the Formica table, the legs screeching against the concrete floor, and sat down.

Dixon didn't appear reassured. He stood by the table, turning slowly to scan the room apprehensively. "Then why isn't he here?"

"He'll be here." A short plump Hispanic woman shuffled up to the table. Cooper smiled at her. "Iced tea, please." He jerked at Dixon's jacket. "Sit down and have some iced tea. It's sun tea."

Dixon hung his jacket on the back of the chair opposite Cooper and lowered himself into it. "No tea. Diet Coke, no ice." As the woman shuffled away he lowered his voice. "You can't be too careful. The ice melts, it's the same as drinking the water."

Cooper frowned at him. "Dixon, you're in L.A., not Tijuana. There's nothing wrong with the water. What's gotten into you? You've been all over the world, eaten all kinds of food in all degrees of nonsanitary conditions. A little hole-in-the-wall Mexican food joint should be nothing to you."

"Have you ever had food poisoning?" Cooper shook his head. "Last year Watson took us on a cruise down the east coast on his yacht, *Rosinante*. Livy got it in a place just like this one." He shook his head slowly. "You can't imagine. It took her a week before she could even eat toast. The thing she had, one in a thousand cases results in paralysis." He leaned across the table. "One in a thousand, Coop. You realize if the lottery had that kind of odds there would be over three thousand million-aires in L.A. alone."

Cooper smiled.

"Laugh if you want, but it's no joke when your digestive system develops the China Syndrome."

Roberts arrived the same time as the drinks, still looking like Christopher Lloyd in a Colonel Sanders suit. Cooper made the introductions, and Roberts ordered for them all. They ate chips and salsa while Roberts educated Dixon on the work of Global Adventures and Cooper described how their grassroots network located the safe house in Chicago.

Dixon eyed the chile relleno the old lady set in front of him and opted for a corn tortilla and packaged butter. "So you're suggesting we take advantage of the network again."

"It's less than a week before the deadline." Cooper pushed aside the mound of chile peppers and cut off a chunk of his Chicken Diablo. It was aptly named.

Dixon shook his head. "And given our recent difficulties, extending our exposure seems to be counterproductive to our interests."

"Pardon me for butting in," Roberts said, "but if you're concerned about sensitive information, we would not have any nor would we desire any. We simply receive a profile and likely neighborhoods. We report the activity in those areas to a central office. No information is shared between neighborhoods, and nobody with Global Adventures knows what you do with the information."

Cooper wiped the sweat from his forehead with a napkin. "What's not to like?"

"I guess it's worth a shot. We seem to have stagnated with our usual channels, and with Claire in seclusion, we need something to jump-start things. Not that I object to pulling Claire. That was the right decision." Dixon stood up. "I shudder to imagine the condition of the facilities in this place, but I'm afraid I'm going to need to use them. Which way?"

Roberts pointed to a doorway in a back corner. As Dixon disappeared into it, he turned to Cooper. "Speaking of surveillance, I talked to Bernie this weekend. He's been staking out a Lebanese guy up in Calabasas, one of his customers at Eye Spy."

Cooper raised an eyebrow and took a sip of tea to cool the fire on his tongue. Bernie was an odd sort, but after meeting Roff up in Chicago, he was willing to listen. "Find anything interesting?"

"The guy was buying surveillance gear and remote control electronics. He seems to run some kind of import/export business. Friday Bernie tailed him to the L.A. Greyhound station. He went to a locker and picked up a large briefcase and took it to his house. Bernie didn't like the looks of it. Thought it might be heroin or something."

Cooper set down his fork and looked at Roberts. "Friday? Three days ago Friday?"

"That's the one."

"Has the house been under surveillance since then?"

"Not continuously. Bernie is doing this solo."

"Do you have his number?"

Roberts looked it up on his cell phone. Cooper called Bernie, got the details on Basil el-Amil, arranged for a meeting, then called Perkins and directed him to get a team on the house and an immediate background check to identify other locations. As he hung up, Dixon returned from the bathroom, walking quickly but gingerly.

"I knew it." He snatched his jacket from the back of his chair. "I've got all the symptoms. I'll never eat here again."

"What?" Cooper asked. "Symptoms?"

"Campylobacter jejuni. I'd bet money on it." He shrugged the jacket on. "It's the hole-in-the-wall places. They're the worst."

Cooper laughed. "Dixon, food poisoning has an incubation period. You don't have symptoms for several hours, sometimes even a couple of days. If you have it, you didn't get it here."

"Easy for you to say. I'm going straight to the doctor. You can get a ride with Roberts." He rushed out the door.

Refugio Elementary School, Los Angeles, California. Monday, 10 March 2003. 16:30.

Basil pulled the black Audi into the loading area, let his father out, and watched him disappear into the building. The old Mexican would help out and would receive his just reward. Instant and painless annihilation. A quick death. Not that he deserved better than the death Kalila had experienced. The old fool wasted his compassion and money and sweat on the Jews. On the infidel dogs who sent a tank shell into the Palestinian settlement home of Basil's in-laws, ripping them to shreds. And his wife, visiting her family, trapped in the rubble, crushed, bleeding to death. That's the kind of fate the old Mexican fool deserved.

But Basil could afford to be generous, to grant him a better death than he deserved. The old fool's death was but a fraction of the payment of suffering he would exact from the interfering Americans who supported Israel in their butchery.

He leaned against the car, scanned the schoolyard nervously, and lit a cigarette. What was taking them so long? A lone man lurking around an elementary school attracted attention. Finally the door opened, held by his father as the old man pushed a cart over the threshold and onto the driveway. What was his name? Oh yes, Emilio.

"Emilio, thank you so much for your assistance." He pulled the cart from Emilio and pushed it quickly to the trunk of the Audi. "Mother's birthday is Friday, but I must leave for another trip in the morning." He popped the trunk. "I'm afraid if I try to hide it in the house somewhere she will find it before her birthday." He pulled out a large cardboard box with pictures of a home theater system on the sides and set it on the cart. "If you have room for it in a corner somewhere, Father can pick it up Friday morning."

He closed the trunk, smiled at Emilio, and ferried the large box into the door, through the halls, and to the maintenance room. They found a spot for it by the cabinet. Basil declined the cup of tea, citing a late business meeting, and left the two old men sitting around the large wooden spool. Tomorrow he would surprise his parents with a trip to San Francisco. Wednesday at noon he would surprise Emilio and a million other people with a trip to eternity.

Van Nuys, California.
Monday, 10 March 2003. 17:23.

The red circle popped up on Cooper's monitor just as he was shutting down. He sat back down and opened his secure e-mail. A new message from Alexia Mantrova. He checked his

watch. It was after 2:00 a.m. in Vienna. He would skim it to
see what would bring her home early from the clubs to send
an encrypted e-mail. Then he would drive by the surveillance
teams on el-Amil's Burbank warehouse and Calabasas home
to see how things were going. The team had been set up at his
house by three. An hour later they located the warehouse for
his import business and got a team on it. El-Amil had not been
sighted.

The contents of the e-mail had him standing in a few seconds.

> Date: 11-Mar-2003 02:19:43
> From: aem9321@emeanet.com
> To: mcooper@irig.com
> Subject: Spring Break
>
> I'm thinking of that trip to Cuba. Things could
> become unpleasant here soon. Heavy weather
> is expected and I'm not prepared for it. I send
> you the names of four friends interested in the
> trip. Please contact them to find out if they will
> be available. Without them, I know the party
> will bomb. You should contact them before
> March 14 or it might be too late.
>
> Saeed al-Ghamdi, Washington D.C.
> Ziad Jarrah, New York City, New York
> Ahmad al-Haznawi, Chicago, Illinois
> Basil el-Amil, Los Angeles, California

Los Angeles was the final city. He ignored the sudden emptiness in his chest as the threat suddenly became personal.
Thoughts of getting the girls out of town interspersed themselves with the beginnings of a response plan as Cooper locked
down his computer and sprinted down the hall. Perkins was

still in his office. He looked up from a pile of reports when Cooper burst through the door and closed it behind him.

"Any sighting of el-Amil?"

"None."

"I just got a message from Boris identifying all four cities and the names of the receivers. L.A. is the fourth city, and el-Amil is the receiver."

Perkins jumped to his feet, sending his chair rolling back. It bounced off the wall. "OK. How will we do this? Do we hit the house immediately while he's gone to see if the nuke is still there?"

"No, we have four houses and four nukes. We hit them all simultaneously. And we do it with skeleton teams. I want this hit so clean that even the insertion teams don't know the address until they're a block away." Cooper looked at the closed door. "Right now, only you and I know about this. We get addresses on the other three houses and personally co-ordinate the raids. You take New York and D.C. I'll take L.A. and Chicago."

"Chicago? I thought they were out of the picture."

"We hope the detonation in North Dakota took them out of the picture. However, I'm not willing to bet the life of a few million people that the device wasn't meant for another city and Chicago is still on the map. Or that they didn't acquire another device from those still left in the country after the cold war ended."

"I'm with you."

"Then there's the suspect in Chicago. When the other targets are hit, he'll fade. I'd rather have him where I can talk to him." Cooper checked his watch. "It's almost 9:00 p.m. on the East Coast. Do what you can tonight on those addresses. Just give generic reasons for getting the information. Make it sound as routine as possible while moving as quickly as you can. We should have all the addresses in twelve hours. That gives us tomorrow to work out the logistics, and we can hit tomorrow night. I'm leaning toward a March 12 D-time of 4:00 a.m. in New York and D.C., 3:00 a.m. in Chicago, and 1:00 a.m. in L.A. That's a bit early for L.A., but we'll just have to live with it."

"What about the Feds?"

"We'll bring them in tomorrow. Once we have teams for each city set up, we'll give them layouts with no addresses so the logistics can be planned. A few hours before, we will narrow it down to a neighborhood and get the teams within a mile or so, both ground and air teams. At D minus ten minutes we'll release the addresses and let them get positioned for simultaneous hits. I'll contact Dr. McKinney. We'll need a NEST presence in all four cities."

Cooper was out of the door before Perkins could respond.

Outside Tecate, Mexico.
Monday, 10 March 2003. 21:30.

He was wearing Levis, boots, a black shirt, and an L.A. Dodgers cap. He had a backpack containing six liters of water, two dozen tortillas, a half-dozen cans of tuna, a Walther PPK, and $5,000 in cash. He would make Doghouse Junction before dawn.

His beard was gone. His mustache was trimmed, black and neat on his brown skin. He had a Mexican passport and a green card with a Los Angeles address. He would find Matthew Cooper and kill him. He would assure that millions would die in the American capital and its two largest cities.

He flicked on the flashlight, checked his compass, and flicked it back off. Time to head north and strike the deathblow to the Great Satan. Then he would return to Iran and kill al-Suri. He smiled in the darkness and crossed the road.

Chapter 44

Van Nuys, California.
Wednesday, 12 March 2003. 01:00.

Cooper poured more coffee and pointed the carafe at Perkins, who shook his head. He sipped from his mug and sat back down at the table. The indirect lighting from the corners of the IRIG war room left the people seated around the table in a gloom. It was a small crowd—Perkins, Montoya, McKinney, Watford, Gilberts, and Wagner, filling in for Dixon, who was at home semi-delirious from food poisoning. Cooper didn't replace Claire, choosing to cover her duties himself.

Most eyes were on the screen on the far wall, where maps of the four cities zoomed in on the safe houses targeted for the raid. Circles with numbers indicated the location of the teams awaiting the signal. Cooper scanned the room, wondering if they had been more successful in getting their families to take an unplanned spring break trip out of town. Nikki liked the idea, but when she asked for the urgent reason that would be sufficient justification to John to affect their schedule, he couldn't give her the real reason. He saw immediately that Stevie discerned the motivation behind the spur-of-the-moment vacation. He saw the fear skitter across her features before they resolved into an unnatural calm. She asked if he would be joining them on this trip. His silence told her everything. She said she wouldn't go without him, and that was the end of the discussion. His only hope was that the target was not near Hollywood.

It was time. He went around the room, asking each person if they were ready. He received six affirmatives. The final checklist sounded on the conference phone, which played the traffic on the radio frequencies used by the strike teams.

On Cooper's signal, seven teams in three time zones hit their targets simultaneously. One team in D.C. hit the home of Saeed al-Ghamdi. He was in custody and the house secured in forty-five seconds. Two teams in New York hit the two residences of Ziad Jarrah, taking four men into custody. One team in Chicago hit the apartment of Ahmed al-Haznawi, apprehending two men.

Three teams in California targeted Basil el-Amil's Calabasas home, his Burbank warehouse, and his father's home in central L.A. The rent-a-cop at the warehouse was detained while the team searched it. The two homes were empty, as expected.

El-Amil and his parents were in San Francisco. Tuesday morning the surveillance team reported that el-Amil dropped a carry-on bag into the trunk of his Audi and drove to a home a quarter-mile west of the L.A. financial district. By the time he escorted an elderly Middle Eastern couple to the car and stowed their luggage, the surveillance team had determined that the house was owned by Amil el-Amil. They took I-5 to the Bob Hope airport in Burbank. One agent followed them in and verified that they boarded a flight to San Francisco International Airport.

When they landed, a team from the Bay Area IRIG office picked up the surveillance. They had lunch at Paul K and spent the afternoon in museums in Golden Gate Park. That evening they checked into the private apartment at the Clift Hotel at Taylor and Geary.

Just before the raids were executed, Perkins checked with the Bay Area team. The older couple was in the apartment. El-Amil was on a leather couch in the Redwood Room, drinking martinis and talking to a woman. Two FBI agents were circulating through the bar, keeping an eye on him. Cooper instructed the team to take el-Amil when he left the bar. Until that time they were to keep close surveillance but not to intervene unless he used his cell phone or was approached by someone appearing to attempt to pass information to him.

By 1:30 a.m. the teams began to report the results of the searches. The D.C. house, one New York apartment, the Calabasas house, and the Burbank warehouse all showed trace amounts of radiation but no device was found at any location. They found a wealth of documents, but those would take time to process. All the suspects were taken to FBI facilities for interrogation.

After the last team reported in, Cooper instructed the San Francisco team to keep him informed when the status changed and disconnected the conference bridge. He looked around the room at a group of weary, red-eyed men.

"It will take a few hours to get usable information from the suspects. Let's plan to meet back here at seven. If anything breaks, I'll contact you immediately."

The room cleared slowly until only Cooper and Perkins were left. Cooper leaned back in his chair and exhaled loudly.

"That sounded ominous," Perkins said. "I'd say it's time to celebrate. We finally caught a break."

Cooper picked up an empty coaster and spun it absently on the conference table. "That's the problem. Three raids in a row are compromised. Then I remove Claire from the picture and we hit four houses and get seven suspects. No last-minute escapes, no snipers, no leaks. Even el-Amil seems to be completely unaware that his house, his warehouse, and his parents' house are all swarming with federal agents right now."

"It's circumstantial. Could be something else." Perkins shook his head. "I just can't see Claire turning."

"The best double is the one that seems impossible."

"Of course, but that's obvious, Matt. It's like saying the best conspiracy theory is unprovable and then presenting an unprovable theory."

"Yeah, I know. But the facts are that the first raid we do without Claire works."

"What about Dixon?"

"What about him?"

"He wasn't here either."

"Dixon? Can you seriously think Dixon would ever turn?"

"Then that makes him the better suspect. More impossible to believe, better double agent."

Cooper threw the coaster at Perkins. "It's too late for this. How about another cup of coffee?"

At 1:55 a.m. the phone rang. Perkins pushed the button on the conference phone. The San Francisco team reported that el-Amil was leaving the Redwood Room alone. Cooper instructed them to have the agents apprehend him before he got to the apartment. Thirty minutes later he received a report from the Bay Area coordinator.

The team followed el-Amil and moved to take him as he waited for the elevator. He was standing with his hand in his pocket. The two agents cornered him at the elevator door, drew guns, identified themselves as FBI, and ordered him to move away from the elevator. He looked at them blankly as if not understanding. They repeated the order. The elevator door opened behind him. He stepped backward into the elevator.

One agent stepped forward to put his foot against the door to keep it from closing. As he did so, el-Amil lunged, pulling a knife from his pocket, and slashed the agent's gun hand. The agent fired but his shot went wide. El-Amil kicked him in the chest, and he stumbled backward out of the door. El-Amil pressed himself into the front corner. As the doors began to close the second agent rushed the opening, firing to keep el-Amil away from the door. The agent shoved his foot against the door by el-Amil, his back against the other and forced them apart.

El-Amil threw the knife. The blade disappeared into the agent's throat and he collapsed, blocking the door open. El-Amil went for the gun and turned it on the first agent. They both fired. El-Amil staggered against the back wall of the elevator and slid down to the floor. The elevator buzzer went off, complaining because the door was blocked open.

The first agent cautiously approached the elevator, stepped over the second agent, removed the gun from el-Amil's hand and threw it into the hallway. He verified el-Amil was dead then checked the other agent. He was still alive. He was calling 911 when backup arrived.

Perkins disconnected the call. Cooper looked at him.

"We have a problem. The one person who knew the location of the L.A. nuke is dead."

Van Nuys, California.
Wednesday, 12 March 2003. 09:15.

The wait was maddening. FBI interrogators worked the seven suspects. Information was reported back to the IRIG office where the expert teams evaluated it, attempting to separate facts from misdirection and identifying cracks in the stories.

Inconsistencies were analyzed and possible lines of questioning were suggested as the larger picture emerged.

Cooper called a status meeting to hear what had been discovered from the suspects. Based on the braggadocio of the terrorists, it was verified that the bombs were planted in technical and financial centers with a high population density as expected. Like many other terrorist bombings, they would detonate upon the call of a cell phone. In addition, they had prepared for the contingency of capture. If no call came to detonate the bombs, they would detonate on their own when the cell phone battery died.

As Watford turned a page on the report, Cooper slapped his hand down on the conference table.

"Cell phones," he said.

Watford looked up, startled. "Yes, cell phones. It's very common. A simple, mature, and pervasive technology."

"Yes, yes. Were any cell phones recovered from the raids?"

"Yes. We have checked all the numbers in the address book of each phone. No unaccounted or rogue numbers."

"Do you know the numbers of the cell phones that were recovered?"

"Yes, they are in the report."

Cooper pushed a button on the conference room phone. "Sarah, could you bring me the most recent report from the Lone Ranger immediately?"

"Sure," she answered.

Cooper looked around at the questioning faces around the table. "Last month our office in Tel Aviv received copies of documents recovered from a raid on an al-Qaeda safe house in Baria. There was a list of cell phone numbers in the file."

Sarah walked in with a folder, handed it to Cooper, and left. Cooper dug through it and pulled out a piece of paper. Watford pushed a page from the report to him.

"Bingo. We have several hits." He handed the list to Watford. "Get these numbers disabled immediately."

La Jolla, California.
Wednesday, 12 March 2003. 12:15.

He found the pickup on Otay Mountain a few hours after sunrise, waited half an hour to make sure there was no surveillance, then walked into the clearing. The driver said nothing, just waited until he was settled, started the truck, and drove down the mountain. The drive took a little over an hour. Then a shower, a change of clothes, and a meal with the TV tuned to CNN. When the noon hour passed without any bulletins, he knew something was wrong.

He called al-Ghamdi's cell phone and received a message indicating the service had been discontinued. He received similar messages when he called Jarrah, al-Haznawi, and el-Amil. Then he tried the number of the device in L.A. Same message. With a mounting sense of rage, he called the other three devices. All disconnected.

He shot the tube out of the television, took the keys to the truck, and headed north.

Chapter 45

Stevie didn't bother with the dining room. She set the plate on the bar in the kitchen, pulled up a stool, and began dismantling the steamed artichoke, dipping it in the mysterious paste Rosa prepared only after banishing everyone from the kitchen. Stevie never needed to be asked twice to have artichoke, but Rosa's secret paste elevated it to a mystical experience. And tonight she needed a mystical experience.

It was only Wednesday, but already the week felt like it was a month long. She hadn't seen Matt since Monday morning when he left for IRIG to deal with some crisis on the case or some breakthrough. Either way, it meant he worked through the night, catching occasional naps in the apartment attached to his office.

Then there was the movie. The on-location shoot went so well that it seemed this would be the easiest project of her career. Then everything fell apart in the studio. A third of the cast and crew fell victim to the flu. Since it swept through California while they were in Morocco, at first it appeared they had escaped it. But then a makeup girl got it from her

.ate bloomer, and that was it.
.es weren't working and dragged
.hem, resulting in several rounds
satisfied. And that was just in a

dragged her to a small group in Santa
.l like going. The Vail weekend and the
.y were up against had sucked out all mo-
.he point of making a movie when four mil-
die in a week? If Matt might die tomorrow?
⁄ relieved when the shooting slowed down. It
.n't have to apologize to Russell for lackluster
.

.la was relentless, so Stevie went, sat quietly in a
.d watched. Somebody had a guitar and they sang
.e had never heard, but the words stirred the sense of
⁄ and significance she had experienced in the desert. She
.ecognized some of the lyrics, words Paula had read in the
.ght before dawn. She hid in the safety of the corner and
.sed her eyes and let the invisible arms surround her like the
.notion of the sea and let the tears trickle down her face. Then
somebody prayed and somebody else prayed. Then somebody
read from the Bible and they discussed it. Nobody bothered
her, but it wasn't like they were ignoring her. They just let her
be there. It was enough for them and enough for her.

When they left, she blurted out some polite words to the
host, the first she had spoken since she was introduced. Then
Paula drove her back to Malibu in silence. Stevie felt like she
had been cranked through an old-fashioned washing machine
wringer and all the hopelessness and confusion was squeezed
out. She was limp and exhausted and euphoric. When they arrived at the Malibu fortress, she mumbled thanks to Paula. She
also agreed to go next week.

Tomorrow was Thursday. As the frustrations and delays continued at the studio, she found her mind drawn back to the catharsis of last Thursday, longing for another taste. In the mornings out on the deck she began reading from the Psalms, starting where Paula left off in Morocco. It gave her a sense of perspective, a grounding that seemed to carry through the beginning of the day, although it usually faded by lunch.

Maybe Matt was right. Maybe it was a crutch. Sometimes it felt like a drug, a relaxing effect that reduced the pressure and pain circumstances caused. She felt a pull to experience it again, like the craving for a fix addicts felt. But the renewed energy and enthusiasm enabled her to face the frustrations at the studio and the gnawing fear that haunted her whenever she thought of Matt and nuclear warfare. And there didn't seem to be any unwanted side effects.

The opening of the swinging kitchen door disturbed her reflections. It was the door that led to the back of the house and the guest wing. Claire crept in almost apologetically, as if hoping to find the room empty. She hesitated when she saw Stevie. It was the first time their paths had crossed since her arrival on Sunday. Claire looked so small and vulnerable, almost wraithlike in a black cotton T-shirt dress. Stevie felt a spring of tenderness push up through her. She felt the frown of concentration fade from her face, replaced by a gentle smile.

Claire's rigid frame relaxed almost imperceptibly, and she let the door swing closed. "Rosa said there was artichoke in the kitchen." She looked at the bowl on the island piled with artichokes. "She usually brings meals to the room, but this time she told me to help myself." She smiled absently. "I guess she's tired of waiting on me."

Stevie returned the smile and got up to fetch a plate. "No, that's just Rosa's way of making you do what she thinks is good

for you." She handed a plate to Claire and spooned some of
Rosa's secret sauce into a dish. "Nikki thinks she's tamed her,
which of course is exactly what Rosa wants her to think. If she
thought you needed it, Rosa would wait on you for a year without complaining. If ever there was a saint in Malibu, which is
unlikely, it would be Rosa." She opened a cabinet of glassware.
"Wine, beer, tea, soft drink, fruit juice?"

Claire looked at Stevie's plate on the bar. "What are you
having?"

"Water."

"That's good enough for me." She placed an artichoke on
the plate. "Do you mind if I join you? I'm going crazy back
there." She nodded to the guest wing.

"Sure." Stevie set the glass of water at the place next to her
own and slid back on the barstool.

They ate in awkward silence for awhile. Stevie couldn't decide on a topic of conversation. Should she bring up the murder or leave it alone? Would Claire want to talk about it with
someone or pretend it hadn't happened? And other than the
emotional reception three days ago, the only time they had
spoken was the Christmas party. Not exactly the best topic for
dinner conversation.

Claire solved the dilemma by speaking first.

"I probably shouldn't say anything at all, but I want to apologize for my behavior at the Christmas party. I'd like to blame
it on the martinis, but the truth is, I'm just spiteful."

Stevie was about to dismiss the apology with some triviality,
but she was stopped cold by Claire's blunt honesty. She realized her mouth was open for the unspoken word and closed it.
Claire continued.

"It's true. I don't do well with other women. I was raised in
a military family with a domineering father, competitive brothers, and an invisible mother. Nobody ever taught me how to be

soft and feminine, which turned out to be a good thing for my career. I wouldn't have made it so far so quickly if I had learned to bat my eyes and control men by playing the weakling."

Stevie started to say something, realized she hadn't the faintest notion what to say, pulled a leaf from the artichoke, and scraped it across her teeth. Claire didn't seem to notice her as anything more than something to talk to.

"You discover quickly which are weak, which are strong, which pretend to be strong because really they are weak, which appear to be weak because really they are strong and don't have to prove anything. If you know what you're doing, that is. If you don't push them, stretch them until the surface thins out, and you see what lurks underneath, you might never know the truth."

"Which was your boyfriend?"

Stevie blurted it out, using Claire's tactics against her. She didn't seem to notice at all.

"Oh, he pretended to be strong because he was weak. It's the cliché of the Arab culture. The only way the weak ones can survive is to pretend to be strong. They figure it out or die. The strong ones don't have to bother." She tossed an artichoke leaf on the pile.

"And which is Matt?"

That stopped her. She paused with a leaf in midair and looked at Stevie. "Oh, I think you know. You wouldn't be here if you didn't."

The voice startled both of them. "He's strong."

Nikki was standing in the doorway to the dining room. She glared at the two of them. Claire looked at Stevie, shrugged, and pulled off another leaf. Stevie slipped off the stool.

"Artichoke?"

"That's what I'm here for," Nikki said but didn't move from the doorway.

Stevie set up a place at the end of the bar next to her own plate. She fixed a Diet Coke without asking and set it next to the plate. Then she sat back down and resumed eating. Nikki hung back for awhile then hesitantly climbed on the stool and sat facing down the bar, looking over the women's plates.

"This theory of yours," Stevie said. "Does it extend to women too? Four categories—weak, strong, strength masking weakness, weakness masking strength?"

Claire was silent for a few moments. "Women are more complicated. You can try to fit them into the four categories, but there are so many variations, it breaks down quickly. The problem is that in the human species, the female is physically weaker than the male. As a result, she is forced to learn how to negotiate for power rather than simply exert power, like the males. She has to translate strength and weakness into contexts beyond physical strength. Men do this too, but by choice. Women do it from necessity."

Claire kept working through her artichoke. Stevie looked over to Nikki. Nikki rolled her eyes and shook her head. Stevie flared her eyes open and nodded slowly. It was like a shared secret. It was such a small thing, and Nikki didn't seem to notice it. But Stevie recognized it for what it was, a milestone. A threshold crossed. In the two-year battle it was the first sign that a DMZ might be possible. She decided to establish a beachhead. She turned to Claire.

"So you think it's all about power? What about love? How does that figure in?"

From the corner of her eye, Stevie saw Nikki nodding. She smiled inwardly.

Claire snorted. "Love figures in the same way drugs figure in. It's an escape from reality that clouds your judgment."

Nikki responded, outraged. "Love is real."

Claire looked at her as if deciding how much to say. "I didn't say love isn't real. Drugs are real, aren't they?"

"But you said love is an escape from reality. What about all those love songs? What about all the romantic movies? How come they're so popular?"

"Why are drugs so popular?" Claire waited, but Nikki didn't respond, so she continued. "We want something to tell us the pain will go away, that the world really isn't as bad as it seems. But the truth is that the world is as bad as it seems and reality bites. So we find something to medicate ourselves with, our drug of choice."

"I don't have a drug of choice," Nikki said with contempt. She pulled a leaf and dragged it through Rosa's mystery paste in an exaggerated motion of dismissal.

"Oh, I suspect if we dig deep enough we'll find one," Claire said. "Maybe not a controlled substance, but something else. Young girls are much more creative with their opiates than boys. For the timid there are romance novels, romantic movies, love songs. For the traditional there is religion or exotic religions for the nontraditional. For the socially insecure there is sex. For those with greater pain to escape there is anorexia, bulimia, self-mutilation."

Stevie noticed that Nikki grew more subdued as the litany continued. Claire seemed to notice it too. She leaned forward to get a better look at Nikki.

"Do you still insist you have no drug of choice? I'd peg you for one of the exotic choices."

Nikki looked at her plate without comment. She seemed to shrink. Stevie turned on Claire.

"So what is your drug of choice?"

Nikki looked up expectantly as if hoping to see Claire embarrassed.

"Martinis and sex," Claire said. "And yours?"

"So you're admitting you can't take reality either?" She glanced at Nikki, who nodded, acknowledging the barb.

Claire turned and looked at her, surprised. "Did I ever say otherwise? Believe me, reality hasn't been any kinder to me than it has to anyone else. I'm here, aren't I?" She smiled bitterly. "I choose my drugs carefully so they don't spill over into the rest of my life and screw it up. Until now." The fire seemed to suddenly go out of Claire. She picked up the spoon and began eating the artichoke heart.

Stevie shook her head. She suddenly felt pity overwhelm her outrage. "Do you really believe what you're saying? How can you live that way?"

"It's called reality, Stevie. A successful person is one who has learned to manage his drug of choice so that it doesn't affect his ability to succeed. Then there are people like you."

"Me?"

Claire nodded. "Some people find a way to make their drug of choice the source of their success. How does it feel when you're in the middle of a scene and everything is working?"

"It feels great," Stevie said cautiously. She looked at Nikki. "It's a feeling like no other." Nikki nodded.

"Sort of like being high?" Claire asked. Stevie didn't respond. "See? You have chosen a profession where the more often you achieve that state of bliss, the more successful you will be. I did the same thing. There's nothing like the thrill of the hunt."

Stevie shook her head sadly. "You're sick, you know that? You've reduced every little joy and pleasure we can experience to a sordid desire to escape reality. I think you're wrong. There is good in life, and we can find it if we choose it."

Claire ignored her assessment and continued, almost as if she were speaking to herself. "The funny thing is that even those who have merged their success with their escape find it isn't enough. We still need more. It never ends. It's like the great void, consuming all. The eternal darkness that never rests."

Stevie turned to Nikki. Their eyes locked. Though no words were spoken, Stevie heard Nikki. There was pain. There was a drug of choice. And there was a desperate hope that Claire was wrong and Stevie was right.

I'm right, Stevie thought as she stared into Nikki's eyes. *I've experienced reality in bits and pieces. I'm learning to live in it more each day. And reality is love.*

Chapter 46

Van Nuys, California.
Wednesday, 12 March 2003. 20:32.

Since no radiation was detected in the Chicago apartment, Cooper suspected the lost nuke was indeed the one targeted for Chicago and no replacement had been made. Transcripts of the al-Haznawi interrogation confirmed his suspicion. The New York team combing through the documents recovered from the apartments identified three likely locations of the nuke. The NEST team located the nuke in the basement of an office complex a block from the New York Stock Exchange. Access had been gained from the utilities right-of-way tunnels. After twenty hours of nonstop interrogation, al-Ghamdi broke. A NEST team found the nuke in the locker of a health club two blocks from the White House.

But there was nobody to ask about the location of the L.A. nuke, and no telltale documents to sift through. At Cooper's request, Dr. McKinney had the L.A. NEST team begin a systematic scan of buildings in the financial district, starting with sweeps from vans, then a building-by-building sweep with handheld detectors. Neither had much hope that the search would yield results. Too much background radiation and the likelihood that the nuke was well shielded made it little more than a token effort, but Cooper was unwilling to overlook any avenue, however futile it might seem. There was no question that the bomb was deployed, and even with the cell phone number disabled and el-Amil dead, it would still detonate when the cell phone battery died. He had even asked Roberts to mobilize his network. They might succeed again where the pros were floundering.

Malibu, California.
Thursday, 13 March 2003. 06:32.

As she drove the Jaguar out of the gate of the Malibu fortress, Stevie didn't pay much attention to the road worker with the walkie-talkie fifty yards down the hill. She was distracted by digging under the seat for a cap for Nikki to keep the hair out of her face. The fact that she was driving Nikki to the studio was enough to distract her. It was as unlikely an event as California falling into the sea.

When Nikki joined her on the deck for breakfast, she was surprised. When Nikki asked about her schedule and then for a ride to the studio, she was speechless. Nikki interpreted her hesitation as reluctance and backpedaled self-consciously, but Stevie interrupted and said she'd enjoy it. Nikki spluttered into embarrassed and relieved silence and then left abruptly to get ready. Stevie looked down at the Bible in her lap.

God, she prayed, *help that girl. If I can help her, show me how. Bring me the opportunity.*

Then Nikki was ready and they were on their way down to PCH. Stevie had just pulled the cap from under the seat when she saw the sawhorses and blinking lights blocking half the road. Another Hispanic man in a hard hat and orange vest held up a stop sign, motioning for oncoming traffic to come through. A white van pulled around the barricade and stopped next to the Jaguar. A dark man in a black suit and sunglasses stepped out. He looked behind her. She glanced in the mirror as another white van pulled up behind her. She looked back to the man in the street. That's when she saw the gun.

"Call 911," she screamed to Nikki and jammed the accelerator to the floor. The Jag lunged toward the Hispanic worker. As they bore down on him, she realized he wasn't Hispanic; he was Middle Eastern. He dove to the side. She crashed against the barricade, and the sawhorses splintered. She thumped over them and heard fragments scrape against the bottom of the car. It didn't sound good. Something was damaged for sure.

As she pulled free from the wreckage a motorcycle appeared from a side street and pulled next to the Jag. There were two men on it. The second had a machine gun. With a few bursts he took out both driver-side tires. Stevie lost control of the car, and it ground to an earsplitting stop against the rock wall of an estate. The air bags deployed, and before she could recover from the confusion, rough hands dragged her from the car. She got a glimpse of Nikki struggling with another man and then a white cloth was placed against her face, blocking her vision. She resisted, holding her breath as long as possible, but as she was forced into the back of the van she lost consciousness.

Van Nuys, California.
Thursday, March 13, 2003. 08:09

Cooper asked the Los Angeles County deputy to repeat his statement, but it didn't sound real the second time either.

"We found an XKS Jaguar Champion registered to Matthew Cooper at the bottom of Topanga Canyon."

He looked at his calendar. It was 2003, not 1997. This was not happening.

"Sir?"

Cooper turned back to the phone.

"Was there a . . . anybody with the car?"

"No sir. We didn't find any bodies in the car or anywhere near it. Just the car. When did you last see it?"

No bodies? His mind flashed through a million scenarios, but none of them made sense. Then he remembered he was on a phone call. "Uh . . . Monday morning."

"Who normally drives this car?"

Car in the canyon. No bodies. What could it mean? "Stevie. Stephanie Zorn."

"When was the last time you saw Ms. Zorn?"

"I talked to her last night."

"Mr. Cooper, I seem to remember a similar incident. Didn't a car of yours end up in the canyon five or six years ago?"

"Meaning?"

"Nothing, sir. I just recalled it. I suggest you attempt to contact Ms. Zorn immediately. And you might want to contact whoever pulled your last car out of the canyon."

Cooper was already reaching for the disconnect button. He hit the speed dial for Stevie's cell phone and got the voice mail. He left a quick message, called Nikki's cell phone, left a message, and then called the house. Rosa answered.

"Rosa, is Stevie there?"

"No, Mr. Cooper. She left with Nikki over an hour ago."

Cooper was concerned before. Now he was astounded. "With Nikki? Stevie and Nikki left together?"

"Yes sir. They both had the studio this morning, so Nikki asked Ms. Zorn to take her."

"Nikki asked?" The impossibility of it temporarily drove other thoughts from his mind. "That's strange."

"Yes sir."

"Did they take the Jag?"

"I don't know about the car, sir. I never left the kitchen."

"Is Alex there?"

Rosa retrieved Alex, who confirmed that Stevie had taken the Jag as usual and that Nikki left with her. Cooper told him about the wreck and asked him to take care of recovering the car. Then he called the studio. Nikki had not checked in, but shooting was due to start in an hour. He called the other studio. They were also attempting to contact Stevie and wondered if he could help them. He couldn't.

He hung up the phone and wondered what it could mean. He suspected that Nikki still nursed guilt over Lola's death. Would she try to reenact it somehow? But then where were the bodies? What did Stevie say about Nikki—that she was barely hanging on? He should have done something. But he had tried. He talked to her, tried to get her to open up, to tell him if something was bothering her. It didn't work. She didn't cooperate.

He slammed his fist on the desk and turned to look out the glass wall of his office. He should have tried harder, should have pushed her. Maybe he should have taken her to get counseling. A doctor. A hospital. That was it. He should check the hospitals. Somebody might have found them and taken them to the hospital without stopping to inform the police.

He turned and rushed back to the phone and then realized he would need help. He would get Perkins involved, the rest of the team. They were going stir crazy anyway, waiting for results from the Feds' interrogations. The thought of the team led his mind to Claire, and he felt a coldness run through him. Perhaps . . .

He called the house again.

"Rosa, is Ms. Moquard still there?"

"Yes sir. Do you want me to get her?"

"No. But you're sure she has not left the house today?"

"No, she has not left the house since she came Sunday."

"OK. Thanks."

He called Sarah in. After she recovered from the shock she gathered the team in the conference room. Perkins got a team working on the hospitals and police stations. Cooper took Montoya with him to backtrack the route to Malibu. They came up empty until a quarter mile from the house they found a damaged rock wall and traces of blue paint matching the Jaguar. Not far away they discovered a pile of smashed saw horses and orange cones. A call to the city offices indicated that no work was scheduled for that location.

He was getting into the Porsche, fighting the sense of panic and nausea that was slowly building as he learned more, when his cell phone rang. It was Nikki's ring. He scrambled for it, snatched it from his pocket, and yelled into the mike.

Chapter 47

Missile silo north of Cheyenne, Wyoming.
Thursday, 13 March 2003. 11:15.

He was glad he had the presence of mind to pick up the girl's cell phone from the floorboard of the Jaguar before Azhar took it to Topanga Canyon. The little things could have the greatest effect. He scrolled through the address book to the "DadzCell" entry and pressed the Send button and put it on Speaker. It was answered on the first ring.

"Nikki, where are you?"

He looked across the room at the girl and smiled. She didn't seem reassured, but she couldn't say much with the gag on. Her eyes flared open and tears welled up. The woman next to her glared at him. In the silence, Cooper's voice rang out across the Quonset hut.

"Nikki? Are you OK?"

"She is OK for now. Whether she remains that way depends entirely on you, Mr. Cooper."

There was a short pause as the mind on the other end recalibrated. Then it came swiftly. "If she has a scratch, just a single scratch, I'll kill you personally."

He smiled. "Come, come, Mr. Cooper. There is no use for your bragging words. You have something of mine; I have something of yours. I'm sure we can come to some agreement."

"I don't have anything of yours."

"Of course you do. You have the devices."

"You know I can't cut any deals for those devices."

He could hear the desperation. Either Cooper hadn't found the bombs or the authorities already had them. He was not surprised, but it was good to get as much information as possible.

"Then it appears you are not in a position to bargain. I have something you want, and you have nothing I want. I'm holding all the cards. So a little less swagger and a little more humility is in order."

"Cut the games, Berkowitz. Why are you calling me if I don't have anything you want?"

He looked at the phone on the table, then over at the women. They looked back blankly. "Berkowitz? Why do you call me this?"

"You know my name. I don't know yours. I have to call you something, don't I?"

"You may call me Nadhir, the one who warns you."

"OK, Nadhir, let's get this over with. What do you want?"

"I want to see you beg."

"Pardon me?"

"Do you want to see your women alive? I will give them to you. If the proud American Christian will beg on his knees before the servant of Allah, he will show mercy." There was silence. "Mr. Cooper, are you unwilling to do this simple thing to save the lives of your women?"

"I'm just trying to figure the angle. That can't be all you want."

He smiled. Of course not. But that would come later. "Mr. Cooper, you do not know much of our culture, do you?"

"I know enough to know I don't want to know any more."

"In our culture, humiliation is a fate worse than death. I will take images of the proud American bowing before the servant of Allah."

"A picture. All you want is a picture."

"Not just any picture, Mr. Cooper. A picture of the humiliation of the Americans. It will serve my purpose as a hundred bombs could not. And you will have to live the rest of your life with the knowledge that the picture of you bowing before a Muslim will be used to bring many young men to my cause." He paused, but Cooper didn't respond. "I am willing to trade two women for this."

He waited. The answer finally came—the one he knew must come from an American, however proud he must be.

"OK, I'll give you your picture. When? Where?"

"Within one hour your Gulfstream IV should leave the Burbank airport. File a flight plan for St. Louis, Missouri, and keep 134.125 megahertz open. I will give you instructions when you are in the air. And do not contact the authorities. I will know the moment you do, and then the women will be dead."

"How do I know you have them and they're alive?"

"You must trust me. Even so, can you afford to refuse and take the chance that your decision killed them? I think not. You follow my instructions and I assure you that you will see both of your women alive and unhurt, standing before you before the sun sets."

This much was true, and he was scrupulous about such matters when he could afford to be. They would be alive when Cooper landed. He disconnected the call, confident his men would report Cooper on the IRIG jet leaving Burbank before the hour was out. He looked at the woman and smiled.

"Don't worry. He'll come."

The woman ignored him. She was watching the girl. He followed her gaze. The girl was looking at him with a strange expression that was hard to interpret, even taking into account the gag. Just when he thought it might be fear, it seemed to look more like resignation. But when he looked at her closer, looking for resignation, the look seemed more like fear, a primal fear, like the fear of a thousand nightmares. It was both and yet neither.

He turned to Naji. "Take them to the back room and feed them. If you harm either I will cook your entrails slowly while you watch and feed them to you."

Naji nodded without comment, pulled the women to their feet, and herded them to the back. Al-Huzayfi watched them go, impressed by their stamina. He expected the American women to be softer, weaker. Of course, they were unconscious for the drive from Malibu south on the 101 to Canoga Park. They were still unconscious when they were transferred from the stolen white van to the black van in an abandoned self-storage parking lot. The drive up I-5 and 14 to the airstrip northwest from Acton was only an hour. They didn't wake up until the Beechcraft King Air hit turbulence coming down over the Rockies.

But then, instead of being panicked and compliant as al-Huzayfi expected, the woman resisted and they had to drag her off the plane. The girl just seemed dazed. But as the drugs wore off, she was as uncooperative as the woman. Until she heard her father's voice.

He turned to the door to put the rest of the plan in motion. She would hear her father's voice again. At sundown, it would be the last thing she would ever hear. Her father screaming.

Malibu, California.
Thursday, 13 March 2003. 11:29.

Cooper flipped the phone closed and turned to Montoya. "Did they get it?"

Montoya spoke into his cell phone, listened, and then nodded. "Eastern Wyoming. Northeast of Cheyenne. Almost Nebraska."

"Get in. Let's go." He shoved the phone into the mobile cradle, started the Porsche, and raced down the hill. Montoya scrambled to buckle his seat belt. Cooper called Perkins. "They made contact. Tell Morse to have the Gulfstream ready and file a flight plan to St. Louis. Bring me a set of full body armor, a field wire kit, and a deep-cover wire kit. Get the Feds on this. We need a Special Forces team in Wyoming in three hours. Montoya can give you the coordinates of the target. We'll need a drone to relay the signal from the wire to the satellite."

Perkins sounded doubtful. "Matt, why would the Feds put all these resources on a kidnap case? An assault team? Reposition a satellite? I know you realize how much red tape that will take."

"Frank, the guy who got Stevie and Nikki is the guy who masterminded the HuJI plot. He is in Wyoming right now. This is not just a kidnap case. This is a chance for the Feds to take the guy who knows where the L.A. bomb is."

There was silence as Perkins processed this information and Cooper took the turn onto PCH much faster than recommended by the authorities.

"So, why not just send in an assault team right now and take him?"

"Call me sentimental, but I'd like to have a shot at getting Stevie and Nikki out of there alive at the same time. Take some notes." Cooper relayed the conversation with Nadhir, the instructions, and his plan.

"I'll get everything rolling," Perkins said. "We can have a last-minute briefing in the hangar."

"No, they'll be watching the hangar. Meet me at the Commons in Calabasas."

Perkins was parked near the Ralph's Grocery. Watford and Gilberts were in the backseat. Cooper slid into the front seat. Perkins handed him a set of satellite photos.

"He called from an old Atlas F missile silo in eastern Wyoming decommissioned in 1965. In 1998, it was sold through Twentieth Century Castles to a Yusuf Mazen, who told the agent he was going to convert it to a retreat to get away from his day job as a CPA in Cheyenne. Mr. Mazen is at this moment in his office in Cheyenne and has not placed or received any unusual phone calls in the past forty-eight hours.

"The Atlas F silo features a 15,000-square-foot underground complex consisting of a command building and a launch silo connected by a 100-foot tunnel. The call was most likely placed from one of the Quonset huts, since he would get no signal inside the silo unless he had installed relay antennae inside."

Perkins pointed to the photos. "You can see here and here the movement of people between buildings. Note the weapons." He pulled other photos from the stack. "There doesn't appear to be a perimeter defense or any surveillance of the approaches. It looks like they feel pretty secure in their location."

He pulled more papers from a satchel. "Here's some documentation on the layout of the Atlas F bases and the realtor's materials for this site." He nodded to a bag in the backseat between Watford and Gilberts. "The armor and the wire kits are in there. And your Glock."

"I doubt I'll get a chance to use it." Cooper twisted around and looked at Watford and Gilberts. "I don't want anything visible to the bad guys within five miles. If the team can come in on foot with zero chance of detection, fine. But we need rapid-response teams in choppers nearby. Also two trauma doctors and any help they need." He flipped through the photos and pulled one out. "It looks like we could get the Gulfstream in and out on this strip if we have to. Takeoff will be tight, but the modified Rolls-Royce engines are designed for this kind of situation."

Cooper looked over the photo. The car was silent for several seconds. Then he looked to Perkins and dropped a hand on his shoulder.

"Frank, I really appreciate everything you've done. There's no way to know what will happen out there. Thanks for everything."

Perkins looked startled, blinked, and looked away. "Sure," he said, looking back at Cooper. "But it will work out. You'll bring them back. I know it."

"Right." Cooper nodded to Watford and Gilberts. "Gentlemen."

He gathered up everything, returned to the Porsche, and drove to the Van Nuys airport. Morse acknowledged him as he came onboard and returned to his checklist.

On the flight he took off his clothes, put on the flesh-colored body armor and then his clothes over it. He put on the conventional wire under his shirt, a tracking device next to it, and the buttonhole camera in his jacket. He expected these to be detected and removed, giving Nadhir a false sense of security that all attempts at surveillance were defeated. Just before they landed, he would put in the contact lens that was a remote camera and the miniscule in-ear transmitter-receiver that was undetectable without a flashlight and very close inspection. He would also shove the Glock 23 into his waistline in the small of his back. He expected this to be detected and removed too.

He went up front with Morse. As they approached the Grand Canyon a transmission on 134.125 MHz gave them new coordinates.

As they turned toward Wyoming, Cooper looked over the photos again, thinking about the risks. The entire scheme relied on Nadhir thinking he had complied with all the conditions until he was close enough to do something. So much depended on chance, on elements he could not foresee or control.

He thought back to the conversation with Stevie. He was always confident when walking into the valley of the shadow of death. He was willing to stake his life on his training, experience, and instincts. But he had not considered the possibility that this case would take Stevie and Nikki into that valley also. Was he willing to stake their lives on his abilities? Or should he appeal for intervention and support from some higher power? He shook his head to clear his thoughts. It was too much like superstition. But he couldn't stop a rogue thought from escaping.

If anybody is listening to this transmission, this is a Mayday alert. If ever you were going to step in, now is the time.

Chapter 48

Missile silo north of Cheyenne, Wyoming.
Thursday, 13 March 2003. 12:21.

The chain clinked as Nikki reached for the can of Dinty Moore stew. The guy, Naji, opened it right in front of her, so it must not be poisoned or drugged. She looked at Stevie for reassurance. Stevie held her can in one hand and looked at Naji.

"Can't you heat it up?" Naji shook his head. "How about a spoon?"

"Drink." He made motions with his hands. "Drink it."

Stevie looked at Nikki. "We might as well. No telling when we'll get to eat again."

"But Dad should be on his way here by now. It's been almost an hour. He should be here before dark, right?"

Stevie looked at her without responding. It was a lot like the look from last night when that woman wouldn't shut up. Like she was trying to tell her something without talking. What was she trying to say? That Dad wasn't coming?

"Nikki," she said with her voice lowered.

Nikki looked around. Naji was gone. The door was open. She could see him in the next room. He could see them, but he couldn't hear them unless they talked loudly.

"Nikki," Stevie said again. "He'll come. But there's no way to know what will happen when he comes. They might . . ." She glanced around. "They might not let us go right away. But whatever happens, we have to be ready to take advantage of the opportunity. So, we eat when we can." She raised the can and took a slow sip of the brown sludge, opening her mouth to catch the chunks.

Nikki looked at the can in her hands. Then she looked at the chain that ran from the manacle on one hand down through a metal ring in the concrete floor and back up to the other hand. It was just long enough to allow her to stand up if she stooped over a little.

She couldn't believe she was chained in a metal shack in the middle of the desert, that her worst nightmares had actually come true. The crazed bomber had come for her, and his eyes were two windows into hell, just like she always knew.

But then, as she thought about it, she could believe it. It was her fault. She was cursed, had always been cursed. She would bring death and ruin to anyone who came too near.

She looked at Stevie.

"Nikki, it's OK. Don't be afraid. We'll make it through this."

Nikki took a sip of stew. She wasn't afraid she would die. She knew she wouldn't. But she was pretty sure Stevie would die.

It was funny, really, this curse of hers that destroyed those around her. If only she could control it, that would be different. But there was only one way to make it work. She had to start liking them. She couldn't curse those she hated. She knew because she had tried it on Stevie. She willed her to die. She had willed her to go away and leave her alone. Just like she did with Mom. That was how she had killed Mom. She had cursed her.

After Mom died, she thought it was the power to curse, to destroy. So she cursed herself with the calm assurance that her power would bring about the catastrophe that would end her own life. But she lived. She didn't make a mistake on the ski slopes and break her neck. She didn't have a wreck on the freeway. She didn't get run over, even when she didn't look before stepping out in the street.

She wasn't sure why it worked on Mom but not on herself. Then Tony broke his arm in a mountain bike accident that could have killed him, and a year later Dad lost the edge of his ear from a bullet that could have gone through his head. That's when she figured it out. It wasn't a power; it was a curse. She didn't have the power to curse others. She herself was cursed, and the curse only hurt the ones she loved.

Even when she wished Mom would go away and quit yelling at her, she loved Mom. It was her love and the curse that killed Mom and almost killed Tony and Dad.

Which explained why the curse didn't work on her. She hated herself. She was certain that if she ever began loving herself, she would die. But that would never happen, so she was doomed to live knowing that she would eventually kill everything she loved.

That was why she panicked last night. She saw the look Stevie gave her, knew that Stevie loved her. And she felt her own hatred begin to crumble. And at that moment, she realized that if she let the hatred fade, let herself return the love, then Stevie was doomed. That was the curse, to look at the thing that would save her and then to destroy it.

So she resisted, but the love from Stevie was irresistible, which was puzzling. She had successfully waged war against Stevie for almost two years. No problem. But suddenly in the past few weeks, since she came back from Morocco, it was different. There was something that slipped past the defenses like a nerve gas through the bars of a cell and numbed the raw nerves in her soul.

Even now, as she tried her best to hate Stevie in order to save Stevie's life, she found it impossible. She looked at Stevie and loved her and hated herself for loving her, for not being strong enough to keep on hating her, for wanting her love so much that she would love her back and therefore doom her. A tear fought free and ran down her face.

Stevie dropped the can, reached as far as the chain would permit and grabbed Nikki's arm. The half-empty can of stew fell from Nikki's hands, and she clutched at Stevie's arm.

"Nikki, it's going to be OK. Fear no evil. He is with us."

"I'm sorry," Nikki whispered.

"Sorry?" Stevie looked confused. "Sorry? Nikki, this isn't your fault."

Nikki nodded. She had no words, only tears.

"Nikki, you listen to me right now," Stevie whispered fiercely. "You aren't responsible for this. There's only one person responsible for this, and he's sitting out there right now with your cell phone."

Nikki shook her head. "No," she said in a squeaky voice that sounded like someone else. "It's my fault. I couldn't stop myself. I needed you too much. I'm sorry. I didn't mean to love you. I didn't want to love you. And now it's too late."

"No, it isn't," Stevie said.

She pulled Nikki's arm, dragging her body to her so that Nikki's head rested in the crook of her left arm, and stroked her hair with her right hand. Nikki could hear the links in the chain as they dragged back and forth against Stevie's jeans.

"It's not too late, and it's not your fault," Stevie said.

Nikki tried to wipe the tears, but the chain didn't reach anymore. They ran across her face and into her hair and down Stevie's arm. Suddenly the hand quit stroking her hair.

"Did you say you love me?" Stevie asked in a whisper.

Nikki nodded her head. There. It was done. It would happen now, and nothing could stop it.

"Nikki," Stevie whispered. "I love you too."

Nikki felt a tear fall on her ear. "I'm sorry," she said.

"Why are you sorry?"

It felt stupid to say, *Because now you are doomed,* but it was true. How could she say what she knew would be?

"This is all my fault. You were safe as long as I hated you. But now you're not safe anymore. And neither is Dad."

"Nikki," Stevie said softly. "I am safe. I know I am safe. And there is nothing you, or that thug out there, can do that will take me from the shadow of his wing."

Nikki didn't know what it meant, and she still knew Stevie would die, but the words sounded so calm and Stevie seemed so certain that her panic drew back slightly.

"Let me tell you something I learned in the desert. The Lord is my shepherd; I don't want anymore. He gives me rest in green fields. He walks with me along quiet streams. He restores my soul. He shows me the right way to go, the way that pleases him. Even if I walk into the shadow of death, I will not fear any evil, because he is always with me."

Nikki felt a hand rest lightly on her head. A peace seemed to pour down from the hand, over her head and down through her body like water.

"Do you hear that, Nikki?" she whispered. "He is always with me—even in the shadow of death, he is always with me."

The hand pressed down. Nikki began to think that it might be true after all.

"Always," Stevie whispered fiercely. "So I am safe and you are safe and Matt is safe, no matter what happens."

Nikki felt her moving, sat up, and looked at her. Stevie was crying but also smiling.

"The shepherd loves his sheep. Even the smallest lamb."

Nikki nodded, wanting to believe it. For Stevie's sake, she wanted it to be true. She wanted the curse to be broken.

"The Lord is my shepherd," she said. "I don't want any more."

Somehow she knew that it was too good to be true, but at the same time, it was true.

Chapter 49

Alliance, Nebraska.
Thursday, 13 March 2003. 15:07.

Morse put the Gulfstream down at the Alliance Municipal Airport. Cooper went through a final check of the gear. The team north of Cheyenne confirmed they were receiving clear audio and video signals. Cooper found the white Ford F-150 in the parking lot, the key duct-taped to the top of the back right tire. As instructed, he drove it north on US-385 to Berea, then took NE-2 through Hemingford and pulled up in front of the brown van on the left side of the road at the junction with NE-71.

As he got out of the truck, a man appeared on either side of him. Each wore jeans, a flannel shirt, boots, a denim jacket, a baseball cap, and sunglasses. From a distance they looked like a couple of ranchers. Only their faces gave them away—dark and uncompromising.

The man with the Johnson Feed Supply cap escorted him to the side of the van away from the road and instructed him to remove his jacket and face the van with his hands on the side, while the man with the John Deere cap covered them with an AK-47. Johnson found the Glock immediately, took it away without comment, shoved it into his belt, and continued the search. Next he felt the wire under his shirt. He turned Cooper around, pulled his shirt open, and removed the wire. He gave Cooper a look of reproof and tossed the gear into the van. The GPS transmitter followed it.

Then he looked closer at Cooper's undergarment, pulling it up and rolling it between his fingers. He locked eyes with Cooper.

Cooper shrugged. "I heard it was cold."

He looked at Cooper without amusement and turned him back against the door. He pulled a bulky belt from the van and snapped it around Cooper's waist. Cooper looked down. It was a series of explosives wired to a radio receiver. That complicated things. A voice whispered in his ear by transmitter.

"Give us a good look at the receiver. When we get in range, we'll attempt to jam the frequencies it will likely use."

Cooper kept his hands against the van, head dropped down, looking at the belt. Behind him the buttonhole camera was discovered and removed and the jacket returned to Cooper. Then he was shoved inside the van and handcuffed to a strut. Johnson drove the van, Deere the truck. They headed west on NE-71, then took US-26 into Wyoming and turned south on US-85 at Torrington. They made no attempt to conceal the route by blindfolding him. Cooper surmised that they didn't expect him to leave the site; therefore, no secrecy was required.

As the sun approached the horizon, they turned off the highway onto a dirt road near Meriden and headed west. They drove through prairie covered with grass and scrub brush. Cooper looked out the windshield, assessing the landscape for its possibilities for cover for the assault team. As if reading his thoughts, the voice whispered in his ear.

"We have the silo area surrounded. Men within one hundred yards of the Quonset huts and closing in. Our readings show eight bad guys, including your escorts, and two stationary marks in the back of the southern hut. Probably the girls. Once they come out we'll get into better position."

The van pulled into a large dirt yard and stopped twenty yards from two metal structures that formed a *V* on the western side of the yard. The truck stopped beside the van. His handcuffs were detached from the van, then Cooper was dragged out and had his hands cuffed behind him. Johnson turned him toward the hut on the left and held him by the upper arm. Cooper stood still and his arm was released. They stood on his left, slightly behind him but still in his peripheral vision.

Cooper scanned the huts. The sun was setting behind them, making it difficult to pick out details. He detected two men at the door of the left hut, both obviously guards.

"Your boss must be the most cowardly Muslim in history. Four of you with assault rifles. One of me. I have no weapon, and you've strapped me with bombs. Then you handcuff me, like you think one guy with no weapon can take you all out." He nodded his head toward the huts. "What's he going to do, hide inside there and blow up all three of us?"

Deere tensed up. From the corner of his eye, Cooper saw his fingers ripple over the stock of the AK-47. Johnson just grunted, as if used to taunts from infidels.

Still they waited. They were losing light. The assault team was equipped with night-vision gear, but Cooper wasn't. There would be only one chance, and he wanted enough light to recognize it and respond.

"Hey, Nadhir or Berkowitz or whatever your name is. Come on out here with your Polaroid, and let's get this over with."

John Deere turned toward Cooper, whipping out the butt of his assault weapon, but Johnson growled something at him and pushed him back with one hand. John Deere grumbled, but resumed his stance.

The door of the hut on the left opened, and Stevie was shoved out by a man holding her arm. He followed her out the door, pulling Nikki behind him. Cooper stepped forward involuntarily, but a word from Johnson restrained him. The guards on either side of the door stepped up to the girls and held guns to their heads. He peered through the gloom at the girls. Neither appeared to be restrained beyond the hold of the man standing between them. As far as he could tell, they were unhurt.

Nikki saw him first and yelled, "Dad, I'm sorry." Stevie looked up and stared at him. He saw her lips moving but didn't hear anything.

"Hold on," Cooper shouted. "Let's get this over with, and we'll all go home."

Cooper heard a chuckle behind him. He felt a desire to kick John Deere's Adam's apple through the back of his throat but stood motionless. A white form appeared in the dark doorway. Nadhir emerged, wearing the white robes and headdress of a sheik. In one hand was a digital camera, in the other a small box with an antenna on it.

"How good of you to come, Mr. Cooper. As you can see, I have kept my word. The sun has not yet set, and here you see your women standing before you, unblemished."

"OK. You kept your word. I'm delighted, but as much fun as it's been so far, I don't want to stand around here any longer than I have to. Give your camera to one of your goons and let's get this over with." He took a single step forward, heard a gun being readied behind him, and stopped. "You want me to come there, or are you going to come here? I don't want John Deere over here to get nervous and spoil your picture by shooting me."

"You may stay where you are. You may wonder why I brought you here by such difficult means. It is so that you will be in the proper condition to hear what must be said. You have interfered in the plan to strike the fatal blow to the chief of the infidels and to bring glory to Allah, so you must be made to suffer that you may learn the way of truth before it is too late."

"Can we just cut to the picture? I'm sure it will be suffering enough."

Nadhir ignored him. "For over eighty years the Islamic world has suffered under the banner of the Crusader. For almost a century our brothers and sisters in Palestine have been tortured, killed, imprisoned, and maimed. In Chechnya, our brothers and sisters have been annihilated, forced to flee to mountains where they were assaulted by snow and poverty and disease. In Bosnia, for years our brothers have been killed, our sisters raped, our children massacred in safe havens. Our brothers in Kashmir have been subjected to the worst forms of torture for over fifty years. In Indonesia, Crusader forces landed to separate East Timor from its Islamic brothers. In Somalia, thousands of our brothers were killed. In Sudan, hundreds of thousands.

"But when we move to Palestine and Iraq, there can be no bounds to what can be said. Over one million children died in Iraq, and the killing continues. Indeed, hundreds of thousands of Crusaders are poised even now on its borders, impatient to exceed the sins of their predecessors in war and violence.

"As for Palestine, what is taking place cannot be tolerated by any nation. The Jews are the foremost and original enemies of Islam, and one can make no difference between Israel and America. They are the twin brothers bent on the destruction of all Islamic people. I remind you of what our Prophet, may God's peace and blessings be upon him, said . . ."

A voice whispered in Cooper's ear. "How long do we have to listen to this? We have shooters within fifty yards of all six targets and others covering all exits of the huts. Can't we just take him out now?"

Cooper turned his head to the right slightly, away from Johnson and Deere and spoke softly.

"We want him alive if we can get him. You have the frequency to the remote?"

"We think we do. Looks like a standard 460 MHz receiver. We're bracketing the likely frequencies."

"He wants to use it. When he tries, take out the other five guys. I'm going to roll backward. When Johnson Feed Supply goes down, I'm going for the pistol. Don't shoot me."

"Thanks for the warning. We'll just target people with caps."

Cooper smiled and returned his attention to Nadhir.

". . . Allah bear witness that I have conveyed the warning."

Nadhir raised the remote in his left hand. Nikki screamed. Cooper heard the men behind him scrambling to get away. He dropped down and rolled backward, tucking in his legs and pulling his hands over his feet. When he came back up on his feet, his hands were in front. He saw Nadhir drop the camera and press repeatedly on the button of the remote, cursing. The three men around the girls staggered backward, the backs of their heads blossoming into explosions of blood. There had been no noise as the shots were made with a silenced sniper rifle. He heard the whine of bullets passing by and heard the men behind him fall.

As the man to the left of the girls collapsed, his weapon fired. Fortunately it was no longer pointed at Stevie's head, but the descending arc of its fall raked across her body. She screamed and dropped to the ground. Nikki turned to face Nadhir, arms open.

Chapter 50

Somewhere in Wyoming.
Thursday, 13 March 2003. 18:11.

Cooper spun around, dove for Johnson's body, and pulled the Glock from his belt. Then he rushed the Quonset hut, pistol raised.

"Stevie's been hit!" he yelled into the twilight air. "Get that chopper and med team in here!"

He saw Nadhir throw the remote aside and reach into his robes. A pistol emerged, and he turned to the girls. Only then did he seem to realize that the men were dead. He swung the gun around and seemed startled to see Nikki staring right at him as if daring him to pull the trigger. He recovered, raised the muzzle of the gun to Nikki's head.

The delay gave Cooper time. He dropped to one knee, sighted, and fired. The gun flew from Nadhir's hand, and he screamed in pain and rage. Then his eyes followed the red dot of the laser sight as it played across his white robes and came to a stop above his heart. He looked up at Cooper and waited, looking past him at the two dead men on the ground by the van. But the shot never came. He looked back at Cooper, startled, then confused, then amused. He retrieved the gun, whirled away in a flash of white, and disappeared into the doorway of the Quonset hut.

Cooper was up and running toward the hut. As he did so he scanned the area. The door of the other Quonset hut slammed open and the burst of an automatic weapon flashed from the darkened doorway. Cooper dropped and rolled as a volley of fire from the surrounding scrub brush silenced the shooter. As Cooper rolled to his feet he heard the thumping of the chopper.

He slid to a stop next to Nikki. She was crouched over Stevie, crying. She looked up at Cooper, disoriented.

"I'm sorry. I didn't mean to. I'm sorry," she said over the noise.

Her statement confused him. He dropped to one knee beside her.

"Little dove, you have to be brave and stay with Stevie. The doctor is coming." He nodded to the chopper that was descending into the dirt yard. "I'll be right back."

He jumped up and ran toward the door of the hut. Nikki screamed at him.

"Dad! The curse!"

He stopped and turned.

"Don't go in there. The curse. You'll die."

He could see that she was desperate, but he couldn't let Nadhir get away. "I'll be right back, dove." Then he plunged into the darkness of the doorway.

Before his eyes had time to adjust, two Special Forces team members were at his side, one wearing night-vision gear. "There." He pointed to a door at the back of the hut. Inside the back room they found a trapdoor.

Cooper looked at the handcuffs.

"Oh. You might want these." The guy with night-vision goggles held up a key for the handcuffs and smiled. As the other guy helped him with his cuffs, the night-vision guy went down the ladder from the trapdoor, which led to a tunnel. They followed. A hundred yards away a dim light illuminated a metal door set in a concrete wall.

When they pushed it open, a burst of gunfire peppered the doorway. The night-vision guy went down. The other guy tossed a flash-bang grenade through the doorway. After the explosion Cooper shoved the door open. A man lay sprawled on steps on the far side of a landing, an AK-47 at his side. On the left another set of steps led down. Cooper picked up the gun. He was evidently in some part of the silo complex. He could see lights shining from both stairways. He turned as the Special Forces guy stepped in.

"You take care of him and get your buddy out there. There's only one guy left, and I'm going after him."

He ran up the steps on the right without waiting for a response. After ten feet they turned up to the left, went another ten feet and then opened into a corridor ten feet long with doors at either end. He ran through the far door and up a couple flights of stairs. He hit a dead end. A reinforced door was padlocked from the inside.

He retraced his steps, rushing past the curious soldier and down several flights of stairs that corkscrewed down past doorways that he kicked in and peered through before continuing his descent. After a half-dozen flights he hit the bottom and had the choice between a doorway and a tunnel. He tried the door. It appeared to be a launch center. It was empty. He turned to the tunnel. It was round, lined with corrugated steel and pipes that ran its length. It appeared to be empty so he ran to the other end.

A doorway opened into the empty missile silo itself. It extended eighty feet above him and a hundred feet below. There was a narrow catwalk that circled the shaft. A white robe was draped over the railing. He stepped through the doorway, swinging the AK-47 around.

He was stopped by the barrel of a gun against his forehead. He crossed his eyes and looked at it. It was a Walther PPK. The last two fingers on the hand holding it were wrapped in a cloth glistening with blood. He followed the arm down to the face of Nadhir. The expression was one of amusement, but behind the eyes was a barely constrained fury, or perhaps madness. He was dressed in a black suit, white shirt, black tie. He looked like he had just left a stockholder's meeting.

"Mr. Cooper, I see you are still a walking bomb. Do you not feel uncomfortable? Perhaps a little nervous?"

Cooper looked down. He had forgotten about the belt. Then he saw that the barrel of the AK-47 rested against Nadhir's chest. He shook his head, the barrel of the gun moving along with his forehead.

"No. But how about you? Doesn't this make you nervous?" He pushed the gun forward slightly.

"No. If Allah wills it, then we will die together. I will die a martyr, and you will die an infidel."

"Why must anyone die? Why can't you just believe what you believe and let us believe what we believe and leave it at that?"

Nadhir studied him, looked into his eyes. "You don't believe anything, Mr. Cooper."

"I believe you're crazy."

"Come, come, Mr. Cooper. This is unworthy of your final words. Surely you believe in something."

Cooper couldn't believe he was standing here in a missile silo with a gun to his head, being asked to explain his personal philosophy of life. He frowned.

"Humor me," Nadhir said.

Cooper sighed and scanned his mind for an answer.

"I believe that freedom is the natural state of man and that those who thrive by oppression of the human spirit, people like you, are doomed to fail. I believe that you make your own choices and you live with them. I believe that if you don't find things the way you want them, you change them. You don't blame it on the will of Allah or God or some fairy tale."

He stopped. There was silence for several seconds.

"That's all?" Nadhir asked. "You believe in yourself? That you can recreate the world in your own image?"

"If you want to put it that way, yes."

"And this is enough for you? This sustains you in the night when the jackals howl in the desert? This gives you the strength to oppose your enemies and emerge the victor? This saves you from despair when men plot against you and seek your life?"

"It's all there is."

"It's nothing. It is a delusion."

"It'll do until something better comes along."

"And if I had pulled the trigger? If your daughter had died? What would sustain you then?"

He clinched his teeth. "The thought of digging your intestines out with a dull blade."

"Now is your chance," Nadhir whispered. They glared at each other. "Your concubine may be dying right now, Cooper. Think of that if you lack the courage."

Cooper growled and squeezed the trigger. There was a loud click that echoed in the silo. Nadhir smiled. The concussion grenade must have damaged it or perhaps it was empty.

"It appears Allah does not will that I shall die today."

The bloodstained finger squeezed the trigger. There was a loud click that Cooper felt reverberate against his skull.

Nadhir's eyes grew wide. Cooper shoved the AK-47 forward, putting his weight behind it. Nadhir went stumbling back, rolling against the concrete wall of the silo. He recovered and ran along the catwalk to an opening on the opposite side.

Cooper raced forward, tossing the AK-47 aside. He reached for the Glock, which was tucked into his waistline at the small of his back. It slipped from his fingers and clattered to the catwalk, skittering to the edge. It came to rest against a post supporting the railing. Cooper stopped then approached it carefully to avoid dislodging it and retrieved it. When he looked up, Nadhir was gone.

He ran to the opening. As he looked down another tunnel he heard the sound of an engine being started. He ran down the tunnel. It emerged from the wall of a larger tunnel. He saw the taillight of a motorcycle disappear around a curve in one direction. He ran to the curve, but Nadhir was out of range by the time he rounded the corner.

It took him a few minutes to get topside. As he emerged from the last tunnel he regained signal on the earpiece. He informed Gilberts about the tunnel and motorcycle, recommending they get something down there to find the endpoints. It would be faster than scanning dozens of square miles of prairie honeycombed with other decommissioned Atlas silos.

They held the chopper for him as he removed the explosive belt. He climbed through the door and Nikki hurled herself at him, clutching as if she were afraid he might disappear if she let go. He squeezed her hard, looking over her head at the gurney strapped to the far wall of the passenger area. He caught the doctor's eye as the chopper lifted off and the door slammed behind him.

"She's stable, but it's touch and go. She took a shot through muscle, but a second went through the abdomen. No way to know what was hit until we get her into the emergency room. We've radioed Cheyenne. They're ready."

Chapter 51

**Refugio Elementary School, Los Angeles, California.
Friday, 14 March 2003. 14:30.**

Emilio was startled when the phone rang. Most teachers came to the maintenance office or sent a student to track him down when they needed something done. It was rare for anyone to call. He set down his pen, pushed aside the form for reordering supplies, and pulled the phone across the desk.

"Maintenance, Mr. Silva speaking."

"Emilio, it's Bernie."

"Bernie?" He didn't recall any teachers or staff named Bernie.

"Bernie Whiteman, from the Global Adventures trip."

"Ah, Bernie." He hadn't seen this strange man since the Holy Land trip over three months ago. He didn't look forward to seeing him again, in truth. But it was not always most polite to speak the truth. He let silence say what it will.

"So, Emilio, you remember how I told you that Cooper guy wasn't all that he seemed?"

Emilio remembered. He said nothing.

"Turns out I was right. He's got this investigation going, something big. I've been doing a parallel investigation. Turns

out we've both been working on the same thing. So, I'm helping him out. George is working with him too."

"George?"

"George Roberts. You know, Global Adventures. So this
Cooper asked George to use the Global Adventures network
to comb the city for suspicious activity, especially any Middle
Eastern types, if you know what I mean."

He paused. Emilio waited.

"So, he's especially interested in anything unusual downtown. Now get this. I've been tracking this guy who comes to
my store by the name of Basil el-Amil. Turns out Cooper is also
tracking this guy and he finds out this Basil guy gets himself
killed in San Francisco Tuesday night."

Emilio's annoyance turned to alarm. Amil's son was dead?
How could this tragedy have happened? Why did Amil not
come to him? After all that Amil had done for him when he
lost Juanita, how could Amil deprive him the privilege of making a small attempt to repay that debt?

"Now this is where you come in. Turns out Basil's parents
live a few blocks from your school. So, we're wondering if you
might have seen Basil or the parents in the neighborhood."

"Yes," Emilio said.

"Yes? You mean you've seen them?"

"Yes. Amil el-Amil is my friend. I have met his son, Basil."

"Wow. What are the chances? So did you see anything
suspicious?"

"Amil is a man of honor. He would not be doing the suspicious things." Emilio felt a weariness that he should be forced
to answer such questions when he knew his friend was in need.
He must go to him immediately.

"What about Basil? Any suspicious activity?"

"No, no suspicious things."

"Did he have a small suitcase or maybe a large briefcase?"

"No."

"You're sure?" Emilio could hear the disappointment in his voice. Bernie wanted to play spy. He had the store. He had the restless burning for digging where it was better to not dig. Emilio would not encourage such uncharitable practices.

"I am sure. Now I must go. Thank you. Good-bye." Emilio heard Bernie's protest like a buzzing insect as he returned the handset to the cradle.

Emilio sat and thought. Amil did not come for tea since Tuesday morning. Emilio thought it strange, but sometimes things happened. People had unexpected emergencies or became ill or any number of things. Now he knew.

It was perhaps the most tragic thing that could befall a man, to lose a child. A parent you expect to lose one day. Knowing it would happen did not lessen the pain, but it was the natural order of things. Even losing a wife—that one might expect. But for a child to precede the parent in death, this was not natural. It was pain beyond what could be borne.

He stood. He would go to Amil now, even during his workday. If only for a moment, to assure him he was not alone. He was turning to leave when he remembered the gift. He went to the corner where it was stored and removed the tarp. Amil might find comfort in this last gift from his son. It was too heavy to carry for three blocks. He would use the cart.

He wheeled the gift out, locked the maintenance office, rolled the cart down the hall, and bumped it over the threshold onto the drive. He chose to take the street instead of the sidewalk, even though it was rough, because he wouldn't be able to get the cart up and down the curbs. The few cars that he encountered swung wide, giving him plenty of room.

It took several minutes to reach Amil's house. He rolled the cart up the driveway, onto the sidewalk, and up the front walk to the porch. Then he saw the yellow police tape. The windows were dark. No one answered the doorbell.

He reluctantly turned the cart around and pushed it slowly back the way he had come. He bounced it over the threshold, back up the hall, unlocked the door, and pushed the cart inside. Then he made some tea, sat down, stared at the gift, and thought of his friend. He prayed for his friend, asking that even a fraction of the comfort Amil had brought him might be repaid. He prayed that, if it were possible, he might bear some of Amil's pain, to lighten the load he must bear.

And then he felt it, a sense of inexplicable loss, a gazing into the void from which nothing can return, not even hope. It was a black hole that swallowed everything, even tomorrow. From this point forward, nothing continued. He shuddered, his shoulders convulsed and a deep groan crawled out of his closed throat. His head dropped into his waiting hands, and the tears streamed through his fingers like he was being squeezed dry, as if his future were pooling on the floor between his scarred work boots and evaporating away.

He did not know how long he sat there. It could have been seconds or hours, but in those measureless moments an eternity of suffering was encapsulated. The pain he felt at the loss of Juanita was the pale, sickly cousin to this roaring monster of grief. And by this sign he knew his prayer had been answered. He knew that to some degree, however slight, he had been granted to bear a measure of the pain of his friend. And knowing this, he was somehow able to bear the unbearable.

Then, almost without him noticing, the nature of the pain began to change. The dull bludgeoning of his senses became the sharp pinpricks of a thousand needles, the oscillating drone in his head resolved into the screeching of a thousand souls in torment. This was not the suffering of his friend. It was a different evil. The tears receded like a waning tide, leaving his senses raw and defenseless. He lifted his head from his hands, looked up and saw it.

The gift. A large box with the picture of speakers and a DVD player on it.

He stood slowly, turned to the workbench, picked up a box cutter and strode to the cart with purpose. Deliberately, as if performing a ceremony, he cut through the tape. Inside he found packing peanuts. He swept them aside. Underneath he did not find a home theater system. He found a briefcase. A large, silver briefcase.

His heart sickened within him. With a heaviness that he felt would never abate, he dialed the phone.

Bernie set the phone on top of the list of contacts and stretched. Time for his fourth Diet Coke of the day. On his way to the fridge he poked his head through the doorway to check on Merv. The store had a couple of browsers. Merv was reading a Mickey Spillane novel and occasionally glancing at the monitors as the customers strolled through the aisles.

Bernie closed the door carefully to avoid attracting Merv's attention. He didn't want to hear another whining recitation of how all the extra hours were wrecking Merv's social life. After all, Merv was between girlfriends. He should be thanking Bernie for the chance to build up his reserves before he hooked up with another Valley vampire who would drain him of cash before tossing him aside. He stepped into the kitchen, opened the freezer, and stared at the Fudgsicles for half a minute. He closed the door with a sigh and took a Diet Coke from the fridge.

The phone was ringing when he returned to the office.

"Eye Spy Surveillance. Bernie." There was silence on the line. "Hello?"

"It is Emilio Silva."

Bernie dropped into his chair, set down the Diet Coke, and grabbed a pen. He waited, but nothing else came.

"Emilio? What's up? Did you get some dirt on el-Amil?"

"Amil's son, Basil, bought a present for his mother. It is her birthday."

"Yeah?" Bernie shook his head. He could see this Emilio character was going to be a time-waster. He still had two pages of names to go through. He leaned back and took a sip of his Diet Coke.

"Yes. But he desired me to keep it for him until the day. So that she would not discover it before the day." Bernie heard a long sigh over the phone. "It is nothing. I do not think anything of it until today."

"Well, the son won't be coming to pick it up. You'll have to get el-Amil to come get it." He pulled the list of names to him and ran his finger down the check marks.

"Then, when I pray, I get a bad feeling about the gift."

His finger stopped on the first unchecked name. He set the pen down under it. "OK. But you'll probably have to keep it a little longer. I think the old man is still in San Francisco."

"So I open the gift. It is not a home theater system. It is something else. Something that should not be in a home theater system box."

Bernie sat up in his chair. "What do you mean?"

"Inside is a large silver briefcase. It is very heavy. Something must be inside it, but I do not open it."

"What did you do with it?"

"I do nothing with it. It is still in the box on the cart."

"OK, Emilio. This is what you have to do. When you hang up, call 911 and tell them there is a suspicious package in the school. They'll want to evacuate. I'll call Perkins and get Cooper on this thing right away." He reached to turn off the phone but stopped and put it back to his ear. "And, Emilio, you did the right thing. I knew I could count on you."

"Yes."

He heard the phone go dead.

Chapter 52

Nagle Warren Mansion Bed & Breakfast,
Cheyenne, Wyoming. Friday, 14 March 2003. 16:52.

Cooper was sprawled on the armchair in the Teddy Roosevelt room, eyes half closed. Nikki was propped up on five pillows on the couch, flipping through the channels on the TV with the sound off.

Now that Stevie appeared to be out of danger, Cooper could relax. It had not been a sure thing. She had lost a lot of blood. The doctor didn't say much in the chopper, but Cooper could see that he was counting the seconds to the hospital landing pad.

The surgery went past midnight. When Stevie was asleep in recovery minus one spleen, Cooper and Nikki found the rooms Perkins had booked for them at a bed and breakfast a half a mile from the United Medical Center. At dawn Cooper sneaked out and waited at Stevie's bedside while Nikki slept. Stevie awoke, weak but smiling when she saw him. She didn't say much, and a few minutes later she was asleep again.

Alex brought Nikki to the hospital at noon, and they ate in the hospital cafeteria, which had surprisingly good food. After lunch they waited for Stevie to wake up, had a short visit, and then returned to the bed and breakfast to get some rest.

Nikki stopped on a station with a TV preacher shaking a Bible at the camera, a mane of silver hair swept back from his forehead. She set the remote down on a pillow.

"Do you think Mom is in heaven?"

Cooper opened his eyes slightly and looked at Nikki. Surrounded by the pillows, she seemed a desert princess reclining in her tent. "You never asked me that before."

"Do you?"

He hesitated. It was not an easy question to answer, loaded with assumptions and traps. "If anyone is in heaven, she is."

Nikki studied him for a minute. "You don't really believe in heaven, do you?"

Cooper smiled and shook his head slowly. "How is it I can bluff my way past border guards and ex-cons and federal agents but I can't get anything past you?"

Nikki settled into a self-congratulatory smile. "That's because I know you. Those other guys, they think they have you figured out. But I really do."

"That's scary."

"Why?"

"Because I can't get away with anything around you."

Nikki nodded. "That's right. But that's a good thing."

"It is?"

"Yes, because you shouldn't get away with anything."

They watched each other in silence for awhile. On the TV, a big-haired woman clutched a microphone in two hands and sang with closed eyes. Cooper struggled to an upright position in his chair and brushed his hand through his hair. He started to speak, stopped, took another breath and continued.

"Nikki, last night you said something about a curse. What curse?"

She leaned back in the pillows and closed her eyes. "Dad, I don't want to talk about that."

"You think I'm going to let you get away with anything?"

She lay silent, breathing slowly and deeply for so long, Cooper thought she was asleep. Then she spoke without opening her eyes.

"You remember when you talked about changing jobs?" She opened her eyes. "At that diner?"

Cooper nodded.

"Were you really serious?"

"Little dove," he began. Then he fell silent, realizing anything he said would sound like an excuse. Perhaps that's all it was, anyway. Was he serious? Would he really change careers? His phone broke the spell. It was Perkins.

"They found the L.A. nuke. It's in an elementary school a quarter mile from the financial district."

Cooper got to his feet. "Confirmed? Is NEST there?"

"They will be in twenty minutes. Here's what we have. Basil el-Amil left a package with a friend of his father. A janitor at Refugio Elementary School off Wilshire."

"A janitor? You mean that old man—what was his name?"

"Emilio Silva."

"Right. Emilio. He's a friend of Amil el-Amil?"

"Yes. And the school is just a few blocks from el-Amil's house. Basil left a package with Emilio Monday, just before he took his parents to San Francisco. Today Emilio got suspicious and opened the box. It contains a silver briefcase. He called 911."

He shrugged an apology to Nikki and stepped to the bedroom. "I'm on my way. Have Morse get ready."

"He's already filed a flight plan to Van Nuys. We'll have a chopper waiting for you."

"I'll call you from the air." Cooper shoved the phone in his pocket, stopped in the doorway, and turned to Nikki. "I have to take care of something back in L.A. I'll be back by midnight, tomorrow morning at the latest."

"I'll come with you."

"No, you have to take care of Stevie. We can't leave her in Wyoming alone, can we?"

The question was met with silence. He wanted to promise her that things would be different, that she would never have to worry about him again, but he realized how absurd it would sound saying such things as he was preparing to leave her one more time. He turned quietly to the bedroom and closed the door.

He was in the air in ten minutes and back on the phone with Perkins. "What's our status?"

"Gilberts is working with LAPD. The city command has issued a citywide tactical alert. All officers have been called in, and an evacuation plan is in process, centering at the school and extending out for a one-mile radius."

"Two miles would be better, but that would take until midnight or later. We had better be done by then. No telling how much longer the cell phone battery will hold out. How about NEST?"

"They're approaching the site. McKinney is concerned about booby traps."

Cooper went to the galley to fix some coffee. "He should be. It could be set to go off if someone opens the case. I don't think we can rely on disarming it, and he can hardly try to detonate it in a controlled environment. Something that can level every building for a kilometer can't be remotely detonated in a steel box."

"What about the underground nuclear testing grounds in Nevada?"

"Get McKinney on the line. We'll see what our options are." Cooper measured out a few scoops and poured the water before he heard Perkins' voice again.

"Matt, I have McKinney on the line."

"Dr. McKinney, I agree with your concern about booby traps. Perkins had an idea. The bomb is only about three hundred miles from the Nevada Test Site. We could probably have it there in less than an hour. Don't they have facilities for underground testing?"

"They did, but it's not a permanent facility. The test sites are custom-built for the test, take months to build, and are destroyed by the blast. The U.S. agreed to a moratorium on nuclear weapons testing over a decade ago, so there are no unused test shafts in existence."

"Isn't there an above-ground test area out there?"

"Above-ground testing was abandoned a long time ago. Plus, you'll be transporting a one-kiloton nuclear weapon above the western U.S. for almost an hour. If anything goes wrong, you will have an atmospheric detonation, which maximizes the radioactive dispersion in close proximity to the most populous area of the nation. Not to mention killing the crew transporting it."

"To make it worse, we have no idea how much time we have left," Perkins added.

Cooper nodded. "No digital readout of a countdown like in the movies. How inconsiderate of Nadhir to omit that detail. So what is the plan, McKinney?"

"Do you know how a nuclear bomb works?"

Cooper got out a coffee cup. "A conventional explosion is used to cause a mass of fissionable material to achieve critical mass, causing an uncontrollable chain reaction in the material."

"You also need free neutrons, but it's good enough for our purposes. Radioactive material is unstable, which means that it will emit particles as it decays to a more stable state. This happens all the time, not just in bombs. Nuclear weapons design takes advantage of this and compresses the material so that a neutron released from one atom strikes another, which splits, releasing energy. The free neutrons strike neighboring atoms and so on. If you have what is known as a critical mass of fissible material, then the chain reaction can be sustained and can be used by nuclear power plants to generate energy. However, if the material is dense enough, it achieves a supercritical state, which means the process escalates beyond control and an incredible amount of energy is produced.

"There are two designs. One shoots a bullet of enriched uranium into an enriched uranium core to achieve supercriticality. The other forces a sphere of uranium to implode around a mass of plutonium, compressing it so that it goes supercritical. The trick is to keep the material together long enough to generate the maximum amount of energy. If it is not controlled, it blows apart before all the potential energy of the device has been exploited. In fact, it is difficult to get a full yield because extreme precision is required. Unfortunately, even an inefficient device can be devastating."

"I'm sure at some point you're going to tell me how this will help us."

"I was just getting to that, Mr. Cooper. If we use conventional explosives to destroy the bomb instead of detonating it, we might be able to cause the components to be damaged in such a way that a supercritical mass is not achieved. Or, if it is, it will be less precise and much less efficient and therefore less deadly."

"You're saying we might be able to blow up a nuclear bomb without detonating it?"

"That's the basic idea. The blast will still destroy anything within a few hundred meters, even if it doesn't go supercritical. But that is considerably less than a kilometer, and the dispersion of radiation will be significantly less."

"And where exactly would we do this?"

"Ten miles west of Catalina Island, at a depth of three thousand feet. A fifteen- or twenty-minute flight instead of an hour."

"What about the effects of the blast? Won't it create a tsunami?"

"We'll place the bomb in a robo-sub that will allow us to accurately place it at a specific depth. We can suspend the bomb several hundred feet above the ocean floor, so there won't be any seismic activity as a result. There might be some high surf for a few minutes. We would want to order evacuations of the immediate coastline for a hundred miles or so."

"How long will it take to get everything ready?"

"It will take us an hour, maybe a little more, to get the sub on-site and set to go."

"I'll be there by then. Let's do it."

The sunset chopper flight from Van Nuys gave Cooper a good view of the evacuation. The 101 and 170 were gridlocked within a mile of the 110. But the circle around downtown L.A. circumscribed by I-10, I-110, I-5, and US-101 was a ghost town of skyscrapers and barrios. There was a UH-1 Huey on the school playground, rotors spinning, so they put the IRIG chopper down on the field behind the school. Perkins met Cooper at the back gate.

"McKinney is inside. The briefcase is in the sub, and they're bringing it out."

"Good." Cooper scanned the schoolyard. Soldiers in assault gear lined the periphery every ten yards. Gilberts stood in the doorway to the building. Cooper wasn't surprised to see him there, even though he had a high position in Homeland Security. His life would be over if this went badly, whether he were here or back at the office.

There was a noise from inside, and Gilberts stepped aside. Four men in Hazmat suits carried a strange device the size of a jet ski, surrounded with a series of turbines, lights, and a set of articulating arms. Dr. McKinney followed them. Even though it was a mild March evening, his shirt was soaked with sweat. Cooper joined him and nodded at the procession.

"Aren't those suits overkill?"

McKinney shrugged. "If they survive this . . . if we survive this, then the precaution doesn't hurt anything."

Cooper looked at Gilberts, whose eyes followed the pall-bearers as if he were wishing for a Hazmat suit for himself. He turned back to McKinney.

"Ready for a ride in a Huey?"

McKinney inspected him. "You don't have to go on this trip, you know. We have it covered."

"Dr. McKinney, I created this investigation. I'm riding shotgun on this flight if I have to straddle that contraption like Slim Pickens in *Dr. Strangelove*."

McKinney shrugged a tired smile and walked to the Huey. Cooper followed. The Hazmat crew tumbled out of the chopper and waved to them on their way back into the building. Despite his speech in the schoolyard, Cooper yielded the right seat to McKinney and got in back with the robo-sub. He donned a set of headphones as the door slammed shut and they lifted off. After the pilot completed his communications with the civil and military authorities, Cooper asked a question over the local channel. McKinney twisted in the seat to face him and answered.

"We put the briefcase in the sub and packed it with C-4 and a remote detonator. The sub is controlled with the console in that case." He pointed to a large briefcase behind his seat.

Cooper nodded and looked out the window. They were moving past the evacuated area, toward Santa Monica and the coast. In a few minutes the evacuation could be called off. If the cell-phone battery held out a few more minutes, they might all live to see tomorrow. Dr. McKinney opened the case and booted up the robo-sub control. It would take them at least ten minutes to get past the coast and turn southwest toward the target ten miles west of Catalina Island.

With Nikki safe and Stevie in recovery and out of danger, he allowed his thoughts to return to the salient points of the case. There was no longer any doubt that Claire was the mole. The moment she was removed from the picture, the dominoes fell one after another to a swift resolution. It might be difficult to piece together a chain of evidence that would convict her, but Cooper vowed to make her conviction his next and only project. If she were still at the Malibu house, he would convince her that it was the best place for her to await the grand jury verdict. She would be under his constant surveillance until he had sufficient evidence to guarantee a conviction.

Then he would . . .

That was the question. IRIG was his life. Could he walk away from it? Did he really have to? Nikki had proven her resilience in the most dire of circumstances. Only a few years remained until she became an adult. Did it make sense to abandon the business he had spent almost twenty years building for the last few years of Nikki's time at home? In four years she would graduate and begin her own life and he would be adrift, having forfeited the very thing he had spent his adult life building.

And then there was Stevie. He tried to imagine a future with Stevie but without IRIG. He would be drawn into her plans. Would she still respect him, or would he become nothing more than a flunky to advance her career? Last year he would have been sure, but now he didn't know. She was changed since the trip to Morocco. Nothing was certain anymore.

A change of direction drew him from his reverie. They were over the ocean, well past Catalina Island. McKinney was preoccupied with the controls for the sub. Cooper took a closer look at it. A winch line hooked onto a ring on the top of the sub. A lump in the line indicated an explosive charge that would allow release of the sub once it was safely in the water. The pilot's voice sounded over the headphones.

"We're approaching the target. Mr. Cooper, can you open the door?"

Cooper inched around the sub and slid the door back. The pilot brought the Huey lower until they were only a few dozen feet from the surface of the Pacific Ocean. Cooper blinked back the salty spray that wafted through the open door.

The pilot's voice sounded over the headphones. "I'll winch it up. You and Dr. McKinney will have to swing it out over the door, and I'll let it down."

McKinney climbed back over the seat and helped Cooper push the sub out of the chopper. They both watched as it descended to the surface ten yards below and was engulfed in the choppy waves created by the backwash of the rotors. The winch stopped, the cable veered for a few seconds, a surge of bubbles appeared and the cable went slack, proving the first explosion of severing the cable had gone according to plan. McKinney returned to his seat and retrieved the console as the winch pulled in the cable and Cooper closed the door.

Cooper stepped behind the right seat and braced himself as the chopper tilted and lifted away at a sharp angle. As they gained altitude he watched the display that tracked the descent of the robo-sub. The chopper reached five thousand feet as McKinney leveled the sub at twenty-nine hundred feet. The pilot brought them to a hover and nodded at the point where they had detached the sub. McKinney looked back at Cooper and pulled the headset microphone to his mouth.

"You want to do the honors?" He held a remote out to Cooper. "It's steady five hundred feet above the floor and almost three thousand below the surface."

Cooper took the remote, looked from the pilot to McKinney, and pressed the button. Nothing happened. He looked at McKinney.

McKinney nodded at the console. The display had gone blank. "Wait for it," he said.

Cooper waited. The world seemed to pause on its axis. The sound of the rotors was the only thing that existed. After an eternity, the surface began to bubble. Then it erupted into a geyser five hundred feet high. They watched it fall back to the surface. Cooper looked at McKinney.

"Conventional explosion," McKinney said. "If it had been nuclear, the spout would have exceeded our altitude. That device is no longer capable of achieving a supercritical mass."

Cooper nodded, handed the remote back to McKinney, and dropped into his seat in the back.

Chapter 53

Westlake Village, California.
Saturday, 15 March 2003. 11:23.

Cooper crumbled crackers into the tortilla soup. He saw Dixon wince and look away, off the balcony to the waterfront. He looked back at Cooper and pulled the robe tighter around his throat. They ate in silence for awhile, listening to the flapping of the umbrella over the table. Finally Dixon spoke.

"You don't have to eat soup. Livy can get you something else."

"No, this is fine." He set the box of crackers down on the patio table and shook salt into his soup.

"If it's so fine, why are you desecrating it?"

"What?" Cooper looked up. "I always put crackers in my soup."

"Even tortilla soup?"

"What is a tortilla anyway but a soggy cracker? Besides, I don't want to taunt you with something you can't eat yet."

"Believe me," Dixon said between slurps, "I'm happy just to be eating anything with chunks in it at this point. It's the first day I've had anything besides straight liquids. How is Stevie doing?"

"She's doing well. The first shell just went through muscle. The second hit her spleen on the way through. Lots of blood and it was a near thing getting her to Cheyenne in time, but the wounds were clean and she's going to be OK."

"That's good. And Nikki?"

Cooper blew a lungful of air out. "She's been through a lot for a kid. A lot for an adult, even. We had a long talk last night. She's going to see a counselor. Actually, we'll both go. And I might cut back on travel for awhile, once I wrap up the loose ends."

"There are plenty of loose ends, I gather. I spent the last two days catching up on status, reading reports, making calls," Dixon said. "Do we have all the nukes?"

Cooper shrugged. "All the ones we know about. I watched the last one fall into the Pacific. And the chatter's dead. We put a serious dent in the organization, took out major players on both coasts. Based on tapes of the interrogations, there's been mixed success with the terrorists we have in custody. I think al-Ghamdi knows more than they've been able to get out of him. A lot more. I intend to have a conversation with him myself tomorrow." He spooned soup into his mouth. "But Berkowitz got away."

"Berkowitz? Didn't he call himself Nadhir?"

"My name for him. It's funny. I could feel a single mind on the other end, pulling all the strings. I knew it even though I didn't have any hard intel on the organization. I needed a name for him, so I called him Berkowitz."

"Any particular reason you picked Berkowitz?"

"Because I knew it would annoy him if he knew."

Dixon nodded. "Good enough for me. But even though you don't know much about him, he seems to know a lot about you."

"That's the price of freedom. I don't go slinking around like a sewer rat, hiding from the world, so it's easy to find information on me."

"Too bad you didn't get him in the silo. If that gun hadn't jammed, there would be one less loose end."

"What?" Cooper dropped his spoon, splashing soup onto the table.

"Your Berkowitz guy. If your gun hadn't jammed, he would be dead."

Cooper felt cold. It couldn't be true. He had told no one about that moment. There was only one way Dixon could have this information about Berkowitz. He leaned across the table, grabbing the sides with both hands, glaring into Dixon's eyes.

"How do you know that?"

Dixon looked back as if Cooper had lost his mind. "It was in a report."

"No, it wasn't. I didn't put it in any reports." The fact that he had been so thoroughly fooled, had been so quick to suspect Claire, increased his fury.

"I'm sure I read it in a report somewhere." Dixon set his spoon down. "I've been through a lot of material in the last two days. It might take me awhile to track down where I read it."

Cooper shoved the table aside, umbrella and all. Bowls and glasses shattered on the tile of the balcony. This man had attempted to take his life. He had let him into his home, trusted him with his family, and he had repaid that trust with betrayal and murder. He stepped forward, put his hands on the arms of Dixon's chair, and leaned into his face.

"I didn't put it in the report," he whispered fiercely. "I didn't tell anyone. Not even Stevie. Nobody knows that but me and Berkowitz. And you didn't hear it from me."

Dixon shifted uncomfortably in his chair, craning his head back away from Cooper. "Matt, calm down. I'm telling you, it's in a report." He pushed at Cooper's arms. "Here, let me up and I'll get the files and we'll find it."

"Oh yeah, that's a great idea," Cooper sneered. "I'll just let you go back into your office and get your Glock. Or maybe a knife, like you used on Bactar. Maybe Claire was onto you so you had to get her out of the way, set her up to take the fall."

Dixon looked at Cooper steadily. "I'm not going to dignify that with a reply. Now back off and start talking sense."

Cooper grabbed the front of Dixon's robe in his right hand and jerked him nose-to-nose. "I'll talk sense. You're the leak, the perfect double agent. Nobody would suspect you, least of all me. And you took advantage of it. Tried to have me killed when I got too close."

Cooper saw Dixon's eyes shift to the side and focus past him. He noticed somebody at the extreme edge of his peripheral vision.

"It's OK, Livy, just a little work disagreement. Put down the gun."

Cooper flicked his eyes to the side and saw Dixon's wife, standing with her hand to her mouth. She didn't have a gun. Dixon suddenly pushed up from the chair, head-butted Cooper, and grabbed his right arm. He spun to his left, taking Cooper's right arm with him and knocking his left arm free of the arm of the chair.

It was the arm Cooper was using to support himself. He was thrown off balance. As Dixon continued to spin around, pulling the arm with him, Cooper was thrown onto the chair. Dixon followed through, pushing Cooper and the chair over then releasing his arm. He crashed against the railing of the balcony with the chair atop him. He looked up to see Dixon standing over him, panting and leaning against the rail of the balcony.

"Coop, you've gone soft when an old, sick man can take you. Too much emotion, not enough discipline." He pulled the chair off of Cooper with his free hand and tossed it aside. "If I wanted to kill you, I could have done it dozens of times over the past decade. And believe me, if I wanted you dead, you would be dead. I wouldn't have used the nitwits Berkowitz hired. Drive-bys from the back of a Ninja? Some third-rate soldier of fortune who can't even take out a target in the clear?"

He shook his head and held out his hand. Cooper pointedly ignored it, rolled to his side, and climbed to his feet. He looked at Livy, who was standing just inside the sliding glass door, frowning at him with a look approaching hate. He glared back and turned to Dixon.

"You didn't try to kill me before because I never got close enough before. What was it? How did they get to you? How long ago? Back when you were working the KGB? Or after the cold war ended and a domestic position didn't hold enough excitement?" He wiped a trickle of blood from his lip with the back of his hand. "Or was it when you were getting close to retirement and the pension looked too small compared to the money you went through for a single operation?"

Dixon shook his head. "Coop, I'm the one who should be delirious, not you. I'm not going to hold this against you because I know you'll regret it later."

"You haven't explained anything."

"To the contrary. You just don't like the explanation. When I locate the report where I read the information, I'll show it to you. If I'm allowed to actually go get it, that is." Dixon sighed and sat down in the one chair left upright on the balcony. "I'm afraid I used up more energy than I actually possessed. You should probably go, if Livy will let you out in one piece."

Cooper stared at him, not trusting the calm manner.

"Coop, I'm not going anywhere. I'm barely alive, for crying out loud. When you come to your senses, I'll still be right here, eating tortilla soup, if there's any left."

Cooper looked from Dixon to Livy and then shoved the chair aside with his foot and strode out of the house and down the stairs to the Porsche without a word. Now that he knew, he was certain he would find the evidence he needed. Dixon was right about one thing. He wouldn't try to stop him. He couldn't without bringing more suspicion on himself.

He pulled away from the curb, making a mental list of the lines of inquiry that should be pursued. He would put Perkins on connections between the Bactar murder and Dixon. He would personally handle the HuJI-Dixon connection. The D.C. suspect, al-Ghamdi, was his best lead. He would fly to D.C. and talk to him.

Chapter 54

It didn't help that none of Cooper's contacts was at the CIA safe house where al-Ghamdi was being held, even though he called ahead before his arrival at sunrise. Or that the Washington, D.C., FBI and CIA liaisons to IRIG weren't available. Or that he lost his temper when the CIA agent baby-sitting al-Ghamdi on Sunday morning wouldn't let him question the suspect without authorization.

After several phone calls came up blank, Cooper left to find a Starbucks and cool down. He returned an hour later to a friendly face. Hugh Carter was the FBI liaison for IRIG and had coordinated the near-miss raid two weeks earlier and the successful raids early Wednesday morning. Carter took him to a conference room, offered coffee, which Cooper declined, and gave him al-Ghamdi's file. Cooper skimmed over the background and the details of the raid. He passed over the transcripts from Wednesday through Friday, which he had already studied closely, and read the notes from Saturday. Nothing new, just extended periods of silence interspersed with occasional religious monologues and predictions of the destruction of the Great Satan and the victory of Islam.

Cooper agreed with the assessment in the file. There was little question that al-Ghamdi was a central figure in the HuJI organization, probably the lead sleeper in D.C. Twelve years of residence with various jobs that gave him mobility—interpreter, cultural consultant to university Middle Eastern programs, procurer, taxi owner-operator. And resources that could not be explained by his irregular self-employment—multiple sets of ID, multiple bank accounts with significant balances under various names, real-estate holdings under most of the identities.

Questioning centered on uncovering his communication lines to Iran, but the going was slow. They got nothing from al-Ghamdi, but footwork at banks and other locations was slowly bearing fruit. It wasn't fast enough for Cooper. He closed the file and took it back to Carter in the lounge.

"I want to talk to al-Ghamdi."

"We can't get much out of him. Don't know what more you could do, but you're welcome to try." Carter got up from the couch, muted the political jousting match on the TV, and held the remote out to him. "I'll get him moved to the room. It'll take a few minutes to get the tapes set up."

Cooper waved away the remote. "I want to see him in his cell."

Carter stopped. "It's not procedure."

Cooper knew it wasn't procedure. But procedure had produced four days of drivel. Even Carter should be able to figure that one out.

Carter frowned. "We're not set up to tape in there."

"I don't like the sound of my voice on tape, anyway."

Carter waved the remote. "We've asked him everything at least a dozen times."

"Then he ought to know the answers by now, and it'll be fast." Cooper looked at his watch. "In that case I should be done before ten." He figured it would take longer. He knew a few things the FBI didn't. Like what al-Ghamdi's boss looked like. That he was willing to kill two of his faithful servants because they happened to be standing by his enemy. They would have lots to talk about.

Carter was still frozen in indecision. Cooper slipped the remote from his fingers, dropped it on the couch, and clapped a hand on his shoulder.

"Hugh, let's just get this over with. I'll shake him up a little by sitting in his cell with him, show him I'm not afraid to take him on in his own space. Maybe he talks, maybe he doesn't. We find out, I go home. Done, just like that."

Carter shrugged, and they walked up the stairs. An agent sat at the top. He looked at Cooper, stood up, and looked to Carter.

"We'd like to look in on our guest, Rich. He up yet?"

Rich looked them over again. "Of course," he said, looking back to Carter. "He's always up at daybreak with those prayers. It's like five times a day with him. I just brought him some tea." He stepped to the door, slid back a panel, and looked in. He frowned. "That's strange. He never sleeps during the day."

He unlocked the door and opened it. Cooper looked in. Al-Ghamdi was on the bed, but the tea cup was shattered on the floor. He pushed Rich aside and was beside the bed in two steps. He heard labored breathing whistling between al-Ghamdi's teeth. His lips moved as he muttered something. Cooper leaned over.

"Rosie . . ." He breathed as if resting from the effort. "Auntie. Rosie . . ."

Cooper leaned closer. He could smell the fetid breath wheezing in and out of his throat.

"Auntie . . . Rosie Auntie." He shuddered. "The stallion."

Cooper felt a hand gather his shirt and jerk him backward.

"What do you think you're doing?" Rich demanded. He leaned over al-Ghamdi, looking around suspiciously.

"Where did the tea come from?" Cooper asked.

Rich looked at him. "They brought it up from the kitchen."

"They?"

"They. The people in the kitchen. They."

A tremor from al-Ghamdi caught their attention. Another seizure shook his entire frame, then he lay still.

Cooper turned to Carter. "Let's talk to the kitchen staff."

Downstairs in the kitchen two Puerto Rican women were preparing lunch. When Carter finally got them seated and Cooper asked his questions, they discovered that neither of them had made the tea. One found the tea made and took it upstairs, assuming the other made it. The other assumed the first made the tea and then took it up. They began looking at each other and muttering in Spanish. Cooper couldn't tell if they were calling each other liars or warning each other of evil spirits.

A survey of the two remaining agents in the house determined that nobody made the tea. Cooper left with the conviction that someone in the house had been compromised by HuJI or the mole or both. He had lunch as he formed a plan. The greater part of the afternoon was consumed in a hunt for Watson, Dixon's boss.

Chapter 55

Columbia Island Marina, Washington, D.C.
Sunday, 16 March 2003. 18:27.

Late in the afternoon he finally located a restored house off New Hampshire Avenue in Foggy Bottom and a housekeeper who told him Mrs. Watson and the children were in Charleston for spring break and Mr. Watson was on the boat. Cooper got directions to the Columbia Island Marina, a phone number, and a slip number.

It was just after sundown when Cooper pulled off George Washington Memorial Parkway into the empty parking lot of the marina. The boat was berthed on Dock A, facing the Potomac. It was a Searocco 1500, one of only two fifty-footers in the marina. The extruded metal door to the dock was locked. He stepped to the side, vaulted over the barrier, and walked down the dock.

He boarded through the aft gateway and stepped to the door of the cabin. It was dark, but light spilled up from the stairwell to the right of the bridge. He walked through the cabin without a word and stepped quietly down the circular stairway. The light was coming from the master stateroom at the bottom of the stairs.

Watson was inside, angled away from the door, a gun in his hand. He was talking to someone out of Cooper's field of vision. He took another step and saw Dixon, pale and defeated, sitting on the bed facing Watson. Cooper was temporarily caught off guard. When he had heard Dixon describe those private moments in the missile silo, he knew with certainty he had found the mole. Dixon's reaction had created a small seed of doubt, but it was easily overwhelmed by the evidence. And now Dixon was here with Watson. What did it mean?

Perhaps Dixon knew that Cooper would uncover hard evidence and he had come to take countermeasures. The fact that he was in D.C. meant he could have made the tea or instructed the person who did. And if Watson also suspected him, he could have come to remove that threat as well, but in his weak condition was overpowered and captured. Cooper looked at the gun again. It was Dixon's own Walther PPK nine-millimeter compact. The silver one. He had seen it on the firing range many times. It looked like Dixon had finally run out of luck.

Cooper stepped into the room. Dixon saw him and started in surprise. Watson jerked his head toward the door. In an instant Dixon was across the room, hands locked around Watson's wrist.

"Matt!" Dixon yelled. "Take him!"

Cooper lunged forward, grabbed Dixon, and pulled him off Watson. It wasn't difficult, given Dixon was still weak from the effects of food poisoning. As Cooper pushed him back on the bed, Dixon struggled and cursed at him.

"Now you've done it, you fool!" He pushed Cooper back toward the door and collapsed to one side on the bed, panting. Sweat beaded on his forehead from the exertion. "It's him, you idiot, not me!" He swung an arm weakly at Watson. "He's the mole."

Cooper turned. The gun was now pointed at Cooper.

Dixon tried to sit up, but slumped back. "After you left I went through all the reports, looking for the one that had the information about the gun jamming. I couldn't find it. Then I realized why. He's the one who told me about the gun jamming. Over the phone."

Watson smiled. "Thank you for the assistance, Cooper, although I could have managed without you. He really shouldn't be out of bed."

Cooper stared at Watson and then looked at Dixon. He was breathing heavily and shaking his head. "One of these days," Dixon croaked. "One of these days your impulsiveness is going to get you into real trouble."

Watson chuckled. "That's Dixie. Old school. Soldier to the end. I knew I could count on him to follow the chain of command and keep me informed. And he would have if he hadn't been at death's door rattling the doorknob." He smiled at Dixon. "I suspect this time you won't find the door locked."

Cooper was suddenly filled with an overwhelming rage. He was barely able to restrain himself from rushing Watson, even with the gun.

"I should ask why, but I don't care why," Cooper said. "There is no why that can justify what you've done."

"It all started in Brooklyn." He nodded to the wall on the other side of Dixon. "Would you like the stool? It's a bit of a story, and I've never had the chance to tell it before. It might take awhile, and I'd like it to be a bit darker before we take Rosie out for a cruise."

Cooper just glared, jaws clenched.

Watson shrugged. "Suit yourself." He leaned on the counter that angled along the walls out from the bed. "I was a prodigy, you see. Reading at age two, graduated high school at age seven. My older brothers were normal, ended up on the police force like my father, who had no idea what to do with me. Fortunately, my mother's family had a better idea. Her brother took me on as a project and managed my higher education. I completed college when I was twelve. Double major, physics and political science. Guided by my broad-minded uncle, I read extensively on every aspect of the human condition, but it was the ideals of Marx that captured the imagination of my youthful mind. The struggle of the human spirit against the greedy machine of capitalism. I imagined that the brick walls of the brownstones in my neighborhood concealed all sorts of horrors and abuses of the common man.

"And then Kennedy faced down Castro that October. The rest of the country saw a hero; I saw a bully. I celebrated silently a year later when he died. Even at my young age I knew what was safe to tell and what was better kept secret. As the various theories ran their course I began to see where the real power lay. It was not with the supposed brokers in the Oval Office or Capitol Hill or even the nine men in black. It lay with the men who did their deeds in the dark, did the necessary things that others shrank from.

"As the cold war progressed, I groomed myself for a position with the agency. I kept my record spotless, free from all questionable associations and organizations, disavowed my uncle, and continued my study of world politics and international finance. By the time I was old enough to vote, I knew more than most of the analysts in Washington. But I wanted practical knowledge to supplement my education. I volunteered for Vietnam. That was where I met Dixie."

He nodded at Dixon. Dixon had caught his breath. He wrestled into an upright position and glowered at Watson.

"Our careers were made together in those jungles. But utopian vision and my talent for politics were an irresistible force. Even though he was four years older, I quickly passed him and eventually brought him into my organization as a right-hand man. Faithful to a fault, old Dixie was. It blinded him, as I knew it would."

"I don't get it," Cooper said. "What does this communistic dream have to do with Islamic terrorists?"

"Instability. Chaos," he said, as if stating the obvious. "I knew the Soviets were finished when they began striving for stability. Stalin, now there was a man who knew how to keep you guessing." He shook his head. "But I didn't mourn when the wall came down and the Soviet bloc collapsed. It was corrupt, merely the exchange of one exploitive tyrant for another."

"Chaos is not utopia."

"No, of course not. But only by razing the current world order to the ground, taking it down to the bare metal, can we rebuild the utopian society. You could say I'm a dreamer, like Lennon, but I can imagine it. I am unashamedly, if secretly, quixotic in the truest sense. Hence the name of my yacht."

He nodded to the life preserver on the wall by the door. Cooper looked. It was inscribed *Rosinante*. He looked back to Watson, puzzled.

"You don't recognize the reference? No, probably not. Few people read the classics anymore. It is the name of the noble steed of that famous dreamer of literature, Don Quixote."

"Rosinante?" When he said it, something clicked. "Rosie Auntie," he said. "You're Rosie Auntie."

"Very good. I see you got some useful information from our friend despite my efforts. I had to move fast on that one. Lucky for me the CIA man called me for authorization while you were out gnashing your teeth. It gave me just enough time to respond. I missed breakfast but made it in time for tea."

It happened so quickly Cooper had little time to react. Dixon hurled from the bed, clawing at Watson's arm and screaming, "Matt! Run!" Watson swung the gun away from Cooper and

Dixon threw himself over his entire arm. Cooper started to join Dixon in the attack, but Watson fired. The noise was deafening in the tiny stateroom. Dixon clutched at the counter and fell to the floor.

Cooper darted up the staircase. He heard another shot. A bullet ground into the wall behind him. Then he was out on the bridge. He grabbed the heavy swivel chair behind the pilot's wheel and pushed it down the stairwell as Watson rounded the corner. Watson was sent tumbling back against the doorjamb between the fore stateroom and the bathroom. Cooper heard the gun clatter across the bathroom floor.

He scanned the main cabin for potential weapons. He rejected the knives in the galley. Not very effective against a man with a gun. He slammed the door open and raced down the exterior walkway aft to the ladder to the top deck. He found a Zodiac, a jet ski, some fishing tackle, a fire extinguisher, scuba gear, and an assortment of life vests. The oars on the Zodiac were lightweight plastic.

Lights came on, and the engines rumbled to life, startling him. He crept to the back of the upper deck and saw Watson toss the tether onto the dock and return to the cabin. *Rosinante* pulled away from the dock and made for the Potomac. Evidently Watson didn't want interference or witnesses while he stalked his victim. Cooper crept forward on all fours on the roof of the cabin and peeked through the windshield. He could see Watson's left hand on the wheel. The right presumably held the gun ready for intruders. On the bridge, surrounded by large windows, Watson had a 360-degree view. There was no way to sneak up on him.

Cooper looked up. They were nearing the parkway bridge that marked the end of the marina and the entrance to the Potomac. It was near enough for him to touch. He could scale it and escape to the roadway above, but Dixon might still be alive. Cooper turned from the bridge and resumed his search for a weapon. Soon they would be on the Potomac. Watson would probably turn right toward Reagan National Airport, where the noise of the jets would mask his activities. Then he would put the boat on autopilot and begin his search.

On the deck at the bow, about fifteen feet in front of the bridge windows, he saw a Danforth anchor with its twin pointed blades and a few hundred feet of rope coiled next to it. It might hold possibilities. He returned to the scuba gear and briefly turned the valve on a tank. It was charged.

He shrugged on a scuba vest, stuffed a wrench into his belt, and stepped to the ladder. He dropped to his stomach, braced himself on the rails and lowered himself headfirst until he could see in the cabin. Watson was faced forward, navigating the inlet.

Cooper slipped down the ladder and crouched at the aft door to the cabin. Verifying that Watson was engrossed in navigation, he pulled a life vest from a pile by the door, propped one of the scuba tanks on it, bottom facing the cabin, and inched the door open. With a swift and forceful blow of the wrench he snapped the valve off the end of the tank and dove to the side. As the tank rocketed into the cabin, careening off the walls and destroying the furniture, Cooper raced up the port side of the deck. A few gunshots shattered windows in the aft cabin.

Reaching the stairs, Cooper crept forward on all fours, keeping below the level of the windows, past the door to the bridge and along the hull of the fore stateroom, to the foredeck and the anchor. On his knees he set the remaining scuba tank aside and assessed the weight of the anchor. About thirty pounds.

The motion of the yacht changed as they hit the choppy waves of the Potomac. Cooper peered over the roof of the fore stateroom. Watson was dividing his attention between navigating the turn south toward the airport and scanning the aft cabin. Cooper suspected that Watson would wait until they were past I-395 and the railroad bridge before he left the cockpit to begin his hunt.

Cooper crouched, reached for the scuba tank, and pushed it to the top of the fore stateroom roof. As he steadied it with one hand and reached for the wrench, he heard gunshots. He looked up to see the windshield shatter and Watson lowering the gun toward him. Cooper swung the wrench as he ducked. The scuba tank skittered along the roof and slammed against the windshield crossways, shattering several panes.

As Watson dropped back in reaction, Cooper hefted the anchor and took a deep breath. Then he stood, took a wide stance, and hurled the anchor at the window where Watson was raising his weapon. Watson threw up his right arm, but the anchor tumbled over his arm and into his head. He staggered back. Cooper raced down the starboard walkway and through the door to the cabin. He kicked the captain's chair aside, back into the galley.

Watson was sprawled on the deck. The gun was three feet away. Cooper retrieved it and returned to Watson. A gash ran from his temple to his cheek. He lay with his eyes open but unseeing, his chest rising and falling rapidly with shallow breathing. Cooper cut the engines and turned back to Watson, who muttered quietly. Then his voice suddenly became louder.

"Not so fast," Watson rasped. "In last year's nests there are no birds this year."

Cooper dropped to one knee next to him, cautious.

"Ah, now I see it, Antonia," Watson exclaimed. He took several quick shallow breaths, as if excited. "Blessed be Almighty God, who has shown me such goodness. In truth His mercies are boundless, and the sins of men can neither limit them nor keep them back!" His hands moved aimlessly along his body.

"What?" Cooper said. "Mercies? You? If anybody burns in hell, it'll be you."

"The mercies, niece," Watson stated flatly, as if quoting Scripture, "are those that God has this moment shown me, and with Him, as I said, my sins are no impediment to them. My reason is now free and clear, rid of the dark shadows of ignorance that my unhappy constant study of those detestable books of chivalry cast over it."

Cooper ground the nose of the gun into the gash in Watson's temple. "The only mercy you'll get is a bullet." He clenched his teeth and his hand shook. He thought of the hundreds if not thousands of lives Watson's philosophy of chaos had likely ended. He thought of Stevie curling into a ball of pain in the Wyoming desert with two bullets in her side, of Nikki turning to a terrorist to welcome the bullet, of Nadhir's taunting look of contempt when Cooper didn't shoot him in front of the Quonset hut. His finger quivered on the trigger.

The voice of Skaff played softly in his head. *Do not follow the enemy into hate.*

Watson continued to mumble. "A doughty gentleman lies here, a stranger all his life to fear."

Cooper ignored him. He thought of Skaff's family—the wife of many years, faithful, devoted, trusting; Rafik, reckless and uncertain in his manhood, devastated by the knowledge he had failed his father; the innocent Hayat, shy and tentative in a confusing world of hide-and-seek. All slaughtered by this man's partners in chaos.

Again Skaff's voice whispered in his head. *I kill them if I must. But I pray that God have mercy on their souls.*

How could a man like Watson ask for mercy? But he wasn't even asking. He said he had already been shown mercy. It was unthinkable.

"Nor in his death could Death prevail in that last hour, to make him quail," Watson continued. It was as if his mind were playing back random tidbits.

But if this man, this traitor, this monster is not beyond the reach of God's mercy, then . . . He could not finish the thought. It was incomprehensible. To apply it to himself was to place himself on the same plane as Watson.

The damaged brain continued to leak its absurd fantasies of redemption. Cooper released the pressure on his trigger finger and stood. He looked back at the stairwell. Dixon had crawled around the corner. He sat on the third step, leaning against the wall and watching. They looked at each other for a long moment.

"You did right, Coop, although I would back you either way. The world is better off without that traitor, but it never does to play God," Dixon said. "Best to leave that to the experts. Tie him up and find a radio. I need a pint or two."

Chapter 56

Honolulu, Hawaii.
Wednesday, 19 March 2003. 16:34.

They were on the balcony overlooking Waikiki when Cooper overheard the announcement from the TV Nikki had left on. He stepped back in and watched the president's statement. It had begun. He watched some of the initial footage, the talk of shock and awe, wondering where Nadhir was. Nowhere near Iraq, he guessed.

Nikki called to him from the balcony. He stepped back out.

"They're bringing the canoe in on the surf." She pointed to a large, yellow outrigger canoe catching a wave.

He sat down in the deck chair. Nikki dropped into his lap and leaned her shoulder against him, watching the canoe ride the wave onto the beach. He circled one arm around her and reached the other out to Stevie. She was leaning back in a chaise lounge, a floppy straw hat shading her eyes.

"How are you doing?" he asked.

"Beats a hospital room."

He watched her as she watched the surf. The afternoon light glowed on her face. The dark circles under her eyes were almost gone. She still looked tired, but tired was a significant improvement from her appearance on the helicopter ride. That night he had held Nikki in his arms much like this afternoon, and watched Stevie, strapped onto the gurney and unconscious.

At that moment he knew he couldn't do it again. When Lola died, he had lost himself in his work. But he had already let Lola go, long before she drove over the edge. It was different with Stevie from the beginning. If he lost her now, it would be much more than losing a piece of himself. It would be losing a part of the future, a part of reality. Losing the chance to say the things he told himself he would tell her *one day*. The day when he had finally wrestled the demons down, had slain the beast within, when he was safe and acceptable.

But now he knew that *one day* would never come. He would have to decide to do it or not, just as he was, demons and all. He watched the ocean breeze run its fingers through her hair and thought maybe he would. Maybe this day would be that *one day*.

Stevie turned to look at him suddenly, as if he had called her name, and caught him staring. He felt an unexpected embarrassment and looked away. Then realized it was the reaction of the old Matt, not the Matt who sat in a chopper and cursed himself for all he had left unsaid and undone. He turned back to her and watched the frown on her face relax and melt into a smile. He smiled back and let her watch him watching her, let her read what there was to read in his face as the thoughts strolled through his mind.

Maybe this was the day. He dragged a fingernail down Nikki's back and watched her squirm. It seemed that somehow Nikki had learned the secret. In the hospital he had seen something he thought impossible–Nikki visiting Stevie, talking to her about girl stuff, reading to her. From a Bible, no less. Maybe she would teach him the secret of how to let go, how to relax the defenses, how to begin demolition on the fortress.

He looked back at Stevie while tracing Nikki's spine with his finger. Nikki squirmed again, and Stevie laughed.

Nikki turned around and looked at the two of them looking at each other.

"Did you guys ever think about getting married?"

Stevie's mouth dropped open, and her eyebrows disappeared under her hat. Cooper laughed, closed his arm around Nikki, dragged her the rest of the way into his lap, and tickled her. She squealed like she used to when she was six. Back before.

Yes, maybe this was the day.

ACKNOWLEDGMENTS

It was about a year after 9/11 on a beautiful fall southern California day when I was having lunch with longtime friend John Tayloe. John has been an enthusiastic supporter and was encouraging me to write about my experiences and knowledge in counter-terrorism. I kept saying I am an action guy not a creative one.

John's persistence paid off, and that week I prepared an outline for what ultimately became my first book, *Hostile Intent*. As I was writing that manuscript, another longtime friend, Susan Wales, read some of my manuscript and took it upon herself to find me a publisher. Her frequent calls to both David Shepherd and Leonard Goss landed me at Broadman & Holman Publishers. Susan, you are a true friend, and I thank you for your faith in me.

On that first meeting with David and Len, a friendship was started. It was in that meeting that Len said they also wanted to do fiction with me, based on my work in the field of counter-terrorism. *Hell in a Briefcase* is the first result of their faith in me. Thank you, David and Len, and all the great staff that have supported me with such passion—including Lisa Parnell, the project editor for my books. When I have had questions, Mary Beth Shaw, B & H author relations specialist, has handled every one with timeliness and attention to detail. In fact, every department at B & H operates with great integrity and professionalism, and I have a high level of comfort in the whole team supporting me. Saying "thank you" just doesn't seem to be enough.

Brad Whittington, a successful novelist in his own right, helped me get inside the hearts and heads of the people in Matt Cooper's life. Without Brad's help I could not have opened the joys, hurts, struggles, and the desperate search to find happiness and purpose for life in my characters. Thank you, Brad, for your brilliant touches and for your friendship. You are a true professional.

Most of all I thank my family, whose lives come alive in this story—especially my sons Wayne and Wade and my daughter Nicolette. Kids, you are loved because you not only love me but you are friends and good critics, and you have encouraged me to follow my dream. Believing I can accomplish whatever I set out to do comes from my saintly father, who is ninety years old and who still believes in me and prays for me every day. Daddy, you are a saint. I love you.

Finally, I thank you, my reader. I hope you enjoy Matt Cooper's journey balancing single parenthood, developing a romantic relationship, and working in his chosen profession to save our country from nuclear disaster. May God bless America.

Brad's Acknowledgments

Thanks to Phil for all the dinners; Lanny Hall for the law enforcement advice; Mike Favazza for the medical advice; Clyde and Marsha Combs for the guest house writing retreat; Tuan Nguyen for dinner at Solley's; Susan Powell for all the cross-functional meetings; John Kennedy Toole for Ignatius O'Reilly; the Mushroom Club for the showdown advice; Graham Allison for providing a wealth of information in *Nuclear Terrorism, The Ultimate Preventable Catastrophe;* Mom for a copy of *The Haj;* Nick for your last name; Daniel and Chris for an unforgettable evening at the Redwood Room; and Jody Kline for the artichoke.